The Ka

The
Ka

The portion of the spirit of the dead
that remains inside the tomb.

Mary Deal

Titles by Mary Deal

Fiction
The Ka, a paranormal Egyptian suspense
River Bones, the original Sara Mason Mystery
The Howling Cliffs, 1st sequel to River Bones
Legacy of the Tropics, adventure/suspense
Down to The Needle, a thriller

Collections
Off Center in the Attic – Over the Top Stories

Nonfiction
Write It Right – Tips for Authors – The Big Book
Hypno-Scripts: Life-Changing Techniques Using Self-Hypnosis and
Meditation

For **Ron Holte**

…who had more faith in me than I had in myself in the beginning. His encouragement has had a profound effect on my writing life.

Acknowledgements

My son, Dean Alan Deal, for his unending encouragement and support, having read and critiqued every major book manuscript I've written.

Elizabeth English, Founder & Executive Director, Moondance International Film Festival; for her continued advice, expertise, encouragement, and friendship.

Lori Kikumoto, whose keen-eyed scrutiny helped polish the manuscript.

The late Richard D. Robbins, MD and Writer, for constantly exchanging roles of student and mentor with me during the all too brief time we wrote together.

Letisha Teserak, Librarian, who pushed me to get this manuscript started, and who supplied me with every book and video about Egypt found in Hawaii's libraries across the Islands.

Magda Batstone, who shipped nearly her entire private Egyptian library from California to Hawaii, and who allowed me to retain it for research for over a year.

Author photo by *Faces Studio and Salon*, Honolulu, Hawaii.

1

"Witch!" Randy Osborne said as he strode around the room wearing a contemptible smirk. "You're an out 'n out witch."

"Your choice of labels defines your ignorance," Chione said, not backing down from his stare. Witch was his mother's terminology. He always listened to her. Randy seemed unable to form his own opinions. If pressed, he always quoted his mother.

"Here, here," Clifford Rawlings said in her support as he threw a fist into the air.

Others in the group expressed mixed reactions, but Chione Ini-Herit had grown emotionally strong enough to withstand Randy's cruel taunting. Shortly after they met, and she learned of interning with him, she decided that anything Randy said would not tear at her equilibrium. Her passive attitude, till now, kept him in line.

This was the first time Chione had a chance to see all the members of the archaeological team together in one room. They were older and, at times, a little intimidating. Her own demeanor was quiet, meditative; maybe passive-aggressive, and she sometimes became overwhelmed with their high-spirited personalities. Yet, being allowed to accompany these professionals to the dig site in Egypt was the chance of a lifetime. Presently, she would be happy to sit back and watch the team members goad one another. Information came at her so quickly it numbed her senses. With the whole team together, their voices assaulted her eardrums in round after round of quips and retorts that would send the meek fleeing. Getting to know these people could not wait until they arrived at the dig site when work would proceed at full speed. The only way to get to know them as a team began here. Now.

Aaron Ashby stepped up behind her. "You don't know the meaning of witch, Randy." Chione felt Aaron's hand touch her shoulder, but he removed it right away, minding his manners. "What gives you the right to label anyone?"

"Because she predicted our discovery," Randy said, "and danger near some small tombs. What did she say… that the bone yard is haunted, and that our find could change history? Ha!" He rocked back on his heels. "Sounds like a typical psychic reading." He glared at her again. "Even your Egyptian looks spook me. Why don't you crop that black hair of yours about ear length like the Egyptians used to—?"

"If Chione's appearance spooks you, Randy," Kendra Laker said succinctly. "Maybe you need to scrutinize your own image."

Chione became flustered and wondered why they stood up for her. She could hold her own in her quiet way. The group seemed too willing in their zeal to pounce on Randy. During the planning stages of the expedition, envy among some of the lesser staff at the California Institute of Archaeology predicted the team would not hold together. It would not be because of the diverse backgrounds of each in the field of archaeology, but due to the clash of personalities and ego opposites.

"Excuse me, Mr. Osborne," Aaron said. "Any learned archaeologist knows that in Egypt those small tombs are *mastabas*."

"And what you so unprofessionally label the boneyard," Clifford said, "is a *necropolis*."

Eager anticipation, as well as irritability, hung heavy in the small conference room at the five-star Re-Harakhty Hotel in Cairo. Jet lag had gripped them all. Despite air conditioning, the crowded conference room was stuffy. The moment for which all had waited was upon them. The small group of colleagues milled around impatiently awaiting the arrival of Dr. Sterling Withers. Before the team made their way south along the Nile to Valley of the Queens, he was to deliver one final briefing on this, the first advantageous opportunity to befall the Institute and that tempted to be the find of a lifetime.

Archaeologist Dr. Sterling Withers inherited a fortune in croplands in the California Central Valley. Yet his interest had never been in what grew from the soil but what lay buried beneath it. He quickly leased out most of the land to crop farmers but retained the residential portion to manifest his lifelong dream of a privately held archaeological institute. The Institute's monstrous old Victorian main building, with its attendant, renovated and new smaller structures that comprised the facility, sat off the main road. Situated on a verdant patch of green acreage, the cluster of buildings was canopied and sheltered from the heat and dust by decades-old shade trees. Perfectly timed, the Institute opened its doors with the New Millennium. Lathrop, California became a bigger dot on the map. After several years of hoping to find a new dig site, the Institute's exploration team auspiciously happened upon a tomb that had remained sealed for how long, no one yet knew with certainty.

Chione glanced out the window of the top floor hotel conference room and over the resort grounds, replete with monstrous swimming pools and lavish amenities. Though she detested commercialism, just being in Cairo, or anywhere in Egypt, made everything right. Still, she could not shed the luxury fast enough. Something had taken hold of her. She yearned to get to the dig site and down into that hole in the ground.

Off in the distance, clouds of sand blew on air currents. They reminded her how summer lingered in the California Central Valley. The late fall season had not been the traditional mild Indian summer like many others. There was no escape. Everyone suffered. Any place in the world would have offered a reprieve from the antagonizing heat, but traveling to the Egyptian desert was not where anyone would seek respite from the sizzle of the California Central Valley. Now that they had finally arrived in Egypt, having to wait to learn last minute details of the project fueled impatience and made tempers flare.

Randy's snicker brought her thoughts back into the room.

Aaron sighed. "You don't get it, do you, Randy?"

"What's to get?"

"That's what makes Chione so gifted. She has no skeletons dancing in her closets."

"You mean because everyone knows her secrets?"

Chione felt pangs of anger at being taunted by Randy and freely talked about. She harbored no illusions about the condition of her life. She glanced at Kendra with a wry smile. They were aware of the fact that her reproductive organs were underdeveloped leaving her unable to bear children. She did not care who knew and because of that, in her mind, she felt free. One day, Randy would get his comeuppance. Now, she intended to let the scene play out, partly to get to know the team, and because Randy could make a fool of himself without any help from her. Randy's inclusion in the project deterred any emotional high the team might experience. Intolerance would be tempered by the work.

Tall, muscular Aaron passed a handkerchief over his forehead, then over the back of his neck as he paced at the rear of the room. Finally, he took a chair at the end of the conference table. Chione knew Aaron had to force himself to bite his tongue as he watched the mixture of amused grins and disapproving frowns exchanged among the others. She watched Aaron vent anger as he slashed random crosshatch lines on a notepad. This was not the first time Randy tried to trash another person's reputation to enhance his own. He was trying to discredit her into losing her place on the team. She lacking a Ph.D. like the others, Randy voiced disbelief at her being chosen to work on the most significant archaeological exploration in recent history.

"The fact that Chione's so open about her private life," Bebe Hutton said from across the room, "doesn't give anyone permission to make a mockery of it." Bebe's habit was to remain quiet and observe, saying only enough to quell a situation or incite further interest when needed. She would hold her composure and watch the turning of events.

"You belittle her because she happens to outdistance you in practical intelligence," Clifford Rawlings said as he stared at Randy with disgust. When the mature and learned Egyptologist Dr. Rawlings spoke, everyone respected and listened, despite frequent lapses into the satirical. To look upon the man offered a view of a person approaching old age with a stately posture and whose clothes were always trendy and fresh. He had gray at his temples and a demeanor sculpted by time. Except when in one of his frequent comical moods. Then it was difficult at best to take him seriously. People said he turned over the management of his Napa Valley winery to a management team because he did not need the bottle to enhance his humor. In reality, the winery was only a tax shelter.

"I agree," Kendra said. The natural sparkle of her green eyes teased. "Chione does have a special sense of intuition." Kendra's wiry energy resonated on every word, driving a point home.

"But—"

"Leave it alone, Randy," Clifford said.

Randy stood supported with a hand on the back of a chair, flagging a leg back and forth as if his underwear might be caught in the wrong place. Then he lifted the leg a couple of times in a last-ditch effort to end his discomfort. His personal habits were reason for a good snicker among the team, who could politely ridicule one another, then laugh. At times, criticism from any of them seemed in jest, a way this group of high-strung colleagues dealt with stress. At other times, Randy's behavior was repulsive. He seemed to take great comfort in eating all the time and, thanks to his mother packing his lunch, he always had an ample supply of food nearby to pick at. His continual weight gain and lack of personal hygiene turned people off. He always looked sweaty and wrinkled, with matted hair. No one relished the idea of sharing a tent with him in the heat of the desert. Finally, he reached behind himself and gave the seat of his pants a tug. Not the kind of professional posture one would expect from a Physical Anthropologist who worked with genetics and biochemistry.

Chione wished Randy would get the point that his taunting could not discredit her accomplishments. She tried to be exacting in anything she did and had no plans to change her ways. He probably found that intimidating.

Aaron glanced at her and smiled secretly at the comments tossed on her behalf. Chione was well aware that Aaron still loved her, yet contained his feelings, sometimes behind indifference, which she easily read because she had always understood him. Aaron, too, hoped Randy would not be included in their upcoming expedition.

Kendra persisted. Her love of limelight would not allow her to turn her back on anything as attention-grabbing as a paranormal prediction come true. "Chione's dreams predicted this tomb would be found," she said, "predicted that mournful sound would lead our exploratory team to it."

"Similar to the singing Colossi of Memnon at Thebes," Bebe said, referring to the two north statues which some thought to be Amenhotep's mother, Mutemuia, and Queen Tyi. She had learned to rattle off the Egyptian names as easily as she spoke English. "Tyi's statue was the one thought to emit the singing. Our tomb was discovered because of similar noises emitting from it." Bebe was old-fashioned and skeptical of the paranormal, even as she talked about the recent incontestable events. She would be eager to put her knowledge of Egyptian history to work. Her professionalism as a historian was reputed to be unequaled. She looked the.part, serious and educated, but with a matronly figure. Her brown hair would erase years if lightened and styled otherwise. Yet, she was the epitome of today's professionally groomed middle-aged businesswoman.

"You see?" Randy asked, seizing the moment and raising his voice. "Only a witch could prognosticate finding a hidden tomb."

"Or someone with a sixth sense finely tuned to what she's doing," Aaron said, standing again.

"But to predict? Tell me, did she forecast this tomb dating to the 18th Dynasty before those first relics were unearthed?"

"Does it really matter?" Clifford asked. "Fact is, Chione dreamed it all, from the mournful sounds to someone stumbling over a stone and falling into a hole."

"A hole that led to the passageway of a tomb," Aaron said. His smile was smug and showed he was thoroughly pleased about her extrasensory abilities. With Aaron partially in command, he would not let Randy's personality throw the proverbial wrench into the mechanism every time he opened his mouth.

She was glad she had not told anyone but Aaron that she had caught strange flu-like symptoms a couple months back, about the time she began having those revealing dreams. She thought that, perhaps, the dreams had a deep psychological effect on her nervous system and hoped her unpredictably queasy stomach and other symptoms would pass. Luckily, Aaron was trustworthy and had not told anyone. Knowing that someone in the group understood her and how she received her extrasensory information was helpful too. Her occasional nausea was gradually diminishing. Had Randy learned about the lingering malaise, he would have seen to it that she was prevented from accompanying the team anywhere.

Chione discreetly glanced at Aaron, and then quickly looked away. She needed to hide the fact that she remained quite taken with him. The desire for some degree of intimacy recently returned. His promotion to becoming Dr. Withers' understudy and second in command meant they would now work side by side. That was all she could allow. Somehow, she knew that while working closely he would try to gain back what they shared and try to convince her to give him another chance. He was a decent guy; the only one to comprehend what she was all about. Not only that, she had shown him that with a little more study and self-knowledge he could develop his own unique abilities. The possibilities fascinated him.

As an adopted child, she endured an unfulfilled need to know who she was and clung to her adoptive mother and father. Their divorce left her devastated. Then came her second adoptive father, an Egyptian, whom she adored and whose name she took. Yet, his nurturing only made her more dependent.

Soon after she and Aaron met came the most disparaging news of all. How devastated she felt after learning she would never bear children. She interpreted it as an omen to share her life with no one, and to find strength in being alone. When she and Aaron parted, she made it clear that she could not cling to anyone any longer. Perhaps her consolation did come with solitude. After all, self-imposed seclusion perfected her special mental gifts. No one truly understood those peculiar qualities and that cinched the concept of separatism in her mind.

The fact that Aaron had been open-minded and made a gigantic effort to broaden his understanding of alternate realities offered hope, especially since his own awareness expanded with the experiences. She believed it wise that his and her lives remain separate. He might fall in love with someone else and have the family he desired. However, the thought of him loving someone other than her created a confused sinking feeling in the pit of her stomach. Recently, she began to yearn again for him and that was forcing her to confront her feelings. Clearly, Aaron seemed not about to give up on her, or on the development of his extrasensory abilities. She felt rushed to sort things out.

"This whole paranormal thing baffles me," Bebe said. "Can we run through it again to help me understand?"

Kendra eagerly picked up the momentum and described how Chione first had a dream about mournful sounds connected to a tomb in Egypt. Chione had not told Dr. Withers, but told his wife, Marlowe, who later related it to him. Dr. Withers thought nothing of it. About the same time, Clifford heard from a friend at the Madu Museum in Cairo relating that a grave robber looking for tombs to plunder heard a sound like whimpering near some mastabas.

"Coincidence," Randy said, drumming his fingers against the backrest of a chair.

"Lucky for us," Clifford said. "The grave robber claiming the necropolis was haunted scared people out of the area."

"Gimme a break," Randy said.

Clifford continued, saying the people from the Antiquities Society of Egypt thought something had shifted or been unearthed which caused the sounds to be made by the wind. His friend at Antiquities knew he was looking to organize some work in Egypt and suggested the Institute send an exploratory team. "Which we did," Clifford said. "But I, myself, hadn't heard about Chione's dream. And I didn't tell our illustrious leader about the mournful sounds, only about the possibility of a new dig site."

Clifford helped himself to a drinking glass and bottle of water kept cool in a small tub on the credenza against the wall. He poured himself a drink but passed the water to Bebe holding out her hand. Chione produced her pocket flask and poured a drink of Egyptian Karkade, a scarlet tea made from the hibiscus flower, which could be drunk hot or cold.

Aaron explained that after Dr. Withers sent the exploratory team, Chione told Marlowe of her second dream about a guy stumbling over a block and falling into a hole that led to finding a tomb. A few days later, Clifford heard that one of the men on the exploratory team stumbled over a block and fell into a hole. "When Dr. Withers was told—confirming Chione's dream that none of us had heard," Aaron said, "Dr. Withers and Ginny rushed here to Egypt to be with the exploratory team."

"Ginny McLain got to see before any of us?" Randy asked.

"She's our photographer," Clifford said, smiling his most ridiculous grin as if sticking a pin into Randy's inflated self-worth.

"I'm glad Dr. Withers was present when they discovered the entrance," Kendra said. "He himself was down on knees in that hole scraping away rubble with his bare hands."

Bebe listened intently. "As I understand it," she said. "Chione knew none of the details happening at the site, or even about an exploratory team being sent."

Randy sighed pathetically and looked out a window. "We'd have found the tomb without Chione's dreams. If she's such a great seer, why does she need any of us?"

Again, Chione only rolled her eyes at the others and caught a glimpse of Aaron hurting for her. Someone would surely comment, so she decided to withhold and simply watch the fireworks.

"If Chione's senses are so keenly honed that she dreams what we're about," Kendra said in her no-nonsense way. "It's we who need her."

"She's obsessed with things Egyptian," Randy said, flagging a hand as if he could not be bothered. "She kept her lunch under that shiny black diorite pyramid on her office credenza instead of in the fridge like the rest of us."

"If I remember correctly," Clifford said. "You used to store your lunch with hers when she interned with you."

Randy smiled sheepishly. "It was novel."

"Sure it was," Kendra said. "But you claimed the mayonnaise in your sandwich never melted and that your salad stayed crisp."

"The salad wasn't cold, though."

"I wouldn't take pyramid power lightly," Bebe said, surprising everyone. "Truth is, weren't all our knife edges keenly honed when Chione brought in her glass pyramid and demonstrated its effect?"

"That convinced me," Clifford said. Good hearted Clifford would give anyone the benefit of the doubt.

"Aaron changed when he met you," Randy said, turning and finally addressing her directly. "And the birthday party for Rita. Were you trying to cast spells with that party you threw for Clifford's wife? Even your tiny place is cluttered Egyptian."

"I'm Egyptian," Chione said, though she wasn't born Egyptian.

"Egypt appeals to her, Randy," Kendra said quickly. "She grew up with Egyptian history and culture—"

"Because her mother loved Egypt and gave her an Egyptian name that means Daughter of the Nile," Randy said. "How is it that American woman adopts an American child who grows up looking like Nefertiti's sister? Chione even uses her stepfather's name."

"Chione Grant Ini-Herit," Bebe said, enunciating. "She's never given up her first father's name."

By now, Kendra and Bebe had moved to stand beside her, opposite Randy on the other side of the conference table. She was beginning to feel claustrophobic. She did not need anyone standing up for her and would have to do something about Randy, and soon. He was getting out of hand.

"At least she claims her roots," Kendra said, pointedly reminding Randy how he openly blamed his shortcomings on a domineering mother.

"Chione wishes she were Egyptian," Randy said. "Heaven knows if she could have a baby, it would probably look like that heretic Akhenaten."

Aaron slammed a scratchpad onto the tabletop. "Wrong again, Randolph. Chione's too beautiful. The child would probably more resemble Nefertiti or even King Tut. Certainly not your mentor."

"That's right," Randy said. "It's been said you resemble the Boy King."

Aaron lunged, clutched Randy's shirtfront and drew back a fist.

Clifford grabbed Aaron's wrist. "Enough!" he said as he stepped in between. "Here comes Sterling."

2

Dr. Withers walked through the doorway in a huff. His average build was slightly stooped. His suit jacket flapped open at his sides. "Good morning, everyone," he said in a voice that took command and stopped cold anything that might be going on. He dropped his briefcase onto the tabletop and motioned for Chione to sit in the seat closest to him. Then he took his seat opposite Aaron at the other end of the long table.

No one spoke. They waited eagerly to hear about the excavation site. Due to flight delays and other snafus, he had not had time to deliver a final briefing before the team departed to Egypt. Dr. Withers pulled at his mustache and made eye contact with each person over bifocals. He took a good look at Randy who sat sweating profusely. Aaron glared at Randy and gritted his teeth as the muscles in his jowls tightened.

"Aaron," Dr. Withers said suddenly. "Give me a recap of things on your end."

Aaron flipped through a few sheets of his notepad. The margins of the pages were covered with random crosshatches. When had the articulate Aaron Ashby begun the messy habit of doodling? "Only a recap?" he asked.

"That's all I've got time for. I want to hear your report and mentally," he said, motioning toward his temple, "put the pieces together."

"Well," Aaron said. "If our find had garnered the type of publicity we anticipated, we'd have been assured of additional grants to help fund this project." Others in the group could not contain their disappointment and slipped snide glances in Randy's direction. "Other than those already on board," Aaron said, looking doubtful, "most professionals in our field have voiced an unequivocal disinterest."

"Disinterest?" Dr. Withers asked, grabbing the edge of the table with both hands. "Dis... interest? Even the biggies back east?"

"Especially the biggies. The rumors, sir. They don't like the rumors about Chione's dreams, let alone believe in her abilities overall."

"When the hell did that get out?"

Aaron stared straight into Dr. Withers' eyes and would not disclose the rest. It would not be his style to inform on Randy regardless of personal disgust for the man. Finally, Aaron shrugged. "After Clifford and his contacts managed to pull this find in our direction, we were getting flooded with offers for funding." He shook his head. "However, the upside is that after the leak, the ones who are with us now, regardless of rumor, will be unequivocally supportive."

Dr. Withers' lips tightened. His deflated expression changed to that of a person conjuring retribution. "The press, what are they saying?"

"Making light of the paranormal, I'm afraid."

Just then the lights flickered. They flickered again then went out, leaving the room strangely lit from sunlight filtering through the window curtains.

"Good ol' predictable Cairo," Clifford said.

The lights flickered on and off several times. Dr. Withers lips pinched together again. While he had a sense of humor, he also detested interruptions.

Clifford leaned back in his chair and raised both arms up toward the ceiling lights. "Dah-dah-h-h!" he said. They flicked on again and stayed.

"Magic," Kendra said.

Randy's head flopped from side to side with an expression indicating he could not tolerate another allusion to anything paranormal.

"Aaron," Dr. Withers said, calling everyone to attention again. "Anything better than that?"

"We've awarded first news release rights to the San Francisco Sentinel," Aaron said as he flipped through pages. "Besides showing positive interest, they will vindicate us even if our find turns up empty."

"What leads you to that conclusion?"

"We're giving them first rights. They wanted exclusive coverage, but they won't refuse any deal. They're already on their way to the site and will probably accept whatever we offer. This is a biggie for them. It's usually the East Coast or international papers that get handed this type of privilege."

"How do they feel about Chione's influence?" Kendra asked.

Aaron smiled. "They'll take it all in stride. After all, one of their journalists plays the stock market...using numerology."

Dr. Withers settled back and twitched his mustache, a sure sign he was thinking. "Would be nice if we had a Lord Carnarvon." Finally, after another silence, which meant he had shifted mental gears, he adjusted his glasses and began again. "I want you all to prepare yourselves for one of two events." Everyone leaned forward. "Either we're about to unearth a barren tomb long ago plundered of its riches—"

"Or?" Kendra and Bebe asked in unison.

"Or... hopefully, we stand to unearth the greatest Egyptian find since Howard Carter's time."

Pandemonium broke loose. Dr. Withers sat patiently waiting till their reactions calmed.

"Just how far into the dig are we?" Clifford asked finally.

"We dug out the hole that our guy fell into. We suctioned out and strained the backfill from inside the entrance passageway," Dr. Withers said, relating in his methodical way. "Farther in, we discovered a portcullis, which we left in place. I made sure the tomb was sealed before I left. In the interim, workers are setting up yurts for our use."

"And those first artifacts?" Clifford asked.

"The day we left, Ginny was filming those few relics found buried inside the entrance. She also shot the entire area before we so much as lifted a shovel."

"What tantalizes you into believing this could be a rich discovery?" Kendra asked.

Dr. Withers thought a moment and then leaned up close over the table as if he did not wish anyone else to hear. "Because those few 18th Dynasty artifacts hint... at a royal tomb."

Everyone had something to say. How well they knew the feeling of digging till disappointed or excavating into pay dirt. Suddenly the atmosphere was charged again.

"What more, Dr. Withers?" Bebe asked.

"We all stand to make history," he said, barely able to contain his excitement. "The fact that those first menial relics were not already plundered, and that the portcullis is intact, tells me the tomb beyond has remained sealed for thousands of years. Till now, till someone tripped."

Aaron rocked back in his chair smiling at the whims of fate, something he always claimed had a powerful force all its own. This was the news everyone needed to hear. Confirmation of Chione's premonition dreams was the reason Dr. Withers rushed to join the exploratory team, but gloating was not her style. This was reality for her and her ego had nothing to do with it.

"Sterling?" Bebe asked, prompting him.

"Oh, excuse me," Dr. Withers said. "When I heard about the mysterious sounds, like you, Bebe, I fixated on the Singing Colossi." He shook his head thoughtfully. "One thing we don't explore is the wind." He chuckled. "I'll bet that guy who first heard those sounds got scared right out of his turban." He threw a fist into the air. "I'll bet that put an end to one grave robber's career." Everyone cheered, but Dr. Withers quieted and leaned forward over the tabletop with a pensive gleam in his eyes. "When I was down on my hands and knees in that hole," he said, "I had a déjà vu experience."

"Really?" Kendra asked.

"I felt like we had just finished sealing that tomb and here I was opening it again."

Hearing his paranormal experience left the others speechless. Quiet filled the room. Chione hoped no one resented the importance

Dr. Withers placed on her presence. She was being used for some sort of channeling. She, too, felt overwhelmed.

Dr. Withers again broke the silence. "Let's not forget Clifford's part in all this," he said. "Without his affiliation with the Madu Museum and that inspector buddy, Paki Rashad from the Antiquities Society, this exploration could have been bequeathed to some big university."

"Or to a well-known museum," Aaron said. "Because they have financial clout."

"Or to some wealthy patron who cares not one iota about digging in the hot sun," Bebe said. "Unless there's a reward for personal coffers."

"Wish we had a filthy rich patron on our side," Dr. Withers said.

"Let's hear it for Clifford and his contacts," Kendra said. "Here, here."

They toasted, raising water glasses. Randy only smiled.

"You gonna be a part of this group or what?" Aaron asked, prodding Randy to toast.

After taking a sip, Clifford waved his hand to be heard. "You may not understand what I'm going to say," he said, looking around the group. "But listen up. The negotiations went too easily, just fell into our laps, like this was meant to be—like there's another reason it's all happening specifically to us."

"Uh-oh," Randy said. "Chione's mumbo-jumbo's gotten through to you."

Clifford nearly choked. "Until you learn how to read your own gut," he said. "Don't condemn others who do."

Chione stared at the tabletop. From her dreams, she gleaned other reasons why each of them may have been chosen. They came from varied backgrounds and had reputable experiences. Having ended up together at the new and unproven California Institute of Archaeology did not feel coincidental. Until the visions provided clearer answers, she would not disclose any fragments of information and risk sounding like a fortuneteller. She would watch each in the group deftly play out their parts as events unfolded in the days and weeks to come.

"Even the funding obtained, Dr. Withers," Aaron said. "The donors just about dumped the cash on the table."

"Still," Dr. Withers said. "It's only enough to get in, do the job, and get out."

"What about delays?" Bebe asked. "Unforeseen events, cost over-runs, things like that?"

"Our benefactors aren't that wealthy. It's all we have now, considering the leaks that got out," Dr. Withers said, shaking his head again. "Our Institute's too new, still got a reputation to prove."

"Wish we had a bigger cushion," Clifford said, shaking his head thoughtfully.

"Regardless," Dr. Withers said. "As a professional group, this is our expedition to what might well be the most intriguing Egyptian find since Howard Carter persisted."

"If not now, we'll at least be poised for future grants," Bebe said.

"So, let's get on with our meeting. I need to count heads." Dr. Withers flipped through his paperwork. "Let's go around the table. Bebe Hutton, you've decided to postpone your surgery for the duration of our stay here? You're very much needed, but let me stress," he said, pointing into the air again. "You'd better consider your health."

"It wasn't I who chose to delay the surgery," Bebe said. "My new gynecologist insists my symptoms will diminish with natural remedies." She rolled her eyes. "Wish they'd hurry."

Bebe could be so reserved, yet at times, curiously open about her female problems that caused many absences from work. The entire group knew of Bebe's post-menopausal malaise. In fact, they all knew one another on fairly personal levels. Understanding each other was what made them bond together as a tight-knit team despite the bickering. They could not help themselves. Or, according to Chione's dream fragments, these particular people might simply be acting out predestined scripts.

"Okay, so you're on board. Did Kenneth come along?"

"He had hoped I'd slow down after our years in South America," Bebe said. "His back's been acting up, but he never let a little bullet stop him."

"Next, Clifford Rawlings, with your wife?"

"Need you ask? I should have retired five years ago, but Egypt again?" His grin stretched ear to ear. "Rita says when I do retire, we should just move here and buy our burial plots in Garden City."

"Aaron Ashby? Did you bring a friend?"

Aaron glanced quickly at Chione, and she pretended not to see. "Just me, and raring to go."

"Oh, yes. I learned something about you before you joined the Institute," Dr. Withers said. "You've been through the Holy Land, so the Nile should be right up your alley."

"Yes, sir. The Holy Land was totally a spiritual experience. I'm eager to see Egypt as well."

"Next, Randy Osborne?"

Randy puffed up his chest and pulled back his chin. "I'm also rarin' to learn how much of Chione's so-called predictions come true."

"Randy," Dr. Withers said. "What I'm attempting to learn is who brought a significant other and who didn't. That's all."

Randy looked sheepish again. "Just me," he said. "I work better alone."

Dr. Withers raised an eyebrow then continued. "Kendra Laker?"

"Royce wouldn't miss this either. It's like coming home again."

"How many times does this make you?"

"We've already logged a dozen trips along the Nile. This is lucky thirteen."

"Well now," Dr. Withers said. "With Chione, that makes eleven of us, counting Marlowe and me—"

"Why was Chione allowed to come?" Randy asked, blurting it out too forcefully.

Chione's ire had been triggered. Before she could respond for herself, Dr. Withers dropped a fist onto the tabletop. She had never known anyone as belligerent as Randy. No one said a word as Dr. Withers struggled to maintain his composure. Randy had overstepped his bounds and the only person to take the situation in hand would be Dr. Withers, who stood and leaned on his knuckles as he glared at

Randy. "To those who know her," he said, "Chione... is... Egypt. Period."

Kendra turned and smiled at Aaron as she always did as if to confirm they had gotten the best of Randy again. She always looked to Aaron for assurance. Stranger still was how people said he and Kendra resembled one another. No one would guess Kendra was nearly forty. Aaron once asked if that made him look older than his thirty-three years. He and Kendra both had pale green eyes and wavy brownish-blonde hair, but he saw no resemblance and wished Kendra would consider changing her hair color. Luckily, his pastimes enabled him to spend time outdoors where the sun streaked red through his.

Dr. Withers sat down again. "I've heard enough," he said in a tone that left Randy to stew in his despicable attitude. He looked up from his notes and pursed his lips as he studied the group. Finally, he said, "As much as I hesitate to delay, I want all of us to take a few days' vacation—"

"First?" Randy said, blurting again. "Let's just get into the dig."

"First," Dr. Withers said as he glared at Randy over the top of his glasses. "You'll allow me to finish." He took a moment then smiled again at the others. "I propose we spend a few days touring Cairo or other points of interest. You've all been working just as hard on this project back in California as anyone at the site. Those of you who have not been to Egypt, Bebe and Kenneth, and you, Aaron—"

"And me," Randy said, waving a hand.

"And you, Randy," Dr. Withers said, rolling his eyes, "will have a chance to experience some of the Nile Valley with the rest of us. During this time, you can put jet lag behind you and become acclimated to the drastic change in climate. October in the desert may be a little warm but cold at night."

"Are you proposing we take some excursions along the Nile together?" Kendra asked. Her excitement was infectious.

"That's if we can stand one another," Dr. Withers said, almost laughing. "This morning, though, we're scheduled to go to the Madu Museum to meet the curators and see where our tomb's relics will be housed. After that, you're on your own." Despite his business as usual attitude, it was known that he, too, enjoyed the camaraderie of a finely tuned group. He had a reputation for being fair and fun around the campfire when the day was over. He shot a finger into the air, and raising his voice said, "Lastly, there's a crucial little matter on which we must come together."

3

Conversation ended abruptly. Dr. Withers looked at her again. He had the kindest eyes. She could read him well. He was about to discuss her and his eyes begged for patience. "At issue here is whether or not some of you can work with Chione Ini-Herit without letting personal resentments get in the way." He stared straight at Randy.

She knew that Dr. Withers had grown fond of her and her abilities, especially since her premonitions had provided the chance to validate his dream of a private institute that held its own. He had toyed with the idea of retiring but changed his mind at the first sign of opportunity. Then too, his wife, Marlowe, who held a lifelong interest in the paranormal, had been fascinated and befriended her a couple of years earlier.

Dr. Withers waited. Finally, he said, "I don't have time to hear any of you privately. If you don't care to comment out in the open right now, after today you can put a lid on personal grievances."

There was a moment of silence but then Bebe raised her hand. "I don't have a grievance," she said. "I used to see Chione as excess, even felt intimidated by her knowledge. But the more I learned about her, the more I realized she's a self-taught historian. Egypt is new to me, and she's fluent in hieroglyphs. I could learn from her." Her smile seemed sincere and, for the first time, Chione felt a rapport with Bebe.

Dr. Withers seemed pleased to hear something positive. "Your exceptional reputation as a historian precedes you, Bebe. I'm glad you feel that way."

"So? We already have one historian," Randy said. "Chione's assignments can be covered by any of us."

Kendra shook her head as if she could not believe what she had just heard. "What exactly do you see as being her assignments?"

"So far as this trip is concerned, she's assigned to hieroglyph interpretation and to transcribe Bebe's manuscripts which will document our work. And logging, secretarial stuff with you, Kendra, as conservator of artifacts and inventories."

"A valuable person indeed," Clifford said.

"Minor stuff," Randy said.

"Is that your grievance, Randy?" Dr. Withers asked.

He reached over and took hold of her hand. The moment their hands met, a shot of energy assaulted her nervous system. "Oh!" Chione said as she pulled her hand away. She had just received a psychometric impression from the touch. That was one way her extrasensory perceptions occurred, unexpected, spontaneous, in the middle of a thought or conversation. Vivid or vague, suddenly there, quickly gone.

"What happened?" Kendra asked.

The others looked inquisitive. Except Aaron. He understood all her token expressions. They had been close once. He refused to accept the reason she needed to be independent. He still studied her as if he might further learn to emulate her abilities. With what she knew of him, his paranormal awakening was about to explode without direction from her. Aaron knew her well, knew when she perceived things in her extraordinary ways. Others in the room had no inkling about what made her tick. Now Aaron would not take his eyes off her for fear of missing something. The others noticed them staring at one another.

"Chione, you received something, didn't you?" Kendra asked again.

"Yes," she said, feeling embarrassed at having to explain to the entire group. "I've seen myself at the excavation site."

Randy let out a coarse burst of laughter that the others ignored.

"I don't know how you intuit all that information," Clifford said. All but Randy seemed sincerely interested. "Try to grasp this concept," she said, ignoring him. "Everything that's ever happened, that's happening now or yet to occur, happens all at once."

"I'll never get it," Bebe said.

"On different planes of existence," Chione said. "Practice mentally changing planes. It's like this. Imagine playing all the notes of the scale at the same time, then focusing on hearing the sound of only one note while hearing all the others simultaneously."

Everyone quieted as if practicing the technique. At least they tried.

Aaron doodled, drawing grids on a note pad. He must have begun the habit to keep his hands busy when he felt nervous. He, too, was eager to get to the site.

"I get it," Clifford said. "Then we try to hear other notes separately."

"Each note is like a different plane of existence," Chione said. "Happening along with all the others."

"Like the quality of your jokes," Bebe said, teasing Clifford.

Offering extraneous information was a bold stance on her part. She shared her inner self with a trusted few. But something new had been happening since she began dreaming of the tomb. The team being part of those dreams, she felt the need to make them aware of certain facts and knew, in time, she would have to divulge more. She wondered how much Aaron might perceive. When they had been close, at times they shared virtually the same dreams. Now she was growing, rapidly developing her skills. She introduced him to strange and enticing realms, then as he put it, deprived him. She could tell he both loved and abhorred her. Yet, if they dreamed the same dreams in the past, could he know that she was aware of the erotic dreams he recently began to experience? Dreams of her? And who was the other woman who recently began appearing in those dreams?

Silence filled the room as the others noticed Aaron and her avoiding one another. Finally, Bebe said, "Tell us more about the tomb."

Chione looked to Dr. Withers who made a gesture of approval and said, "Far be it from me to discredit anything you've seen in that mind of yours."

"Is it a rich find?" Kendra asked. "Beyond our wildest dreams?" Kendra would like nothing less than to have the discovery turn up lavish rewards and for her to be known as having been a major part of it all.

"Go ahead, Chione," Dr. Withers said. "I'm sure none of us so much as dabbled in altered states before meeting you, but your gifts have done right by us. We're believers now, at least in you, and willing to listen. Tell them what you told me on the phone."

"Something new?" Kendra asked, leaning forward.

Chione hesitated. Why was she being given this information if not to share with them in the discovery? She had difficulty believing the strange new scenes. What if she told them something that did not come true? She had no recourse but to continue, though carefully. She took a deep breath then quietly said, "This find affects each of us." Excitement broke out again with everyone begging to hear more. For a group of professionals who had been trained to control their emotions regarding their work, they were certainly an expressive bunch. "I've received only fragments," she said, elevating her voice above the others.

"We'll take 'em," Clifford said eagerly.

She began again. "There is... much gold."

"Yeah," Randy yelled.

"Incredible artifacts and jewels."

By this time, Randy was standing and leaning over the tabletop excitedly banging a fist. Dr. Withers suddenly redirecting his attention forced Randy back into his chair in a spell of regret.

Chione moved her eyes upward from side to side, something that came naturally to do as if reading messages in the highest corners of her mind. When she did this, information flowed in. "A strange pyramid," she said. "Some danger averted, some not." Then she looked at the group again and forced a weak smile and flinched.

"What is it?" Kendra asked.

"An eerie feeling, like we're being watched."

"Watched? Here?" Bebe asked. "By whom?"

"Not here," Chione said. "In my mind, I'm already at the site. There's a sense of foreboding like we're being watched."

Randy sighed heavily. "Oh, sure. A curse, like at King Tut's tomb."

"Will you shut up," Clifford said sharply across the table. Then he turned to the others. "Excu-use me," he said, affectedly teasing and knowing he had done something the others lacked the courage to do.

Dr. Withers pinched back a smile.

Sensing herself in Egypt, Chione gasped. She had just received more extrasensory input. As was her habit, she looked in the direction from which the thought or vision appeared in her mind.

"Is there more?" Bebe asked from the edge of her chair. "How will history be changed?"

Chione blinked slowly then gazed downward. She did not want anyone to try to guess anything from her expression. "Better to let it play out," she said, averting full disclosure of more incredible clues that were, as yet, only fragments. She could not disclose all the bits and pieces of events she might receive. Doing so would force her to admit that even she did not understand how they fit together. The others would lose faith in her. "Each one of us plays a part," she said, nonchalantly smiling at Aaron as Randy squirmed again from want of attention. To Dr. Withers, she added, "We won't need sensors, however, to locate the new pyramid."

"Radar, sensors?" Randy asked, cutting in. "They're standard modus operandi for finding formations beneath the sand. We, of course, will need sensors."

"Not even a simple magnetometer will find this pyramid," Chione said.

"A pyramid," Randy said. "How does she know?"

Everyone quieted, this time giving her the opportunity to speak. "My dreams have given us this find, Randy," she said quietly. "This information comes from the same source."

"You don't have the kind of knowledge needed to aid in the dig," Randy said. "Sensors certainly are not your area of expertise." He turned to the others. "It's ludicrous. How does Chione know we will or will not need a magnetometer or seismic devices?"

"First of all," Chione said, answering despite Randy not addressing her directly. "A magnetometer has proved most effective in the dry limestone cliffs of the Valley of the Kings, primarily used for locating tomb entrances near the surface."

"We aren't digging in Valley of the Kings," Randy said, sounding like a know-it-all.

Aaron smiled, knew what she was about to say.

"Exactly. And we've already found our entrance," she said. "We won't need to be measuring magnetism for gaps in rock formations."

"If there's another pyramid buried some place," Randy said. "You can bet we'll need sensors."

"Radar and seismic devices," Chione said, continuing undaunted, "are used for locating greater rock formations below the surface."

"That's my point."

"But you didn't get mine," she said, watching the others reacting to Randy's insistence. "I said we'd find another pyramid. You assumed I meant one like the Great Pyramid at Giza and that it would be buried."

"How do you know what I was thinking?"

"Need you ask?" Aaron almost laughed at Randy's refusal to recognize Chione's abilities. Her talents never surprised or intimidated him, but she wished he would soon find someone else to dote upon.

"The pyramid will not be found near the surface," Chione said, innocently digging into Randy's flagging self-confidence. "This tomb, representing one unique breath of history, contains all kinds of inconsistencies."

"We're looking for something different now?" Randy asked, whining. "Haven't you heard? We're already inside the burial complex."

"Unless we remain open to unusual possibilities," Chione said to the others, "we'll miss the most important hidden chambers."

Everyone snapped to attention after becoming distracted by Randy's fear of being supplanted. Except Randy who sighed, disgusted, as he tipped back in his chair. "Sure, hidden," he said and then snickered.

"You mean," Dr. Withers said, pausing to raise fingers signaling quotes, "you've seen something else?"

"Unless we heed the messages of this tomb, we could be forced to abandon the dig."

"No!" Aaron said. "This is too important."

"Agreed," Chione said. "But much beyond our present stage of entry, sensors won't help."

"If you think we're going to have difficulty finding something unusual buried in the desert," Randy said. "Leave that to the seismographers, the engineers, okay Chione? That's their job."

No one paid further attention to Randy. Voices hummed again. Dr. Withers reached into his briefcase. "That's it for our meeting. Here are some tour brochures." He flung packets across the tabletop and Bebe tore into hers. Dr. Withers began to rise, then paused. "Uh... there is one last thing I need to make clear here and now." Everyone came to attention and his jovial expression turned dead serious. "Ladies—and that includes the ones not present," he said. "Make no unnecessary eye contact with the locals. Do not become friendly with the local men."

"But eye contact is a sign of integrity," Bebe said.

"Not in this country," Clifford said.

"Especially from women," Dr. Withers said, enunciating every word. "Women stay subdued in this culture. You do the same. If you don't heed this warning, it could cost you your life." He pointed into the air. "No woman from our group is to walk the streets of Cairo alone—night or day—or leave our camp at the dig site without at least one male escort. You hear?" He sighed, sounded tired, then said; "I'd appreciate if you who know Egypt would make yourselves available for those who don't."

"Why can't we just have a private reading from Chione?" Randy asked.

Dr. Withers gathered his papers and closed his briefcase, snapping the clasps loudly. Then he looked directly at Randy over the top of his glasses. "I want to see you privately," he said, thumbing backwards. Everyone gathered their materials and began to leave. Aaron delayed, pouring over his notes. Chione's heart quickened. Recently, with the prospect of working in Egypt, people began teasing saying he resembled Pharaoh Tutankhamon, except that Aaron's teeth were straight and pearly white. Since beginning to dream of Egypt, every time their eyes met or when they touched, she perceived recurring dreams that he must have been having. The fantasy changed little, always him making love to a woman on a woven cot among soft tapestry pillows and red ornate paneling; or under the full moon at a cool oasis; or floating on a barge on the Nile. Why had she felt such rapport with the woman in those dreams? Recently she began seeing the woman as herself.

Sensuality suggested by the visions made her woozy. The dreams, him loving her, and she burning with equal fire, were always the same, but fantasy it was. Dreams acting as a pressure release valve. Who was the new woman who recently began appearing, usurping the place she thought of as her own? How was it so easy for her to also feel like she was the new woman as well?

The woman in the first few dreams dressed in the Egyptian style clothing Chione sewed for herself. She wore subtle modern-day makeup that made her look Egyptian. She wore the same golden ankh that dangled on a chain around her throat. In the latest dreams, she became the other woman wearing a golden scarab. Aaron, too, became someone else. They had made love with unbridled passion, each appearing as the foreign other, returning to themselves before the dream faded. The glorious Egyptian man in the dreams worshipped her slender body and lithe legs. The dreams were why she felt renewed interest in Aaron. If they were his erotic dreams, she needed to allow him privacy and block them out of her mind. Each time she caught him dreamily staring at her, were those dreams permeating his daytime fantasies as well? She was not sure she wanted to renew the relationship with Aaron. The dreams were his, and she was simply psychically tapping into them.

She and Aaron once loved one another, nearly committed all. He departed, thwarted by her decision to remain single so that he might find someone else and have a family. Yet, she could tell by his actions that he would try again to win her. It would be subtle. He was not one to appear as a love-struck puppy. He would wait and keep his erotic secrets. If her dreams came true, why wouldn't his as well? The thought made her both want him and wish to repel his interest.

After the others left the room, and Chione began to leave, Aaron hastily gathered up his things and caught up with her. "Your eyes are black as onyx gleaming," he said. His voice contained a hint of an accent most peculiar. His gaze was piercing.

The golden ankh at her throat caught the glint of the sun through the window and beamed brilliantly across his face. He seemed caught in a spell. "Aaron," she said.

"Uh… yeah?" he asked, blinking. He seemed to have difficulty coming back into the moment.

"When the going gets rough, don't let them give up, okay?"

"Okay…."

"Promise?" She had to make sure he understood.

"You've seen more than you let on," he said. "What else do you know?"

"I couldn't mention it to the others. You understand? It seemed as if there was too much happening. I couldn't see it all, as if there was a haze right in front of my face." She passed her hand back and forth in front of her eyes.

"Like a premonition that didn't quite come in?"

"More like a haze, that I couldn't see through. Don't know how else to describe it. A feeling of near defeat."

"That doesn't sound promising."

"It's one of those pieces of the puzzle that will eventually fit," she said. "But it would frighten the others to know. Promise, Aaron? Don't let them give up."

He reached to touch her shoulder then caught himself. After a moment of them staring into each other's eyes, he said, "I promise, Chione. I'm good at that. There'll be no giving up."

4

A young boy strolled along the road at the periphery of the camp. He rang a bell that called the Islamic faithful to morning prayers in an area set up for the purpose lower down the hill. "Good morning," he said, yelling up to her and waving.

Chione waved in return, curiously surprised that a young Egyptian child's mannerisms could seem so western. Something about him was gregarious and cute. He disappeared beyond the large airtight mud-brick shack that had been erected for the electronic equipment. She saw him again as he entered a portable toilet. It was also curious that he took such liberties using their facility.

Dr. Withers referred to the mud brick structure as the tech shack. He had paid a fortune to have a single phone line stretched from the small Theban village down on the flats to the south. The ancient village had sprung back to life due to the hundreds of Egyptian workers and families helping to restore various dig sites. Some of the line simply lay stretched across the rocky dunes. It was hoped no mangy jackals, starving dogs, or other animals might chew the line and knock out phone and fax capability at the CIA site. However, the FAX line transmitted only intermittently, if you had patience to keep trying. The single telephone might be used for emergencies since the connection was nearly nonexistent. The tech shack would also house the developing of film on site and save valuable monies and time wasted on outside film developing when still shots were immediately needed.

Ginny McLain's cameras would electronically capture most of what they needed to document during their entire stay, no matter how long it took. The tech shack housed its own generator solely for the purposes of keeping her equipment charged and keeping the FAX machine running. Cellular phones were stored there as well, the team having learned that connections in the desert, and inside a tomb, to be non-existent.

A gigantic colorful Egyptian tent had been rounded up to house the artifacts brought out of the tomb and readied for shipment to Cairo. The inventory tent was erected nearest the tomb entrance and in front of the tech shack to shelter it from dust from the road. The dust and grit threatened to be uncontrollable. The cook tent and dining area, also used as their meeting room, sat in sight of the tomb entrance. The portable toilets and shower tents sat between the business area and the personal yurts where the team slept. They were also positioned according to which way the wind blew.

The wind whipped down off the stark neighboring hillsides and made strange noises that rumbled between the hills. In the Egyptian Book of the Dead, the roaring wind at Abydos called the noise of the dead, made sounds at times like high voices, at other times, deep rumbling. It was a result of fine, clean Aeolian sand rolling down the slopes that produced the eerie music. Chione fantasized at the similarities between ancient times and what she now experienced as she looked out to the hills.

The laborers' camp was erected across the road at the nearer end of the mastabas. Their ragged tents sheltered woven sleeping cots. Many men slept in the open air. The team slept on the same type cots. Wool blankets were welcomed to stave off the cool night chill. An added feature Clifford learned over the years was to place the legs of each cot into wide-mouthed vessels filled with water. Footers, he called them. They prevented scorpions and other creepy crawlers from climbing up the legs and into the bed. Unfortunately, they wouldn't be any help in deterring snakes.

Instead of having shanties built, and because of budget constraints, Dr. Withers and other decision-makers opted for second-hand yurts that Paki Rashad rounded up. The white canvas domes dotted the hillside and actually afforded each person or couple some privacy. Other than diet, meager generator electricity or lanterns and some personal items, they would live no better than the locals and Chione felt so much a part of it all.

She longed to walk barefoot in the rock and rubble but heeded well the warning about scorpions and snakes that could show up anywhere. Groups of local people were hired for the ongoing task of keeping the site clear of pests until activity scared the crawlers out of the area. Boots were part of the daily uniform, to be removed only before evening showers. Later she could wear the Egyptian sandals she had purchased in Cairo. The sturdy khaki pants and shirts the team would wear throughout their stay were surprisingly cool in full sun.

Dark men and women scurried everywhere. Egyptians, a mixture of African and Middle Eastern nationalities, always had a ready smile and talked incessantly or sang while they worked. In the cool crisp morning, as one man intoned a work chant to the prophet Muhammad, the workers threw out their mats in the dust and bowed down where they happened to be.

Siti, a local woman, and cook in the laborers camp carried water to the men in a large pot on her head. Her colorful skirts and the sheesh covering her hair billowed as she walked. Many groups of laborers built small fires in the open and huddled around to divert the wind while they cooked their simple meals. Occasionally a mingling of delicious scents from their food cooking wafted around the campsite.

"So many dialects," Aaron said as he, Bebe, and Rita approached her near the tomb entrance.

"And good English too," Chione said.

"Yes," Aaron said. "They speak great Inglizi."

Chione could not help staring at Bebe's new hairdo. Her mousy brown hair had been cut and permed into an ancient Egyptian style with curls nearly to her shoulders. The color was now reddish brown.

All she needed was a perfumed beeswax cone on the top of her head, and she could pass for an Egyptian woman seen in historic etchings. She looked truly elegant though her relaxed appearance indicated that she was going through some drastic changes. Chione could not help commenting. "You make one fabulous Egyptian woman, Bebe." Bebe smiled nervously, as if still in the process of understanding what she had done to herself.

"The tomb's about to be opened," Chione said. "Soon as the workers return from prayers."

"That happens... what?" Bebe asked. "Five times a day? Prayer breaks will slow down our progress."

"Probably not," Aaron said. "They can just come and go as they need to."

Beginning about fifty or sixty feet off the bumpy dirt road, the grade the laborers dug sloped downward toward the tomb entrance. With access to the entrance cleared, a great flat triangular decline pointed to the mouth of the tomb. Crude steps had been carved along one side for foot traffic. Pulleys were rigged in the triangular pit, for ease in moving heavy or bulky artifacts. In light of the specific articles already found, expectations soared. Generators were already in place with lamps and extension cords and a variety of equipment strewn about. The scene looked more like a movie being shot on location. They stood near the road in preparation to walk down to the tomb entrance.

Chione paced nervously. She could not be more ready. Her elation soared after a dream the night before, a scene of many children loving her.

"What's that cleared area up on top?" Bebe asked.

"An excavation from lifting out the portcullis blocking the passage-way," Aaron said.

The multi-ton granite obelisk with its one irregular geometric end had been lowered to the foot of the slope. It was left at the side where the backfill from the entrance had been deposited. Wedged in sand and chips, it looked like a cousin of the Unfinished Obelisk in the Pharaonic quarries at Aswan, a left-over from the Graeco-Roman period of the 6th Dynasty.

"That's one of those blocks they let slide into place when they seal the tomb after burial," Rita said.

Rita, whose education had not been in Archaeology or any related field, worked with little or no pay alongside her husband, perhaps longer than most of the others had been in the career field. She knew as much or more about Egypt. Despite her folksy, down-home way of expressing herself, she had a way of endearing people to her. Clifford always credited her for his successes.

"We're hoping we won't find another," Aaron said. He was serious as usual as he voiced concern for any aspects of the work.

"Won't we just follow the passageway to see where it leads once we're inside?" Bebe asked.

"If the passage is long," Rita said. "Farther in, they could have blocked it off again."

"It seems that when the neighboring necropolis encroached on this ancient tomb," Aaron said as he looked toward the rows of monuments, "debris from digging for placement of the mastabas was heaped on top of this burial site."

"This tomb was simply forgotten?" Bebe asked.

"Looks that way," Chione said.

Aaron turned to her. "Is that the reason you said the dig could be abandoned?"

"One of them. If debris had been allowed to swallow the tomb's entrance," she said. "It's almost certain the burial took place during a much earlier period." Since they already knew this tomb was 18th Dynasty, past digs predicted the tomb would be carved downward inside the mountain. "This being an older tomb with many years' rubble piled on top," Chione said. "The burial chambers may be much deeper than our sensors can detect."

Given the fact the portcullis looked like another rock wall inside, the dig could have been abandoned. Anyone might think the passageway had not been completed, a common practice meant to discourage grave robbers.

Historically, to seal some tombs, the shafts were filled with sand. The sand was released slowly at the bottom allowing the portcullis block to lower. The entrance tunnel to this tomb slanted too steeply downward to hold and release sand. Neither did Dr. Withers and the others find any trace of sand under the portcullis area.

The engineers reported finding the portcullis and its shaft were a bit smaller on the lower end. The Ancients were experts at block cutting. With the shaft narrower at the bottom, the block was eased downward until it came to a stop. A slightly V-shaped rock squared off at the bottom to match the floor, sat inside a hole carved with the corresponding shape of the portcullis. When the block was dropped in place, it looked like just another outcropping on the surface of the hillock.

"Why was the tomb closed again yesterday after removal of the portcullis?" Rita asked, rubbing her temples. Finally, she turned away from the sun.

"Waiting for the team to make their way here from Cairo," Chione said.

A Norwegian archaeological group was restoring a site nearby at Dier el-Medina, west of Queen Hatshepsut's Dier el-Bahri, and closest to the Institute's location. Dr. Withers arranged to borrow some of their equipment. They moved it over to coincide with the return of the California team. Paki Rashad from the Antiquities Society joined them from Cairo for the lifting of the portcullis.

"Were you inside, Chione?" Bebe asked.

"No, but that's the reason Dr. Withers wanted to return early," she said. "He was inside with Rashad when they lifted that rock. He got so excited, and he's been giddy ever since."

"Why? What happened?" Bebe asked. She treated every incident like a good piece of gossip.

"He said once that block started to lift, impatience forced him down on his belly to see underneath. He said the passageway goes on forever."

"No kidding," Rita said. The way she squinted against the sun, she should have worn sunglasses.

"See anything else?" Bebe asked.

"Painted walls and a chamber door."

"Oh," Bebe said. "I can't wait."

"After we've removed the artifacts from the First Chamber," Aaron said. "While we're cataloging and all that, the engineers will do some testing farther in."

"To identify if there are any more of those granite blocks?" Rita asked, fanning herself. Beads of perspiration glistened in her curly red hair.

"That, too," Chione said, smiling reassuringly. "It has to be done while we're out of the tomb, in case there's a collapse."

"Everyone's eager to find your pyramid," Bebe said.

"Help them have patience!" Chione said, begging understanding from the overzealous teammates. Then, to divert attention away from her abilities, Chione asked, "Bebe, why was Kenneth limping?"

"I told you about his war wound," she said. "He took a bullet in Nam."

"You never said he took a bullet," Chione said. She felt Kenneth's pain and hugged herself. "Can we do anything for him?"

Bebe suddenly wrapped an arm around her shoulders. They watched a group of men clear equipment from in front of the makeshift doorway at the tomb entrance. "Kenneth is tough," Bebe said. "Just leave him be."

"Does he suffer?" Chione asked. She stepped back and placed a hand over her eyes to shield her face from the sun.

"The camel excursion we took was a bit much. Don't pamper him, though. If he had to admit to pain, he'd begin to fail."

"He walks in pain. I hadn't noticed that before."

"Sometimes it bothers him. The bullet's lodged near his spine. Some people joke saying he got hit running away. It actually entered through his side." The tone in Bebe's voice expressed great empathy for a husband she never quite seemed to trust. The way Bebe studied everyone could be a byproduct of the education of her career field. Perhaps she understood more of human nature than she let on.

As the penetrating Egyptian sun burned away last wisps of the night's fog, hearing about Kenneth caused a chill to transit Chione's body. Aaron touched her shoulder in silent recognition. She wished that somehow Aaron would force himself to disconnect from her. Aaron being able to translate what she was experiencing would be as difficult to turn off as her own abilities. He seemed to intuit her every whim. She held her composure and smiled at Bebe. "So that's what makes Kenneth push himself, always wanting to do more?"

Chione also knew that Kenneth was trying desperately to make something of his life, such as it was. He wanted to gain back the love and admiration he once received from their son, Kenneth, Jr. The son they doted upon had turned pacifist and renounced his father. His injuries were living reminders of war. Chione realized that she was staring at Bebe and looked away quickly.

"Why aren't you wearing your hat?" Bebe asked.

Chione pulled the crumpled headgear from her back pocket.

"And you're not wearing your ankh," Rita said.

"I'm wearing this now," Chione said. She tugged at the chain around her neck and pulled up the plump golden scarab pendant from inside her shirt. "A trinket Mom and Dad brought home from one of their trips." As far as she knew, it was not real gold, and she did not think it important to have it tested. Her parents had given it to her. That was all that mattered.

5

Randy sped up in a jeep skidding to a stop in the sandy rubble dangerously near them and throwing a billowing dust cloud.

Chione jumped back and fell into a sand drift.

"Hey! What's with you, Randy?" Aaron asked as he offered to help her up.

Bebe beat the dust off her pant legs with her hat. "Randy!" she said. "Will you ever grow up?"

"Loose soil," he said, shrugging and climbing out of the jeep.

Three noisy laborers rode in the back of the jeep. Like some of the other men, they wore turbans loosely bound with the ends drooping around their necks. The ends could be quickly wrapped around the face should the wind kick up. They also wore the common loose fitting gallibayas over trousers and lifted the skirts to throw themselves over the tailgate. Then they noticed her and stopped short as Aaron pulled her to her feet.

Chione accepted Aaron's hand but released it immediately upon righting herself. Egyptians detest public displays of any kind between men and women and the team wished to respect those traditions.

Suddenly the laborers backed away and smiled pleasantly yet averted their gaze. Then they turned and quickly walked toward the other workers and talked low among themselves.

"What was that all about?" Bebe asked.

Chione only smiled. She knew that she and Bebe looked Egyptian. The workers saw it too. She shrugged.

"It's just like what happened aboard that old dhow on the Nile when we first set out," Aaron said. "With the wind blowing through your hair? The navigator wanted to bargain for you so he could tie you under the bowsprit and use you for a figurehead."

Everyone laughed, except Randy. "So where were you last night, Chione?" he asked. "Afraid your powers wouldn't protect you from the bucktoothed witch? Afraid you're going to be sick again and have to hide it from everyone?"

She and Aaron exchanged knowing glances.

"Chione's not ill?" Aaron said. "How would you know what she's feeling?"

"She interned with me, remember? I got to know her. She had some really weak days in the months before this trip was announced."

Chione was aghast. Someone had noticed her malaise. Why did it have to be Randy? She wondered why he had never used the knowledge to his advantage, as would be his habit. She and Aaron again exchanged quick glances.

Then Bebe, perhaps sensing Chione's discomfort, stepped forward and in a taunting manner asked, "How would you know about the bucktoothed witch? You didn't tour Giza."

"You did?"

"Wouldn't have missed it for the world. We even crawled through the labyrinth of tunnels and read graffiti dated 1837."

Randy leaned back against the jeep and crossed his arms. "So how much *baksheesh* did you have to fork over to bribe your guide into taking you that deep?"

"We didn't have to bribe anyone. We pay for services rendered."

"Well, did the apparition make an appearance?" Randy's attitude said he did not really wish to know.

"You should have come. Some things are better experienced first-hand."

"I had other plans," he said. His effort to dig at Bebe and remind her that she did not believe in spirits fell short.

"Other plans?" Bebe asked, shaking her head. "Kenneth and I rather liked the excitement of sleeping inside the Great Pyramid."

"I don't need to know if the Pyramid is haunted," Randy said. "I don't believe that stuff; mysterious visions, chanting, whistling and fluttering sounds. Gimme a break."

"Where did you stay, Randy?" Rita asked.

"I booked myself in at the new Khepri Oasis," he said proudly. "It's out near the Pyramids."

So what if Randy chose another night of relative luxury? His lack of participation in the experience at hand showed how much he was not a part of the group. He would be the one least likely to become acclimated now that they had all bedded down in the tent camp.

Aaron looked smug, ready to dig at Randy. "I understand only the most diligent can make it through some of the passages found in many tombs," he said, subtly reminding Randy that he was out of shape.

"Hope we don't experience any of the difficulties encountered by Giovanni Battista Belzoni in the early nineteenth century," Bebe said.

"Belzoni and his team inched downward on their bellies in a dim passage not much wider than their own bodies," Rita said. "They crawled through piles of mummies, having to breathe their fetid dust."

"Not to mention the putrid taste of them in the air," Bebe said, making a face. "Neither to mention damaging them."

Randy ignored the hints being thrown his way and persisted. "Where did you stay, Chione?" he asked nicely. His effort to be friendly came across more as an insult.

"I hadn't heard that we're accountable to you," Chione said.

"I understand no one knew your whereabouts either, Aaron. Could it be—?"

"Can it, Randy! Go fall into a hole somewhere," Aaron said, gesturing toward the hills.

Randy always seemed startled anyone should speak to him in that manner. "I guess you pale skinned ladies ought to be careful here in

Egypt," he said, climbing back into the jeep. "I understand kidnappings are common occurrences."

Rita threw up her hands and turned away.

"That's mostly in Cairo," Chione said. "Usually if someone's worth a hefty ransom."

"Guess that leaves all of you out," Randy said quickly. "But they could use someone like you, Chione, in a harem."

Aaron took a quick step toward the jeep. "Like I said, Randy, go fall into a hole!"

Randy smirked, shifted the gears and sped away. If Aaron could have gotten close enough, he would have finally thumped Randy's head.

"Clifford and Rita and I stayed in Cairo," Aaron said, wrapping an arm around Rita, whom he had always been fond of.

"I'm always stunned at the noise level in that metropolis," Rita said. "I've had a headache ever since."

"I'm glad we didn't stay," Bebe said. "We played like locals, took Bus 14 through town, public transportation out as far as possible, and rode camels around Giza."

"You took the famous 14?" Rita asked. "Wasn't that some trip? The locals hanging onto the sides like San Francisco cable cars?"

"And riding the bumpers," Bebe said. "The real flavor of Cairo."

"Quite a lengthy excursion, wouldn't you say?" Rita asked.

"Actually, no. Cairo is sprawling, creeping close to the Pyramids," Bebe said. "It's really an illusion out there in that expanse, a real paradox. The closer you get to the pyramids, the smaller they look."

"I had no idea Cairo was such a bustling place," Chione said. "A big step back in time for me."

"You mean the donkey carts, animals running loose and so forth?"

"That, the throngs of people in traditional dress, the crowded suqs, and the beggars," Chione said. "Despite traffic that's worse than New York City."

"And all those high rises," Bebe said. "Who would've guessed?"

"You two didn't like Cairo?" Aaron asked. "Is that why I lost track of you?"

"On the contrary," Chione said. "I feel as if I've come home. Definitely, Egypt is now the center of my world. But I felt such a pulling toward Thebes. Couldn't get here fast enough."

That was not the real reason to rush to Thebes. She began seeing bits and pieces of scenes of Ancient Egypt and experiencing many new premonitions. The flashes of scenes were not dreams. They happened in the normal waking state, like switching a channel on TV, then quickly switching back to the channel previously watched. The occurrences began intensifying since arriving in Egypt. She smelled a certain perfume again and again but could not find it in the perfumeries. Children in Cairo crowded around her and clung to her for no reason. The strange occurrences left her with a sense of needing to get to the dig site. She surmised that since the visions occurred with greater frequency in Egypt, they most certainly had to do with her purpose for being invited along. She felt motivated to reach the tomb site and arrived early with the Witherses. "Dr. Withers and Marlowe and I already walked the mastabas."

"Walked the mastabas?" Rita asked. "Following up on some of your dream clues, right?"

"Sort of."

"More dreams?" Aaron asked.

"Strange," Chione said, thinking deeply and remembering. "Ancient Egyptian scenes..."

"In your dreams?" Bebe asked. "What? How?"

"Just dreams, I'm sure," Chione said, shooting a glance at Aaron, warning him not to corner her for an explanation.

"Some dreams are just rehashing of the facts," he said, helping her out of a situation she did not wish to again explain. "But what happened to Kendra and Royce?"

After visiting the top of the Cairo Tower and looking out over the Great Green, the team had scattered.

"They went visiting friends in Heliopolis and Garden City," Rita said. "Must have lots of friends. They arrived in camp separately, Kendra late last night and Royce this morning."

"Hey, hey, over here!" Kendra said as she approached from the direction of the tech shack. She hurried to meet them. "Isn't this wonderful? The expansiveness, the stillness?"

"You've got to be kidding," Marlowe Withers said as she, too, approached. "I hope my face doesn't prune up."

Marlowe looked much pampered wearing tailored khakis, subtle makeup and straight raven hair pulled smoothly back into a knot. That was not the way Dr. Withers would describe her. True, they lived the good life. However, she would get down and dirty in a dig with the best of them.

"If it gets really hot," Kendra said. "The dry air can burn your nostrils."

Marlowe sighed and looked out across the cemetery. "I had no idea mastabas were so large until we walked the rows. It's like a subdivision of mini-houses that goes on forever." She made a sweeping motion with her arm.

If pharaohs, being wealthy, built pyramids and tombs of grandeur, the burial places of the nobles and commoners would also be as big as they could envision and afford.

"That's why some were built up here on the hillside," Rita said. "More space and all."

Chione studied the distant view, which from that height included sharp crested sand dunes planed off by the eerie howling winds. A deep lavender haze blanketed the hills and the towering al-Qurn, Peak of the West, deemed by the Ancients as a natural pyramid created by their Gods. Al-Qurn was one reason the Ancients chose the craggy hills north of Thebes for burial sites.

"Look at these," Kendra said. She fanned the photos as they huddled around. "This is what the area looked like on day one."

One picture showed nothing more than a high sandy hillock being invaded by clumps of starving alfa-grass above the last row of mastabas.

Rita crowded in and took shade in Aaron's shadow. "Who'd have guessed what lies beyond the end of a dusty rutted road in Valley of the Queens?" She glanced out over the distance. "I wonder if anyone ever searched the remote outlying gullies like they did in Valley of the Kings. I'll bet there's much more to find."

"They've already found seventy-five to eighty tombs here, but there are many hills, many possibilities," Aaron said.

The idea was plausible, considering the necropolis represented commoners who lived and worked the tombs. The throngs of laborers had to be working on many sites.

The next photo showed a close up of a nondescript hole straight down in the ground near a random square stone looking cast aside from some ancient burial. Backfill in the cavity settled over time, creating the gaping hole that a man fell into.

Chione snatched the photo. "Yes!" she said and turned to face the tomb entrance. "Shows exactly what was in my dream!" The others could not know how vindicated she felt.

Aaron pointed out the hole in the ground in the photograph. "Dr. Withers and one of the exploratory team were first lowered into that hole—"

"Ginny got to go down, too, to shoot these stills," Kendra said.

"After a little digging around, they found the entrance that we're about to see down there." Aaron gestured toward the bottom end of the pit where others waited.

"Look at this batch," Kendra said, offering more photos. "Eating utensils and jars found buried inside the entry." Traditionally, those would be from the last meal of the tomb sealers after burial.

"These are garlands found in one of the jars," Marlowe said, explaining to Bebe.

Rita crowded closer. "Look at the flowers," she said. "Part of the celebration of the final meal. I'll bet they found them in the jars." She stepped back and fanned herself again. She had begun perspiring heavily.

"They're perfectly preserved. The arid sand does that," Kendra said. "It can dehydrate, make you skinny."

"Ha!" Bebe said as she flattened the front of her clothes. "For that, I could like it here."

"The artifacts are what convinced Sterling there was a tomb here," Marlowe said. "Combined with Chione's information."

Though the others seemed to bubble over with enthusiasm, Chione felt distracted with her attention impatiently pulled toward the workers. Having removed the padlocked chain from across the crude wooden doors ordered put in place by Dr. Withers, the tomb was about to be reopened. "The whimpering sounds," she said. "The crying. It stopped."

"How do you know that?" Bebe asked.

"From the men in the jeep."

"That's right. You understand Arabic."

"They said when Dr. Withers left for home, the strange crying stopped." Chione's heart wrenched, wishing not to miss anything. She felt ready to cry out and then realized the others would not understand how much she was beginning to feel connected to the tomb.

"It could have been the wind," Kendra said. "Excavation might have removed whatever was catching the breeze across it."

Suddenly Dr. Withers passed by in a huff with Rashad, the ASE Inspector, at his side. He waved an arm. "Come on, everybody. This is our big day."

Others in the team rushed past, accompanied by a handful of engineers; also in the group, Madu Museum historians, Dakarai and Masud. Both looked to be in their early forties, their dark mustaches stretched thin by eager smiles. Dakarai's blue gallibaya looked as if he was digging in dirt elsewhere. With everyone showing up neat and clean for the opening, where could he have been working to accumulate so much dust on his clothing?

Following came Carol Stockard and Edmond Hale from the San Francisco Sentinel and Radcliffe Stroud and Hadden Bourne from the London News-Herald. Surprisingly, the latter four seemed quite cohesive despite the San Francisco paper conceding partial rights to the London newspaper and also to Exploration Magazine. They made their way en masse down toward the entrance.

"Where are Royce and Kenneth?" Aaron asked.

"Photographing sunrise among the mastabas," Bebe said of Kenneth.

"In the tech shack," Kendra said of Royce. "Collecting e-mail from his office. He needs something to do while I'm working. I don't know how he'll keep busy."

CIA photographer Ginny McLain, along with the Antiquities photographer, the camera crew from Exploration Magazine and other media members, rushed past. They pointed cameras and zoomed in as the throng descended the rough-hewn steps. Laborers stepped aside.

A large square hole, shored up with wooden beams, framed the newly excavated entrance that sat back a few feet inside. As the temporary doors were slowly swung open, the group clustered in front of the exposed cavity leading into mysterious darkness.

Clifford stepped up from behind sounding a noise through cupped hands like a trumpet-call leading a charge. "Prepare to enter the underworld!" he said in a ghostly voice. Peals of laughter rang out.

The original small entrance hole had been carved into stone and each would have to bend or crawl to pass through. Early morning sunlight cast sideways shadows, making the interior darker and even more mysterious.

"Chione?" Dr. Withers said, calling out to be heard. "Where's Chione?"

Chione, too short to see over the heads of the others, hung onto tall Aaron's shirt as he pushed his way forward.

Rashad's presence and the procedure they were expected to follow was standard protocol. Dr. Withers made a brief speech of gratitude to Egypt to be captured on video. He concluded by saying, "In respect for the Egyptian government and for safety purposes, it's customary that only designated persons be allowed inside during the first walk-through inspection. Paki Rashad here," he said, placing a hand on Rashad's shoulder, "needs to document the present condition of the tomb, after which, viewing time will be set aside for all."

Rashad stood beside Dr. Withers wearing designer jeans and a blue long-sleeved cotton shirt. Like the shirt, his jeans were pressed. His turban was perfectly wrapped over shiny black hair. His mustache glinted in the sunlight. He was inscrutably clean despite anticipated entry into the tomb. He looked somber, unlike the other locals, whose facial gestures and flashing eyes led one to believe they could burst into laughter. Yet, Rashad had been quick with a warm smile as he greeted them. He was all business, at times pensive, and underneath it all surely harbored some deep personal opinions about the work at hand.

Dr. Withers took Chione's hands as the others made room. Aaron stayed put beside her.

"As much as this find belongs to Egypt, the world, and to history," Dr. Withers said for all to hear. "Chione. I dedicate this discovery to you. This is your tomb." A burst of laughter cut him short. "If you'll excuse the pun," he said, laughing at himself.

This was surely a joyous day. Chione cupped her ears, bent slightly forward and strained to hear. The crowd hushed. Low mournful wails, eerie and faint, resounded. The wailing did not sound like the high-pitched hum people reported hearing from the statues at Memnon when they sang. Yet, hearing sounds represented how much the gods respected the person who heard them. A couple of laborers, who had heard, seemed frightened and fled. Several devout believers fell to their knees in the rubble, arms outstretched toward the entrance, and kissed the ground.

"What's going on?" Kendra yelled above the questioning of the crowd.

"Sh-h-h!" Aaron said as he turned to face the others. He put his hands up asking for silence. The sound came again. "I hear it," he said. "I hear it! Did anybody else?"

No one responded. Dr. Withers' expression told Chione that he, perhaps, would try to understand.

A moment later, with eyes closed, Chione felt hands on her shoulders, felt her own arms drop limply to her sides.

"You do belong here," Aaron whispered softly in the same foreign accent she had heard from him before.

Chione opened her eyes and looked into Aaron's, which had deepened, like dark emeralds. "So do you," she said, not recognizing the peculiar accent in her own voice.

He blinked hard. "What do you mean, Chione?" he asked. "Chione?"

She shook her head. "What happened?" she asked as that perfume again floated seemingly from the tomb opening and right into her nostrils. She wondered if Aaron had noticed.

"I heard it too. Is that what you mean?" Aaron asked. "I... hey, Chione, what's going on?"

A sudden gust of wind came up and rustled everything moveable and showered a desert baptismal of sand down on everyone. Then, as quickly, everything became eerily still and hot.

With the silence, Chione became aware of something that had never happened before in her life. She felt consciousness uncontrollably slipping and everything going black.

6

"How did I get here?" Chione asked weakly from her cot.

"Aaron carried you," Rita said. Her red curls drooped from perspiration.

"Where is everyone?" she asked, hearing only an occasional voice outside.

"Inside the tomb."

"How long have I—"

"You slept a bit, mumbled like you were dreaming."

Chione sat up, turned to the small electric fan and rubbed tension from the back of her neck. Fleeting scenes from a dream flickered through her mind. Scenes of a beautiful priestess, Pharaoh's concubine, throwing herself at his feet... waiting for his command to rise... or to sensually creep up his muscular legs. How she could bring mighty Pharaoh to his knees. "Oh, my!" Chione said.

"What is it?"

Chione realized again that she was inside her own yurt and closed her eyes to dispel the erotic scene and the desire the dream aroused in her. "I-I wanted to be inside the tomb too. I—"

"They're only documenting right now," Rita said. "The film will have to be developed before they move even one artifact."

"But I want to be a part it all," Chione said, standing and testing her legs.

"You haven't missed much. Marlowe told me it took a bit of time lowering some equipment down the portcullis shaft."

"But to be inside when—"

"Yes, lucky you," Rita said as she offered a frail but steadier arm. "You feel up to it? Shouldn't you rest?" She looked like she could use a bit of rest herself.

"You don't understand. Do you remember what you told me about yourself?"

"Specifically?" Rita asked as she poured water from a bottle into a paper cup.

"How you had to struggle to prove yourself when you began to work with Clifford."

"Oh, that," she said. "No one thought I was smart enough to make the switch from nursing." But she had, with her caregiving skills ever present.

Rita quit nursing when the medical field could not save the daughter she and Clifford lost. Rita's gynecologist blotched the Cesarean birth of their daughter leaving her unable to have another child. Because Rita could not provide the son Clifford yearned for, he devoted his life to raising their daughter. She followed her father's footsteps into archaeology. On her first flight to the Andes, her small plane crashed. All others on board, including the daughter's husband, were killed. The daughter had lingered, strapped into her seat for four days before rescuers found the wreckage. In the hospital, the medical team failed to save her. She slipped into a coma and passed away weeks later.

"That's right," Chione said. "You always felt you had to prove yourself in archaeology."

"Why do you bring that up?" she asked, handing over the cup of water and pouring another. Her hands shook as she lifted the cup to her lips.

"It's the same with me. Don't you see? I don't have a degree yet."

"But quite a brain, I believe," Rita said, raising an eyebrow.

"That's not the point," Chione said. "Fact is I have this other ability that most people think is hocus-pocus."

"It can be intimidating."

"Intimidating? The whole world is coming to this. Mankind is becoming more and more intuitive."

"Some of you are way ahead of the pack," Rita said. She stepped closer to the fan.

"Okay... okay, but don't you see what I have to prove here?" Chione asked. "I can't pretend I get my information from books and studying. I'm real and so are my abilities. I need to be recognized for the person I am."

"I understand, Chione. But don't forget. You're just as much like the rest of us. You fainted, remember?"

"Why did I do that?"

"Egypt affects me the same way." She eased down onto the edge of the cot. "What were you feeling?"

"I-I'm not sure. I felt a pulling into the tomb like I needed to be inside. Then I smelled that perfume—"

"Perfume?" Rita asked. "What perfume?"

Chione wished she had not mentioned the heady scent. "Never mind," she said. "I must be confused."

Rita stuck her fingers into her hair and massaged the top of her head. "Do you think they'll eventually allow the wives and husbands inside?"

"Being a spectator is difficult, isn't it?"

"Frustrating," Rita said. "Just like this headache I can't get rid of." She stared at the floor. "Marlowe will get in."

"You will too," Chione said as she french-braided her hair into one long plait and retrieved a rubber band from her pocket. Finally, feeling stronger, she stepped outside the tent on Rita's arm as Aaron appeared. "Aaron, your clothes," she said.

"Pretty grubby, eh?"

"It's that messy in there?"

"Well, you have to scoot on your belly through that narrow passage," he said. "In and out."

How had Bebe made it through that narrow opening, considering her matronly figure? Still, Bebe could do anything once she put her minor insecurities aside and set her mind.

Chione looked at Rita, whose years were taking their toll; frail Rita, whose drive and intentions far exceeded the strengths of her aging body. Rita would have to muster all her stamina to crawl on hands and knees or to climb up or down through the portcullis. After all, the spouses had helped on previous digs. In their late sixties, Clifford and Rita Rawlings were the eldest of the group. With extremely active minds, both had much to offer science and history and felt no need to retire simply because the years had crept up on them. Their philosophy was that in today's world, why stop discovering as long as you can maintain a presence and function accordingly?

"Let's go," Chione said, catching Aaron's unwavering excitement.

"I'd like to be in there too," Rita said as she clipped a water flask to Chione's belt loop.

At the tomb entrance, Aaron said, "We'll have to use this route. They're still rigging the portcullis."

"This way it is," Chione said. "Let's get in there."

"You're pretty small. You might be able to crawl on your knees and elbows. I have to scoot on my gut."

"How far?" she asked.

"About sixty feet to just under the portcullis," he said. "By the way, we're only inside the First Chamber right now."

"You've seen another?"

"Topside on radar, just after that one."

"Anyone entered the Second Chamber yet?"

"Of course not. The camera crews are still recording the First Chamber, the artifacts and all. Plus, we couldn't see the entrance to the Second Chamber by only flashing our lights."

Chione stooped down and peered into the darkness of the tunnel. "I guess this is the death and rebirth canal," she said. "We're like babies going back in." Then she smelled that odor again; a sweet provocative scent full of memory and closeness, seeping out of the tunnel. She had not smelled it before arriving in Egypt. She wondered if Aaron had detected the beckoning fragrance.

"I calculate the slant about fifty-five degrees all the way," he said. "I'll go first in case you begin to slide."

"You kidding?" she said. "I can handle myself. Hand me your light."

Aaron hesitated, probably at her assertiveness, something she needed to practice. Or was it despite being able to take care of herself, she forgot her flashlight? "Grab hold of the rope along the floor we've installed for a handrail," he said. "On your right."

She stuck her head into the entrance and said, "C'mon, Aaron."

Instead, he grabbed hold of her back pocket and pulled her back. "Uh-uh," he said. "Feet first."

"Feet?"

"Yep. It's too steep. If you go up-side-down and begin to slide, you could land on your head on the stone floor at the bottom."

"That steep?"

"Slippery too. Be sure not to pull on the conduits by your left arm."

Chione turned, dropped to her hands and knees and backed into the square hole. She eased downward using the rope. In a few seconds, Aaron entered and blocked out most of the light from above. As he maneuvered his body, sunlight intermittently broke through and cast short flexing shadows each time he changed position.

"Be careful of those limestone chips," he said. "They cut like shards of glass."

The sturdy khaki clothing the team wore had doubled knee and elbow patches to pad the body parts coming in contact with the ground and rock.

The axial corridor through which they maneuvered had been hollowed out of solid limestone and slanted more steeply downward than Chione anticipated. Prior to the exploratory team's entry, five tons of debris filled the passageway to the portcullis. The smooth hewn floor showed grooves from the equipment carriers sliding down. Remaining patches of sand slipped downward and small pebbles rolled. Light disappeared, except for the one dimly seeping up from below. The going was slow. She tried to hurry, feeling as if the tomb was pulling at her. Pulling her in. The deeper she moved, the thicker and more stagnant the air became.

"Pity the claustrophobic," Chione said as she clicked on the flashlight. "Hey, slow up, Aaron," she said, directing her voice up to him. "You're kicking sand in my face."

"Sorry," he said. "I was hurrying, hoping to hold my breath till we were under the portcullis."

"I know what you mean," she said. "The smell is incomparable."

"Wait till you get in deeper," he said with a chuckle. Past midway, he called out. "You okay? Not faint anymore?"

"I'm too excited to care."

"What about your queasy stomach? Symptoms you've had for a couple of months?"

"It went away, especially since arriving in Egypt," she said. "Stop worrying. I can't let myself be sick anymore." She continued to creep backward. Though the dreams had intensified, her nausea and symptoms eased. She felt relief not having stomach problems that would get in the way of her work performance.

"This tomb is definitely New Kingdom, 18th Dynasty," he said. "As we suspected from those first relics."

Their voices reverberating off the rock walls had an all too close feeling about them. Her eardrums vibrated as she suddenly heard a feminine but otherworldly voice say...

"Waiting... inside the coffin... waiting... waiting... through all of time."

"Wow!" she said while exhaling a forceful gust of air, and then feeling glad she could inhale again. A sense of confinement accompanied the vision, a vision so strange; it was as if she were lying on her back like a mummy inside a coffin. Waiting.

"Wow... what?" Aaron asked.

"It's... bad air," she said, finally continuing to descend.

Sunlight pouring through the portcullis area below became brighter as they neared the bottom. Muffled voices projected an eerie drone from the First Chamber beyond.

Just before the portcullis opening, the floor leveled off and the ceiling heightened. Some equipment was stacked to the side. Directly under the shaft, thick boards and loose rags were positioned to keep stones from marring the floor when they fell from above. Chione rose to her knees as Aaron backed up beside her and took his flashlight.

"Look up," he said, pointing and pulling at her sleeve. "Be careful of falling debris."

Chione shielded her eyes and looked up into the huge gaping square hole of the massive portcullis shaft. "I get it," she said. "This opening would be how a sarcophagus or larger object was introduced into the tomb." At the top, two turbaned heads appeared over the edge and looked down at her. She waved and they smiled and waved back. Tiny pebbles fell and embedded in the pile of rags. Sand drifted down like measures of poured salt.

"Passage will definitely be more accessible on a ladder through this opening," Aaron said. "We'll also build a ramp with rungs for the axial corridor we just passed through."

"That'll make things easier."

"We're installing grilled gates with locks to secure both accesses when we're out of the tomb at night."

"To ward off looting, of course," she said.

Aaron looked up again. "Can you imagine being inside a tomb when that block was lowered once and for all? Can you imagine the horror of knowing you might die in here if no one noticed you missing?"

"Better to be dead when it happened," Chione said.

It had been known to happen. When some tombs were entered after centuries, human remains of probable grave robbers or unwary workers were found trapped inside. When a portcullis was lowered into an airtight position, it sealed the tomb for eternity.

Just beyond where the portcullis came to rest, six descending steps added more depth to the space. With the area now lighted, carved and painted walls displayed their cryptic messages in a profusion of color and design, recorded not for worldly posterity but for continuance in the Afterlife. Their flashlight beams cast farther ahead illuminated more of the ancient splendor, and a dust-laden floor continuing down the passageway.

Chione felt stickiness on her face and turned to Aaron who chuckled. "Here," he said, whipping out a handkerchief. "It's a good thing you don't wear makeup. Perspiration's already caked the dust on your cheeks." He flashed his light into the passageway again and onto the floor. "Look."

She wiped sticky black grime from her face. "What'd you expect to see? A portal into Ancient Egypt?"

"No," he said, chuckling and aiming the beam again. "No footprints past ours."

She smiled. "I expected that." Workers always broomed on the way out. It was a gesture of cleanliness and respect for the departed.

He looked at her suspiciously. "Listen, I have to say this... I felt a presence in here."

"You felt it too?" Chione became excited at the implication, then calmed. "It's the Ka, Aaron. You know what that is?"

"Can't say I remember."

"Ka is a portion of the spirit of the departed that stays behind in the tomb with the mummy." She continued to strain to see down the passageway. "Direct that light again," she said, having seen something down the passageway that made her heart pound. "Down there."

"No," he said, teasing and clicking off the beam. "Better you wait and see with everyone else."

7

More loose cloths for the cleaning of footwear lay before the opened double wooden doors of the First Chamber.

"So far, no sign of white ants," Aaron said.

They dusted their boots and squeezed through the busy engineers glutting the doorway. Bubbling over with excitement, the others welcomed them.

Chione's eyes widened. She could only stare at the splendor, replete with history. Borders of hieroglyphs and a profusion of colorful lotuses framed each wall. Varied delicate scents wafted through the chamber as if a breeze had blown them through. There was no draft and evidently no one else detected the new odors. A mysterious voice lilted again.

"The treatment room."

The words resounded in her mind. Judging from the unchanged expressions of the others, they had not heard. Chills ran over her body. She had just stepped back in time, like entering a room visited before. She felt utterly empowered as she drank it all in.

Clifford flagged her attention and pointed upward. Others tipped their heads to look. Lighting was redirected exposing a pyramid rising above them. "Carved right into the ceiling stone," he said.

Four square pillars rose from the floor at each corner to the top edge of the walls. From there, leaning, they met at a point in the center of the vaulted ceiling. Around the top edge of the tall walls, a border had been carved around the room, connecting the lower ends of the leaning beams. Beams of the pyramid structure were painted black.

"The ceiling's Egyptian blue," Kendra said. "With gold stars. The pyramid form looks like it's been shoved up in there."

"Carved in," Clifford said. The realist in him would not let the facts be distorted.

"This isn't an ordinary tomb," Bebe said.

Chione smiled upward, staring with her mouth agape, again silently validated.

"Where's Randy?" Dr. Withers asked as he counted heads. "I want the whole team in on this."

"He hasn't been with us since he sped off in the jeep," Aaron said.

"That figures," Dr. Withers said, rolling his eyes.

The chamber was small and crowded, roughly fifteen by fifteen feet. Each had to squeeze past one another to move around without touching the artifacts. Dakarai and Masud, who had abandoned their loose gallibayas for denims and cotton shirts, spoke among themselves in Egyptian and inched around the room taking notes and drawing sketches. Long-legged Dakarai stepped over artifacts instead of inching his way around. Something about his actions made Chione wonder about his respect for the items. Masud was more careful. He was shorter and stockier and couldn't have stepped over anything.

"Look at these artifacts!" Chione said. Taweret, the ferocious-looking pregnant hippopotamus and goddess of childbirth, stood in one corner. "To ward off evil during childbirth."

On an elegantly carved wooden table in another corner lay various size scarabs placed in a circle. A magical knife shaped like a boomerang lay in the middle. It would have been used to draw a line of protection around an area or a person.

"A lion, an Eye of Horus, serpent with a knife and a jackal," Masud said, studying the carvings on the blade as he stood beside Chione.

"All those creatures gave the knife its power," she said.

"O Little One," Masud said. "You know."

Several of the others laughed at Masud's understatement.

"One of our resident experts," Bebe said. Her smile was amicable.

In the opposite corner stood another table on which lay a gilt hand mirror, face down, the backside bordered with lotuses delicately etched and one large bloom in the middle. A gilt pyramid about a foot tall and inlaid with stones stood beside the mirror. An enormous faience ankh carved with a dog-headed scepter representing power lay nearby. The scepter was said to be the pillar of the god Osiris and held the power of a god over millions of years. On the floor near each table and between the legs, stood faience vases, jars and containers, some inlaid with gold and jewels. Several draped garlands, though withered and faded, held together and withstood time. Small stone steles with inscriptions leaned against the walls. Fragile papyri bearing more writings lay scattered.

One glorious wall was totally etched with a painted relief of a man and woman sitting facing one another. The female wore a long closely fitted, pleated white skirt. The cloak over her shoulders attached to the front of her skirt between bare breasts. The male wore only a pleated white calf-length kilt. Both sported beautifully braided wigs of differing lengths with perfumed pomade beeswax cones on top. Both faces were etched with broad lines depicting the use of kohl around the eyes, which was a decorative way of deflecting harshness of the sun's rays away from the eyes.

"Look at this," Chione said. Her excitement brought the group around in front of the giant-sized figures. "The woman wears a sacred menat around her neck."

"And holds a sistrum," Bebe said. She carried a pen and notepad everywhere and had an extra pen clipped to her pocket. She began to sketch the image, perhaps to later verify it in some texts.

"Yes," Chione said, agreeing. "A sacred rattle carried by noblewomen and priestesses."

"She looks to be counseling the man," Kendra said. "Could it be we've found the tomb of such an important woman?"

"Let's not speculate," Dr. Withers said, smiling his well-known witty grin. "Let's take it one day... uh... that's one chamber at a time."

In the mural, a five-stringed harp stood on the floor beside the woman's chair, colorfully decorated with dancers and lyre and double-flute players.

On the opposite wall, two women faced each other. One, the same woman from the first mural, appeared to be administering to another who looked to be with child. Her face was painted black.

"The black woman, a Nubian, perhaps?" Bebe asked. "A lady from Punt?"

"Not when she's dressed like an Egyptian," Chione said, studying hieroglyphs bordering the scene. "The rest of her skin is pale."

"Check the woman's expression," Bebe said. "She looks committed to what she's doing."

Chione wanted to offer a bit of information, hesitated, then decided no reason existed to withhold from this group if she had something solid to consider. "The ancients believed the heart was the center of their being. They thought with their hearts."

"No kidding," Ginny said. She listened and spoke, all the while doing what she did best. The camera eye was seldom more than an inch or so away from her eye, if not pressed against it.

"It's my guess ancient Egyptians were a very emotional people," Chione said, "by the look on this woman's face."

Ginny had great curiosity and learned a lot during her shoots. She had worked all over the world until Dr. Withers nabbed her for the Institute. Though she, at times, dressed like a man and was husky, the sparkly earrings she wore, a diamond-studded pinkie ring, and her dainty perfume told a different story. Still, she was wondered about. She could shoulder a heavy camera like any man and compete with the strongest of them.

Wadjets, Eyes of Horus the Hawk God, occupied both reliefs. Bowls, vases, winged scarabs, and other amulets filled the spaces. The spell caster also carried a long incense burner with a head of the Hawk God on one end.

"Listen," Chione said. "I'm not going to interpret every glyph right now, but I'll give a few English interpretations, okay?" All nodded eagerly. She began by pointing to a cluster of glyphs. Bebe stepped up beside her, ready to write. Having studied ancient pronunciation, Chione sounded out a few glyphs phonetically in the old language and then pointed as she translated.

Blacken your face
with Hapi's mud
like farmer's fields
new life will bud

"A spell!" Kendra said.

Chione's better judgment told her not to describe the thick earthy odor of Hapi's mud she just inhaled.

"But wait," Ginny said as she relaxed the camera on her shoulder and pointed. "Why did you begin reading from the right? The next row, you read from the left."

"See this?" Chione asked, pointing to a bird figure. "When any figure of life faces left, you begin reading from the left. Facing right, begin right and read left. Up or down, whichever way the live figure faces, start from that direction."

"I knew that," Ginny said, teasing to hide embarrassment.

"What the spell implies," Clifford said. "Is that the tomb's occupant believed in the magic of the times, such as it was."

In both murals, a sun disk with long beaming rays and hands at the ends holding ankhs pointed toward the woman's face. "This tomb is from Akhenaten's era," Chione said. "The main god is Aten!"

"Would you look at that," Dr. Withers said. He had a playful way of acting surprised at times, though he had probably already seen the symbols, having been in the chamber a while. He never missed much.

"God Aten, as opposed to…?" a technician asked.

"You can answer that, Bebe," Chione said, gesturing for her to speak.

"Thank you, Chione," she said, turning to address the group. "When Akhenaten became Pharaoh, he banished all other gods, especially

Amon-Ra. Amon was divine protector, principal god of Upper Egypt, Thebes, and toward Africa. Ra was the sun god of Lower Egypt toward the Mediterranean."

"Amon by itself stood for the midnight sun, the hidden mysteries," Clifford said. "Ra represented the sun's life-giving rays."

"Aten represented the sun itself as a disk in the heavens," Bebe said, motioning upward to the brilliant golden orb in the murals. "This is the Aten symbol!"

"Go-o-od, good, good, good!" Dr. Withers said, dancing around. "If this is Akhenaten era—"

"And worship of the Aten was banished during the reign of Tutankhamon," Bebe said and waited.

"Then we've narrowed down our time frame," Dr. Withers said with joy. "Let's review our information."

Bebe agreed. "Tutankh-Amon's name was first Tutankh-Aten."

"I remember reading that," a technician said.

"If I may, O Teacher," Masud said to Dr. Withers and nodded to the others. He paused for any objections to him speaking. Everyone waited so he continued. "King Tutankhamon's full name was first Neb-Kheperu-Ra Tutankh-Aten," he said with a heavy accent. "He married a niece, maybe half-sister, named Ankhesenpa-Aten. Older than him, she was believed to be the third daughter of Akhenaten and Nefertiti."

"I remember," Aaron said. "It's not known for sure if Tutankhamon was Akhenaten's youngest brother or a son by Akhenaten and his minor queen Kiya."

"They sure knew how to complicate their lives, didn't they?" Ginny asked.

"Actually, they simplified it," Clifford said. "Or tried to. Intermarriage assured the kingship would remain a family matter."

"How does this narrow down our time frame?" Another technician asked.

"Speculation has it," Chione said. "Though reared in the Aten tradition, King Tut changed his name to Amon, restored Amon worship, and wiped out the religious dogma established by Akhenaten."

"Why would he wipe out his father's traditions?" Someone asked. Everyone had become enthused. "Or a brother's, if that's what he was?"

"That's what I've always asked," Bebe said. "I speculate that since King Tut assumed the throne at age nine, he was presumably advised by Aye, Nefertiti's father, and who could have been Tut's grandfather. It was Aye who forced Tut to change his name and restore Amon."

"Tut, being a child, had no real choice," Dr. Withers said thoughtfully.

"King Tut was reputedly deposed," Clifford said.

"That's only theory, O Professor," Rashad's cameraman said, stepping close. "His mummy does have a hole in the side of his skull from some sort of blow perhaps. The resultant bone fragment lies deeper inside. There are also bruises on his temple. Close up pictures and x-rays are on file at Madu Museum."

Chione hugged herself listening to the conversation. At the mention of the blow to King Tut's head, she moaned quietly, then heard...

"All must change. It's the new order."

The warning echoed through her mind as if she had heard it many times. A feeling of urgency overtook her as if so little time remained, but for what? Again, she looked at the others. They had not heard. No one heard the words or saw the pictures that appeared inside her mind.

"The theory of murder is only speculation," Dr. Withers said, reminding everyone to remain open-minded.

8

"What is it, Chione?" Kendra asked, coming to her aid. "You look pale."

"I-I'm just too close to this, can feel it all, but I-I'm okay."

"So, after that?" Dr. Withers asked, waiting for a response. He had a way of denying any reason that disrupted progress, even Chione's frailties. "After that... no other Aten worshipers?"

"Correct," Clifford said. "All of Akhenaten and Nefertiti's temples and artifacts at Akhetaten were abandoned, destroyed or defaced. Even the Aten symbol."

"Wait a minute," Ginny said. "Akhenaten named a town after himself?"

"Not really," Bebe said.

"But, Akhenaten or Akhetaten? What's the difference?"

"I see why you're confused," Bebe said. "It's like this. In any Egyptian name, remove the prefix or suffix 'Aten' or 'Amon' which signifies the god the person worshipped."

"I get it. The basis of Akhenaten's name is Akhen. The town is Akhet."

"Ahken meant, *He who serves the sun,*" Masud said.

"And Ahket meant, *Horizon of the Aten,*" Clifford said. "Based on how the sun rose over the distant hills as seen from El Amarna, Ahkenaten's town."

"We've got it," several in the group said. Their excited voices filled the small chamber.

"Oh, yes," Dr. Withers said. "We're such a team."

"So, what we have here," Chione said. "Is a tomb constructed sometime between the reign of Akhenaten and possibly through that of Tutankhamon. Not very long."

"Definitely from the Aten era," Bebe said. She had studied and learned well, easily making the switch from South American to Egyptian archaeology.

"How'd you figure?" Ginny asked.

"Because Aten era tombs have side chambers, like this one. Amon worshippers carved the rooms of their tombs straight in."

The Egyptians listened as the Institute's group of professionals proved their knowledge.

"Who ruled during that time?" Ginny asked.

"Akhenaten for seventeen years," Bebe said. "Then as speculation has it, possibly Smenkhkare, his younger brother, for about three years; then Tutankhamon succeeded by his wife, Ankhesenpa-Aten who became Ankhesen-Amon, who married her grandfather Aye."

Kendra continued to study the walls. "By that latter marriage," she said, "Amon was restored."

"Somewhere in a period of about twenty to twenty-nine years," Bebe said.

"I'm sure this tomb is going to clear up a lot of speculation," Aaron said as he studied the murals.

"I can feel it in my bones," Dr. Withers said.

The other walls contained hieroglyphs and more reliefs. Rows of spectacular lotuses bordered the panels in bright blues, reds, and greens. Brilliant yellow hues glowed as if freshly painted.

"Work your magic for us, Chione," Dr. Withers said, directing his light to the hieroglyphs.

She moved slowly around the chamber, forcing herself not to contaminate the paintings by touch, which she really wanted to do; touch, feel, and perceive ancient history in one of the best ways only she knew, with psychometric impressions. But body oils, carbon dioxide from breath, photography lamps, exhaust fumes, and fresh air could begin deterioration of tomb art.

Chione stopped suddenly, gasped and could say nothing. Everyone as well seemed suspended in anticipation.

Finally, totally out of character when addressing her, Aaron said, "Don't keep us waiting."

"Some of you know what's being told by these glyphs," she said, teasing and drawing out the moment.

"Bits and pieces," Clifford said. "Chione, please!"

Methodically, she examined one row of hieroglyphs. "Beware," she began, pointing her way along.

Beware, and be ready
Two who would enter
The spell is cast
to last
till all of time has passed

"Magic!" Kendra said again. "But that sounded like a warning."

Chione looked away quickly. "Guess in time we'll find out. Magic and spells were common." For some reason, Chione felt utterly triumphant, as if having completed one of the most important acts of her life.

"Two who would enter," Aaron said. "Pretty specific."

"Tombs weren't built with the expectation others would enter," Kendra said. "Till all of time has passed suggests—"

"Maybe this priestess, if that's what she was," Bebe said, "saw into the future to a time when two people would come here for a purpose." She shrugged. "Maybe."

"Could these reliefs be showing us the two specific people?" Kendra asked.

"I doubt it," Chione said quickly. Drawing quick conclusions was not her habit. She hoped that no one noticed, and then wondered why she responded in such an abrupt manner. "These are probably scenes from her life and work."

Aaron had learned much about glyph interpretations from her. What little the others knew was learned from their experiences. They spent a few minutes deciphering the overall message of the chamber. Quiet mumbling filled the room as each sounded out different symbols, like subdued repeating of chants and prayers. When Dakarai and Masud joined in, the team members trying to emulate their accents and pronunciation made the hum of voices sound ancient.

"The mummy in the burial chamber," Clifford said finally, "was either of royal personage, maybe a royal relative, or high courtier."

"Almost certainly a female," Kendra said. "Judging by these murals." The Egyptians expected to take their lives with them into the Afterlife. Decorating their tombs was a way to assure that their earthly lives went along.

"Which great women are not accounted for among the Eighteenth Dynasty?" Bebe asked.

They looked to one another, searching memories for any royal female mummies not found during the decades of discoveries.

"Some of the queens," Clifford said. "Specifically, Ankhesenpa and many minor queens and daughters. Nefertiti's tomb was found recently."

"And her mummy," Dr. Withers said.

"Nefertiti vanished two years before Akhenaten's demise," Kendra said.

"There's a rumor that Nefertiti became Smenkhkare, the so-called brother of Akhenaten," Clifford said. "In order to accede the throne."

Dakarai and Masud exchanged curious glances, seeming surprised by the vast amount of knowledge shared by the team members.

"All speculation," Dr. Withers said. "Let's not get our hopes up. From this chamber, it's my guess we've not discovered a queen's tomb." He rubbed his stomach. "For now, let's go topside for lunch," Everyone concurred. "You folks," he said to the two filming teams, "can complete your video documentation of the room and contents without us being in the way."

After lunch, they re-entered the tomb and took another peek into the wondrous First Chamber.

Kendra and Clifford's tasks, along with clerks supplied by the Madu Museum, would be to tag and number each artifact. Photographs would be taken to document placement within the room. Once artifacts in the front were removed, any concealed behind those would be identified in place. Such procedure provided a permanent record of the placement and condition of each artifact. Between various steps of the procedure, film would be developed to assure information was factually captured before another layer of artifacts could be moved from its resting place. Cleaning and preservation would begin on site should some pieces begin to deteriorate in the fresh air and sunlight.

After again viewing the First Chamber, they quietly began to leave when suddenly a low moaning resounded. Kendra grabbed onto Aaron. Bebe seemed more interested in seeing to whom Kendra would turn in a time of distress. The groan was so stunning, Dr. Withers placed a hand on Clifford's shoulder. Both Aaron and Chione looked to each of the others to determine who was playing a joke.

Then it came again. A low muffled tone, almost like someone calling out for recognition. This time, all had heard. No one moved or said anything. Finally, Chione said, "That's not the same sound I've been hearing. A male voice? Which one of you guys are trying to pull one over?"

The men looked to one another. The sound came again, vague and indistinct, but none of the men had opened their mouths.

"The wind," Aaron said, shrugging.

"There's no air current in here, O Pilgrim," Masud said.

"The tomb is no longer sealed, however," Aaron said.

After that episode, no further sounds were heard, and they slowly exited the spectacular First Chamber. They made their way into the passageway and down the short flight of steps.

Aaron pulled Chione aside. "Why did Masud call me 'O Pilgrim'?"

"The Egyptians are very respectful of others."

"But why, specifically, 'O Pilgrim'?"

"Someone must have told him you've been to the Holy Land. Anyone who's been there is revered by the Egyptians."

"So, if they respect you, they tack on some sort of title?"

"Better than saying 'Hey you', right?"

Against a backdrop of walls displaying scenes of the times with artistic splendor, Ginny's lens continued to record their every move, videographed for posterity.

Clifford flashed his light to the ceiling. He flashed again. He motioned for a man to bring a ladder, which Clifford placed precariously close to the priceless wall art. He climbed and again inspected with the light. Finally, he said, "Just as I thought. This dark ceiling contains residue of the oil lamps used by the Ancients when they carved and painted."

"No kidding," Aaron said. "Let me see." He held the ladder while Clifford descended. Aaron climbed and gingerly picked at the edge of one spot. He held up fingertips for all to see. "Right again. The restoration people can analyze this grime."

More stair steps took them deeper into the passageway.

"According to radar scanning," Aaron said. "One wall of the next chamber lies adjacent to the first, though several feet deeper."

No visible doorway could be found where radar indicated the next chamber.

"Oh, great," one of the engineers said. "Just what we need."

"What is it?" Clifford asked.

"Look for a sealed passage, anything," the engineer said. "Radar picked up a good-sized chamber on the right. We'll have to locate the entrance."

"Just look," Aaron said. "Try not to touch."

Each of the team took a section of the wall and visually examined. Lamps were brought close.

"Strange," Bebe said. "I'd heard limestone in this valley was too poor to do much carving. Look at this art."

"We're higher up than Valley of the Kings," Clifford said. "Way back into the hills. Might make a difference."

"Hey, I've found something," Kendra said in a few moments. "Right where it should be." She pointed along several deep slashes. "Right about here."

"How do you figure?" Clifford asked, straining to see.

"Look closely," she said, nudging him to bring his face up to the wall. "These cracks were purposely made to look like artistic tool marks, then painted over." Again, she traced up one side, across the top and down the other. "Here's our doorway."

"A solid block wedged so tightly you'd think the seams were carved in as part of the design," Clifford said, shaking his head in amazement.

Everyone stepped back for filming of the mural before the engineers would cut through. Chione accompanied Bebe and Clifford to sit on the steps near the portcullis shaft allowing a breath of fresh air. Words and exclamations in mixed languages floated through the passageway as the crews worked. The job of loosening a disguised stone block without damaging surrounding portions of the wall would be tedious. More equipment was needed. A nimble Egyptian scaled a notched rope hanging in the portcullis shaft. Soon, he returned with his equipment lowered to him. After what seemed hours, they heard stone grating as it slid loose, excited voices, and Dr. Withers calling them back to the fold.

Two muscular laborers strained to pull the loosened granite block outward; taking what precautions they could to avoid scratching the stone floor. Using tenuous finger holds, they pulled and rocked the stone side to side. No one wished to cause damage that could be avoided.

With the two-foot thick block almost free allowing a small opening into the chamber, a thick gush of putrid air escaped. Suddenly that moaning came again! Clearly, the noise originated from inside that chamber.

They covered their noses and mouths with facemasks. For all their effort to clear, preserve, and enter through the only passage available, who or what could possibly be inside that chamber making those moaning sounds?

They waited. No more noises. Finally, Aaron shrugged and began helping to dislodge the stone. More putrid air belched out. He grimaced, cheeks puffing as he paused to blow out a couple breaths to clear the odor from his lungs and sinuses.

Unbelievably, the block began moving by itself! A dirty hand slipped around the edge. Aaron took two paces back, grabbed a tripod and raised it like a club. His eyes bulged in their sockets. They stepped back. Way back. Several workers fled.

"What is it?" Dr. Withers asked, straining to see from a distance.

A dirty arm, with blood on a torn sleeve poked through as the block moved again. Then dirty, disheveled, and favoring the bloody arm, a figure hobbled into the passageway like the dead coming to life.

9

"Randy!" Dr. Withers said as his voice screeched in frustration.

Perspiration dripped profusely from Randy's scalp, creating muddied streaks in the dust covering his face. His clothes were soaked with perspiration. Blood on his torn shirtsleeve had dried and darkened. The wound had stopped bleeding.

Those who had not done so, immediately slipped into gloves, but not because Randy might contaminate them. With the foul air oozing out of that chamber and not knowing the cause but that something had surely rotted in there, they needed to keep their bodies covered because of a fungus called Aspergillus Niger which infected many tombs. Randy wore no protection of any kind.

"How did you get this?" Aaron asked as he ripped Randy's sleeve apart to get to the laceration.

"Never mind that," Dr. Withers said, leaving Aaron to tend the deep gash. "How the hell did you enter that sealed chamber?" He fumed. This discovery was the most significant of his career. To have a member of his own team corrupt the site, or destroy parts of it, would be disastrous.

"I found another passage," Randy said meekly. Then he yelped when Aaron tried to move his arm.

"Who approved of you going off on your own?"

"It was an accident."

"You're an accident, Randy!" Dr. Withers said, screaming it, unable to contain his rage.

"We'd better get him to a doctor," Aaron said. "His arm could be broken."

"I just bumped something," Randy said, eyes wide in denial. "It doesn't hurt anymore."

"Don't be stupid," Aaron said. "Your shoulder's swollen all the way over your collarbone."

Dr. Withers had stopped pacing to take a look. "Before you even move," he said, "I want to know where you got in."

"I went up the incline behind the portcullis," Randy said. "I saw what looked like a hole or depression. When I bent down to examine it, the whole thing gave way."

"You fell into the chamber?"

"Head first… or… shoulder first," Randy said.

"What we have here is another Giovanni Belzoni," Clifford said.

Dr. Withers shook his head and paced as the others looked on. "Well, someone get him across the river into Luxor," he said, thumbing a direction. "If they can't treat him at that hospital, get him on a plane to Cairo."

Dakarai smiled. "Please, O Teacher, my cousin nearby is a doctor."

"No," Kendra said quickly. "Peter Vimble is a British physician in Cairo. He's got a clinic at the hospital in Luxor just across the river. Doc's got medical records for all of us at both locations."

"Yes, O Teacher," Dakarai said, avoiding Kendra's eyes and nodding his agreement to Dr. Withers. "I myself was to go to Cairo later today. I'll go along now."

With a look of resignation, Randy limped away beside the tall, lanky Dakarai who had to slow his stride as pudgy Randy struggled to keep pace.

Chione tugged at Aaron's sleeve pulling him aside. "Do you remember what you said to Randy earlier?" she asked in hushed tones. "You told him to go fall into a hole."

"I did, didn't I," he said with a crooked smile.

"How did you know that would happen?"

"I didn't. At least, I don't think I did."

"Sterling?" Clifford asked, placing a hand on Dr. Withers shoulder.

Dr. Withers took a deep breath and calmed himself before saying anything. "I don't want you all to think I'm being callous toward Randy...," he said. A flagging hand waved off the rest of his sentence. He was perspiring heavily. Finally, he said, "So whatever condition that chamber was in—"

"Excuse me, Sterling," Clifford said, fanning his face and moving away from the putrid air still oozing through the chamber opening. "I think we should do a little investigation on the hill before we enter this chamber."

"How's that?"

"This entire valley experiences what's known as *ten-year floods* from torrential rains. If this chamber was laying open up there, it's been flooded."

"Might explain the stench," Bebe said, pressing her mask against her face. "Everything's probably rotted."

"In that case," Dr. Withers said. "Somebody catch up with Randy. Have him request another crate of surgical masks and gloves. Tell Kendra's Doc friend to send the bill along."

They had no choice. Paki Rashad's men stayed in the passageway to assure no one entered the chambers. Outside, everyone gulped fresher air and fanned each other. Except Chione, who found the air inside the tomb, laced as it was, with fragrance the others had not detected, to be quite pleasant most of the time.

Once outside the tomb, Clifford started toward the incline. "Sterling. Aaron," he said. "Let's get ourselves up there on that hillock."

"Uh-uh," Dr. Withers said, grabbing Clifford's arm. "Lets you and me just stay put while the younger, sure-footed billies climb up there on that slippery rock."

More than an hour passed by the time Aaron and the engineers came off the slope. "See that abutment up there?" Aaron asked, pointing. "Our crews have already set too many footprints up to that point.

Randy's gateway is about a dozen feet in front of it where we found a long crack in the rock."

"What you're saying then," Dr. Withers said. "Is that it's possible the ceiling of the Second Chamber is wide open?"

"Maybe," Aaron said. "Looks like some small boulders block the hole now." Dirt backfilled over the boulders, prevented more rubble from pouring into the chamber, and hid the hole. "We traced the water run-off pattern. Water runs off the upper part of the hill down toward the abutment. When it hits the abutment, it separates and runs off in either direction away from the hole and down the sides of the hillock."

"Is it possible little or no water got into that opening?"

"Since Randy fell in, the area around the hole's been disturbed, so we couldn't tell if any water passed through."

"Maybe the hole sealed itself," Chione said. "Maybe no water ever seeped in."

"There's always a chance," Clifford said. "The diurnal temperature variation caused air to seep into the chamber and affected what's inside."

"Then let's get down there again," Dr. Withers said. He started toward the tomb entrance. "I'm ready to face whatever's in that room."

"Please, O Teacher," Masud said. "With the passageway right above that chamber, we should first vacuum away the debris on top. Please, O Teacher, let me suggest to build a retaining wall to keep further earth from entering Randy's hole."

"Yeah," Dr. Withers said, giving a couple of tugs on his mustache. "Whatever you have to do, make sure nothing else slides into that chamber."

Masud called out the order to workers nearby, instructing with arms waving, fingers pointing and always with a smile and flashing eyes. The workers scrambled to get started.

At the entrance to the Second Chamber, more loose cloths were about to be laid on the floor. Aaron said, "Look, Randy left footprints. Whatever's in that room, the floor's filthy." They laid the cloths over Randy's marks. Dr. Withers shook his head and took a couple of swipes at the cloths with his boots before he and Rashad stepped in with a lamp.

"Phew!" echoed out of the room.

Masud followed, having drawn his shirtfront up over his nose. He backed out fast. "What is it you say in English? Stinky?"

The others crowded the doorway, choking on the foul air. Their flashlights immediately showed the reason for the stench.

"Mummies!" Dr. Withers exclaimed, backing up. "Piles of baby mummies!"

The photographers were allowed in to do their job before another footprint was set down.

"It's late," Dr. Withers said. "We won't be able to fully enter this chamber till tomorrow."

Later that evening as the encampment was being secured for the night, Aaron asked, "Why didn't they finish carving steps in that first entryway we had to slide down through? Other tombs in these valleys all had steps inside the entries."

"Good question," Dr. Withers said. "I can't remember any other tomb having such openings. Things do look somewhat incomplete."

"I agree," Chione said. "There's a sense of urgency that I perceive from the glyphs too. Some are unfinished. Some have been reworked."

"I've got a theory," Dr. Withers said, looking up the hillock. "Let's just say the men carving this gateway to the Underworld started with that axial tunnel we first backed through. Once far enough into the rock, they discovered the first of those holes like Randy fell in."

"Could be," Clifford said. "In their haste, finding that hole more accessible, they enlarged it for the portcullis."

"Because they had to hurry," Chione said. "For whatever reason. A definite sense of urgency exists here. So, in addition to abandoning the axial entry, they left the glyphs unfinished."

"And used the wide portcullis shaft from that point on," Clifford said.

"Why the hurry?" Dr. Withers asked.

Later, word came that a couple of photo technicians became sickened in the Second Chamber. When Dr. Withers asked what was inside, the only response he received was that he had to see for himself. If what was in that room made them sick, how had Randy lasted?

The prayer bell early the next morning called the Islamic faithful to worship. After breakfast, the team scampered to the shaft for re-entry. Once inside, technicians were also expected to follow protocol and donned gloves and masks as well. "With these mummies lying exposed to the outside," Dr. Withers said. "I don't know what we'll be breathing."

At the Second Chamber doorway, Chione heard that voice again.

"Come... meet the children."

This time the voice was full of patience and dignity. It was female and soft, the offer irresistible. Chione eagerly pushed her way in and fell to her knees in the dust before a pile of tiny linen wrapped bodies. "Babies!" she said. Upon closer inspection as the room filled with light, the scene was one of near horror.

Baby and children's mummies were strewn everywhere on the floor, scattered by the intruding rubble. Many had been stacked against the walls. Dismembered arms and feet were strewn about, even a head or two! Worst of all, many were burned.

"Grave robbers," Bebe said. "Grave robbers burned the mummies for torches."

"Barbarous disrespect!" Clifford said.

"That's what Randy stepped in," Kendra said, pointing to the floor. "Ashes."

A quick glance through the dim light disclosed a rectangular room about twelve by twenty feet in size. The hole Randy fell through was near the corner adjacent to the First Chamber. Rubble had fallen into the chamber in a steep triangular spill, spreading out over a third of the floor space.

Not much attention went to the decorated walls at that point or to another pyramid ceiling. More pressing to learn was what had taken place inside the chamber. It had evidently been breached. Hunched over, Bebe began inching her way around studying the confusing scene. "Aha!" she said. "Look here."

"What have you got?"

"Bones of fowl, I think. Coarse paper wrappers, and an old cup."

"Someone brought take out?" Aaron asked. Everyone laughed, all the while trying not to breathe too much of the sickening hot fetor.

"Grave robbers might have spent the night," Rashad said, showing embarrassment for the actions of his countrymen.

"Or spent a long time trying to locate the passageway," Kendra said.

Remnants of the meal would be analyzed. Something as simple as bird bones could help reveal the time period the robbers had been present. Spices and seasonings on the remnants would reveal what types were being used in the common diet of the day. Bebe looked as though she might write some notes but gave up in the dimly lit space.

"The same pyramid ceiling," Ginny said, pointing her camera and lights upward. Curious, too, was the fact that another pyramid was constructed over a rectangular room.

"Lucky for us. See that?" Clifford asked, pointing to the hole in the corner. "Another foot over, and they would have found the First Chamber, too, with its easily opened doors to the main passageway."

"Let's not be too sure of ourselves," Dr. Withers said. "If cunning grave robbers were able to access this chamber, who knows what we'll find deeper in."

Clifford and Bebe began to carefully poke at the rubble to learn what might be underneath.

"Don't," Dr. Withers said. "If you disturb that pile of earth, more could pour into the room and pin us all. And I'm still fond of breathing." He fanned his face. "Even if the air is putrid."

Chione stood at a wall and again hugged herself, perceiving memories intended for no one to see.

"What is it?" Aaron asked quietly over her shoulder.

"This goes against all tradition," she said, whispering.

"More magic?"

"Magic would be traditional. These glyphs describe a room meant to hold babies and children dying the same day as the person in the Burial Chamber."

"Wha-at?"

She followed several rows of glyphs with her fingertips but did not touch. "A spell was cast and any child buried here would share in the afterlife of the main occupant."

"Did I hear you right?" Dr. Withers asked from behind.

"Yes, sir," she said. "Evidently this chamber was built to hold as many of the young as would fit. In sharing the Afterlife of the tomb's main occupant, their families would be elevated in social stature."

"That implies the mummy we've yet to find held a high position in life," Aaron said.

"Could also mean she loved children," Chione said.

"Oh!" Bebe said, pointing. "Look in that corner,"

All at once, everyone noticed the statue of Bes, god of the family.

"My, my, my," Dr. Withers said, carefully picking his way over to hover close, head cocked, inspecting through bifocals.

The wooden three-foot figure, painted with grotesque features and a protruding tongue, carried a sword to repel danger. The other hand held a tambourine. A foot of the figure danced on a base of painted lotus blossoms.

"Part lion, part dwarf," Bebe said. "God of the welfare of newborn children and families."

Another quick look around the room showed walls with scenes of many, many children and babies. Two of the few adult women were depicted as pregnant.

"If I had to judge it on these two chambers," Clifford said. "I'd say the life of the main occupant focused around children and childbirth."

Cribs and children's beds poked out from under the pile of rubble, broken under the weight of the intrusion. Small beds supporting additional piles of mummies lay against the far wall. Toys were strewn everywhere, even sandwiched in bed with the mummies and intermixed in the heaps. Painted dolls with hair made of clay beads, balls, and rattles, mice and cats, even tiny horses on wheels, skillfully carved from wood and symbolically painted.

"Oh, look," Bebe said in a voice that foretold something special. They bent down in a circle. "A top. Over there's another."

"Made of powdered quartz. Look," Clifford said, pointing. "Traces of papyrus twine."

Though the first impulse was to pick up something and feel it, each knew the dangers inherent to the object in doing so.

As Chione studied one of the tops, a vision seemed to pour itself into her head.

A sunlit day, a young Egyptian woman with much younger children spinning tops on the marble floors, fortunate children, whom the woman had birthed.

Chione grabbed Aaron's sleeve to steady her as the stunning vision faded.

"Wonder why the robbers didn't take all this loot," Kendra said.

"It's not gold," Chione said.

If grave robbers had gotten into this chamber, perhaps they found a way into the others. Everyone seemed momentarily deflated at the realization they could be facing another tomb long ago plundered of most of its artifacts.

A mechanical drone sounded overhead. Sparse light beamed down from above as a thin skin of sand entered at the ceiling and poured down over the rubble like a wave. The area overhead was being vacuumed out, exposing the length of the crack in the rock.

"Shoo! Everybody out," Dr. Withers said, waving his arms. "It's not safe in here right now."

10

The team and camera crews proceeded to the next level of the passageway, down a long flight of perhaps some twenty steps. The camera crews scrambled, at times seeming dramatic as they first filmed the floors with a layer of undisturbed dust. After the floor was walked on, they filmed the footprints. With photographers capturing every aspect of the dig, the world would share the team's first impressions.

Everyone marveled at the glory of the walls and ceilings and stopped to examine both sides of the passageway. Scenes depicted children at play, children in the fields, children being taught. She and Bebe would have a huge job of documenting the glorious reliefs.

Whenever possible, Chione avoided facing the cameras. Emotions were illogical in the archaeological profession. How might she hide the alternating tides of elation and disappointment that welled up unexpectedly, brought on by the increasing numbers of dreams and visions? Emotion might be interpreted as exaggerated, especially now that jealous competitors waited for a chance to further denigrate them being in Egypt. Too, if Aaron had heard the sounds when she did, and smelled the perfume, had the cameras caught him wearing some questionable expression?

Just as they aimed their lights deeper into the passageway and proceeded on, Chione saw the tip of something familiar on the wall farther down. They came upon a supporting rail, a balustrade. Its supporting balusters were etched with hieroglyphs. Another half dozen descending steps appeared. The lower they dropped the hotter and heavier the air hung.

A clank and clatter followed them as camera technicians manipulated awkward lighting equipment and wiring while trying to keep up. Chione flashed her light as the full scene came into view. "Look," she said.

All flashlights were directed to the wall. A technician turned on flood lamps. In view was another gigantic painted relief, ceiling to floor, of a woman sitting inside a black pyramid. God Aten's hands reached down. The woman's countenance was one of serenity, composure, and bearing.

After the oohs and ahs, Clifford asked, "How did you get painted up there, Chione?"

"Good grief," Kendra said. "She looks like she could climb down and become one of us."

Chione felt another bone-deep chill.

"Look opposite," Bebe said.

More oohs and ahs filled the passageway as the lighting was focused on yet another mural showing the same woman bedecked and leading other priestesses in a ceremony.

Chione heard the inviting chant, felt compelled to join in and heard words come out of her mouth, foreign yet native. The scene on the wall opened out and took her in. The sweet music from a lyre and harp came from somewhere in the corner of a dimly lit room. She danced slowly, sensually at first until her body came alive. Soon the ritual dance made her blood rush. She became drunk on the perfume of sweet incense. Desire coursed through her veins. She danced for someone in waiting. She was being made ready. For what? Then the scene let her go. Chione staggered then caught her balance. Of course, no one else in the passageway perceived the spectacle. Aaron turned away hiding his face, but she had already seen his expression. It was clearly one of sexual hunger.

At the end of the passageway, they came face to face with two massive doors. The wood had dried, separated in places at the grain. Both doors were deeply carved and richly painted. An Eye of Horus stared, mute, from above. A golden Aten sun disk illuminated and hieroglyphs filled every vacant space. Securing the doors, a wooden cross member lay between handles, wrapped around and around with heavy woven papyrus twine. A large dollop of mud pressed into the twine knot was stamped simply with an ankh.

"An unbroken seal," Dr. Withers said, giddy as he danced around with clenched fists.

They cheered, having found another hopefully unbreached chamber, and took turns inspecting the glyph pressed in.

"Why would the symbol of life be used in this manner?" Kendra asked.

"An awful lot about this tomb breaks with tradition," Clifford said.

"Did you see this entry in your dreams, Chione?" Dr. Withers asked.

"Sorry to disappoint anyone," she said. "I didn't see these particular doors. All I can say is I saw quite a few entryways."

"Many doors?" Kendra asked. "Inside maybe?"

"Possibly. And a huge main hall."

"Do you know what that means?" Kendra asked joyfully. "What lies beyond these doors could be quite expansive, elaborate."

"Then let's get cracking," Dr. Withers said, gleefully rubbing his hands together. They stepped back momentarily for filming.

Use of the dollop was to prevent loose ends of the twined rope from unraveling. The sure way to save the impression would be to cut the opposite looped ends of twine. Destroying a relic was something all archaeologists dreaded. They chose to preserve the precious ankh seal and leave the cut twine ends dangling from it and would bind them, so they would not unravel. With deft fingers and small hand tools, Masud clipped the strands; carefully unwound them from the crossbar, and began to tease the dollop away from the handle.

"I remember part of a dream," Chione said.

"And?" Dr. Withers asked, preoccupied with Masud's skill.

"Something about a portal that we overlook." She cocked her head trying to remember the elusive scene.

No one said a word, perhaps because they dared not breathe. All were tense with excitement and packed close before the massive panels. Someone bumped Rashad's cameraman, who nearly lost his grip on the camera. Only a few tiny chips of the clay fragmented around the edges as the dollop popped free.

Though the wooden doors had dried out and contained cracks, the seams remained tight on all sides and required much coaxing. Once loosened, they stepped back as the massive panels creaked and slowly opened, laying bare a hermetically sealed universe. Again, thick, old air, gaseous and hot, oozed out. Everyone retreated, sniffing for fresher air.

"The smell's not as bad as the mummy chamber," Kendra said finally.

"Wait," Clifford said, sniffing conspicuously and moving toward the doorway again. "Scents of wood... and food?"

"Perfumes," Kendra said, also sniffing. "And oils."

More cloths were thrown down before Dr. Withers, Rashad, and the camera crews entered. The others remained at the doorway straining to see into the massive Pillared Hall as lights were cast about. This was the best yet, more beautiful than anyone had imagined. Kendra choked back overwhelming excitement. Bebe could only say, "Oh my! Oh my!"

Electricians set up stationary lighting inside the doorway, then more inside the Hall. The team waited as the videographers made their cursory sweep.

"Are you to blame for all this, Chione?" Dr. Withers asked teary-eyed as he rejoined the group.

"No, Dr. Withers," she said. "My dreams only served to spark your interest. The choice to follow through was yours."

Tall Clifford bent down and hugged Chione. "The world owes you," he said. "Mmmm... How is it you smell like the perfume that's oozing out of that room?"

"Egypt owes you," Paki Rashad said, nodding his appreciation.

The filming crew caught their reactions. Finally, they entered and silence overtook the group. The chamber was immense. Six square pillars stood in two rows in the middle of the room, reaching up to the inclined ceiling.

"This chamber must be over three hundred fifty feet into the ground," Dr. Withers said.

"No sign of the Burial Chamber doorway," Clifford said as he strained to see into each dark corner.

"Look up," Bebe said. Lighting was redirected. "Another pyramid makes the ceiling."

Clifford strained. "Sculpted in like the others."

The ceiling was indeed pyramid shaped, but with a lower gentler slope over the pillars. Unfortunately, patches of the Egyptian blue covered with gold stars had fallen to the floor and shattered.

Chione, standing directly under the center of the ceiling, had a sudden startling vision of four columns. The vision flicked into her mind, then disappeared in less than a second. "Not six columns," she said.

"What's that you say?" Kendra asked.

Chione caught herself. "Just thinking out loud."

The wall to the south offered two sets of double doors and another set on the west wall at the rear. All the doors were wooden and separating at the grain.

Chione's mind reeled. In yet another elusive vision, she caught a glimpse of a different chamber. It did not look anything like the Hall where they presently stood. She came back into the moment. Unlike in the vision, the wall murals and pillars in this hall were flaking. The floor under her feet was solid rock etched with shallow grooves forming large squares and resembled a gigantic white limestone checkerboard covered with dust. The floor in her vision had been smooth but unfinished.

She concentrated upon familiarizing herself with where she stood. The gleam of pure gold glinted off everything. Shoulder high columns displayed busts of ancients that would need to be identified. The Pillared Hall was uncluttered, with furniture strategically placed. Children's chairs were included. The furniture was exquisite. Painted hues were fresh and vibrant in the magnificent artwork. The Pillared Hall, with its riches, reflected a glimpse of the opulence of Ancient Egypt.

Eager to inspect everything, their voices all speaking at once rose in swells to an excited pitch, then calmed till someone found yet another relief, another relic, and became excited again.

"Is this the grand chamber you dreamed about?" Clifford asked. He stood beside one of the massive pillars looking ganglier than ever.

The vision of a large empty chamber with four pillars flickered through her mind again. "No, but it'll do," she said. Colorful visions, glimpses of different chambers, transited her mind like intrusive random thoughts.

"Look, but don't touch," Dr. Withers said. He kept his hands clasped behind his back.

Silence filled the room as they spread out in all directions.

Aaron spoke first. "Solid gold foil," he said in quiet understatement. Chione went to his side as he pointed. "That desk and chair by the second pillar. Covered with it."

They also noticed a long couch and chair against the north wall, carved from wood with woven seats and decorated with richly painted scenes. Various parts of the furniture were overlaid with sheets of gold foil. Nearby, gilded statues of various Gods stood mute watch.

"Would you look at this?" Clifford asked suddenly, leaning forward at the hip to examine the wall behind the couch. "Here's that same woman. And isn't this Tut?"

Another chill transited Chione's nervous system and it was not because of any cold air in that oven of a room.

"Tut?" Bebe asked. She hurried to Clifford's side and studied the wall. "Oh, my. It certainly resembles his likeness."

"What's Tut doing in here?"

"Good question."

"He looks like you, Aaron!" Chione said, laughing.

Aaron seemed embarrassed. Randy accused him of resembling the Boy King. Now she had innocently said it too. Why was Aaron's face reddening over simple off-hand joking?

In jest, Aaron struck a pose similar to that of the young man captured in time on the mural. Everyone had a good chuckle.

"You do look like him," Dr. Withers said. "But if that's Tut, who is this woman?"

"Considering these inner chambers call our attention to the tomb's occupant," Bebe said, gesturing to the woman's many images on the walls. "My guess is that we're seeing the likeness of the person buried here."

The filming crews were just as enthused. "Look at this," Ginny's technician said while shining a flashlight beam onto a bust painted black and perched on a pillar. His enthusiasm bubbled over, and he evidently could not wait for anyone else to speak. "I photographed her mummy years ago."

"When? Where?" Dr. Withers asked. "Who is she?"

"This is Queen Tyi."

Crowding close to see, they concurred. Chione felt compelled to reach out, but Aaron quickly jerked her hand away. "Uh-uh!" he said. "No touching the relatives." It was strange how he consistently happened to stop her from doing something she might regret.

"Just like Tyi's other heads they found," Clifford said. "Carved from the wood of a yew tree."

"Why would she be in here?" Dr. Withers asked as he bent close to study over bifocals. "They've already found her mummy."

"And her tomb," Clifford said.

"Well, this is not a Queen's tomb anyway," Dr. Withers said. "Unless they broke from tradition."

"Oh, and don't forget to say hello to Amenhotep III," the technician said of the bust on a neighboring pillar. "Tyi's husband and Pharaoh."

"Would you look at that," Dr. Withers said as he edged closer. He turned to the technician. "I wouldn't want the Exploration Mag people getting wind of your expertise. We need to keep your keen eye on our team."

"Stranger still," Bebe said. "Tyi's statue at the Colossi of Memnon was the one emitting strange sounds. Not only does this tomb sing, but we find Queen Tyi in here."

"Don't say it's magic," Dr. Withers said, but with a curious smile as he eyed Kendra. "My level of belief can't be stretched that far."

"The connection's to be found elsewhere," Clifford said.

The remaining busts were of children and unidentified adults.

As if in sequence, each person was drawn to a special artifact. "Get a look at this chair," Chione said, breaking the silence.

Carved and colorfully painted on the backrest of one chair were replicas of two decorated chairs and a standing man and woman.

"Hey, it's me again," Aaron said jokingly.

"What are you doing on all this furniture, Aaron?" Dr. Withers asked.

"Wait," Bebe said. "This is King Tut. And look, he's offering a seat to a non-royal woman."

"She's depicted nearly as tall as Tut," Clifford said. "Which signifies she was high in social stature."

"This has got to be her tomb," Kendra said. "But why would Tut be offering her a seat beside himself?"

"That's right," Chione said. "She's not Tut's Queen."

"This tomb was definitely not meant for Ankhesenpa," Clifford said. "And Tyi's tomb's over in Valley of the Kings."

"Good, good, good!" Dr. Withers said in his inimitable fashion. "So now we're looking at the resident of this not so humble abode of the afterlife."

"Maybe young Tut had a clandestine affair," Clifford said, suggestively raising his eyebrows a couple of times.

"That would explain the riches of the tomb and him being in here," Kendra said.

"Pharaohs took many wives," Bebe said. "However, documented history tells us Tutankhamon had only one queen."

The others speculated, sniffed the air, and wiped sweat from their brows. Chione picked her way around the fallen debris studying the walls, deciphering pictures and symbols that now relinquished hidden messages left only for the dead. "There's so much written here," she said.

"As if the Egyptians could leave a blank space anywhere," Clifford said. "Like Aaron's doodling."

"Any other clues?" Dr. Withers asked. At times seemed a little too impatient about making progress.

"Have you looked closely at these?" Chione asked, motioning to tall figures in the picture writing. "They represent gods of the Underworld, where the soul goes." She gestured across the mural. "Did you notice out in the passage, the messages got more and more mystical as we moved toward this Hall?" She smiled, onto something the others had not seen.

"What I saw," Aaron said, "had a lot to do with children and life and death."

"What are you saying?" Clifford asked. "That these scenes of a woman administering to others, that was her work?"

"Exactly," Chione said. "Also, here, lots of spells, magic, verses, chants, that sort of cryptography. But many of the glyphs are unfinished." She pointed across the chamber. "That mural over there too."

"What about the finished ones?" Dr. Withers asked. "Do they give a clue?"

"It'll take time to decipher."

"You have all the time you need."

"Did you notice?" Bebe asked. "On all the walls, there's a figure of what looks to be a young boy, always with the woman." She pointed out several scenes.

"Most curious," Kendra said.

"Perhaps when the chambers are cleared," Chione said, "I'll spend some quiet time in here."

"Anything you need," Dr. Withers said. "But for now, take another look around folks." He chuckled. "Then look at yourselves." They did and found themselves drenched in perspiration from captive heat that had stood still for thousands of years. "I suggest we all go topside to cool down and have lunch."

Chione suddenly needed to sit, which she did. Immediately, she heard Aaron calling her name. He sounded far away. Then, unexpectedly, she saw him...

...approaching in sunlight outdoors on the promenade, with naked and near-naked golden-skinned people all about.

Aaron without his shirt? The scene confused her. She froze, not knowing what to do, not knowing if she should try to do anything. Aaron approached again, fully clothed and handsome in khaki, from between the pillars.

"Chione?" he asked. "Why are you sitting in Tut's chair?"

"Chione?" Clifford asked, too, coming up behind Aaron. "Are you play-acting?"

She could not move, could not even blink as she heard Pharaoh softly call her by a different name.

"Chione? Hey, Chione...."

Then that eerie haunting whimper came again, sounding like from another world, yet so close, it could have come out of her own mouth!

"Oh, boy," Aaron said. "Anyone else hear that?"

Clifford had not reacted.

Chione had heard it while hearing the voices in the Pillared Hall. Somehow, she floated between that room and an ancient one as scenes intermingled.

"Hear what?" someone asked.

"The sound, the whimpering," Aaron said.

Dr. Withers looked helpless, but Chione was powerless to explain. "What happened at the moment we turned to leave?" he asked.

The noises sounded confusing. Aaron knelt at her feet with a questioning look. The whimper came again like someone's voice stifled in the middle of uttering a cry of desperation, chilling and muffled. Had that come from her? Again, she heard the whimpering. It ended suddenly. Her head flopped forward as if pushed quite abruptly. In slow motion, she felt herself falling out of the chair.

11

Noontime at the site was quiet, with many being called regularly to pray by a man's voice, at times melodic, at other times staccato, against the backdrop of Egyptian desert stillness. Hearing the bell ringing and the chanting five times a day became synonymous with the camp routine, particularly noticed if it did not happen on time. Many of the laborers took advantage to sleep off the high noon heat. Tarik, the young boy responsible for ringing the prayer bell, did not go with the men to pray. Instead, he hung around camp, helping where he could. Each time Chione saw him he would smile and wave. Somehow, his over-friendliness seemed strange, almost as if he had some sort of hidden agenda. Many young children, who seemed to belong to no one, had already taken to bribing workers, saying they wanted to help, only to gain access wherever they could in order to steal. Tarik also seemed like an orphan, because of his ragged, unchanged clothes. His eyes were those of a child wizened to exploiting every opportunity with stealthiness. Chione felt sympathetic and dismissed her curiosity about his attraction to the group. His accent and mannerisms were cute. When he spoke his attempts at English quite admirable.

Seeking shelter from the hot blowing sands, which never seemed to bother Tarik, Chione and Bebe shared a moment inside Chione's yurt.

"You really should keep an eye on your man," Bebe said softly so no one passing outside the yurt might hear.

"My man?" Chione asked, pausing mid-stroke while applying sunblock on her face.

"You and I will spend a lot of time away from the others, deciphering and all."

"My man?" Chione asked again.

Occasionally, men's laughter could be heard from a distance among those who chose not to pray but to stoop in a circle, throw stones and wager their coins.

"Doesn't it always seem that Kendra is after Aaron?"

Chione was momentarily stunned. "Well, Aaron is not my man." What Chione was more concerned about was that they all thought she was some sort of mental case.

Bebe smiled. "Aaron and Kendra. That is, I mean...." She stopped using the hair pick and looked sideways at Chione.

"Bebe, you surprise me."

"I don't mean to. I certainly don't want to sound like a busybody, but Kendra's all over your guy."

"Aaron and I aren't together anymore, never really were. It's been the better part of a year."

"Oh my, how foolish I am," Bebe said. She rolled her eyes. "I thought... weren't you and... am I the last to hear?" Bebe accepted the tube of lotion.

Chione smiled at Bebe's bewilderment. "I thought you all knew. As soon as one person gets hold of a story like that—"

"Aren't you two just being discreet?"

"Is that how it looks?"

"But why? You belong together."

"We didn't part as enemies, really," Chione said. "When I first told Aaron about my being adopted, he made an innocent statement—said he was thankful he'd never have to tell someone he had raised from childhood that he wasn't their biological father."

"That broke you up?"

"Not really. I learned I could never have children."

"Oh, yes, that."

"I think it's best if Aaron had his own family, don't you?"

Bebe turned to face Chione and looked at her in friendship, something they had both begun to feel. "I have a feeling Aaron would sacrifice the world for you."

"I couldn't ask that of anyone."

"You broke it off? Guess Kendra can have him, huh?"

"If she doesn't lose her rich husband in the process," Chione said. Hearing about a close friend making moves on Aaron made her heart sink, Kendra being married at that. The rumors of Kendra's flirtatiousness might be true after all.

Bebe touched her arm. "Forgive me, Chione."

Chione smiled. "I forgive," she said. She knew Bebe's motives. Bebe's great looking Kenneth had an affair with the nurse who all but forced him back to health at Clark Air Force Base in the Philippines after he was wounded in Viet Nam. That much she knew about Kenneth. Bebe said other affairs came after that. So, of course, Bebe would be preoccupied with who might be interested in whom. "If there was any way I could have a child, I'd marry Aaron without thinking twice."

"Say that again," Bebe said quickly. "Then tell me you don't love him."

"It's a moot point," Chione said. She felt a pang of deep sorrow. "If there was any way I could have a child...." Chione felt like she was about to come apart. For the first time, something someone said forced her to face her feelings. "I wish I could have...." Bebe's look of empathy made her feel rotten.

"Let's get back to the cook tent," Bebe said.

They squeezed in at the tables well shielded inside the largest yurt. The crude kitchen and eating area consisted of appliances, shelving, and dining tables standing on rare hard ground. One entire section near the kitchen had fresh vegetables and other foods being stored under pyramid forms. Irwin, the Chinese-American cook, poured Bebe a cup of coffee. Yafeu, the Egyptian cook, had Chione's favorite Karkade ready and waiting. The tantalizing food odors of both Irwin's cooking and Yafeu's Egyptian delicacies often left the team having difficulty deciding which to eat.

"I meant to ask," Bebe said to the others. "What kind of animals do that scary screeching out in the hills at night?"

"Jackals," Clifford said quickly, taking delight in the fearful look that came over Bebe's face.

"Jackals?" she asked, swallowing hard. "I thought they disappeared with the Ancients."

"Don't anybody worry about scorpions or snakes or jackals," Clifford said, affectedly teasing. "We've got enough activity out there to keep the pests away." He tried hard not to burst out laughing as he watched Bebe's look of despair.

Dr. Withers grinned and shook his head at Clifford being Clifford. Then he announced, "I've just gotten word of Randy's condition from the clinic at Luxor. He might have a dislocated shoulder. The x-ray equipment at Luxor isn't the greatest. They've sent him on to Cairo."

"It's that bad?" Clifford asked.

"If anything's broken, they'll have to operate," Dr. Withers said. "I understand he was experiencing mild shock and fever by the time they arrived across the river."

"Poor unfortunate Randy," Clifford said.

"I guess one of us should go stay with him," Dr. Withers said.

"What can any of us do while he's lying in a hospital bed?" Aaron asked. "What about our tight budget and time constraints?"

"Randy's a grown man," Bebe said. "Certainly, he realizes the nature of our situation."

"That's right," Aaron said. "I'm sure Dakarai will check in on him and keep us posted."

"Okay," Dr. Withers said. "If one of us needs to accompany Randy back here, I'll go, or you, Aaron. When the time comes." Then he flashed his famous beaming smile. "But for now, let's get to work."

"Yeah!" Clifford said.

"We're going to open the three side chambers in the Pillared Hall first. I want the full team present to identify exactly what's stashed.

No sense in sending Kendra and Clifford back to the beginning to start tagging while the rest of us find all the goodies."

"I love you, Dr. Withers," Kendra yelled from the end of the long table.

Bebe raised an eyebrow.

"Randy should be here, too, for that matter," Dr. Withers said, casting a dubious look of regret.

"What about the spouses?" Clifford asked, wrapping an arm around his wife.

"I thought of that," Dr. Withers said, addressing Rita. "If you're going to be helping with—"

"Rita? Helping?" Clifford asked, nearly choking on a gulp of water. "Doesn't she always work by your side?"

"Well, yes, but only when asked to do so by the head honcho."

"Excuse me!" Dr. Withers said. "I guess this head honcho's been taking too many naps." He smiled his silly grin, begging forgiveness. "I just assumed since Rita worked with you in the past, she'd be at your side this time."

"You mean—"

"In fact," Dr. Withers said. "After the crew finishes installing the temperature control equipment, Rashad and I don't see any harm in the entire party going in." Then he quickly raised a hand in warning. "Just our little party though."

"Here, here!" everyone said, lifting glasses. They used any excuse to toast themselves.

"Where's my wife?" Dr. Withers asked, leaning in his seat to peer out the fly.

"Over there with Siti," Bebe said, pointing. "Charming some of the laborers with her chocolate cake."

"Darned woman," Dr. Withers said, shaking his head. "Could bake a cake over two cans of Sterno if she had to."

"It's not the baking I'd be concerned with," Kenneth said, also teasing.

"How's that?"

"The men," Kendra said. "Some of the men are downright charming."

"Is that a fact?" Bebe said, in a voice that accused if anyone should know, it would be Kendra.

"Marlowe's no slouch either," Royce said. He seldom spoke.

While fairly good-looking, Royce always had a wary look in his eyes, like he was onto something, like he knew something no one else fathomed. The set of his mouth combined with those steely blue eyes and quiet self-absorbed nature made Chione feel uneasy. She did not know why, but her intuition always sent caution signals when he was around.

"My wife will have those laborers eating out of her hand," Dr. Withers said with a crooked smile. "They'll work harder."

"Guess we'll be seeing a lot of chocolate cake," Bebe said.

"And fresh vegetables," Kendra said. "Since Chione's convinced our cooks to store items under pyramids."

After both Clifford and Dr. Withers had a snooze, during which time Aaron edited records and Bebe clarified some of hers, the team gathered in preparation for re-entry. This time they would enter via the way they had exited the passageway, on a ladder in the portcullis shaft.

"Chione, you might try to identify where those sounds are coming from," Dr. Withers said.

"Strange no one else heard them," Bebe said.

"Don't forget," Dr. Withers said. "That Egyptian grave robber heard them first."

"Why haven't the rest of us?"

"Would you really want to?" Clifford asked. "Considering how we jumped out of our skins when we heard Randy?"

"Some of the laborers surely heard them," Bebe said. "Among us, why only Chione and Aaron?"

"Well," Dr. Withers said with a sideways smile. "If I were Randy, I'd have to say because Chione looks Egyptian and Aaron resembles Tut."

Everyone had a good laugh. Clearly, Dr. Withers was unaffected by not having heard the sounds. Chione had heard them and was thankful he believed in her.

Aaron believed in her too. Chione needed to be careful not to give Aaron the impression she knew more than she did.

Once inside the passageway, they paused long enough for those who had not seen the opened chambers to view them. Quite adept with a camera, Kenneth's candid photos would provide additional history for Bebe's documented manuscript.

Making their way down to the Pillared Hall, Chione lagged behind, her mind transfixed by the ancient etchings. A sinister voice came up behind her asking, "Are you lost, little girl?" She turned to see Clifford tiptoeing toward her with clutching hands raised.

"Are you the big bad wolf?" she asked.

"Today I'm Anubis, jackal god of embalming, looking for work!" Everyone laughed at the enviable spontaneity she and Clifford enjoyed. Again, he raised his crimped hands above her head as if ready to snatch her and got up close to her face. "Wanna go for a walk in the woods to Granny's house?" As the others laughed again, Clifford ducked inside the First Chamber before Dr. Withers had a chance to sound off his name in frustration.

"Are you able to come up with answers?" Dr. Withers asked finally.

"Getting a feel for the overall message of these spells," Chione said. "I've written down some which seem more significant. I can go over them later."

"Heard anything else?" Aaron asked.

She shot a glance in his direction, and then quickly looked away. "Not really," she said quietly. If he had not heard what she had been hearing or smelled the same odors, perhaps he was only receiving what he was supposed to perceive and no more.

A little later, they were ready to open the first of the three annexes, side chambers to the Pillared Hall. Lighting was strategically placed directly in front of the two doors of the first annex. Quaashie and Naeem, laborers who worked closely with Dakarai and Masud, stepped before the doors that, like the others, were flush against the south wall and looked more like niches carved into the stone in which to place wooden panels. They carefully slipped the long wooden dowel from between the door handles, and gently pulling at the doors until they moved freely. No rope, no dollop of mud had been installed. The doors had simply been closed and remained that way. Accumulated dust in the cracks and seams provided little resistance. The wood creaked and made strange rustling sounds as the wood was shifted to the opened positions.

Kenneth extensively photographed his wife's reactions.

"Gold," Bebe said, stepping directly in front and getting first peek as the two doors came free and opened out. "More gold!"

As flashlight beams probed, gold foil gleamed from furniture haphazardly stacked. Golden treasures and jewels twinkled in response to the photographer's lights.

"Everything looks thrown in," Chione said with dismay.

"Someone was in a hurry to close shop," Clifford said. Though he was tall, he still stretched to see over the others and all the equipment.

Then another vision rattled through Chione's mind.

Ancient laborers hurriedly casting possessions into the chamber and then fleeing lest they be perceived as participating in wrongful worship.

"Run! Run away!" Chione said quietly as the vision faded.

12

"No beams, just a plain pyramid ceiling," Kendra said, crowding in. Above the glut of artifacts, the ceiling rose to a point in the middle.

"Not even painted," Aaron said.

Chione tipped her head back to view the assortment of artifacts that reached toward the ceiling in a claustrophobic muddle. "The pyramid is why nothing's deteriorated," she said.

Clifford moved closer to study some of the pieces. "Chione's right. Nothing's broken. Nothing's sagged and collapsed."

"Most women are happy if they have few precious gems," Marlowe said, pointing. "I can't imagine what it would be like to own as many as adorn that one chair alone."

"In our society," Kendra said. "These are only semi-precious stones, carnelian, lapis, amethyst and so forth. We'll have to identify them later." Something in Kendra's voice hinted that semi-precious stones were not good enough for her.

"Look," Chione said. "There's blue anhydrite! It's so rare... was, even in those days."

"There's a fortune in gold in that one room alone," Royce said.

No one entered that First Annex, not even the photographers. Space to set a foot down inside simply did not exist. One quick sweep of a video camera would not catch what lies hidden inside. As with any of the chambers, extensive photographing during the removal process would prove the best method of documentation.

After they all took a good look, they turned their attention to the Second Annex.

"This is like Christmas," Marlowe said.

"Haphazard placement of the artifacts is so like Tut's tomb," Bebe said. "All of his chambers were heaped with artifacts in disarray."

"Wonder what the hurry was," Rita said. She carried a fan. Stuffiness inside the tomb seemed to be affecting her.

"Whatever reason, it must be why some of these hieroglyphs and murals are unfinished," Kendra said.

"As if this person's burial wishes were being carried out," Chione said. "But stopped with her possible sudden demise."

"Let's try to limit our speculation," Dr. Withers said.

They stepped back to give the workmen space. All lighting had to be moved and repositioned. It made their shadows swing around the Pillared Hall like dancers in a dimly lit ballroom and must have tickled Clifford's wit. He grabbed his wife, and they waltzed across the floor and into the darkness. Then Clifford let out a soft but menacing burst of devious laughter.

Rita came fleeing back into the light wearing a ridiculous grin. "If Randy had howled like that when he slipped out of the Second Chamber," she said. "I'd have died in my tracks."

As archaeologists adept at having patience when finding artifacts representing situations they could not change, anticipation hung heavy in the stifling air. Each knew they could not affect anything found, its condition or history, but each knew whatever was found might adversely affect them. Finding this tomb just happened to be a glorious event, cementing the team's place in history.

Dr. Withers paced and, several times seemed to want to urge the laborers to be quicker at what they had to do. Then even he stopped moving. They waited and no one spoke. Finally, Quaashie and Naeem took their positions in front of the doors. Stillness permeated the Hall. As the doors of the Second Annex were opened, slowly, they offered out the secrets they had kept for millennia.

"Praise be to Allah!" Masud said.

Everyone's attention riveted on the widening crack as the doors swung open. In front, just behind the doors, sat a gleaming life-sized golden statue facing out. Cropped hair accentuated the female figure's uplifted jawline. Open eyes gazed eternally fixed. In one hand, the woman held a large ankh, in the other, a djed-pillar amulet.

"A djed!" Clifford said, standing erect as if honoring the statue. "Representing the backbone of Osiris, conferring stability and firmness."

Chione sighed heavily. She pressed her fingertips against her shirtfront, to feel the golden scarab underneath. Why did the amulets seem so familiar? She could not move, as if the statue had stolen her strength. She felt like she needed to merge with its likeness to gain back her agility.

The others inched closer. The rendition of a very young woman in full priestess decorum sat on a typical 18th Dynasty squared base inscribed with hieroglyphs.

"Look here," Aaron said, bending down and pointing along the bottom. "A cartouche."

At that point, no one so much as glanced at the rest of the contents in the room.

"Can you two decipher it?" Dr. Withers asked.

Bebe bent over, as far as her figure would allow.

Finally able to move, Chione stooped, studying the etchings. "See these?" She pointed to two symbols. "Representing the goddess of pregnant women."

Bebe straightened and whipped out her pocketbook of hieroglyph translations and thumbed quickly. Chione stood and flashed her light onto the booklet. Finally, Bebe said, "Translates to the pronunciation of Tauret."

"Tauret," Chione said, enunciating, looking into the face of the statue....

...whose eyes came alive and looked straight into hers!

"Tauret," several others repeated. It sounded like a chant.

"Would you believe it?" Clifford asked, down on all fours, his face up close to the cartouche. "The inscription is incomplete. What would that mean?"

Someone touched her shoulder and brought her back into the moment. "Couldn't even guess," Chione said.

"Weren't cartouches used only by royalty?" Kenneth asked.

"And nobles and courtiers," Bebe said. "Anyone, for that matter, if they wanted to create one for themselves."

Excited, Dr. Withers finally laid out flat on the stone floor seeing alternately through bifocals, then without them. Ginny would not think of missing such a moment. "Looks like something's been rubbed out," Dr. Withers said over his shoulder. "Someone cast the light at an angle. Masud, what do you make of this?"

Masud dropped to all fours, looked, and then said, "The symbol of Aten has been eradicated."

"Eradicated?"

"Erased. Notice the indentation, please, where it is almost obliterated." He pointed with the long fingernail on his pinky. Chione bent down next to him and followed along.

"Yes, yes," Dr. Withers said. "Rubbed out in the soft gold. But why?"

"Over here are the beginnings of the symbols representing the Amon," Masud said. "But in outline form, as you Americans say."

"Where, how?" Chione asked, irresistibly ready to press fingertips against the lines.

"No, no!" Masud said, pushing her hand away. Then he realized what he had done, rocked back on his feet, clasped his hands and begged, "Forgive, O Little One." He bowed his head. "I did not mean to touch. Forgive, forgive."

"You did no harm, Masud," Chione said, touching his arm, which he withdrew cautiously.

"Please forgive," he said again.

"Masud, it's all right."

"Okay," he said, still cautious. "But see?" He timidly aimed his pinky back toward the base of the statue. "Look closely."

Chione drew her face closer to the base where Masud pointed. She gasped. "A fingerprint! And another!"

Everyone had to look. The photographers had to take close-ups; such as they might be able to do with the deficient lighting. Paki Rashad half stooped, bent forward with both hands on his knees, and strained to see over the heads of the others. Even Kenneth with his back problem would get down on the floor for something like that.

"I want to collect those prints," Dr. Withers said finally.

"But why?" Bebe asked. She feverishly took notes as she tried not to miss anything.

"For posterity. Here's a mark of a person who lived and worked in this very spot over three thousand years ago."

"But a fingerprint?"

"It's all part of the find." Dr. Withers rose to his knees. "We'll gather as much information as we can." He smiled at Bebe. "You historians can make something of it."

"The Museum," Masud said, excited. "We have such equipment for lifting fingerprints."

"That settles it," Dr. Withers said. "Listen up everyone. More than ever, no one touches or comes in contact with anything." He directed his comments toward no one in particular. Chione knew that she, more than anyone, was the one who needed to feel an object, a glyph, to more clearly receive its message.

Again, they concentrated on the obliterated symbols.

"See this shape of a reed?" Clifford asked. "This checkered area and the wavy line?"

"An Amon symbol in an era of Aten worship?" Bebe asked leaning in between the men to closer study the contradictory marks.

"This part's just like Tut's cartouche," Chione said.

"This person, this Tauret, was converting her faith?" Dr. Withers asked.

"Converting one's faith has been going on since the beginning of time," Masud said, evidently proud of the opportunity to contribute.

"Why weren't these completed?" Dr. Withers asked, allowing Aaron to help him to his feet.

"There are more unfinished glyphs around the room," Chione said. "Everything, the haphazard furniture in these side chambers, unfinished murals, they all imply the burial was done in a hurry."

"Like they didn't care if anything got finished," Rita said.

The others stood. "Look, there's the ram-headed god, Khnum," Chione said, pointing into the Annex behind the statue and breaking a silence that had overtaken them.

"Why would other gods be present when all were supposedly denied during the time of Aten?" Kendra asked.

"Not if people were in the process of conversion," Masud said. "By the way, in mythology, the name of Khnum means 'reborn sun.'"

"Makes some sense," Clifford said. "Goddess of pregnant women and reborn sun."

"So here we have the former Tauret-Aten," Kendra said. "That doesn't answer why her name was being changed to 'Amon' if in fact, that's what the obliteration means."

"That confirms what I've already found in many of the murals," Chione said.

"Almost certainly, the mummy was a priestess," Bebe said. "Probably involved in the hidden mysteries."

"As soon as we decode the glyphs and murals," Dr. Withers said. "We'll know her secrets."

Finally, their attention began to focus on other contents of the annex. Behind Tauret were pieces of furniture in rows and heaped with the tools of her suspected trade. Amulets lay everywhere, some carved from gemstone and bordered with pure gold knots, gleaming around the edges. Tiny carved decorated pillars, more djeds, and tiny headrest amulets lay about.

"Now what would all those things be used for?" Marlowe asked.

"Spells," Bebe said. "If I'm not mistaken, these were implements used in Tauret's rituals."

"Chances are we're going to see many more trinkets," Clifford said.

"Look at that dried stuff in those flat open vessels," Rita said, fanning and weakly crowding in for a better look.

"Remnants of plants and powders," Chione said.

"Yes," Bebe said. "Those round dark things are most likely juniper berries. The powders in those bowls, henna, and look. There's garlic."

"Almost perfectly preserved," Dr. Withers said with wonder.

"Because it's under yet another pyramid," Aaron said.

"Garlic under a pyramid?" Chione asked. "Don't any of you say I haven't finished my lunch!" They laughed heartily. Chione was quietly surprised with herself for having cracked a joke.

Scarabs and winged scarabs, wadjet eyes and carved steles were plentiful. Various sized figurines of gods and goddesses were packed in. In one corner stood another statue of Taweret, the goddess of childbirth. In the opposite corner stood a tall stele carved with the likeness of Horus, the child with sidelocks, depicting youth. It was believed to transmit the power of Isis and protect those where the stele was housed.

"Oh, look," Kendra said, as each person crowding in for a look then was crowded out. "Royal vases."

Just inside the doorway to the left stood a small table on which sat numerous utensils and containers. Most were carved from mottled stone with lids of decorative solid gold. Several lids were bound with strings also fashioned from twisted gold strands.

"For lotions and potions is my best guess," Bebe said. "These are definitely items a priestess would use."

"These clues must have a common thread," Marlowe said.

"My sentiments exactly," Bebe said.

Chione studied Taweret, glanced to the various ritualistic paraphernalia, and then to Tauret. She cradled her stomach, which felt strangely full. But she had hardly eaten a thing at lunch due to anxiety beckoning her back into the tomb.

"What is it?" Marlowe asked. "Are you ill?"

"Just nervous," Chione said. "Overexcited." She smiled weakly. The statue that everyone seemed to accept as a full-hipped Amarnian female of Akhenaten's era actually looked pregnant. No one noticed the stomach bulge being too high up under the priestess's skirt. The previous night Chione had dreamed of having a baby but would keep that information a secret. Disclosing such a dream at the same time as finding a pregnant statue would sound to the others like wish fulfillment. Yet, she felt Aaron watching her hug her belly. She dropped her arms and dared not glance over at him just then.

"Each one of these items is a facet in the history of this dearly departed one," Clifford said. "With all our modern methods, we may not take ten years to empty a tomb like Howard Carter did with Tut's, but it might take us as long to decipher the meanings of the artifacts and glyphs."

"You're right about Carter," Bebe said. "He wouldn't allow the next item to be brought out until he finished drawing, cataloging and writing the history of the one just removed." Each time she had something important to impart, she stood more erect and attracted attention. She would make a great classroom instructor as well.

"Well, times have changed," Dr. Withers said. "Can't leave the artifacts to be plundered. With modern methods of documenting, developing the history comes later."

"The museum staff is excellent in that regard," Masud said, always seeming ready to contribute.

"You've got your work cut out for you, Kendra," Aaron said.

"Wanna help?" she asked. Her smile invited.

Aaron looked surprised. "I've got other things to do," he said quickly.

Attention focused on the other set of doors at the rear of the Hall. They were the only remaining doors and the team had yet to find the burial chamber. Clifford excitedly rubbed his hands together. His eyes flashed a message of expectation. As he headed toward the back of the Hall, he high-stepped and repeatedly thrust his head forward, strutting like a chicken. Rita smiled for the first time in hours, rolled her eyes, and shook her head.

Lighting was moved to the back of the Hall.

"Aaron," Dr. Withers said, calling through the dimness. "Get some more lighting down here when we begin our work in this room. It's just too dark in this large space."

"This is it," Masud said. "Maybe the Burial Chamber or leading to it."

"I'm afraid to look," Rita said. "A whole lifetime of thrills in one day makes me weak."

The air seemed electrified with expectation. Once again, Quaashie and Naeem took their places at the doors. Their dark eyes flashed, their smiles beamed. This time the team could not stand back and wait. In eagerness, they crowded up close. As the doors were pulled open all expectation vanished. Another pyramid ceiling protected only kitchen furniture and vessels containing a cache of foodstuffs set in to last an eternity.

Quiet filled the Hall. Dr. Withers began to pace. "Chione?" he said. "While you examined the other walls, did you happen to notice anything that might be another hidden passage?"

"I wasn't looking for any."

"Decipher any clues?"

"Some confusing messages," she said. "Nothing that would direct us to another doorway."

"Well, keep an open mind to any covert messages," he said. "All of you."

"Come out, come out, wherever you are," Clifford said loudly. "Where do you suppose that woman's hiding?"

"If you were playing hide-and-seek with her," Chione said, laughing. "You must have made her wait so long, she mummified in her hiding place!"

13

While awaiting the arrival of the fingerprinting kit from Cairo, the rest of the media were given tours, though photographing was strictly prohibited and cameras not allowed to be brought inside. Aaron and Bebe would release copies of the few photographs the various newspapers would be allowed to print. That was the deal that had been struck. The media could write anything they wanted about what they saw, inside or out, and photograph anything outside the tomb. The Exploration Magazine would publish only those photos approved and given to them by the team. The pictorial expose' of the tomb's contents was reserved for the Institute's future books and publications. That was unless a reporter managed to worm his way into the receiving area at the Madu Museum by bribing an unscrupulous laborer.

After the tours, the three annexes were closed again. The tomb now vacated, soundings were resumed above ground for any variations adjacent to the Pillared Hall that might disclose the location of the Burial Chamber.

Progress being at a standstill, over refreshments Dr. Withers said, "I would've suspected the burial site to be at the far end of the Pillared Hall, where we found the foodstuffs."

The tomb had been carved in a steep downward slope toward the interior of the mountain. The higher up the hillock crews took the sensors, the greater the distance between them and the underground rock formations. Nothing registered.

"We should have listened to Chione about not needing sensors," Clifford said, wrapping an arm around her shoulders. "We wouldn't be wasting time on soundings."

"In the interim," Dr. Withers said. "I've decided to have both the First and Second Chambers cleared."

"Agreed," Kendra said. "Since they've been exposed to fresher air, the mummies might begin to deteriorate."

At original inspection, many mummies were found wrapped haphazardly; the cloths in which they were bundled showed varying stages of decay. Even the utmost care in mummification was unpredictable. Rameses II's Queen Nefertari had immediately crumpled into dust as her sarcophagus was opened. So time was of the essence since the tiny mummies had lain somewhat exposed since ancient grave robbers first made entry. When the hole in the ceiling backfilled and closed off it offered some protection. Now that the mummies would be brought out into the sunlight and strong climate, deterioration would proceed.

"What intrigues me as well," Dr. Withers said, "are those strange glyph interpretations Chione's been coming up with."

No one said a word. Their eyes glazed over. They would have to wait for final analysis to form opinions on that.

The retaining wall above Randy's hole was finished. Rubble had been vacuumed up exposing the cavity ancient robbers used when entering the Second Chamber. Thick wooden timbers were placed on top of the hole at the ceiling level to keep more rubble from sliding down. Determination would later be made as to how to close the hole permanently.

Naeem was to oversee the clerks and laborers assigned to Clifford for tagging and photographing in place and removing artifacts from the First Chamber. Quaashie was assigned to the crew helping Kendra with the removal of the children's mummies from the Second Chamber. Both local men were experienced in the use of preservation chemicals necessary to be applied before the artifacts could be shipped to Cairo.

Kendra later reported that all the little ones would exit the tomb wrapped in thick layers of gauze bandage. Too, the time-honored method of applying hot melted paraffin over fragile and decaying objects to hold them together saved many an artifact, as well as mummy wrappings, from crumbling.

A bucket brigade hand-carried rubble out of the Second Chamber and had it hoisted up through the shaft. Each load would be sifted and searched for any relic or broken piece.

Outside, a great shadow drifted over the sifting bins. Noise from the ever-enlarging crowd of onlookers dropped to nearly no sound at all. Then everyone was yelling and pointing upwards. Like the others, Chione craned her neck. A gigantic hot air balloon decorated with Egyptian symbols drifted overhead.

"That's too low for comfort," Dr. Withers said angrily. He shook a finger in the direction of the balloon.

"Too much Western influence," Chione said under her breath.

Then the mummies were being brought out. In the distance from somewhere among the throng of locals and visitors alike, the plaintiff wail of mourners for the souls of those little ones drifted up the hill.

"I find it strange," Chione said. "That news of everything we do travels so quickly."

"What in particular?" Dr. Withers asked.

"The minute we start to bring out the bodies, the wailing begins. It's as if some of the people were prepared for what will happen next."

Despite soundings turning up no new findings, methodic Dr. Withers needed to assure himself that everyone followed the best scheme of things. Remaining members of the team readied themselves for re-entry. They donned facemasks and gloves since decaying mummies were being moved.

While the first two chambers were being emptied, the rest of the team translating the hieroglyphs and art might provide clues to the whereabouts of the final resting place. Reading began at the front of the passageway as tiny remains made re-entry into the world.

In the passageway outside the First Chamber, Chione again smelled that heady perfume that brought with it a vision so bold it made her feel limp.

A procession of Ancients. Each wore the regal uniform of a striped headdress and white linen kilts. Only royal workers now allowed touching the mummified children. Workers' images intermittent in the dim flicker of oil lamps, bringing in tiny freshly wrapped mummies for positioning inside the Second Chamber, their final resting place. The Ancient worker's chants resonated.

The pad and pen slowly slipped from her hands. Chione stood motionless, hearing the forgotten language. She stared down the passageway. Her heart raced. Her knees almost buckled. Aaron stooped to retrieve her writing materials. Despite the facemask hiding the rest of his expression, he looked straight into her eyes with a look so profound she could only guess he had sensed something too. She turned to the wall, pretended to study the glyphs and took time to gather her thoughts. When able to return her attention back to the others, she said, "When I looked at these reliefs earlier, I found something of a mystery. A big one."

"Then let's put our learned heads together," Dr. Withers said.

"History in this tomb is coded in spells. Magic symbols abound. I stick to our original theory that the person buried here was a courtier or priestess whose life was steeped in magic and mysticism."

"What else?" Dr. Withers asked.

"Follow me as I read our way down the passage. And prepare yourself," she said, hinting at possible surprises. "The figures on these walls confirm something we discovered on Tauret's golden statue."

"Spill it, Chione," Clifford said, poking his head out of the First Chamber. "I can't stand the suspense."

"Be quiet, Anubis," she said. "Or I'll turn you into a statue."

"As long as I'm real gold," he said, bending his knees and assuming Anubis' pose of sitting with hands on his thighs and chin stuck out.

"Will you two—!"

"Sorry, Dr. Withers," Chione said quickly, smiling as Clifford disappeared. "What I've found is a history that continues to the doorway of the Pillared Hall."

"Then what?" Aaron asked. "Stops?"

"Not stops, changes," Chione said. "Changes that coincide with the name 'Aten' being obliterated on the statue."

"Ah-ha!" Aaron said. "Maybe something drastic did happen in this person's life."

"Relative to the belief system the person followed," Bebe said.

"Exactly," Chione said. "But before we get into the change that might have taken place, there's much more to understand." She pointed out a number of women in one mural who looked to be in the first trimester of pregnancy. "These are not rounded full-hipped Amarnian type ladies of the Akhenaten and Nefertiti era. Our lady was a priestess or educated specialist working with women's issues, as we call them today."

"Specifically?"

"Fertility, I believe, generalizing into monitoring pregnancies and childbirth, even counseling husbands. Just like today's midwife."

"Like that spell in the First Chamber," Dr. Withers said. He thought a moment then repeated from memory, " 'Blacken your face with Hapi's mud. Like farmer's fields, new life will bud.' "

"One of her magical treatments?" Aaron asked.

"Evidently it worked," Bebe said, "According to that mural, the woman with the blackened face was definitely pregnant." While Dr. Withers and Aaron studied a row of glyphs, Bebe leaned close to Chione and whispered, "If this priestess worked with women's issues, I wish she'd cast a spell and end my menopausal malaise."

Chione smiled secretly. "Now here's a surprise," she said, returning attention to the others. "These murals depict various other patients—if we can call them that—along with the life in general of the woman interred here. It was a good life, and she worships the Aten."

"The symbol we found being removed," Dr. Withers said.

"This further narrows down the time frame," Chione said. "If Tauret worshipped the Aten, and suddenly it was wrong to do so, that would account for her changing her faith, as we call it."

"That fits," Bebe said. "Tauret's life ended during the time of Tutankhamon, specifically, when the god Amon was being restored."

"Exactly," Dr. Withers said. He could barely contain himself and danced around bouncing fists at his sides and singing, "Good, good, good!"

Chione pointed out specific symbols. "Remember inside the First Chamber about the spell being cast, 'till all of time has passed'? Listen to this one." She pointed to a trail of glyphs, again sounded out a few of the markings, and then translated them to English.

Down this corridor no living walk
no sound in these halls creak
Only Anubis inside doth stalk
till Khentimentiu speak

"Does that mean Clifford is the reincarnation of Anubis?" Aaron asked. No one could keep from laughing.

"Refresh my memory about Khentimentiu," Bebe said, ready with her pen.

"God of the dead's destiny," Chione said. "Thought to be the original god of the Predynastic peoples."

"That god is seldom seen," Dr. Withers said. "What do you suppose he's doing in here?"

"I'm sensing something about all of this," Aaron said. He had that glossy look in his eyes again.

"In the same way Chione does it?"

"Maybe not," he said, looking doubtful. "My intuition tells me these spells imply an expectation that someone would again walk here."

"As if Khentimentiu expects the dead to rise?" Dr. Withers asked, showing some disbelief.

Just then, with Bebe's back to the First Chamber and the others in front of her, Clifford crept up from behind, breathed heavily through his face mask and placed a slow hand on Bebe's shoulder while moaning low. She screamed as they all howled with laughter.

"Sorry," Clifford said. "It's more fun out here with the living." Then he disappeared again.

Chione led the others down the passageway, past walls filled with gloriously painted reliefs, breathed in the heady perfume and felt her ancient sandaled feet on the smooth stone. She slowed and studied a scene. "We'll have to verify this," she said, pointing to an image and knowing she was about to surprise them again. "I believe this woman is known today as *Ankhesenamun*, King Tut's Queen."

"That is her," Aaron said. He drew close and studied the cartouche near the image. "In this tomb, her name's written as Ankhesenpa-Aten."

"Yes," Chione said. "Her name changed from Aten about the same time period because today's scholars read her as Ankhesenamun. *Amun* is a modern-day derivative of *Amon*."

"Plus, she's sitting in a royal chair," Bebe said as she pointed with her pen.

Chione remembered Ankhesenpa's face, knew it well but did not remember how she had become so familiar with that Queen's image, not having paid undue attention to her in any history studies.

"Look what Tauret's doing," Dr. Withers said, pointing. He bounced up and down impatiently. "She's combing the Queen's hair!"

"The Queen's handmaiden?" Bebe asked. "We have reason to believe Tauret was a high priestess, a courtier. Is this how?"

"Why would a hand maiden be lavished so many riches at burial?" Dr. Withers asked.

"Remains to be seen," Aaron said. He sounded as if he wanted to keep something secret for a while. Just how much had he been able to intuit?

Chione led them next into the Pillared Hall. "Tauret's private life is here," she said, gesturing to the walls. "Rows and rows of glyphs express familial bliss. That woman near you, Bebe, could be Tauret's mother."

"This symbol of destiny in the cartouche over the mother's head," Aaron said, "must represent her name."

"Mes... khen... et," Bebe said, reading after pulling a small booklet from her booklet.

"Meskhenet," Chione said. Suddenly she felt another chill. "Mother."

"This man, then," Dr. Withers said, "might be her father. His cartouche translates to—"

"Umi," Bebe said. "Her father's name was Umi, meaning life."

"Bebe, you're really good at this," Chione said.

"These next scenes make Umi look like he was... Pharaoh's clothier," Aaron said. "A noble! That explains Tauret's high standing." The expression on Aaron's face said he knew something more.

Chione called their attention to nearby busts of a man and woman resting on neighboring columns. "Mom and Dad," she said, in a proud voice similar to how she might introduce her family. Everyone scampered back and forth wherever attention was directed, careful to sidestep ceiling plaster still laying on the floor. A strong resemblance was found between the faces on the walls, the features of the sculptures, and the face on the golden statue of the priestess.

"Now look at this," Chione said, again calling them back to a mural. "This Aten symbol, Tauret's history as Tauret-Aten stops abruptly. See? Another cartouche." That cartouche had also been obliterated. Dr. Withers pulled at his mustache. Chione waited as the others inspected the glyphs, trying not to miss anything but neglecting to look farther than the ends of their noses. Finally, she said, "You're all missing someone who's standing right in front of you."

They milled around. Suddenly from the back of the chamber, Dr. Withers exclaimed, "Would you look at this?"

They went to view the pillar at which he pointed. "That is Amon-Ra," Bebe said. "The tall feathered headdress with the sun on it. That's Amon-Ra."

"He wasn't on any of the reliefs out in the passageway," Dr. Withers said.

"Exactly," Chione said. The passageway murals depicted Tauret's life as a priestess and handmaiden to Ankhesenpa in the days of Aten before the restoration of Amon began. "Tauret must have died at the height of the restoration. The walls and such, in the process of being changed, were left unfinished."

"Amazing," Dr. Withers said. "Now, let's put the pieces together." He paced slowly as the others waited. "Would someone contribute something here?" he asked finally. "This place is as silent as a tomb."

Once Bebe stopped laughing, she said, "Tauret's childhood occurred during the Aten period. After she's involved with Pharaoh's family, that's where the obliteration begins."

"It stands to reason that when Tutankhamon came to power and was in the process of restoring the old gods," Chione said, "Tauret and her family, being part of his court, would also convert." Tauret's tomb was already in the process of being built. The Pillared Hall was only half finished by the time Amon-Ra was being reinstated.

"Did they plan that far ahead?" Aaron asked. "How did they know she would be needing a tomb during what looks to be the prime of her life?"

"And if she began as a commoner, why these elaborate digs?" Dr. Withers asked.

"Digs?"

"Wait, there's more to consider," Chione said. "Was Tauret, the priestess of childbirth—if that's what she was—brought to Ankhesenpa because the Queen bore two stillborn?"

"Good question," Aaron said. "Was Tauret to work her magic?"

The more they found the more questions popped up.

"It'll take time to sort," Dr. Withers said.

Silence came again as they spread out in different directions examining the murals. Then Aaron called out from the far end of the chamber. "Hey, everyone, here's Queen Tyi in relief."

They rushed to his side. "That is her," Bebe said.

"She's my favorite," Chione said. "Of all the Queens, she's the one I really have an affinity for."

"What is it about her?"

"I have no idea," Chione said. "I remember reading how she was well-loved, respected, even in death when they finally found her in that cache of royal mummies." When found, Queen Tyi's chest had long before been ripped open, ravaged by tomb robbers for the embedded scarab and jewels. "Still, she possessed this majestic aura." Chione was silent a moment, and then asked, "Haven't you ever felt empathy with someone and you didn't know why?" The others were attentively silent as Chione caught herself expressing emotion, which she seldom did.

Finally, Dr. Withers asked, "Is that similar to Clifford's affinity for Anubis?"

"I don't know who's worse," Bebe said, laughing. "You or Clifford."

They continued to inspect the walls. Nearly every bit of space had been carved or painted. Yet, not one section so much as hinted of a possible disguised entry. "I suggest," Dr. Withers said, "that we tend to matters topside until such time as these chambers are cleared. Maybe passage to the Burial Chamber is through the back of one of those crowded Annexes."

"Quite possible," Aaron said.

"Might be beyond the pantry," Dr. Withers said, snickering. "I'd want to be near food if I expected to live forever."

"You men and your stomachs," Bebe said.

One last look at the glorious furnishings and the walls with yet to be disclosed secrets, and they began to leave.

"Aaron," Chione said quietly, pulling him aside. "Do you think Dr. Withers will let me stay in here?"

"Stay? Now that everyone's leaving, you mean?" He shrugged. "Why not? You're a professional."

"No, during the night."

He leaned toward her and quietly asked, "You want to stay in here by yourself... all night?"

Why should that seem like such a surprise? She realized immediately that she should not have mentioned it to Aaron. Now he would want to stay too. "Just for a while," she said. "I want to listen to the whimpering."

"I haven't heard it anymore." He stuck his notepad under his arm and his hands into his pockets as if to keep from touching her as they shared a private conversation.

"But I have."

"When?" he asked, seeming disappointed. A hand came out of his pocket to tap his chest. "Why haven't I heard?"

"It happens all the time, Aaron," she said. "I can't make an issue of it. The others wouldn't understand."

"Why haven't I heard it again?" Surely his many responsibilities were distracting.

"Do you really want to?"

"I'd like to know too."

"Not just like to know, Aaron. We need to experience what went on here."

He shook his head and looked at her sideways. "If someone's pulling a joke and you stay by yourself all night—"

"Not a joke, Aaron. A joke wouldn't have given us this tomb." Why did she have to remind him of all people?

"Oh, I get it. If you slept in here you might have better dreams and learn more? What else have you heard?"

"Nothing much different," she said, wondering if she should disclose the rest. Then she said, "It's what I'm feeling at the same time."

"You're sensing something in other ways?"

"Yes. I know this sounds crazy, but I believe I was called here." Then she cautiously said, "Maybe you too."

"I'm not sure what you mean," Aaron said as he took hold of her hand and looked into her eyes. "You've always been an enigma, Chione. You've shown me a different reality, but I'd be foolish to expect you'd let me be a part of this."

Chione could not acknowledge him and pulled away while struggling to maintain her composure despite Aaron's tender expressive look that went right into her. The warmth of his touch emanated through his gloved hands. Memories of being in his arms flashed through her mind. Fleeting moments that could have led to consummation. Yet, why had she begun longing for him again? "Do you think Dr. Withers will let me stay?"

"Ask him," Aaron said as he shrugged.

"Hey you two, turn off the lamps before you come out," Dr. Withers said from the doorway.

"Chione," Aaron said, grabbing her hand again. She turned back reluctantly. "Even if you'd rather I didn't share this with you, why have I also heard the whimpering? And where did you get that new perfume you're wearing?"

14

Another Friday meant another Arabic Sabbath. Because of that, most locals were unavailable to work. Many left their cots and tents where they lay in the open and converged on the small tent camp that had sprung up down the road. Dr. Withers had let it be known that he expected more out of his team on those days when fewer workers were around to lend a hand.

"Found nothing?" Aaron asked. "What do you mean 'found nothing'?" Any delay seemed like an eternity. They had hoped to accomplish something, even out of setbacks. To hear no progress had been made taking soundings was deflating.

"Exactly that," the seismologist said. His clothes were dusty from being up on that hill in the breeze. "We've been testing all morning, even expanded the search grid. Radar only penetrates about twenty-five feet."

"I know that," Dr. Withers said. His patience seemed thin.

They stood on the hillside in full sun, something to which all were becoming acclimated. They had learned never to forget their headgear and at times team members blended in with the Egyptian workers.

"We even used the special filters—"

"What about the seismograph?" Aaron asked.

Chione had warned about sensors being useless and Aaron well knew but had to try.

"Nothing. Seismic refraction picks up a good reading till just past the Second Chamber," the seismologist said. "The hollow of the tomb slopes too steeply downward to get more readings."

"How far up the hillside do you get anything?" Aaron asked. He removed the handkerchief from around his neck and passed it over his face. He always wore the top buttons of his shirtfront open with the handkerchief tied around his throat. His rugged image had great appeal.

"As I calculate, above the passageway, just about where it drops down that long flight of steps after the Second Chamber. Beyond that point, absolutely nothing."

Dr. Withers stood perspiring and pondering the hillside. He held out his hand until Aaron realized Dr. Withers wanted to use his hand-kerchief. As he accepted it, he asked, "Aaron, did you see anything else that might look like another hole big enough for a person to pass through?"

"Only the one Randy found."

"Can any of the hillside be cleared off?"

"Maybe we should get Randy up there," Clifford said, joining the conversation momentarily, on his way to the inventory tent. "He's good at making things slide!"

"Clifford, do you mind?" Dr. Withers asked while trying not to smile.

Clifford knew it was best to keep walking. Dr. Withers snickered and shook his head as they watched Clifford affectedly slink away.

"You mean clear away all that rubble?" the seismologist asked. "So our equipment can be in closer proximity to the tomb ceiling?"

"I guess that's what I mean. How about it?"

"Already thought of that and tested the soil. It's too loose. If disturbed, the whole hillside could slide down on you and bury the tomb again."

"And anyone inside," Aaron said.

"Probably your entire encampment," the seismologist said, nodding toward the tents. He took off his cap, rubbed his arm across the top of his bald head, and left a dirt mark from his sleeve. Chione looked away.

"How likely is that to happen?" Dr. Withers asked.

"Not unless you go up there disturbing the natural way it's settled. When we drove our stakes to take the readings, sand and rubble began to skid."

"Then we'll think of something else. For the next few days, we'll concentrate on emptying the chambers."

They followed Dr. Withers inside the cook tent for shade. "I don't like the possibility of landslides," he said. He poured coffee for the others then a cup for himself. "Great," he said. "Just great." He sighed as he sat down, evidently recognizing his own streak of impatience.

Chione retrieved a pitcher from under one of the pyramids and poured herself a cup of Karkade.

"We'll find the Burial Chamber," Aaron said. "We'll go in after—"

"That's not what I'm concerned about," Dr. Withers said. "Chione, I know I just told you that you could spend the evening in there—"

"Alone, I suppose," Aaron said.

"I have to be alone."

"I don't care if you're not afraid of being spooked," Dr. Withers said. "That's not the point." He tweaked his mustache, picked up his cup, stood and stepped out into the scorching sunlight again as she and Aaron followed.

A lot of excitement came from the processing area as yet more trays of mummies were being delivered. Mourners had begun crowding closer among the throng of onlookers. In the distance, their plaintiff wailing continued. With Aaron holding the fly open, she followed Dr. Withers into the inventory tent.

"Hey, Sterling," Clifford called out from his makeshift desk near some crates. "Maybe we should hold back some of these little folks... in case we have a power outage." Everyone laughed as someone threw a pencil that glanced off Clifford's shoulder when he ducked.

Dr. Withers could only shake his head.

Later inside the Pillared Hall, as Dr. Withers and Aaron discussed issues, Chione felt irresistibly drawn to sit again in the gilded chair. That was the last thing she remembered.

"Chione," Aaron said softly. He gently placed a hand on her shoulder.

She looked into his eyes. "Kheperu-Ra," came out of her mouth in a lusty new voice.

"What?" Dr. Withers asked, leaning close.

"Sh-h," Aaron said. They listened, but she had nothing more to say and the silence inside the Hall was unremarkable. "Chione," Aaron said again, nudging her shoulder.

The nudge was gentle and made her feel like she watched two scenes at the same time, each jostling, interfering with the other. With eyes wide open she waited, felt disconnected from the voices she heard, and powerless to respond.

"What's she doing?" Dr. Withers asked, whispering.

"She's in an altered state," Aaron said quietly. "Earlier she said she really gets messages in this room."

"Oh, boy," Dr. Withers said. "I've never seen anyone in a trance."

Aaron put a finger to his lips. "She'll be okay," he said softly. For once, she was thankful for his presence. He would know how to handle Dr. Withers.

"What do we do?" Dr. Withers asked quietly. "This is spooky."

Something that held her finally let go. Chione suddenly bolted out of the chair. "I-I'm sorry, Dr. Withers," she said. "I didn't know I sat—"

"Geez," he said, stepping aside as if to avoid being touched by something he did not understand. "What is going on with you?"

"Guess I fell asleep."

"With your eyes wide open?"

"Must be the heat," she said without looking at him. Particularly, she did not want to look Aaron squarely in the eyes either.

Dr. Withers paced then turned abruptly to face her. "I don't want you staying in here by yourself this evening."

"What's the harm? I'll be okay."

"I don't like this," he said. "You in some sort of trance and not knowing whose around." Something in his voice seemed almost relieved. He glanced at Aaron who quickly looked elsewhere.

"Who'd be around?" she asked.

"Until we know the origin of those sounds you hear, who's to say?"

Certainly, Dr. Withers had already accepted her explanation for the sounds. Why, then, would he use the noises as an excuse for her not to be alone? "I'm not afraid," she said.

"We've just learned the whole side of the hillock could swallow us if we're not careful," Dr. Withers said. "For your safety, I can't allow it. Not by yourself."

"Uh... Marlowe. Can Marlowe stay with me? She's not afraid. We could leave the lights on."

"No lights, no Marlowe," Dr. Withers said. "You're giving my wife too much credit."

"She understands."

"Marlowe's interested in your dreams. To be a part of what Aaron and I just saw you doing? The mummy we'd find later would be my wife."

"Honestly, Dr. Withers. Marlowe knows."

"Marlowe certainly won't know what to do if anything unexpected happens on the hill," he said, thumbing upwards. "Aaron will stay with you if you insist on quiet time in here." Again, his voice contained that hint of victory.

Aaron seemed flustered. "Chione and I already talked this over. It's better if I don't stay."

"See here, you two," Dr. Withers said. "We've got something really special here with this discovery. Admittedly because of your dreams, Chione, which may still provide us with the location of the most important chamber in this hole in the ground. But if you two can't put aside your personal lives for the sake of our expedition, we'll rely solely on traditional methods to find the rest."

"But, Dr. With—"

"Look, I don't mean to lecture the two most mature members of the team, but that's the way it's going to be." He smiled suddenly as if proud of himself.

"I don't see why Aaron has to be the one."

"Because no one else understands you and I don't want you in here by yourself," Dr. Withers said. "That's all."

"What about Clifford?"

"Do you honestly think humor could add to your trance state?" Aaron asked.

"Aaron stays or no one stays," Dr. Withers said. "That's final. You bring in some food and water, just in case." He turned to leave.

Chione sighed. "If Aaron's the only choice."

Neither she nor Aaron spoke as Dr. Withers left looking triumphant.

Finally, Aaron said, "Us being alone together doesn't mean I'm gonna' get personal, Chione."

"You can't tell me your only interest is... is... after the history we have together?"

"I want our job here to be successful," he said. "If it means supporting you in this, I can put my emotions aside."

"Good. You know the reason I ended our relationship."

"But it wasn't strong enough to end your feelings or mine."

She sighed. "I thought that was all behind us." She did not want this to become an issue again. If she got upset emotionally, it would preclude entering any altered state. "I just want to get on with my life."

All through dinner and afterward, Clifford teased about her and Aaron looking for the mummy's bedroom and Bebe flashed victorious looks toward Kendra. Dr. Withers listened but had not joined the conversations, yet neither had he squelched them, as he would usually do to keep a tight rein. He just sat studying some notes and looking triumphant. When she and Aaron finally departed for the depths, whatever comments flew among the others stayed topside sizzling in the heat.

"I'll be sitting between the first and second pillars," Chione said, ignoring his patience.

"Can I at least know what you've planned?"

"Does it matter?"

"Chione, I'm not here for personal gain. In fact, you recently told me that I belonged here too."

Chione remained silent and arranged her sitting mat on the hard floor. Then she pointed in the direction of the sofa and chair against the wall. "That's north, isn't it?"

"Yeah, that's north," he said. Then he smiled. In the days when they had been close, she had told him to sleep with his head to the north and that he would be lined up with the magnetic forces of the planet. Having done so, he reported the quality of his dreams began to improve. Aaron placed his mat away from her, toward the center of the Hall.

Once everything was in place and the lighting much dimmed, she said, "Well, come here if you want to be a part of this."

"When did you start issuing orders?"

"Since you're here, you may as well contribute something," she said. Almost instantly, she realized she was expressing disappointment at having to share her quiet time.

"Just do whatever it is you do, Chione," he said. He finally sat and slipped out of his boots.

She sat cross-legged, sighing, and having difficulty relaxing. She knew Aaron well and surmised the thoughts going through his mind at that moment. Knowing disturbed her concentration. They were once devoted to each other. He previously admitted never experiencing a depth of emotion with anyone else like he felt with her. He was not about to become involved in another relationship if complete devotion was not matched. His feelings for her never weakened. What he would do as they sat quietly was pray the winds of change would gale. Chione recognized a great peace knowing he held no real animosity toward her. "Aaron," she said quietly. "I'm sorry I was irritable with you."

"Sh-h-h," he said in his forgiving way.

After a few moments, she felt even more frustrated, but she would not quit. Any other time, when she concentrated deeply, she would slip into a trance without realizing it until returning to consciousness. Aaron being there inhibited her. Not like in the past when she relied on him for an added measure of peace and stability. Now the fact he was in the same room during her quiet time irritated her. If she could not get through this evening, he would interpret it as them belonging together and needing to make peace. Never before had she felt such mixed feelings about him.

Finally, she slumped and sometime later revived, not knowing how long she remained in the trance. It never really mattered. She tried to speak and tilted her head back and saw someone standing over her, but her eyes were closed! Then she exploded back to the present, though her body had not moved at all. She found herself sitting in Tut's chair! In the royal chair! Nearly unnerved, she quietly went to sit on her mat again and slipped back into a trance, only to rouse a bit later.

"I haven't experienced a meditation this deep in a long time," Aaron said in a whisper. In the dim light of the chamber, Chione opened her eyes and saw him rub the stiffness out of the back of his neck. "I saw scenes the likes I've never had."

By the time he roused fully, Chione had already rolled up her mat. "So what did you see?" she asked.

"Could have sworn I wasn't in a trance," he said. "I saw you sitting in that chair by the sofa." He pointed toward the furniture along the north wall. "The room was different. Must be the power of suggestion."

"You mean because of the nature of our work? You saw some images?"

"About Tutankhamon, I believe," he said. She gasped the moment he mentioned the name. "You got something about him, too, didn't you?"

She pretended to be busy with her things, but he was already at her side and grabbed her arm. "Let go of me! If we must be thrown together, the least you can do is be professional."

He laughed. "Professional? After the history we have together? Even now, as we share the same visions?"

"How do you know what I saw?"

"How quickly you deny the connection between us!"

"Okay, I saw him too. So, what?"

"He came toward you from the couch, didn't he?"

Chione was shocked. "He came from the couch, then sat right there." She pointed to the area of the floor that would have been at the head of her mat.

"I sat there," Aaron said.

"You...?"

"You were having trouble getting into trance. I sat there to balance your energies."

"You weren't... Tut was...."

"How quickly you deny," Aaron said. He walked away a couple of paces, and then came back. "Tutankhamon came to you in your vision and sat in the very place I sat?"

She could no longer hide the truth, at least not from Aaron, and gave in to the moment. "Another time, I sat in a chair and Tutankhamon and I spoke."

"You're sure it was him?"

"Of course, I'm sure. He wore a nemes on his head with a wadjet, a white kilt and carried a crook and flail." How could Aaron question her? It only added to the discomfort of the heat in the Hall.

As if he sensed her uneasiness, his voice softened. "How do you know he was that Pharaoh?"

"Don't doubt me. I just know it."

"How much conversation did you share?" Now he looked ready to grab her arms and shake her.

She stepped back. "It was brief when I first began to quiet down. While he and I spoke, I sat with him. When I came out of the trance, I was sitting in that chair," she said, pointing.

"You just confirmed things I saw you doing in the vision I had. You were with Tutankhamon!"

"You said you sat in front of me... on the floor, where Pharaoh sat."

Aaron looked to be in disbelief. "It's late. We should get out of here."

"Not so fast," she said and grabbed his arm firmly. She knew she had no right to pry into his messages since she did not wish to share hers. Or did she? "What else did you see?"

"Nothing that spectacular."

She knew him too well, knew he was hiding something. "C'mon, Aaron. If you want to share, then share."

"Okay. In my vision, I had gone someplace to find a young woman. I did this in secret. I led her by the hand to a chair to sit and talk." He looked around the area and the dim light cast strange shadows across his face. It did that to everyone, except Aaron's face always seemed to change the most. His eyes got darker, his chin more proud.

"Who were you in the scene?"

"Just a guy."

"You said you dreamed of King Tut."

"I-It was all too confusing," he said quickly. "I saw a lot of confusing scenes."

"Where did King Tut fit into your dreams?" She was seeing a pattern emerging that told her she must allow Aaron to share meditation with her again. Curious, too, despite needing to maintain separate lives, the longing to share with him had intensified and sorely clouded her judgment.

"I'm really not sure," he said quietly.

"In your vision, you were Pharaoh, weren't you?"

"Maybe," Aaron said, shrugging. "Somehow, all this seems contrived."

"That's what I mean, Aaron." She deftly tied up her mat and prepared to leave. "No one believes in trances. Till they begin to have a few themselves."

"Which seldom happens and that's why people won't believe."

"And your rationale won't allow you to totally admit it either, right?" she asked. "Now I'm really curious. How is it that you, as Pharaoh, led a young woman to sit in a chair to talk, coincidentally, all too similar to my vision?"

Aaron only shrugged and went to retrieve his mat. By the time they exited the tomb the moon was high.

The next morning came too soon. In the rapidly changing temperature and humidity of the Egyptian dawn, the encampment was in the process of being moved farther away from the front of the dig site. The area was a swarm of activity. She had to smile. Even at a distance, she knew by Aaron's arm movements and body language that he was explaining to Clifford that she needed to assure her yurt and the head of her sleeping pallet polarized to the north. Aaron would not be explaining if he did not also believe it. She didn't have to guess which direction his cot faced inside his yurt.

Tarik's young friends walked the new areas where yurts were being erected. They looked for scorpions and other creepy things that might need to be removed before the yurts were anchored again. All the footers around their beds had to be emptied and refilled with fresh water before they were put back in place. Tarik volunteered for more paid work, to keep the footers cleaned and filled. He was going to get rich.

Nearby, Royce yelled, "Where the hell is my laptop? Anyone seen my computer?"

"Oh, dear," Chione said as Aaron and Clifford approached. "Royce without his portable office is like a fish in the sand."

"I'd say that's exactly the case," Clifford said. "Given the desert that surrounds us."

"There you are," Marlowe said, walking up with Bebe. "Must have been a thief in camp last night." How could Marlowe always look so perfect? Bebe's new hairdo needed a bit of touch up. And Chione was always concerned about the sand in her braids.

"Actually, Kenneth gets up before dawn," Bebe said. "He noticed the flap on the inventory tent waving in the wind and went over to fasten it. That's when he noticed some containers scattered around."

"Not in the same orderly stacks Sterling demands at day's end," Marlowe said.

Chione's heart skipped a beat. "Anything missing?"

"C-22. A crate of children's toys."

"Now Royce's laptop, too?" Aaron asked.

"That's hard to believe," Chione said. "Is that all they took? One box of toys?"

"Masud said whoever took them will try to get more."

"Oh, great," Aaron said. "While Dr. Withers was concerned about what might happen to us inside the tomb, this was going on out here."

The robbery seemed calculated. All any thief had to do was sneak into camp and take what he wanted once everything was neatly crated.

"Speaking of taking," Aaron said. "How is it they took a crate of toys that are easy to sell, and not a container of children's mummies or larger artifacts?"

"That's right," Chione said. "The boxes are only numbered. How would a thief know what's in each one?"

All gathered around a late breakfast of dry cereal in the open air while waiting for the cook tent and kitchen equipment to be moved. Siti spread out mats in the sand. They would eat quickly because a meal in the hot sun would be no picnic.

"I call your attention to the layout of our new camp," Dr. Withers said to everyone. "From now on, artifacts and inventory, the cook tent, and all supplies will be in the center beside the tech shack. Our yurts encircle the periphery—the team's, the photographers and engineers—everyone's. That one passage between the tomb and our camp," he said, pointing, "is the only way in or out of the business section. Our yurts are close enough now. When you're in your respective tents at night, keep your ears open for anyone passing between."

"Good idea," Clifford said. "These guys must be able to walk on eggshells, considering they stole something from inside Royce's tent with him and Kendra in it."

"That's my fault," Royce said as he sat down and straightened his clothing. "I left the laptop lying on my trunk near the tent flap. All anyone had to do was reach in and take it." His voice was apologetic as he spoke to Clifford. Royce had an intimidating way of looking into a person's eyes when he spoke to them as if he had to be right about everything.

"Inadvertently made available," Kendra said.

"I've still got my back up DVDs," Royce said. "Now I'll have to purchase another computer. I'll go into Cairo for a few days."

"A few days?" Kendra asked.

"Yes, Darling," Royce said, smiling with those cold eyes. "I need to stay in touch with my company."

Kendra pouted but Royce ignored her. She glanced at him sideways. He continued nonchalantly sipping coffee. Bebe watched them both and glanced at Marlowe who raised an eyebrow. Then Bebe took another bite of cold toast.

15

Four days passed. During that time, the fingerprinting equipment arrived by air along with two technicians from the Madu Museum. Nearly a dozen impressions had been lifted from the golden statue alone. Other items with printable surfaces were scrutinized and many more prints gathered.

Additional help was assigned to Kendra and Clifford. Removal of the many small relics in the First Chamber had been accomplished quickly though the work was tedious. Allowing Kendra reprieve from the odoriferous Second Chamber, Clifford now oversaw removal of artifacts from the mummy's room. Kendra would oversee removal of objects in the Pillared Hall and annexes till Clifford caught up.

Quaashie and Naeem were kept busy running up and down the passageway translating and directing the laborers. Their instructions in Arabic resounded off the walls. Peace and quietude of the Underworld had been irrevocably disturbed. Chione felt saddened and decided to leave the tomb while the others worked.

She also needed to stay out in the air for a while. Perhaps the perfume inside was the reason for her bouts of dizziness. How could anything like a delectable scent maintain such a grip?

Later, Rita and Marlowe found her outside the tech shack. Marlowe still looked like she stepped out of a beauty shop. Rita looked wilted. Lately, her red curls always drooped. It seemed the climate had gotten to her. With as much time as she and Clifford spent in Egypt, she should have been better prepared in handling the climate. But she was excited. "You've got to see what's coming out of the Pillared Hall," Rita said.

"Good stuff?" Chione asked with rejuvenated enthusiasm. "Bebe and I have been busy interpreting glyphs."

"It's beyond belief," Marlowe said. "Let's get over to Inventory."

"Yes, let's," Rita said. "This heat makes me woozy."

A string of village women, wearing colorful local garb and head wimples, helped carry artifacts that had not seen daylight for thousands of years. Other workers wore functional jeans and cotton shirts, more conducive to climbing and hoisting than skirted gallibayas.

Chione, Bebe, and Rita entered Inventory alongside the continuing procession. Inside, Chione said, "The crowd of gawkers is growing out there."

"Word of our discovery has spread throughout the world," Dr. Withers said as he poked a pencil over his ear. He and Aaron sat head to head finalizing inventory records.

"Yeah," Aaron said. "Crowds gather as if reaching Egypt was as easy as driving across town."

"The guards will keep onlookers on the far side of the descending pit," Dr. Withers said. "Until we can get that retaining wall finished."

Sentries had already been posted at the portcullis opening. The curious were kept off the hillock. Everyone was to keep a sharp lookout for those stealthy young children who might dart about trying to slip into the burial complex or inventory tent. Their main objective would be to find some trinket, even a painted piece of fallen ceiling plaster, that they might sell for a few piasters. Others had their hands out, begging baksheesh in exchange for small meaningless favors, like sweeping the sand smooth in front of the yurts. Some begged simply to earn a living.

Clifford brought more inventory records and handed them to Aaron.

"It's about time," Dr. Withers said as he stood and stretched. "We must do what everyone else and their uncle has done when visiting Egypt."

"And that is?"

"Break out that case of writing implements that Clifford suggested we bring."

"How about that humongous box of chopsticks Irwin brought?" Clifford asked.

The Institute had long ago received a huge donation of plain writing pencils with plump erasers. Cases of those had been brought along with a case of ballpoint pens, favored by the beggars. Dr. Withers hoped the gifts would stave off those who made it past the guards with hands outstretched. If the younger locals would help keep the site cleaned of garbage and other leavings, they, too, would earn the prized writing tools. Within minutes, word of the pens and pencils brought a horde of beggars with opened palms. Not much clean-up work existed to keep them all busy. Not that all sought work in exchange.

Requests were being received from universities and colleges from around the world asking for accredited tours and work status. So far, the team had only approved two such requests. An elementary school in Cairo had requested that a group of young students, all gifted in studies of Ancient Egypt, be allowed an extended tour. They would arrive by bus with Dakarai and Randy and chaperones. Additionally, students of Museum Science and Antiquities at Kamuzu University were to work study tasks at Clifford's discretion.

Realizing he had not been following protocol, Dr. Withers reluctantly sent responses to major universities and museums around the world telling them they may schedule their resident archaeologists to examine the find.

Reporters from the Institute's hometown paper, the Stockton Journal, which originally had not requested a presence due to the expense of such a venture, now wished to produce their own publication for San Joaquin Valley residents. They would arrive to meet with Aaron and the other journalists about rights. Every television network around the world made demands. Some of their representatives had begun showing up, not waiting for approval to do so.

The fax machine worked overtime when electrical power was strong enough. The world was impatient to hear about the discovery. The intention to open the tomb and collect the relics, leaving the cleanup to the Antiquities Restoration Society, had been a simple dream due to meager funding. Now the endeavor was ballooning into nightmarish proportions, stretching thin the tethers of a tight budget.

Farther down the valley on both sides of the only crude road into the area, the tent camp had swollen. The guards were forced to constantly monitor the size of the spectator crowd and to hold them back.

Standing out on the hillock, Chione said, "Evidently beggars think it worthwhile to stay and panhandle tourists."

"Camel rides are novel," Clifford said facetiously.

Sightseers arrived on horses and donkeys, some in jeeps and van buses that occasionally sputtered and coughed to a standstill. Hawkers brazenly offered guaranteed genuine artifacts from this and other burial sites. Their activities kept visitors entertained.

"That glut of curiosity seekers is way out of hand," Dr. Withers said as he passed on his way to the portcullis shaft.

Tarik was given permission to supervise other local boys to remove the smelly camel dung and other manure from the site. Farther out in the hot desert sand, they laid the patties in rows to bake and dry. Then they sold them to the workers and families in the Theban village who used them as fuel.

"I can't believe we've become such a spectacle," Chione said. She had never been a part of something so important, so grand.

"Wait till the paparazzi arrive," Rita said with disgust.

"Not them too," Chione said. Peering past their yurts to the crowd, thankfully, their encircled universe seemed far removed from the rest of the goings-on in the circus-like tent camp.

"Sterling's accepted aid of the Egyptian Armed Guard," Marlowe said.

"The area police?" Chione asked. "But why?"

"The paparazzi will be after you, Chione," Rita said. "More than any of us."

They began walking back to Inventory.

"That and with people swarming around, Sterling's afraid of more thefts happening before we can get everything to Cairo."

With the growing numbers of people, it would be difficult to keep track of who was a hired worker and who might just slip into the work area to try to steal something.

"Do you really think these people would—" Suddenly Chione took a long deep breath. "Would you look at that!"

Two men carried an exquisitely carved chair. Sunlight beamed off solid gold foil. Inlaid semi-precious stones twinkled. The roar of the crowd told of their elation. With smiling laborers singing happily, Chione put her hands together and bowed her head as the chair was paraded past.

"Why did you do that?" Marlowe asked.

"You mean this?" Chione said, touching her hands together again.

"Yes, why?"

"Can't really say. I feel a strong connection with certain things. I honor them, I guess."

"You mean certain things really touch your heart?" Rita asked.

Chione smiled. "Yes, like you and Clifford."

Women and men struggled down the hillock awkwardly managing large wooden trays of colorful trinkets and artifacts labeled and partitioned off with thick gauze and bubble wrap. Then came more furniture and trays. Faces of workers along the rutted pathway reflected various moods, some smiling, some proud, and some somber as if this was just another job among many in a string of dig sites.

Chione and the others stepped inside the now crowded inventory tent. Every available table, bench, and chair had been pressed into service. Trays were stacked high in the aisles. Chione sighed, dismayed at the sight.

"What's the matter?" Rita asked, fanning herself and sipping water from her hip flask.

"This stuff doesn't look the same in here."

"What do you mean?"

"Bunched up like this?" Chione asked. "Suddenly all these artifacts seem commonplace."

"Not the same as being strategically placed inside the tomb?" Marlowe asked.

"Moving them from their original placement has surely disrupted their purpose," Chione said.

"Do you think anyone will want to dig us up after a few millennia?" Rita asked as she retrieved some of Clifford's paperwork and began to double-check the lists.

"Now that's something to think about," Marlowe said.

"Wonder if they'd be able to tell I had this horrible headache." Rita managed a weak smile. As she gestured toward her temple, her hand trembled.

"You still having that?" Chione asked.

"I don't believe in taking lots of medicines," Rita said. "It's another reason I got out of nursing. But I think I'm changing my mind."

"These are items from only the First Annex," Masud said as he entered the tent and greeted them in the Egyptian way of keeping his eyes distracted. His clothes were pretty limp. He must have needed a break from the stuffy Hall.

"What happened to the columns, the busts and all that other furniture in the Pillared Hall?" Chione asked, not looking into his eyes.

"Too large," Masud said. "Too heavy. We build crates inside the tomb; pack the large items down under, as you call it. Easy for lifting out."

"We're no different," Rita said.

"Ma'am?" Masud asked, always polite.

"We're tomb robbers just like the worst of them."

"But in the name of science and history, don't you agree?"

"Perhaps, Masud," Rita said, still staring at Clifford's lists. "How do you feel doing this in your own country?"

"If not us," he said politely and shrugged. "Someone else."

"We were meant to discover this tomb," Chione said. They looked at her and said nothing. "There's a reason for everything."

"You will indulge me, O Little One?" Masud asked, turning his attention away from the others. "I hear of your dreams." Still, he did not try to look into her eyes. "Do they foretell everything?"

"Everything?"

"Yes, all details?"

"Evidently not," Chione said, "because I don't know the source of the whimpering or the location of the Burial Chamber."

"You don't get everything?" he asked cautiously. "For example, would you expect to know the source?" What could he be leading to? He seemed intent on learning something that he almost looked her straight in the eyes.

"I don't expect anything," she said. "I merely receive what comes through."

"You never see the whole picture, as you Americans say?"

"If you're referring to this particular situation, I might get more as time goes by."

"What is your history, Little One, your ratio of accuracy?"

Why was Masud so interested in her abilities? What was he trying to ascertain? "I've never kept track," she said.

"She's almost never wrong," Marlowe said.

"Hm-m-m," Masud said. "Most curious. I wish to know more. We will speak again about this?"

She shrugged, and then politely said, "Maybe." Masud nodded and then walked away. "I'd better get busy," Chione said, not wanting to have to answer any more questions. "There's a lot of work to be done now."

Just as she picked her way through the artifacts to the other side of the tent, Dr. Withers appeared from behind a stack of crates and pulled her aside. "I understand you and Aaron made headway a few nights ago."

"Is that what Aaron told you?"

"C'mon girl. Don't play coy."

Why, suddenly, was everyone looking to her for answers? "I can't imagine what Aaron might have implied. We both had visions."

"Yes, similar pictures."

"They didn't have that much in common."

"According to him—"

"Dr. Withers, before we begin analyzing our dreams and visions, we need to first understand how to detect the ones which carry those special messages."

"Sounds logical."

They waited till several workers passed with more trays. No one knew which of the locals spoke English. Chione had already made it clear that she wished to keep her abilities known only among the team and close affiliates, but word had gotten out.

"A lot of wish fulfillment goes on in the dream state," she said when they were alone again. "Dreams are presented using symbolism borrowed from the most recent pictures and concepts we've absorbed into our minds during the day."

"You both saw Egyptian type scenes because of involvement with this project, right?"

"Definitely."

"Anything significant about the similarities of what you both perceived?

"Nothing to speak of."

"Will you spend time in there again?" He seemed not able to let it go.

"Does Aaron really have to stay?"

Dr. Withers' slow triumphant smile unnerved her. "Yes," he said.

"What about Kendra, now that Royce is gone?"

"At the risk of sounding sexist and with thieves in our midst," he said. "I'll sleep easier knowing there's a man in there with you. And don't ask for Clifford or me. We've got our wives out here."

"Oka-ay…."

"I could send Randy in," Dr. Withers said, throwing her a teasing glance. "He's returning soon."

"Oh, no," Chione said. "No thanks."

"Guess you're stuck with Aaron," he said, smiling all too much as he slipped away.

Toward evening, contents of the First Annex had been removed. The Second Annex was being readied. As Chione sat and admired relics of an ancient priestess's effects laid out in front of her on the table, she had great difficulty staying in the moment. She picked up a small, carved turquoise box and was, again, aware of floating between the present reality and an ancient one.

"Get a load of Chione," Clifford said, whispering behind her. His voice seemed to come to her out of a fog. Scenes paraded through her mind, crowding and distorting reality.

"You'd think one night's sleep would carry anyone through the next day," Kendra said in a low voice that echoed through a vision of a long ancient funeral procession. Chione heard but could not acknowledge, having been pulled into the historical moment in ways the others couldn't fathom.

"Maybe she didn't sleep well," Clifford said. "How come you're not laid out on a bench somewhere, Aaron?"

Chione pushed their laughter out of her mind. Something more important enticed. The scene opened out as if she had only to open her eyes.

Egyptian priests and priestesses performing a forbidden ritual, speaking in the old tongue. She was being cleansed, body shaved and adorned with only an insubstantial skirt and an amulet to dangle between her bare breasts; her desiring to chant and sway and undulate with other priestesses till elevated to an ecstatic frenzy, then to be handed over to Almighty Pharaoh; the beat of the drums, the music, driving her to wantonness.

Clifford's familiar laughter filtered into her altered state. She tried to block out the noise behind her and to concentrate on the scene that had electrified her senses. Other words were coming now, words from ancient times, intertwined with voices of the present.

"You two are missing the point," Aaron said softly.

Begging for silence, Chione waved a limp hand in the air without looking back.

"Point is, she likes those dreams," Clifford said.

"She's not sleeping now," Kendra said.

"Sure, she is. Just look at her."

I'm not sleeping! she wanted to call out. Be quiet and learn something!

"Come closer," Aaron said, whispering to the others. "I hope she doesn't hate me for this."

Don't do this, Aaron, she wanted to say, aware of them standing behind and peering around her. But her trance was too deep, too wondrous to be broken. She would have to deal with them later. She closed her eyes to focus more deeply and ran a finger over the amulet.

"She's not sleeping," Clifford said softly. "She's studying an artifact."

She tried to repeat the words she heard. "Wear you... box... break... belly...."

"Listen," Kendra said, cautioning softly from behind.

Chione repeated the words, added some, and omitted others. She concentrated, finally getting the whole message. Suddenly, she opened her eyes, picked up a pencil and scribbled the spell over Aaron's crosshatched doodling. Not until she finished did she look around, finding Aaron, Kendra, and Clifford standing behind in bewilderment. Her face flushed hot. She glared at Aaron. "How could you?" she asked through clenched teeth.

"Eavesdrop?" Clifford asked. "This is our workspace too." He smiled that toothy grin that always dissipated tension.

"You don't understand what's happening," Chione said.

"We're trying," Kendra said.

"But you don't believe."

"Believe us, Chione," Clifford said. "We're trying."

Chione let out a long sigh. She felt frustrated, exposed and slowly looked at each of them. "Not at all do I want to hear ridicule or innocent jokes," she said. "If only one of you could be lucky enough to experience what I do, until then, not another word."

"Nobody doubts you, Chione," Aaron said, picking up the inventory sheet and reading.

Wear you this box
Break not the seal
till in your belly
the child you feel

Kendra carefully picked up the tiny amulet and turned it over in her palm. "Something has long ago broken off this little box," she said. "So where did you read that spell?"

"Do you see any glyphs?" Chione asked.

"Only the carving of a lotus blossom," Kendra said. "Where'd the words come from?"

If they could not yet figure that out, they did not need to know.

They worked in silence the rest of the day. Even Clifford, who always had a punch line, stared off in space occasionally and sometimes shook his head. Once, Chione heard him say, "Just when I thought I had life nailed...."

All through the evening meal and afterward, Chione watched Kendra hover close to Aaron. Then Bebe said quietly, "See what I told you? Now that Royce is gone, Kendra will attach herself to him."

"I don't care," Chione said. "I guess Kendra's the type to need a man around." Yet she wondered if Kendra would be so bold as to carry the friendship farther, and would a pining Aaron suddenly find Kendra irresistible? A lump came up in her throat.

16

Chione had showered, as she always did before evening meditation. She looked forward to receiving more information or images. However, her heightened sense of apprehension unnerved her. Inside the Pillared Hall, she approached Aaron as he removed his boots. The only lighting came from their flashlights. "I'm feeling sort of unsettled this evening," she said. "Can we sit together?"

He looked surprised that she had asked. "What's put you on edge?"

"The furniture, the ancient wood," she said, glancing at a few remaining pieces. "Can you hear their noises?"

"They're breathing again."

"Just like in Tut's tomb."

"Or any tomb," he said. "After all the years being in dead space, then to be surrounded with fresh air, the wood makes those sighing noises."

"As it begins to deteriorate."

"All the more reason for us to get these pieces to the Madu for treatment," he said.

Chione deeply experienced every moment, the breathing of the tomb, her own heightened senses, and new feelings on top of the ones that clamored back and forth between her and Aaron. She was caught between resisting him and the recognition that his presence made a difference in her inner life. Irresistibly drawn to one another, despite her rejection of him, neither had been able to let go. It was time she faced it. In fact, being in Egypt seemed to make them more attracted to one another. Suddenly she regretted having been the harbinger of change that forced him to put his life on hold. "So, you want to sit?" she asked again as she rolled out her mats.

"You can do this by yourself," he said. "You don't need anyone else."

"But I do!"

"Don't be so emphatic," he said. "It's not like you to manipulate."

She had never seen him in dim light wearing a sarcastic expression. It was grotesque and she didn't like it.

"Is that what you think I'm doing?" Her vicious tone sliced the stillness and surprised her too. "I just thought… oh, never—"

"Wait, wait, wait," Aaron said, coming to her side. His expression had softened. "You report vivid scenes which have nothing to do with me. Why join together now?"

Chione looked away. "It's your decision."

"What is it, Chione? Why can't you look at me?"

"Make up your mind," she said, still avoiding him. She did not need another unsettling confrontation.

"Wait a minute," he said. "You're hiding something."

"You're imagining—"

He grabbed her arm. "How many times have I actually been part of what you've received about Egypt and this tomb?"

She pulled away quickly. "Don't be so presumptive." Their voices sounded hollow as the sounds bounced off the walls.

"I get it," Aaron said, lowering his voice. "You only received bits and pieces before we arrived here. Solid bits and pieces, but never anything as complete as what you got the other night when we were together."

"Your ego is puffed."

"No ego here," he said. "We had a good thing going, you and me. You might kid yourself into turning off your feelings, but deep down inside, you know the truth."

"I'm a realist, Aaron," she said, looking into the deep shadows over his eyes and enunciating the words.

"Then face it. At least now, we've shared a vision so similar—"

"Don't make that much of it."

"Why haven't you disclosed any more of your dreams?" he asked, not letting up. "The ones I know you're having."

"When I have something worth telling," she said, hiding the truth. "How would you know about my dreams?"

"Because I'm dreaming again. We used to—"

"Share similar dreams," she said quietly. "But what are you withholding?" She really was curious to know what his dreams contained and if they, in fact, still held similar content. In the very least, why had hers become so sensual that she did not dare disclose them?

"Okay, if you want to hear. The other night, while you were sitting on your mat," he said. "I went to sit on the floor in front of you, right where you say Pharaoh came to you." His tone said he still questioned what had happened. "Later, I had a vision that I was talking to a young woman who sat right there." He pointed rigidly to King Tut and Tauret's chair.

She stared at him knowing a revealing series of expressions transited her face. Finally, she said, "You wouldn't lie, would you?"

He sighed hard, quickly. "Chione...?"

"Okay, your being here has helped," she said. "Is that what you want to hear?"

"Only if it's true."

"Then you'll sit with me?"

He smiled. She gestured to her mat, feeling deeply satisfied, yet still wondering what his casual dreams contained. Sitting cross-legged, just as she began to get comfortable, she heard the familiar sounds again and grabbed quickly for his arm. "Did you hear that?"

"Nothing," he said, looking about.

"T-That was strange," she said. "The whimpering... it had a—a ring of desperation!"

He leaned toward her, straining to see in the dim light. "Let's just be quiet."

Again, she heard the sounds as her hair bristled. "Something's wrong," she said, scooting closer to him.

"You're frightened?" he asked, reaching for her.

"I can't believe you're not hearing this," she said as she clutched his hands, a gesture to help both stay connected to the present. Something about his hands felt reassuring.

"Wow!" he said at the moment she touched him. His hands tightened around hers. They sat mentally circling energy back and forth between them. What she perceived, he received. Him not hearing the sounds confirmed that they came from another realm. But he needed to hear them too.

The whimpering was again faint and choked, like someone trying not to cry but unable to keep from it. Then as before, the sounds ended abruptly. Chione felt herself crumple over onto the mat. She cradled her stomach and lost track of Aaron.

She half roused sometime later to find herself lying beside him. Without thinking, she reached and quite naturally rolled into his arms. "Kheperu," she said softly, pressing her body against his. Surrendering to the moment, their lips touched. They kissed a lovers' first kiss, voracious and demanding.

"Tauret," he said, rasping, holding her close. His breathing had quickened.

His hands moved over her body. "Kheperu," she said again. The sound of her own voice saying Kheperu shocked her back to reality. She pushed away and stood quickly. "Not like this," she said, backing up a few paces into the dark. Then he roused. "What happened to us?" she asked.

"Must have been tired," he said, sitting up and passing a hand across his face. He must have thought he fell asleep.

"I had another dream," she said, still sensuously stirred. "Did you?"

"No," he said nonchalantly as he stretched. "Why are you standing over there?"

She came to the mat and dropped onto her knees but kept her distance. "Are you interested in my dream?"

"Tell me tomorrow."

"I might forget," she said, trying to elicit his interest.

"You, forget? That's laughable." After all his insistence that they share, now he wasn't even curious?

"Listen, Aaron," she said. "This was a strange dream."

"I'm sure it was."

"I'm serious."

"Okay," he said, giving in. "Tell me."

"Tauret came toward me from the couch." Chione picked up her flashlight and pointed the beam toward the north wall and saw nothing.

Aaron looked and shrugged when he, too, saw nothing. "That's strange?"

"No, no, she merged into me," Chione said. "I became Tauret!"

"So?" he asked. "It was a dream, wasn't it?"

"A fragment, maybe," she said. "Actually, I spoke to Pharaoh again, sort of."

"What do you mean, sort of?" he asked. "Did you, or didn't you?"

"We were close," she said. "You know."

"You dreamed you were getting it on with Pharaoh?" he asked. He could not hide his broad smile. His great teeth showed in the dim light. "Now that's fantasy manifesting, don't you think?"

"Oh, why should I share with you if you're only going to joke."

"I'm applying what you told me, that some dreams are only dreams."

"This was more than a dream," she said, this time wishing he would listen. "We were about to make...." She stopped short of full disclosure. Suddenly Chione remembered how Aaron had rolled against her. She looked at him curiously. Surely, he had the same dream. That could produce such a reaction. "You called me Tauret."

He looked quickly to the floor and rubbed the back of his neck. "I don't know what to say about that," he said. "That still doesn't make it a premonition."

"Someday," she said, cautioning. "Something's going to appear in your mind and you won't know how to deal with it."

"Well, thanks for the half-compliment," he said. "At least you still believe my mind has capabilities."

17

"You'll never guess what I found," Bebe said, not waiting till Chione invited her to enter. As she entered, a rush of delicate Egyptian scent floated in with her. She carried something in her hands and a small woven bag. Whatever it was must have been special to occupy her time. By this late hour in the evening, Bebe would have been showered and wearing some sort of Egyptian robe which was more comfortable for her to work in while sitting at her computer late at night. And what was that scent she wore now? She was overly excited and that was not like her.

"Must be important," Chione said. She had been working at her tiny desk, transcribing more of Bebe's notes into her laptop. She barely had time to push the computer out of the way before Bebe scattered a handful of photographs in front of her. "What are these?" she asked.

"Ginny photographed these before they were sent to the Madu. Read them. Can you read them?" She pulled up a woven reed stool that creaked as she sat down.

The photos were of papyrus pieces. Each photograph had been marked on the back with the location or vessel in which the papyrus was found. "I saw the record of these when I was logging. What's so special?"

"Read... read." Bebe was so excited she could barely get the words out. She rummaged through the photographs. "This one first."

Chione held the photo close and wished the lighting in her yurt could have been brighter. The photograph was a close up of the writing on the papyrus. She began to sound out the hieroglyphs. Finally, she put the words together in English.

Drink, drink of this potion
Restore yourself to health
Put the spell in motion
Good health is newfound wealth

"These are spells," Bebe said. "That one. That would work for me."

"For you?"

"Don't you see? It's a spell for better health. For my female problems," she said. "My love life with Kenneth is non-existent because of my menopausal problems. Hell, I've had monthly problems all my life."

"But what's this got to do with—"

"Tauret's spells. That's how she healed women. I have to try it. That's why I brought these." She reached into the bag and produced an Egyptian drinking goblet, a modern Egyptian saucer from the cook tent, a vial looking to contain oil and another of black powder, a writing stick, and blank strips of papyrus.

Chione could only watch a desperate woman taking desperate measures. She looked at Bebe's Egyptian hairdo and felt another chill. The discovery of the tomb was affecting Bebe. They were all being affected by the Priestess's spells. "How can these help you?" she asked, motioning to the materials on her desk.

"I can't write hieroglyphs, Chione. Please, please, write the spell for me."

"Can't write hieroglyphs?" Chione laughed and picked up one of Bebe's tablets. "What do you call this?" Bebe's notes looked more like shorthand. Or hieroglyphs. And Chione had even been able to understand Bebe's scribbling!

Bebe ignored being shown her own talent. "Please?" she asked again.

"Me?"

"You know how they used to do spells in the old days. They mixed lampblack with oil and wrote the spells on papyrus, then stuck the papyrus in the water till the ink mixed. Then they drank."

As incredulous as it sounded, Bebe sat there expecting her to go along with it. "You need to think this over," she said.

"I've thought about it. I'm doing this, whether or not you help me," she said. "You're the only one I'd turn to. I even had a feeling you're supposed to be the one to write the spell."

The lights flickered off and on, an eerie prognosticator, but symbolic it was. Chione interpreted it as a sign to go ahead with Bebe's plan. "So where did you get the papyrus?" she asked.

"I had Siti get some for me. It's real stuff."

"Okay," Chione said, still a little hesitant. "We don't have lampblack."

"Charcoal," Bebe said, picking up the vial of black powder. "And cooking oil."

Bebe reached for Chione's bottle of mineral water on the desk and poured some into the goblet. "Please Chione, please write the glyphs."

Chione felt great empathy. Bebe was clearly being affected by the discovery and in her time of need, chose her to befriend. Chione felt compelled and pulled the saucer to her and began to stir the charcoal and oil together with the writing stick. Bebe sat motionless, even seemed to hold her breath. When the writing was done, Chione gestured to the papyrus. Once completed, it would be best that only the person drinking the potion touch the papyrus, but how had she known that?

Bebe stuck the length of papyrus into the goblet and stirred it around as they both watched the hieroglyphs dissolve and dye the water. Then Bebe looked for the trash pail and threw the damp papyrus into it.

They both sat motionless staring at one another. Finally, Bebe said, "Hold my hands, please. I'm shaking so badly."

They sat knee-to-knee and held hands. Chione realized at that moment that she loved Bebe. For all the things this woman stood for, they could not define all that Bebe stoically held inside.

Suddenly Chione was not seeing Bebe but a woman of Ancient Egypt with her beautiful hair and wonderful presence who was about to lose her husband. "Drink now," Chione said. She could not determine if Bebe heard the foreign echo on her words. Even Chione was jolted back into the moment by the accent.

Bebe picked up the goblet with both hands and, without her usual proper table manners, gulped, until all the murky fluid was gone. Then the lights flickered again and went completely out. A lot of disappointed voices came from around the campsite as everyone complained. Then the lights flickered several times, finally staying lit.

When Bebe sat the goblet down, Chione thought Bebe would break into tears. She looked to be losing her composure. Then Bebe straightened as if something had come over her. Her expression returned to her usual one of no-nonsense and self-assurance. She sighed. "Now we wait, and I'd better get this goblet back into Inventory before someone misses it."

"Bebe, you didn't," Chione said, though smiling.

"I wanted this to be real. It just seemed right to use one of Tauret's goblets." She wiped out the vessel with tissues from her pocket, and then gently placed the precious artifact back into her bag. "I'd better go," she said, disappearing quickly through the fly.

Dazed by Bebe's sudden behavior, Chione sat quietly for a moment. Bebe trusted her. Trusted her so much, she did not have to remind her not to tell anyone else. Bebe trusted her. And why shouldn't Bebe try the spell? Who knew if it worked its magic in ancient times? In today's world, many things worked simply by the fact that people had faith in them.

The photos in front of her invited attention. She had not seen the actual papyri before they were shipped. She studied each one, deciphering the meanings. They were spells for all kinds of female maladies. She quickly read the spells in the rest of the photos. Then she jolted upright in her chair. Had she read right? She picked back through the photos and found the one with a curious message that stuck in her mind. Her hands shook as she sounded out glyphs, translating to English, and finally putting together the meaning.

Drink, drink of this potion
It is more than mild
Put the spell in motion
You will bear a child

Chione dropped the photo and sat up rigid in her chair. A spell for childbearing! Bebe had taken a chance on her spell and it was too soon to know if it had taken positive effect if any. Yet, here was a spell Chione could use. If only she could believe. Bebe did. Bebe believed. If nothing happened to clear her menopausal malaise, nobody but she and Bebe would be the wiser. And she would discreetly console Bebe if it did not work. She definitely would.

She looked at all the components needed to write the spell and carry it through. She looked at the photo again and read the symbols. She had to make sure they said what she thought they did and that nothing was lost in her translation to English.

The hour was late. Electrical lighting flickered all over camp. Lights in some tents were off, signifying some had given up working in the dark and gone to bed. Chione found herself inside the inventory tent. She knew what she had to do and did not wish to be mistaken for a thief.

The lights flickered again. She strained to read the inventory lists inside the poorly illuminated tent. She heard footsteps outside. She did not hear voices but the footsteps went first in one direction then another, stopping near the tent flap. It sounded as if they might enter. She dropped down behind a large crate. But what was she afraid of? Her plan had made her a little paranoid. She did not want to be caught inside the tent at that hour although no one would think much of it since she always worked late. When the footsteps went away from the tent, she stood and quickly opened a nearby box and retrieved a small delicate blue faience bowl and left.

Back inside her yurt, she sat down at her desk and placed the bowl aside. Her heart pounded both from having secretly taken a bowl from Inventory and because of what she felt compelled to do.

After calming, she slowly pulled a new strip of papyrus off the stack as the raw edged pieces clung together. She picked up the writing stick to stir the charcoal and oil mixture and had to steady her hand before attempting to write the glyphs. As she wrote, she felt herself slip back in time to ancient Egypt. She was becoming Tauret! As if enveloped in a bubble of light, she sat at a beautifully carved writing table, conjuring a spell. For herself. She did not wish to lose the admiration of her beloved Pharaoh who desperately longed for a son. She had much to offer her King. Surely others too numerous to mention had or were casting spells to put themselves into the graces of Pharaoh. Her spell would be the strongest yet.

When the writing was done and the papyrus swilled in the bowl, in ancient tones, she said, "Pharaoh shall have an heir, a boy child!" Then she held the papyrus to the side of the bowl and drank till she had consumed every last drop of the fluid.

She placed the fragile bowl onto the desktop and slowly came back into the moment until Chione realized what she had done. She began to whimper. Tears ran down her face. If only she could have a baby. Aaron's child. She really did love him. As if to seal the deed, she grabbed up the piece of damp papyrus and ate it.

The lights flickered off again and never came back on. In total darkness, she stripped off her clothes, sensually, one piece at a time, as if readying herself for Pharaoh. For Aaron. Then she felt her way in the dark to her cot and lay in a fetal position, hugging her belly, till she finally fell asleep.

The next morning as Chione headed for Inventory, excited voices came from inside the tent. She heard Kendra say, "It was Tut's bowl. It's gone."

Dr. Withers asked, "How do you know it was Tut's bowl? Is it the only thing missing?"

Chione knew they were talking about the bowl she took. The thought that the bowl was Tutankhamon's was shocking. She examined the beautiful faience artifact and saw no real markings to show that it belonged to Pharaoh. Then she turned it over. There on the bottom was Tutankhamon's cartouche. Again, she shook and waited till she knew she would be able to speak. Finally, she entered the tent.

"Hey, I have the bowl," she said. "I took it last night to study it and when the lights went out... I-I didn't want to try to bring it back in the dark. You know. If I tripped and this thing cracked—"

"Good thinking," Clifford said. He looked utterly relieved. "Glad it was with you." He accepted the bowl and turned it over. "If I may say so, looks like this was one of Tut's lavish gifts to Tauret."

Later, Bebe pulled her aside. "I'm glad you did your spell."

"How did you know?"

"That's why I left the photos and all the other stuff. I knew there was a spell for you. I just wasn't sure you'd try it."

"You're devious," Chione said, smiling.

"And you drank your spell out of Tut's bowl. Should that mean anything?"

18

Considering the strange events and trances of the night before, work went well during the daytime as the sun slipped past and tinted the ever-changing hues of the sky. The beautiful evenings had become symbolic of her shifts in consciousness.

Alone, Chione succumbed willingly that evening in the Pillared Hall. The scene began opening out even as she was yet conscious. Tauret appeared and offered her hand and when Chione floated to meet her and their hands touched, they merged.

In the Sanctuary of the Priestesses, candles flickered and incense wafted on smoke that floated to the ceiling in ever-widening spirals of white haze. Linen fabric panels hung, normally to block the daytime sun but still allow in the light. At night, they held back gusts of wind and sand through the bare windows and allowed the air to circulate.

She stood naked. Handmaidens had arranged her hair, which had been washed and cleaned of the wax from her perfumed cone. Her face had already been drawn, but with lighter shades of kohl to accent her sculptured features at nighttime, when heavier lines were not needed to deflect the sun's rays. With fingertips, two handmaidens flicked perfume from small bowls over her body. Others prepared her clothing then draped her in fine see-through linen. The edges of her garment were bordered with glittering jewels and shimmering pure gold threads. Pleats fell below calf-length. The cloth came together from over her shoulders to under her bare breasts and emphasized their suppleness. Her dark nipples stuck straight out. She wore nothing else and was barefoot. She was handed a mirror of reflective polished silver and saw that she looked the best she ever had. All the handmaidens departed leaving her completely alone in the middle of the room on a smooth stone floor.

While exiting, the handmaidens extinguished most of the candles. Drums began to softly beat. The rhythm infiltrated her being. From somewhere in the dark recesses of the chamber came soft tones of a harp, lyre and double flute. Almost immediately, like her heart, the tempo quickened. Minor priestesses danced into the room, clad only in sheer skirts. They were young, with immature breasts and sparse pubic hair.

Tauret began to sway, slowly at first, in unison with the priestesses whose choreographed movements seemed to throw all energy in her direction. As if to shake loose all hesitation, all pretenses, she allowed the beat to carry her into a more physical dance, even into a mystical state.

Other priestesses had danced as she now did, as they prepared to meet their lovers. Now she danced, but only in hope that the one she loved might one day recognize her. She had cast spells and intoned strong incantations. All she could do was wait. Her spells had brought others the love they sought. Would they also work for the enchantress herself? Her reputation would come under scrutiny if she could not help the High Priestess of all. The spells for her had included much more than she had conjured for anyone else. Only one person could achieve the goals she sought to attain.

She danced, set her feelings free interpreting the music, matching the tempo of the drums as it increased. The priestesses snaked around her and reached out as if desiring to touch her. Their dance became frantic and sensual. In the center of it all, she matched them movement for movement, an integral interpretation of the overall spell. The pace of the drumbeat intensified till she thought she would exhaust all energy. At times she imagined she and Pharaoh swaying together as two cobras wrapped ropelike in a ritual mating dance. Other times she felt only as if she wanted to throw her body towards her beloved. She spread her legs, bent her knees and undulated, while her arms beckoned. She imagined her beloved thrusting his body toward her and yearned for them to connect. She was lost in the moment and continued to dance suggestively and sensually, expressing passion and breathing heavily and perspiring till her skin glowed.

Just when she thought she could not last another moment, the drumbeat slowed. She collapsed to her knees on the floor and rested, curled up, breathing heavily with her head down and hands outstretched together in front of her. She heard a rustling and sat up. From somewhere appeared candles in the darkness that converged and lit up an alcove. Servants pulled back the door drapes and stood rigid with heads bowed as Pharaoh walked in! The minor priestesses fell to the floor, arms outstretched on both sides of his pathway. He stood with arms folded across his chest. Wearing sandals, he carried a crook and flail, wore a regal headdress and only a white pleated kilt around his hips.

A manservant appeared and accepted the crook and flail. That meant Pharaoh intended to stay! His shadow fell across the bowed priestesses as he approached, and one by one they scampered from the room, as did the musicians, till Tauret was left alone with no one to come to her aid.

The minor priestesses had known of her desire to invade Pharaoh's heart. She had, after all, been his confidant, his friend of friends, and he always studied her with thankfulness in his eyes.

Tauret had thrown her entire being into the dance because she could only think of her King. She had no idea how her magic might work. She could only wonder how her incantations affected him. Or if an envious rival had apprised him of her spells and now he meant to put an end to them.

Tauret did not hesitate. Sensual feelings and thoughts still consumed her. She remained bent and put her face to the floor at his feet.

Pharaoh did not move. Finally, he said, "Rise, my Tauret."

She stood and he seemed entranced, full of intention. He scooped her up into his arms and walked out of the room, into a courtyard, and down a long promenade. She could only study the face of her King as he carried her the great length of the building without effort. The slapping of his sandals with each of his sturdy footsteps echoed the beat of her heart. The breeze blew her flimsy skirt up over his shoulder. If he had chosen to have her done away with, being carried to her death by her beloved was worth the price. Yet, how sad it would be that the rest of her conjuring could not be carried out. She had more to give him, had intoned to the gods in his behalf, and beseeched them for the one thing he wanted most.

Finally, they entered a chamber. Oil burned and light flickered from beautifully carved calcite lamps. Red mashrabia panels decorated the area around the soft woven reed bed, covered with sumptuous tapestries and pillows. Flowers filled every vessel and lotuses floated in bowls. Incense wafted. In one graceful swoop, Pharaoh laid her down on the cot. He paused only to remove his headdress and place it on a small table to the side. He kicked out of his sandals, and as he lay down beside her, removed and unceremoniously cast aside his kilt.

His breath was warm and gave her chills. His lips and tongue found her nipples. So did his bite as she screamed both in pleasure and pain. He tore at her linen dress and flung it aside.

"My Tauret," he said in deep throaty tones. "Give me an heir. Give me my son!"

Her spell was working. "You shall have your son, my King," she said. Then she remembered her mother's admonishments about this being a pathway from which she could never return. It could also be a means to fulfillment in every conceivable manner.

Her body shook with anxiety and anticipation and it excited Pharaoh to see her in such a state. He kissed her gently then momentarily stared deep into her eyes. She was at his mercy. Soon his lips found her neck while his hands explored the rest of her body, and she could no longer keep track of anything he might do. When he kissed her again it was not at all like the first kiss. He seemed love-starved and in every way meant to exercise his regal privilege.

Tauret was prepared as she sensed Pharaoh about to take her. He brought up her legs. She separated her knees and held her breath as he pushed into her. Then came the sting for which no motherly advice could prepare. Tears gushed from her eyes, and she cried out without meaning to. He groaned with great pleasure and became wild in his movements. The virginity she had kept secret from him had evidently pleased the one man who might change her life forever. A burning sensation followed, and she was now alone with her painful feelings as Pharaoh expressed his with groans and thrusts of heightened excitement. Despite discomfort, Tauret had to let Pharaoh know that he pleased her. She could not fail in this. If she did, he might simply get up and walk out and by morning her life and the lives of her parents could be relegated to the fields.

She wrapped her legs tighter around him and gave in to the moment and encouraged him to do whatever gave him pleasure. "Oba," she whispered lustily. She clutched desperately at his buttocks. "Oba!"

Something woke Tauret after all the candles had burned down and gone out. Only a dim streak of moonlight came through the window. She felt his warm breath on her neck. Then he was kissing her again as his hands explored.

"You please me, my Tauret," he said as his voice filled the room. "Now give me a son."

Without hesitation, Pharaoh lifted her legs and was inside of her again in one fluid movement. The painful burning returned. She wanted to cry out and say she could not continue. She remembered again what had led to that moment, this night, and knew that she would not fail. She lifted her legs higher and clutched at his hair. "Plant your seed, my Pharaoh," she said. "I will give you a son."

She woke toward morning and found Pharaoh still sleeping beside her. How regal he looked despite his nakedness, without regal accouterments. She had pleased him well. He had not left during the night. She looked about as sunlight began to filter in. She had worked herself into a frenzy with the music and dance and copulating with her Pharaoh had been a lofty goal. It was a dream that she could offer no other man, but one part of the dream was not yet complete.

She reached to gently wake her King. As he stirred, she brought her lips to his and ran her hands over his body and found him already excited. She knew nothing about a man's anatomy. What she found pleased her as she acquainted herself and that excited Pharaoh until he lifted her up and sat her down on top of his throbbing pole.

The stinging pain was still there but so was a new determination because this man, this King of all kings, remained with her through the night. Nothing would stop her now. She would give this King an heir with every conceivable pleasure in the making.

19

Chione felt great disappointment as the scene faded, and she found herself back inside the Pillared Hall, lying on her mat, full of sexual desire and perspiring as Tauret had with Pharaoh. Wishing to go back into the scene but realizing where she was, Chione had to lie still until the disappointment subsided. The Pillared Hall was in total darkness. The air was stifling hot. She put her hand to her heart and found her shirt completely unbuttoned. Undone, too, was the button of her trousers and the zipper! Her skin felt sticky all over. She sat up and patted the floor at the head of her mat till she found her small pocket flashlight and switched on its dim beam. Then she saw him. Aaron lay on a mat over by the next pillar. Though a simple blanket covered his hip area, his shirt and trousers were neatly folded and lay alongside his sleeping mat.

Chione dropped the flashlight. Its small beam illuminated only a nearby pillar to the side. "How could you, Aaron?" she said, screaming. "How could you?"

The sounds reverberated off the stone walls. Aaron bolted to his feet in his undershorts. When he realized where he was and that a light was on, he quickly grabbed up the blanket and tied it around his waist. "What's the matter?" he asked quickly as he came to her side. His expression in the dim light was one of disbelief. "What's wrong?"

She felt her bare chest again and turned away to button her shirt and close her zipper. Her mind flashed on the vivid scenes between

Tauret and Pharaoh, and she wondered how they could have seemed so real. She stood and raised her arm as if to strike Aaron, but he kept some distance. "My clothes," she said. "Did we— did you—"

"What is it? What's the matter?"

Chione felt defeated. "Did we do what I think we did last night?"

"What are you talking about?"

"You weren't in here when I started my meditation. Then I was with Tauret, and she and Pharaoh were...." She could not get the words out. "Did we do anything, Aaron?"

"You mean make love?"

"Yes!"

"Only in your fantasies."

She had nearly broken down but his comment unnerved her. "My fantasies? When you and I both have the same psychic experiences? You tell me, Aaron Ashby!" The room continued to echo. Chione felt as if they had insulted the sanctity of the Pillared Hall. She lowered her voice. "You tell me you didn't take advantage of me!"

Aaron let out a breath of air. His face softened. He made sure his blanket was still wrapped. "Oh, Chione, you've never been with a guy at all, have you?"

The comment took her by surprise. How could he have known? She shook her head. "No," she said.

"If you and I had made love, your body would be telling you so. I mean... there are ways to tell and you...." He shrugged, seeming to have difficulty talking about sex between them.

"We didn't?"

"I'm half naked because the electricity went out again last night. Climate control in here doesn't work without power, so I took my clothes off. It's not safe for you meditating alone in here in total darkness."

It was ghastly hot in the Hall. She was still perspiring. "Then why—"

"It was a strong paranormal occurrence, okay?" His words did not sound convincing.

"That's all?"

"That's all it was. Now, can we just enjoy being Tauret and Tut?" he asked, "together in our other world?" He returned to his mat and turned his back while he quickly dressed. As he walked past, he said, "See you topside." He flicked on his flashlight as he exited into the dark passageway.

So how did he know what kind of manifestation took place in her trance state?

Chione flicked off the flashlight and sat again in total darkness. Paranormal events were happening too quickly and too frequently. She needed to think about how to allow what was happening, yet how not to allow them to overpower her. Much more, and she would not be able to function with the team. Concentrating deeply, she heard the distant sound of Aaron ringing the bell so the guards at the top of the portcullis shaft could let him out when he climbed up. The ringing of the bell slipped her into trance again and Tauret approached.

Tauret carried the same blue faience bowl that she had used while performing her ritual spell. This time, the bowl contained a thick dark mixture that felt sticky as Tauret applied it to her face and then receded into darkness toward the north wall.

Chione roused again not knowing how long she remained entranced. She looked at her watch and found it was just before dawn. The team would be assembling in the cook tent for breakfast and the morning briefing. She had not returned to her yurt all night.

She did not have to ring the bell. The grate above the portcullis shaft had already been opened. However, guards were still in place to keep out those not permitted to enter. As she climbed out, they looked at her as if in disbelief.

Chione felt sticky and would hurry to take a shower. The moment she emerged from the shaft and people noticed, all eyes were upon her. Young boys pointed, giggled. Yafeu stuck his head out of the cook tent and suddenly Dr. Withers and Aaron and everyone were rushing toward her.

"What's with your face, Chione?" Dr. Withers asked.

People gathered around and suddenly she was sitting on a wooden box and touching her cheek with her fingertips. Her facial skin felt puckered, rough, and coarse. Siti rushed up with a hand mirror. Chione peered at herself and saw her mouth drop open. She was just as surprised as everyone else was.

"What's the meaning of this?" Aaron asked.

"I-I don't know," she said.

She felt confused and scared but remembered Tauret with her bowl of a sticky black substance that she had applied to her face. That had happened in the trance state. Surely that could not be the reason her face was now streaked with a muddy substance. Nothing tangible ever transferred from a trance state. Chione trembled at the implication.

Aaron bent to kneel in front of her. His knee must have hit a stone because he flinched badly, but his intense gaze told that he was concerned only for her at that moment. "Do you want to lie down?" he asked.

"Better to wash," Siti said.

Dr. Withers placed a hand on Aaron's shoulder. "After she's cleaned up, I want to see you two in her tent."

By the time Dr. Withers crowded into the yurt, Chione was sitting on the low cot. Her face had been washed after Siti pulled off the sticky mud and piled the pieces on a clean cloth. Chione looked again into a mirror. Her cheeks were rosy and clear.

"Hapi's mud," Siti said.

"Whose?" Dr. Withers asked with exasperation.

"Hapi's," Chione said cautiously. "Or maybe it was just dirt and I perspired and made it turn dark." She could not look either of them in the eye. "It's hot in the tomb at night."

Dr. Withers pulled up the woven stool and sat down as the reeds creaked beneath him. "So, after you and Aaron finished whatever, you spent the night in there... alone?"

"Yes, sir."

"I thought I warned—"

"But Dr. Withers, I'm getting—I've had...."

Aaron's eyes widened as if he had guessed what had happened. Then he looked utterly sympathetic.

Dr. Withers motioned to Siti and Aaron. "Leave me in here for a while." He looked stern. When they were alone, he asked, "Is something going on that I don't know about? Or has the whole world gone wobbly?" He looked at the strips of mud and almost reached out to touch them but changed his mind.

She owed him an explanation, but how could she explain when she, herself, did not understand what had happened. "I think I just got really dirty."

Dr. Withers threw up his hands and left the tent. Now she had to worry that she may have offended him by not confiding in him. What could she say to make him understand? Either way, he might lose faith in her.

Aaron entered and took a turn sitting on the creaky stool. Chione felt like a child about to be scolded. "I didn't ask to have these things happen to me," she said. "Now I'm left to interpret them as best I can." Suddenly, Aaron dropped to his knees on the ground in front of her, and she leaned forward into his arms and trembled as her breath come out in nervous fluttering sighs. "You've got to help me," was all she could say.

"I'm here for you, Chione," he said. "What's going on?"

"I'm into this way over my head."

"Can't you turn it off, slow it down?"

She pulled away and sat back. "Can't... won't," she said, gesturing with her hands as they shook nervously.

He eased back onto the stool. "Okay, tell me what happened."

"After you left, I was thinking to leave too," she said. "Then Tauret appeared again. It's strange. She put this stuff on my face. Then she disappeared. She seemed in a hurry."

"Hurry? Why?"

"Don't know," she said. "We had to hurry, that's all. And Aaron, you won't believe this."

"Try me."

"Tauret put this mud on my face, and when I looked at her, she was me."

Outside, the winds howled filling the yurt and made it balloon then snap harshly. Aaron ignored the distraction. "You were her putting mud on someone else's face?" he asked.

"No, I was her, putting mud on my own face," Chione said emphatically. She glanced at the mud strips again and reached over and touched one.

"You and Tauret were the same person?"

"That's the way I understand it."

"I guess you can be two people at one time," he said. "In a vision, anything can happen, I guess."

"That's what I saw. Now here I am with this makeover."

He could not possibly understand it yet. He had read quite a bit about the experiences of others and about psychic phenomena and the spiritual realm. He still practiced the meditation techniques and disciplines she taught him. At times, he reported that he felt consciousness shift to other realities. Still, he needed more experience.

They were aware of other planes of existence where the impossible might happen and also be real. They perceived the planes as being up in the heavens, the universe or maybe all around them, unseen. Those realities did not intermingle with the earthly plane. One could visit another plane and bring back the memory but certainly nothing tangible like Hapi's mud.

Chione needed to exercise utmost caution. Aaron was too eager to learn and, at times, seemed ready to cast aside much of his life to satisfy his thirst for knowledge about the realms to which he had been introduced. If word got out about their practices, he would be labeled one of "those" people. His career could be jeopardized. From the beginning, he made her aware of the necessity of balance between privacy and practice. "I doubt anyone will say anything about this," she said. "They won't know how to talk about it. Let's keep it our secret."

"What meanings do you interpret from this?"

"I wish I knew," she said, sighing. "Most occurrences seem left to me to decipher in the days that follow."

"You can't glean anything else?" he asked. He finally touched and then lifted the edge of a drying sheet of mud. It stuck to his fingertips, presumably like mud reportedly found at certain locations bordering the Nile. Hapi's mud.

"You know that I couldn't have come up with a supply of that mud," she said.

"Was anyone with you in the tomb?"

"Definitely not, but I know one thing. I slipped deep into another realm this time."

"No kidding."

"It was just as real as you and me sitting here," she said. Then her eyes lit up. "Oh, I remember. I came out of trance knowing that Queen Tyi was not a Nubian. She was thought to be barren, then used Hapi's mud to conceive. That's why her face was depicted black."

At the moment she remembered, Aaron's expression said he must have also remembered the spell from the First Chamber: *Blacken your face with Hapi's mud. Like farmer's fields, new life will bud.* Suddenly, they both realized the implication of the spell. Chione, herself, was barren, but Queen Tyi had several children. They sat staring expectantly into each other's eyes.

"There's no record of Queen Tyi having been barren," Aaron said finally.

"Hieroglyphs couldn't tell it all. We'll never know the personal lives of the Ancients. Besides," she said after a moment of pause. "What happened to me was only another vision."

"Yeah, sure," he said.

20

The sifted rubble from the children's room produced few finds. "A small pile of loose beads," Dr. Withers said. "Papyrus ropes, threads, and tiny broken trinkets."

"They're all a part of history," Chione said. The Madu Museum people would later tediously piece those together.

Plans were made to seal off the hole Randy fell through into the Second Chamber. As little as possible would be done other than seal the ceiling both on the outside and the inside. If complete restoration were to be accomplished, the expert artists of the Restoration Society would be the ones to complete it. A local stonecutter from the Theban village volunteered his services to shape a stone to fit the cavity and a message was sent to Cairo for a few bags of cement.

Dr. Withers decided to hold off on emptying the food annex. Crates were being completed for the larger pieces of furniture in the Pillared Hall. Once the Hall was cleared, they would have more space to maneuver.

Aaron cornered Chione, turned to leave and then turned back again. He was busy, but something must have been playing on his mind. "I should run something by you," he said as they moved to stand in the shade of the inventory tent.

"Sounds important," she said.

"Maybe so." He paused in thought, and then softly said, "I had a phenomenal experience yesterday."

171

She smiled warmly. "Tell me about it."

"Guess I should," he said. "I was inside the children's room, looking at the walls. I know we're not supposed to touch—"

"You didn't."

"Couldn't help myself," he said. "As if it wasn't my hand reaching out. I-I heard a voice."

"Re-eally?" she asked. Chills ran down her arms. All he had to do was mention something paranormal, and she would have a kinesthetic reaction. "What did you touch... hear?"

He took the water bottle off his hip, opened it and took a long gulp. "Not sure where I saw that symbol before," he said. He pressed his shirtsleeve against his lips. "Don't know what attracted me. Maybe you can identify it."

"Was the voice male or female?"

"Definitely male," he said. "A powerful throaty intonation." He shook his head, as if unable to accept what had happened.

"Well, what did he say?"

"Something about the reincarnation process of children." Aaron smiled suddenly. "I'm glad to have you to share this with. It's mind-boggling."

"What exactly—c'mon, tell me?"

"According to a spell, the children will reincarnate."

Chione was aghast. "Do you think he meant the mummies stored in that room?"

"Dunno," Aaron said, shrugging. "This is the scariest thing that's ever happened to me."

She smiled. "But real, isn't it? Because you heard it and you're real, Aaron."

"I'm real...."

Inventory of the glut of artifacts progressed slowly. With so many pieces to be classified, each person working with the relics was provided an aide. Chione was assigned permanently in charge of records and was summoned back and forth. Her calling out instructions in imperfect Egyptian dialect at times provided a good laugh, but energy and a willing attitude eased the tedium. Men and women worked side by side and transcended the traditional Muslin attitude toward women.

Suddenly, Kendra gasped, making sure everyone heard. "Oh, no! Another crate's missing!"

"Another?" Chione asked. "Could it have been mislabeled?"

"It's gone," Kendra said, pointing to the specific pallet where all remaining inventoried items from the children's room had recently been stacked and readied for shipping. "C-23."

"Another crate of children's toys," Chione said without having to check the lists. "A fairly light container."

"Light enough to run with," Kendra said. "I don't remember seeing it here this morning."

Dr. Withers joined them and they explained the dilemma. "Thieves in our midst," he said through clenched teeth.

Chione handed him the inventory sheet for crate C-23 and pointed to the list of contents. "Wooden toys," she said. "Easy to sell."

She and Kendra set about looking under tarps and in other areas in case the container might turn up.

Dr. Withers and Aaron stood within earshot. "She always knows what to do next," Dr. Withers said as if she was not meant to hear the compliment.

Chione did not like the idea of being excluded from the conversation, even if the comments about her were positive. She needed to direct the conversation away from herself and moved close again. "It's you, Dr. Withers," she said. "You always know what's best for everyone."

"For the team," he said.

"Yeah, I noticed," Aaron said. "You quietly withhold and let everyone else make the discoveries."

"Can't claim all the glory," he said. Then came that familiar goofy grin.

"You nudge or prod when you think things should go in a different direction," Chione said, on to something. By now she was sure Dr. Withers was trying his best to throw her and Aaron back together.

"You see something in Chione you'd like to promote?" Aaron asked. "Just what special ability do you think she might possess?"

"Aaron!" Chione had tried to move the conversation away from her. Now Aaron kept it focused on her. But why?

"Well..." Dr. Withers said with a grin that said he would like to get out of the conversation. He hesitated.

Chione knew he was up to something. Refraining from acting like a boss was his nature. So was innocent teasing, but withholding information was not. He was concocting something involving both Aaron and her. That would be why he suddenly drifted to the other end of the tent pretending to be busy.

Taking a break, Chione sat down on a crate beside Aaron and asked, "Are you keeping Dr. Withers updated about us?"

"What's your point?" Aaron asked. He was still slashing those grids in the margins of his note pages. Maybe doodling helped him think, like Dr. Withers always pulling at his mustache before he spoke, or poking one or two fingers into the air.

"Why is Dr. Withers always hovering over me trying to find out what you and I do in the Pillared Hall in the evenings?"

"Why don't you ask him?"

"I did. He claims he wants to learn if I've come up with new information."

"So there. You have your answer." Aaron seemed not the least bit concerned.

"If he's looking for clues to finding the Burial Chamber, why does he always ask how you and I are getting along?"

"How should I know?"

Dr. Withers was curious about more than her extrasensory abilities. "Tell me you didn't put him up to this whole thing," Chione said. "About having to stay with me inside the tomb."

"Ha! I had nothing to do with that. Maybe he thinks if you and I are having difficulties, it might upset your abilities."

"Slim chance, considering I received the original clues when I was alone."

"I don't know, Chione," Aaron said. "Maybe neither one of us knows the man as well as we think."

She had to give Aaron the benefit of the doubt. She sighed heavily and turned her attention to the others who just happened to drift within earshot. "Must be about lunchtime," she said.

"Yeah," Kendra said. "Time to get some exercise too."

Bebe watched Kendra walk out of the tent. Then she glanced at Aaron, then to her, probably wanting to see the look on her face if Aaron were to leave immediately after Kendra. Aaron quickly looked away as Bebe sneaked another glance at him. Bebe's imagination could get out of hand. Aaron knew exactly what Bebe was up to and knew leaving immediately would fuel Bebe's suspicions. Thankfully, he stayed put and looked busy. Bebe would have to find her thrills elsewhere. In the meantime, Bebe would probably make something of each time she saw him anywhere near Kendra.

Over lunch, Chione asked, "We're making better progress than anticipated, aren't we?"

Dr. Withers nodded and then slugged down a healthy gulp of Karkade.

"The good weather makes it easier on the workers," Kenneth said between bites. "Who would have expected a breeze at noontime?"

"Don't let that fool you," Aaron said. "The sun is up there in full force."

The double fly of the tent had been left wide open and a current of air wafted through with the help of electric fans powered by a generator. Aaron glanced out toward the onlookers who had thinned over the noon break. "What's going on out there?" he asked. "Why is everyone looking up here?"

The others strained to see. Just then Tarik and another young boy broke free of the crowd and ran, struggling on the uphill slant. The other boy fell back signaling Tarik to press onward. He stopped a few yards away, panting and barely able to speak. A tall worker pointed in the direction of the cook tent and Tarik covered the distance and burst unceremoniously inside.

"An iznukum, esmaHuli!" his young voice screamed. "An iznukum—"

"What?" Chione asked. "Enta bititkallim Inglizi."

"Oh, English... yes, yes," he said between panting. "Ohrma alaya!"

"Who? Which woman?"

"Rr-r... Rr-r," Tarik said, having forgotten the name. Then he pulled his hair. "Ahmar, ahmar!"

"Red hair?" Chione asked. "Rita? Rita fainted?"

"Iwah... Iwah!"

Without a second thought, they raced out of the tent with Tarik leading. Two men jostled past carrying one of the wooden trays. Out of nowhere came a cushion and a blanket thrown on top as they hurried ahead of everyone else.

By the time they reached the mastabas, Rita had already been lifted onto the padded tray. Her skin was blotched with beet-red mottling, and she looked hotter than the desert sands at midday.

"Pulse is too rapid," Clifford said in a panic as he leaned over Rita. She looked ghastly. Two local women fanned air across her body.

"Hot, hot," Rita said, muttering weakly and flailing a frail arm before going limp.

"Sunstroke," Clifford said, looking up at Dr. Withers. "Damn it all."

"Water, min fadlukum, water," a workman offered. Another motioned quickly for everyone to stand aside. "Cool down," the man said, beginning to pour the water over Rita's limp body. A dark woman grabbed the jug from the man and motioned sharply and all the men stepped away as she poured.

Carrying Rita on the tray, the men scurried back up the hill with the entourage behind. Once inside her tent, Aaron helped Clifford lift Rita to her cot. The local woman, Siti, stayed in the cramped space and flailed her arms to keep the air moving. Chione switched on the small fan.

"Clear the tent," Clifford said. "Give the ladies some privacy."

Aaron and Clifford stepped outside so Chione and Siti could remove Rita's clothing and throw a loose sheet over her. After Clifford was called back inside, he stuck his head out the tent flap and motioned the okay for Aaron and Dr. Withers to follow.

"How did it happen?" Dr. Withers asked as he entered.

"Stupid mistake," Clifford said, kneeling at Rita's bedside. "With all the tepid liquids we've had to drink when the wind came up, she thought it would be okay to have some ice in her water."

"Big mistake," Aaron said. "She had any convulsions?"

"Ice water," someone called from outside.

Siti poured cups of cold water over Rita's body, naked to her underpants under the sheet. Chione dipped Rita's hand into the bucket.

"I'll be okay," Rita said weakly as she roused.

Clifford's concern was written in worry wrinkles. "We need to get you checked over," he said, stroking his wife's bony hand.

"I'll be fine," she said.

"We'll get you to the clinic across the river," Clifford said.

"I'm getting better," she said. "Let me rest, drink." She took sips from a cup.

"I'm not going to leave you lying here."

"I am getting better," she said, sounding a bit stronger.

Clifford kissed her hand but would not leave her bedside. Rita smiled then sighed heavily with labored breath as she continued to perspire profusely.

Having left Clifford and Rita to their privacy, a short while later Aaron walked up behind Chione and pointed. "Look over there," he said. Clifford's own frailty now came to light as he struggled to steady his wife. Siti had gotten Rita into fresh light clothes, and she and Clifford were helping her toward the makeshift toilets. Aaron and Chione ran to help.

"Leave her with Siti and me," Chione said.

"Okay, yes, thanks," Clifford said as he opened the rickety blue door. "Pharaoh's Revenge, you know?"

Afterward, they helped Rita back to her tent. Some of Siti's helpers had exchanged the wet woven cot for a dry one with fresh sheets and repositioned the fan.

Clifford called out for permission to enter the tent. Aaron was with him. "This is serious," he said. "You should go to the clinic right now."

"Let me get some strength back first," Rita said, smiling weakly. "I'll just rest and let you know in a while."

"If you're not up and about in—"

"It's happened before, over the years. Remember?" she asked. "A little rest. I'll be okay."

"Can you drink more water?" Chione asked.

"Maybe."

"I'll be right back," Aaron said. By the time he returned with fresh water, Siti was bending over Rita fanning and curiously studying her face. "Something happen again?" he asked.

"No," Siti said, smiling warmly. "Resting."

Rita could not drink much, and they left her in Siti's capable care. Where would they be without that dedicated woman's help?

Back inside the cook tent, no one cared to finish the meal. Except Kenneth. A couple more bites, a swipe of his plate with a piece of bread, and he excused himself to get back to work. Yafeu and Irwin gathered the plates. When Yafeu saw the food left on them that would be wasted, he shook his head. Chione had never seen any leftover food in the garbage receptacles. She guessed that Yafeu made leftovers look palatable and gave the food to the poor.

Dr. Withers turned to Clifford. "Just why were you two down at the mastabas in this heat anyway?"

"Kenneth mentioned he found a hole alongside one of the mastabas that looked to have something in it," Clifford said. "We thought we'd stretch our legs and take a peek."

"Couldn't have waited till evening when we could all go?"

"In the evening we'd have to use flashlights and draw too much attention."

"So, what?"

"I had this idea," Clifford said "What if whoever took the toys couldn't get them out of the area right away? They'd have to hide them during the day." He shrugged. "Sounded like a logical place to look."

They returned to Inventory to resume working.

"Kenneth," Dr. Withers called out. "Let me see you a minute?"

"Yes, sir," Kenneth said, making his way through the stacks.

"What kind of hole did you see at the mastabas?"

"Just a hole, fairly deep. Looked like a wooden crate or something was in it."

"Can you remember which mastaba?"

"Maybe."

"Clifford thinks you might have found our stolen toys," Dr. Withers said. "Let's go."

"Maybe we should take along a couple of the Guard," Clifford said.

Members of the Guard looked no different than laborers wearing turbans and gallibayas over trousers. Curiously, bulges at the hip disclosed something worn underneath that the others did not have. Yet, how would they reach their pistols under those long tunics if a situation predicated fast action?

Kenneth led them up one lane and down the next as the sun beat down on them. "Strange," he said. "I could have sworn it was this one, right here. I remember those ancient markings."

"Well, there's no hole," Aaron said. He tied his handkerchief around his forehead to catch the perspiration and replaced his cap. "A lot of these mastabas are leaning, though, caving in."

"Watch where you step."

"Probably looks the same as it's been for millennia," Bebe said.

Chione gingerly placed her hands on a mastaba and immediately gasped.

"What are you getting?" Aaron asked quietly.

"A chamber, a sense of dread, of pain," she said under her breath. She turned to the others. "Leave this place!" She spun around and swiftly walked away.

"What is it?" Aaron asked, following. He wanted to know everything and, in this case, had the right to know.

"We're being watched."

"You see someone?" He reached to touch her and stopped himself again.

"No, I can feel it."

"Where?" Kenneth asked, catching up. "From which direction?"

"Just leave," she said as she kept walking.

Dr. Withers began flinging both arms, motioning the group to head in the direction of camp. Everyone scampered. At least they believed in her, knew she would not say something like that on a whim. Two of the Guard summoned a few more Guard members, and they began to walk the rows of mastabas.

"I have to know what you were feeling, Chione," Dr. Withers said as they stood on the hillock watching the Guard make a sweep of the area below.

"We were being watched," she said. "From real close by."

"Do you think the thief, or thieves, may have been hiding nearby?" Aaron asked.

"I-I don't know," Chione said. "I just felt threatened." She shivered, trying to shake off the feeling.

"In what way?" Aaron asked.

"With bodily harm," she said. She was still shaking.

"Was this one of your 'other sense' perceptions?" Clifford asked.

"Yes," Chione said. "It was strong like someone was about to be harmed."

21

Being called away from camp suggested only one thing. Dr. Withers wanted to have a conversation out of earshot of anyone else. Marlowe brought her to the outcropping where Dr. Withers waited. Something behind Marlowe's expression begged Chione not to judge him too harshly.

"You wanted to see me?" she asked.

Dr. Withers stood with chin uplifted and hands clasped behind his back, silently gazing out toward the glowing horizon of late afternoon. He greeted them quietly. "We need to talk," he said.

"For that, we have to hide behind the rocks?" Chione asked.

"The others would laugh, you know? Marlowe won't."

"You're expecting me to intuit something?"

"Not exactly."

"Dr. Withers, what is it?"

It was another Sabbath with the site partially deserted. Occasional noises filtered up from the camp through the clear desert stillness. Dr. Withers came close and bent slightly forward as the three huddled together. "First of all, Marlowe's here because she understands your abilities better than I do," he said with a hushed voice. "I guess there's no other way to say this." Then he hesitated again.

Marlowe put a hand on her husband's shoulder. "Sterling's had a couple dreams you might want to hear."

"You, Dr. Withers?"

No one would hear them being that far away from camp, so no reason existed to speak in hushed tones. Marlowe went to lean against the outcropping and Chione joined her and climbed up and sat cross-legged with her back to the sun. "Weird ones," Marlowe said. "And he usually never remembers dreams once he wakes."

Dr. Withers having dreams did not surprise Chione. Their entire group continued to be deeply affected by the magic and spells of the tomb. Who knew what might happen next? "Okay," she said. "Spill it."

"First," Dr. Withers said. "What I want to know is exactly what you felt while walking the mastabas. Anything and everything."

Chione smiled. "That's really all you brought me here for?"

"No, that's not all," he said. "But before we leave this hillside, I want to know what you perceived, how you perceived it, and how you think it affects us... without the others listening in."

"Thank you for that," she said.

"Okay, so I had a dream as I fell asleep last night." He took off his hat and scratched his head. He looked comical with matted hair on top and the rest sticking out the sides. "It was of Kenneth and Bebe on a hill with some other people and their lives being in danger."

"If it happened while you were falling asleep," Chione said, "it's only hypnogogic imagery." Yet, she felt another chill remembering, prior to the trip, having intuited certain peril existing. *Some accidents averted, some not.* "Not just Bebe and Kenneth. Anyone in the group. That's why we had to get out of the mastabas."

"My dream was about danger to Kenneth and Bebe," Dr. Withers said. "It's strange I should be having near nightmares of danger to anyone."

"Stranger still is that you're remembering any of it, Sterling," Marlowe said. "You always say you can't remember dreams."

Chione sat up straight and stretched her back and welcomed the heat of the sun. "We should be wary," she said. "Kenneth needs to be careful, too, down in that area."

"Then I had another dream that—well, that one's not important right now."

"You mentioned it. So, what was it about?"

"Go ahead," Marlowe said, smiling mischievously.

"Well, Chione," Dr. Withers said. "You may not want to hear this, but I've had this same dream, at least twice, that you and Aaron get back together."

"That really was a dream," she said as her heart skipped a couple of beats.

"Wait, listen," he said, putting up those two same fingers. "The strange thing is that you and Aaron were dressed as ancient Egyptians."

Chione was rocked by the implication. Her heart raced, but she did not want them to know it. "Ancient Egyptians? That certainly wasn't a premonition of the future," she said, passing it off with a wave of a hand. "When did you begin remembering your dreams?"

"Since we've been in Egypt," he said. "I've never dreamed of anyone in this group, ever, as far as the few dreams I remember." His finger already pointed into the air and asked a moment more while he got his thoughts together. "You don't think my dreams of you and Aaron amount to anything?"

"No."

"But the content fits what's happening now," Marlowe said.

Since the first time Marlowe approached her a couple of years earlier, Chione understood her interest in the paranormal was tempered by her husband's need to maintain a professional posture among his peers. Marlowe loved her husband and acquiesced. On her own, she might plunge headlong into the occult. Due to the finding of this tomb, her husband's position had been irrevocably secured in the field. Now she just might find freedom enough to explore her own interests, and due to his nighttime reveries, Dr. Withers might not be able to keep himself from being pulled into it all.

"Some dreams merely release figments of the imagination," Chione said quickly.

"Wait, listen, Chione. We both feel uneasy about Kenneth and Bebe."

"As I said, we were being watched," Chione said. "All I know is that I felt threatened. If we stayed in the mastabas, harm would come to us."

"But from where?" Marlowe asked. "By whom?"

"From very close, judging from the kinesthetic feel of it. Something told me if we persisted in our search, one or more of us would be seriously harmed."

"How?"

"Bodily harm, probably."

"Hit?" Dr. Withers asked. "Beaten?"

"Shot, maybe."

Marlowe gasped. "This is serious."

"By whom?" Dr. Withers asked. "No one but us was out there."

"I can only guess," Chione said. "The thieves?"

"That stands to reason," Dr. Withers said, thoughtfully. "Any of those mastabas are unsealed, considering the ancients used to leave foodstuffs and offerings for their departed." Then he did not say anything for a while.

Marlowe looked at Chione and smiled. Chione felt relieved that had been all Dr. Withers wanted to know. Still, him suddenly remembering his dreams was curious. Something told her this would not be the end of Dr. Withers' nighttime odysseys. "May I go now?" she asked. "We've got a lot—"

"Not yet," Dr. Withers said. "I want to ask you a few more questions."

"About?"

"To put it bluntly," he said, smiling briefly. "Back in California, you received several stunning messages about this discovery. I always felt you weren't telling all."

"How could you think that?"

"By being adept at reading body language," he said, smiling sheepishly at having to give away one of his secrets. "You've never told all and you've received more that you haven't disclosed."

"I haven't received much that I could interpret as meaningful to our purpose," she said, looking him straight in the eyes. From that, he had to know that she was telling the truth. After all, she had received only fragments.

"But you've received," he said. He had a way of staring back that would not let anyone read anything in those wizened gray eyes. He would insist on her revealing more details.

"Sort of," she said. She needed to appease him without embarrassing herself. "I've had one recurring vision and one new dream."

"That's all?" Marlowe asked, glancing to her husband.

Chione quickly looked down and hoped she had not blushed. Under the revealing penetrating sunlight, how could she hide anything?

"Spill it," Dr. Withers said eagerly. "We're here because of you. You can't keep secrets now."

"I should have mentioned it," Chione said. "It seemed so trivial. I had a vision, more than once, of Tauret as a live person, coming toward me from the sofa in the Pillared Hall."

"She was sitting on the sofa?"

"No, she just materialized in the general area of the sofa, maybe."

Dr. Withers pulled back a corner of his mouth and made clicking noises with his tongue.

"She comes out of the sofa?" Marlowe asked.

"It's as if the sofa isn't there. I wanted to wait till the Hall was emptied, to see if she'd still show up once the sofa was gone."

"That's why you didn't say anything?"

"Right. I'd like to provide the best information possible," Chione said. "Not just every little detail that may have nothing to do with anything."

"Then?" Dr. Withers asked. "What happened once you saw her?"

"She merged into me, that is, I became her. Or she became me."

"No kidding." Dr. Withers said. Surprisingly, his eyes lit up. "So, what did she look like?" He paced, his way to let off a surge of anxiety.

Chione did not know how to break the news. "Me," she said quietly.

Dr. Withers abruptly turned to face her. "Wha-at?"

"Now, Sterling," Marlowe said. "You wanted to know."

"Several times I found myself sitting in that beautiful chair by the couch," Chione said.

"The one we already found you in?"

"Yes."

"This happened at other times that I don't know about?"

"Yes, when Aaron and I were in there alone."

"No kidding," Dr. Withers said again. "What does all this mean? What's happening to you?"

"I believe I'm experiencing some of Tauret's life." She felt happy to have declared it.

"No kidding."

Chione spotted a monstrous yellow scorpion beating a path toward a shady hole in the outcropping near her. Even though those pests hunted at night and hid from sunlight or came out only to look for a darker hiding place, Chione bounded off her perch.

Marlowe, too, saw the yellow body with its tail carried high and stood clear. "What was Aaron doing during this time?" she asked.

"He must have had his own experience."

"He intuit anything?" Dr. Withers asked, a twinge of hope in his voice.

"Sterling, you always said he was a lot like Chione."

Suddenly Dr. Withers smiled that sly, wide-eyed smile that told another of his secrets had gotten out.

What Chione suspected was probably true. Dr. Withers was being extraordinarily cautious, but in his own way, nudging Aaron and her together. "You think he's like me?" Chione asked, amused.

"Sort of," Dr. Withers said defensively. "Aaron mentioned that you two had similar experiences in there together. My thinking is that if both of you could validate what you received—"

"Is that why you try to throw us together?" Chione asked, teasing, taking him by surprise.

"For the sake of our work," he said. His proud withholding stare and raised eyebrow told of ulterior motives. "Strange that Aaron had a dream where he experienced himself as Tut."

Loud voices carried through the air up from the direction of their camp. They sounded excited about something.

Aaron had not admitted experiencing himself as Tut to her. Just why were she and Aaron sharing the lives of the two depicted in the tomb? "Dr. Withers, I have to say this," Chione said cautiously. "I don't wish to be manipulated toward Aaron by anyone. We had our time together. If Aaron seems a bit like me, it's because his own intuition is fairly well-developed, but he can make it on his own."

"That could be true," Marlowe said. "Chione introduced Aaron to another level of awareness, just like I'm learning. How can a person simply turn it off after being exposed? He would naturally want to be close to her if only to learn."

"It's awfully strange that you two would have all too similar experiences," Dr. Withers said. "What's the message in that?"

The noise level from the site increased. Shortly, frantic voices called out for Dr. Withers who only then stepped out from behind the outcropping. Naeem found them. "Quick, quick!" he said, pointing back to camp. "See Mr. Clifford. Why he's making bad noises and begging to Allah?"

They ran and found Clifford at the head of the crowd outside his tent crying and ranting like a madman.

"Why?" he asked in a raspy voice, fists clutched upwards toward the sky. Tears flowed down his cheeks. "Why my Rita? Why-y!"

They crowded into the tent and found Aaron on his knees beside Rita lying on her cot. Aaron cried quietly. Rita lay blue in the face, mouth agape, and dead. One leg was bent up at the knee and both arms were rigid and mysteriously crossed over her chest. They rushed out to Clifford's side. All Clifford could do was scream until he had no voice left. "Rita, my Rita!" Then he collapsed to his knees, bent to the ground, and wept.

22

In the distance, screeching women wearing the traditional black folds of modern-day mourners monotonously performed the death wail. Rita's body had to be removed from the hot climate and shipped home immediately. Dr. Withers himself set about making preparations for Clifford to return to California with her. Marlowe was to accompany them and help with funeral arrangements.

A great sadness permeated their joyous endeavor. The team worked teary-eyed. The locals worked in silence. Siti had become despondent, unable to forgive herself, having been inside the yurt when Rita died. She said Rita looked to have been uncomfortable at one point, moved around a bit, and then she settled down. Siti decided to let her sleep. That must have been when she died.

Clifford wandered in as Chione sat during a rare moment alone in Inventory. He looked like he meant to do something but his concentration and intent failed him. She went to comfort him, and they held together until they could hold no longer. She felt a curious sensation on the top of her head, then another and another, and still more. Finally, she pulled away and looked up at Clifford and found him weeping silently. His tears had fallen into her hair.

Clifford pulled out a handkerchief and staggered to take a seat. He sat with his elbows on his knees and stared at the ground, dabbing at his eyes till he stopped crying. Chione tried to comfort him, but he squeezed her hand and then stood and walked out of the tent and back into the hills.

"The wailing's different from when the mummies came out," Bebe said as she entered with Kendra. "I never dreamed I'd hear anything like that."

"They still do that," Chione said. "In the Mediterranean, the Middle East, many areas. Some are professional mourners. It's cultural, a tribute to the departed."

"Sorta like the Egyptians did," Bebe said, "when Victor Loret discovered that cache of royal mummies in 1898."

When the shipment of royal mummies floated down the Nile on the way to Cairo, women on the banks of the river threw dirt on their heads and wailed. Men yelled and shots fired into the air, all in celebration, a show of respect.

"Kenneth's probably out there," Bebe said. "He wanted to capture the wailers on video with full sound."

"It's amazing what Kenneth's done to document our effort," Kendra said.

"Yes, this time around," Bebe said. "We'll have more than just stills to put into a history book." Videos would be sold for both publicity and for funds needed by the CIA.

They paused and listened to the tribute for Rita. She was greatly loved and an undeniable part of Clifford and the group. No joyous cheers went up as more indescribable relics were brought out of the tomb. They silently resumed work as the artifacts were carried in.

Aaron found Clifford and stayed with him. Later, after Clifford calmed, they entered the cook tent. "Sterling, don't bother with flight reservations," Clifford said. He had everyone's attention. "Rita's already home."

"Oh?" Dr. Withers asked.

"We wanted to return here," he said. "Sell our properties, the vineyard in Napa Valley—"

"The vineyard?" Dr. Withers asked. "After that new airport upped the value half a mil?"

"Yeah, yeah." He waved a hand in the air. "We wanted to finish out our lives here in Egypt." The words seemed to stick in his throat. "We could live like royalty.... Could have."

"What about Rita?" Dr. Withers asked.

"I'm going to buy our plots and bury her in Garden City."

Dr. Vimble was notified. He sent a local doctor over from Luxor to pronounce Rita for the death certificate. Dr. Vimble was to examine the body once it arrived in Cairo. Then the site was crawling with men identifying themselves as a new squad of the Egyptian Armed Guard who had come to investigate Rita's mysterious demise.

Still photos had been taken of Rita the way Clifford found her, to provide Dr. Vimble and the Egyptian police with a record. The videographers and reporters were kept away. Clifford allowed a chosen few times to pay last respects in their yurt. He had even spent the night in there with his wife's body. He hadn't slept. Because of the heat, Rita's unembalmed body would deteriorate rapidly. Time was of the essence in transporting her to Cairo for an autopsy. The Witherses accompanied Clifford, along with a few aides.

Soon after they departed, Randy, the students, and their chaperones arrived. Randy wandered about as if getting reacquainted with the site. Then he headed straight to the cook tent where he knew he would find someone. His arm rested in a sling. "Sorry I missed her," he said upon hearing about Rita.

"I'm sorry you're so overwrought," Aaron said.

"So why haven't you all gone to Cairo?" Randy asked. "For the funeral."

"Shut down the whole operation?" Bebe asked. "In case you aren't aware, our little private Institute is on a very tight budget, one which cannot tolerate delays."

"Nor deadbeats," Kendra said.

Randy reached into his sling and produced photos of Rita's body and spread them on the tabletop. "You see her crossed arms?" he asked. "And what's with that leg?"

Chione nearly jumped onto the tabletop and snatched up the pictures. "How did you get those?"

"And that gaping mouth?"

Aaron leaned across the table and got right up into Randy's face. "Would have done you a world of good had you dislocated your head." He stood quickly and walked away, saving himself the consequences of finally punching Randy's lights out.

Randy could resist little. "Look at her mouth," he said, leaning away and keeping an eye on Aaron's whereabouts. "And her hands. Royal burial would have closed the fists or left her hands flat on opposite shoulders. Rita's hands look like they're holding something that's not there."

"For God's sake," Kendra said. "The woman is dead."

"You bet she is," Randy said. "Laying there like an Eighteenth Dynasty royal. But what's with that leg?"

"How dare you mock her," Chione said.

"I'm not saying anything any of you haven't already thought."

Kenneth rose to retrieve a pot of coffee and brought it to the table. He didn't offer any to Randy. "Oh, pray, read our minds."

"That ridiculous whimpering, the thefts, Rita's death," Randy said. "This tomb's cursed just like Tut's was. Who's next?"

"When did this sorry disbeliever turn convert?" Kendra asked as she rolled her eyes.

"Tell me, Chione," Randy said, persisting. "Rita's death is not the tragedy you saw in your dreams. Otherwise, you'd have warned Clifford. So maybe there is a curse and more will come, right?"

"You know, Randy," Chione said. "You only care to learn enough to validate yourself."

Everyone looked to Randy, pathetically attempting to blend back into the group after his absence, a group to whom he had never endeared himself. Evidently, his dislocated shoulder had not been enough to humble him. He had never gesticulated when speaking. Now his free hand and arm flopped about as he spoke. "If there's a curse, we haven't seen the end of it," he said, wagging an index finger. "Chione, I'll bet you haven't told all."

After lunch, Chione and Aaron watched Randy interact with the group of children who were being schooled at the site.

"They seem to get a kick out of his clownish gestures," Aaron said with a twinge of sarcasm. "There's really no purpose for him staying on."

They knew that Dr. Withers would be patient and find new duties for him. "There's a reason for everything," Chione said softly.

Later they agreed to accompany Randy into the tomb with the students and their escorts. They studied the precocious children as they waited in the sunlight for further instructions.

"These children are all gifted," Randy said.

"How so?" Chione asked.

"Look at them. The oldest one is only eight," he said. "They know everything about ancient times. They know it all."

"Even the younger ones?"

"Every one of them," he said. "Even those two little ones sitting over there by the wall."

"They can't be more than four or five years old."

"It's eerie," Randy said. "Like they were born with the knowledge."

"Do you believe in reincarnation?" Chione asked, taking both Randy and Aaron by surprise.

Randy rolled his eyes. "What brings that up?"

"Just a thought," she said. "The depth of their knowledge has to come from somewhere."

Lowering the children into the shaft, two at a time in a makeshift seat, took a while. Making a game of it for the children, Randy took some of the more daring ones down through the original entry shaft, easing himself down the rungs on one elbow. Once inside the tomb, when the wide-eyed, little ones entered the children's room, their elation escalated into playful folly. They ran to pile up on top of one another, lying haphazardly placed, arms rigid at their sides and staring blank stares.

"*Ari, Ari!*" one child yelled. "Mummies!"

The chaperons, caught completely off guard, urged the giggling children to untangle.

Chione stared in disbelief. "Remember what they look like, Aaron," she said. "Remember this!"

"What they look like?"

"Just now, their positions. Hold that image till we can look at those photos again."

He shrugged. "Okay."

Next, the children toured the Pillared Hall and annexes, finally resting, sitting at the north wall near the entrance. As their high-pitched voices echoed through the Hall, the whimpering suddenly came again.

"Aaron?" Chione asked.

"I heard it this time," he said.

A wave of fright rolled through the group. The two chaperones evidently had not heard. The younger ones began to wail and cling around Chione crying, "Ari, Ari!" Beyond their cries, Chione again heard the soft whimpering, cut short.

Randy showed no understanding and exited with the more frightened children.

Once outside, Chione and Aaron went to view the photos of how the real mummies looked in the room when they had been found. "I wonder," Chione said, looking toward the group of children. Then she all but ran toward them with Aaron in tow. "They need to see these."

Upon seeing the photos, again the children gleefully giggled and piled up in a heap on top of one another against the newly built restraining wall. Just as they had done inside the tomb, in the same positions as the mummies lay in the photos.

Randy seemed confused and swatted at dust on the children's clothing when they finally stood.

Aaron shook his head. "I'm understanding less and less," he said, fanning a breeze across his face. "Why doesn't the climate affect you, Chione?"

"I'm home," she said. She smiled and wondered what had prompted her reply. Was that why she had been able to settle so readily into Egypt? From where had all the knowledge come that left her feeling she had lived here before? And why did the California Central Valley now feel like it barely existed? She had not once thought of her Egyptian-decorated cottage.

Aaron stared at the photos, still shaking his head. Finally, he said, "By the way, what did those kids call you?"

"Ari."

"What's that mean?"

"Guardian," Chione said quietly.

During a rest break, she and Aaron returned to the children's chamber. She scanned the glyphs for clues, made notes, and came upon something most curious. "Aaron, look here!" She aimed a flashlight high up the back wall that had previously been hidden behind the pile of mummies and rubble. Some of the paint had been scraped off by the abrasion of the sand, but the carvings remained wondrously intact.

"Don't make me figure this out," Aaron said.

"See the woman?"

He leaned close. "Yeah, same one throughout. What about her?"

"Read upwards on the right."

"Chione, I'm not that quick at deciphering."

She sighed and remembered everyone's impatience. They wanted immediate answers. Absolute facts were not that easy to come by. That is, information that she could validate with dreams and visions then point to a glyph or mural to corroborate her theories. "See these small varied figures?" she asked.

"Children."

"See the women at the bottom?"

He studied, hesitated, and then finally asked, "Pregnant?"

"Now you're getting it," Chione said, encouraging. "Her symbol translates to *beq*, meaning pregnant woman."

"Okay."

"Now here's *ten*," she said. "Symbol meaning to split or separate. And these...." She pointed to figures of *mes, mena* and *renen*. "Women giving birth, nursing and playing with children."

Aaron studied the adjacent section. "Children lying prone," he said. "Why?"

"Death," Chione said quietly. She followed a line of tiny prone figures till finally coming to an adult-sized symbol at the bottom, then waited for Aaron's recognition.

"That's the symbol I touched when I heard that voice I told you about," he said. "Who—"

"*Khentimentiu*," Chione said. "God of the dead's destiny." Aaron looked stunned but said nothing. "Now see this woman?" she asked, pointing to the female next to the god.

"Yeah, seated."

"The sound of this female symbol is *ari*, meaning guardian."

Aaron went to his knees and got up close to the figure and studied it. "She's the same woman throughout the tomb," he said. "If Ari is a term applied to the woman buried here, why did the children call you that name?"

Chione was caught off guard. "I don't know yet."

Aaron looked bewildered. He seemed to be having much difficulty keeping himself from touching the symbol of Khentimentiu. His fingers moved toward the etching. His hand shook.

"Look at these walls," she said, distracting him.

"What are the meanings of all these other glyphs?"

"Spells for children, wishing them well, to send them safely into the Underworld. It's as I suspected," she said, half mumbling, absorbed. "All these children were to share in the Afterlife of the tomb's main inhabitant."

"It's as if Khentimentiu predicts—"

"Exactly as you heard when you touched his symbol."

Nothing more could be said. They looked into each other's eyes in the dim light, both fixated on the same thought. Finally, Chione said, "The way I see it—not the way the others might—but to me, Khentimentiu's presence suggests that anyone entombed here will reincarnate." As incredible as it seemed, Chione now had difficulty accepting what she herself claimed. Suddenly she shivered.

"The children outside?" Aaron asked. "Live children, who piled up in a heap in the same pattern as the mummies? Then again outside, all in jubilant fun?"

"How would those unsuspecting children know to do that?" Chione asked. "Unless those children are the reincar...." An idea struck like a bolt of lightning.

"And the mummy?" Aaron asked cautiously. "If the children are to share in the afterlife of the mummy—"

"And the children are now reincarnating...."

"What about the mummy in the Burial Chamber?"

23

The next day at noon, Dr. Withers returned, driven up in a jeep. After helping unload some packages, the driver sped off to the Egyptian encampment below.

"What are you doing back so soon?" Randy asked.

"I run this operation," Dr. Withers said as Irwin served him a meal. "Or had you in your absence forgotten?" To Irwin he said, "Bring me Karkade, please." His response to Randy showed signs of strain that would certainly be antagonized by Randy's ignorance. "I left Marlowe to look after Clifford," he said to the group.

"You left Marlowe in Garden City?" Aaron asked.

"My wife, my helpmate," Dr. Withers said. "Guess I should know better than to feel guilty."

"Because you left your wife with another man?" Randy asked.

"No, Randy." Dr. Withers clenched his teeth as his jaw muscles flexed. "Because I still have my partner, my right arm, and Clifford's lost his."

"Oh, well," Randy said, gesturing toward his sling. "So have I."

Everyone moaned and quickly left the table. Randy went in another direction. No one knew why Dr. Withers put up with him. Perhaps now Dr. Withers had reached his limit.

"Good thing Randy's assigned to the tour groups," Aaron said when they were outside. "He's good for nothing now as far as our work goes."

Randy's knowledge could best be used on the mummies that had already been sent to the Madu Museum. He was unable to contribute much of anything at the site.

Work continued steadily throughout the day. No one seemed in the mood to speak as artifacts were brought out of the chambers. Fragile relics could not be left in the open air for long so everyone buckled down. The students of Museum Science, as beginners, were slow to put into practice classroom learning of the tedium of artifact preservation, much to Kendra's dismay.

Twenty-four hours later, a fax arrived from Clifford telling that Rita died of simple heart failure. Oxygen deprivation carried her past the point of waking. When they were able to make Siti understand that she could have done nothing, could not have even awakened Rita, Siti wept.

Late the next day, Marlowe returned to camp escorted by the aides. She wore Egyptian women's clothing and a sheesh. At first, Chione did not recognize her with her raven hair covered and the sheesh shadowing her face. Clifford had decided to remain in Cairo a couple more days.

"How's he holding up?" Chione asked.

"Facing it well. Talks openly," Marlowe said, removing her head covering. "All of his local friends came out in a show of support."

"Emotionally, how's he doing?" Dr. Withers asked.

"Well enough," she said. "Making plans for a place to live when he moves here."

"He shouldn't be alone," Aaron said. "Maybe I should retrieve him."

"Give him a couple days," Dr. Withers said. "Then remind me again."

The next morning, Clifford wandered into the cook tent in time for breakfast. He sniffed the air, smelling the food as if he hadn't eaten in a while.

"Jeez, man," Dr. Withers said. "How'd you get back at this hour?"

Clifford shrugged. "As well as I know Egypt? Could've walked it in the dark."

Chione rushed to give him a hug. "Welcome back," she said softly. She poured him a cup of coffee and watched attentively as he wearily sat down. In her special way, she could not help but feel more than empathy for the man. She tried to block out feeling his pain.

"How are my kids?" he asked without smiling.

"We've had to get them to the Museum right away," Aaron said. "Everything from that chamber went in the same shipment.

"Why 'had to'?" Randy asked.

"The *museum spirit*," Bebe said.

Randy sighed quickly and said under his breath, "Museum spirit? A spirit?"

"An insect," Chione said. "An insect that decays mummies."

"Known to the locals as the Museum Spirit," Bebe said. "You need to bone up on the facts, Randy."

"I've heard of it," he said. He smiled away the tension. Then he surprised everyone by asking, "How long is Chione going to be with us?"

From the rest in the group came expressions of outrage. Dr. Withers' lips pinched tighter than ever. "Run that by me again," he said through clenched teeth.

This time Randy knew he had better clarify himself. "Chione's not really part of our team," he said. "She works on staff toward her degree. She's not legit like the rest of us."

Clifford choked on his water and glanced at the others. Seeing everyone stuck in exasperation, he asked, This again? It's your opinion that because we all carry degrees, you think she's not as learned as any of us?"

"Something like that."

Dr. Withers relaxed into his chair, expectantly watching Randy walk into the trap Clifford had baited. He signaled Chione with a hidden wave of his hand, begging for patience.

"Tell me," Clifford said. "Have you studied Egyptian history, Randy?"

"I took a crash course about Thebes from the library at the Institute," he said, looking proud.

Aaron swallowed quickly. "Do you speak Egyptian Arabic?"

"No."

"Understand any?" Aaron asked again before casually taking another bite of food.

"No."

"Do you read hieroglyphs?" Kendra asked, pointing at him with her fork.

"Doesn't everyone?" Randy asked.

"No, but do you?"

He had started to take a bit of food but paused. "Well, not much," Randy said, squirming and making no eye contact.

"Do you know any Egyptians or people who've lived here, other than us?" Clifford asked, taking another turn.

"No."

Dr. Withers stuck an index finger into the air claiming the moment. "Have you intuitively or otherwise contributed to the finding of any significant excavation?" That was his way of reiterating he would accept a find by any means. Especially since his career was nearing an end, and he longed to go out in a blaze of glory.

Finally, Randy caught on and did not answer the last question.

"Chione can answer an emphatic yes to everything," Clifford said, sucking his teeth, a mocking gesture toward Randy. "And more."

If ever Randy faced the fact that his opinions were too different to be accepted by the group as a whole, it was now.

The wind whipped up and sent rushing sounds down out of the hills. Bebe cringed. "Those noises, the sounds in the tomb," she said. "Sometimes I feel like we've all been swept up in the Ka."

"Caw?" Randy asked with a mocking grin. He stood like he would leave, knew he was not too popular, yet danced around, flapping his one good arm like a lame bird. "Caw, caw!"

"The Ka, Randy," Kendra said. "As in the spirit of the tomb."

"More hocus-pocus!"

"Haven't you felt at times that most of what we're all experiencing has already been choreographed?" Bebe asked, ignoring Randy and speaking to the rest of the group.

Randy threw his eating utensils onto his tray and tucked his cup between his chest and the splint. "Ha! If Chione has anything to do with it, we'll all be doing the dance of the dead." He left quickly carrying his tray to sit outside with the children.

Chione looked out to see the children being entertained by Irwin who was showing them how to use chopsticks. Their laughter was infectious. She sat quietly finishing her meal. Randy could be more a part of the group if he would stop giving everyone a reason to pounce on him. A little understanding of his deranged sense of humor would go a long way. On the other hand, she detested the way he always singled her out and belittled her. Maybe Randy, realizing now that no one cared to have him around, might begin to get the message.

Clifford finished his meal and surprisingly helped himself to a cup of Karkade. Seems everyone had started drinking the Egyptian beverage. When he realized everyone was watching him, he said, "I sat for a long time watching feluccas on the Nile."

"Did that bring you peace?" Marlowe asked.

"Rita loved to sail. We have this enlarged photograph hanging over the fireplace back in California. Rita's in it. Feluccas on the Nile with those lateen sails, some tattered and decaying, barely able to catch a breeze."

"Sounds like an idyllic setting," Chione said.

"Yeah, with the light of dusk showing through those shredded sails—"

"That's how you'll remember Rita? Sailing?"

"Maybe so. That was her favorite thing to do in Egypt, sailing in one of those fun boats as she called them." He fumbled with something that sparkled between his fingertips.

"Guess we should tell you," Dr. Withers said. "Some of those mourners got into your yurt to do their wailing."

"And?" Clifford asked.

"I sent Dakarai and a couple of the Guard down to get rid of 'em, but they wouldn't leave. Finally, I took Chione. She spoke with them and they left."

"You're saying they actually invaded Clifford's yurt?" Bebe asked. "Did you check afterwards to see if they took anything?"

Clifford only waved a hand to pass it off. He loved the Egyptians and when it came to them, he was one of the most allowing persons on the face of the earth.

"Nothing had been touched that we could tell," Chione said.

"Doesn't matter. Rita and I didn't bring anything of value, except these." He held up two rings on an extended pinkie.

"You kept Rita's wedding rings?" Kendra asked.

"Yeah," he said. "With grave robbers doing a landslide business, I took them off so people could see her in her coffin with no jewelry. Didn't want anyone digging...." He swallowed hard. "I want my Rita to rest in peace."

"You did the right thing," Chione said.

"Now I don't know what to do with them, where to hide them, and this." He produced a small plastic bag from his shirt pocket.

"Red hair?" Dr. Withers asked.

"I couldn't leave the rings with her. I gave her a lock of my hair," he said, gesturing sideways so some could see where he had cut a lock of his own hair to leave in her coffin.

"Then this," Kendra said, pointing to the plastic bag. "It's Rita's hair? You exchanged hair?"

Clifford nodded with eyes begging for understanding. The swatch of Rita's hair had been bound together at one end with braided shiny gold thread.

Tears began streaming down Marlowe's face as she examined the hair swatch.

"That's so Egyptian," Chione said. "You and Rita belong here." She tenderly squeezed his hand.

"You don't want to lose those," Kendra said, pointing to the jewelry.

"Or have them stolen from my tent," he said. "Not sure where I'll hide them."

"Here," Chione said, touching her shirtfront. She lifted the chain from around her neck and over her head bringing out the fat scarab pendant. Everyone leaned closer as she unfastened a tiny clasp and opened the back.

"Hey, it's like a box in there," Kendra said.

"I wear this night and day," Chione said. "It never leaves my body."

"Where did your mom and dad buy that?" Kendra asked. "It looks like real gold."

Kendra would know real gold, but this pendant being real was only wishful thinking. "From a scruffy street vendor," she said. "The guy claimed it was real, but it's probably gold-plated at best." She again signaled her offer to Clifford.

"You want to take care of these?" Clifford asked, holding the rings up again on his pinkie. The brilliant ruby heart surrounded by a bevy of baguette diamonds needed little direct light to flash their message. "I'd hate to lose them. They're part of my Rita."

"Well, that's a big responsibility, Clifford," Chione said. "But it's better than carrying them around in your pocket."

Clifford allowed her to remove the curl of hair from the plastic bag and place it into the back of the scarab along with the rings.

As they watched her replace the necklace over her head and stuff the scarab into her shirt, Dr. Withers turned to his wife who gulped down some pills. "What's that you're swallowing?" he asked.

"For my headaches," she said. "Vimble gave me a prescription."

"How long have you had headaches?" Chione asked.

Everyone looked to Marlowe remembering Rita had a headache for days before dying. What could be affecting them? No substantial evidence of a curse existed for those who believed in such possibilities, but they would have to monitor anyone who came down with any temple throbbing. Still, the mention of another person with a headache, and one death already, sent an unspoken ripple of anxiety through the team. Everyone was fully aware of the multiple deaths that occurred with Howard Carter's group.

"Only a short while," Marlowe said. "Vimble said it's probably the heat."

"Okay everyone, listen up," Dr. Withers said suddenly. "All the chambers have been emptied. The loose rubble and sand topside have been removed. None of our technology points in the direction of the Burial Chamber. Any suggestions?"

"Let's walk it," Bebe said.

"With magnifying glasses, if we have to," Chione said. "Kendra found one hidden doorway. We can find others."

They went back into the tomb, except for Clifford who went to catch up on inventory records. The entire tomb now stood bare and offered an intimidating invitation.

"What I don't understand," Kendra said, "is why we didn't find any insects, especially white ants in the food annex or gnawing at the wooden doors and furniture."

"The tomb is hollowed out of solid rock," Chione said. "No seams anywhere to come apart." Stranger still, the years had not created settling cracks.

"Too mysterious," Dr. Withers said. "Very few signs of aging. It's as if someone's cast a spell to make this tomb stand still in time."

"Oh-oh. Looks like Chione's gotten through to you," Chione said of herself, imitating Randy. Someone had to do something to break the tension. Aaron laughed the loudest.

By noon, no sign of a passageway, secret or otherwise, had been found.

"Okay, Chione, you're our strongest hope," Dr. Withers said with a half-smile, beginning to return to his usual self. "Tonight, you sleep in here again. Then we get to know exactly what you dream."

"As long as none of you becomes over eager and creeps in on me in the middle of the night," she said, joking. Then she realized Dr. Withers might insist again that Aaron stay with her all night and how that might look to the others. "I want to be completely alone."

"You know the rules," Dr. Withers said.

She felt cornered, frustrated, and did not wish to spend another night with Aaron. "I don't need to sleep in here," she said. "I'll just sit awhile like before."

"But you get so much more from dreaming, don't you?" Bebe asked.

"It's unpredictable," Chione said. "I don't have to be inside."

"I don't care what it takes," Dr. Withers said. "We can't be one day in this desert without measurable progress. The bad news is if we don't find the Burial Chamber soon, our funds will run out."

"No," Bebe said. "That's what Chione cautioned about. We could miss something. We can't let that happen."

"Then let's go topside and brainstorm," Dr. Withers said.

When they emerged into daylight, the throng of onlookers and visitors had thickened. People craning too far forward threatened to spill over the retaining wall into the pit. The sea of spectators spread down the hill to the beggars' camp. The noise level had risen.

Randy found them. "Just what we need," he said. "A bunch of those New Age phonies have joined the camp down the hill."

"As long as they don't bother us," Aaron said. "We have no say over who shows up."

"They've heard about Chione's supposed gifts. They're doing spells and incantations."

"How do you know that?" Bebe asked.

"I went down there," Randy said. "It's a circus. Even the local magicians and spellcasters have set up business selling potions and ripping off the tourists."

"You actually allowed yourself to get that close?" Kendra asked. "Maybe they put a hex on you."

"No one can do that to me," Randy said. He pulled back his chin and wagged his head side-to-side. "I don't cow-tow to the whims of fate."

Dakarai found them in the cook tent and politely delivered several rumpled fax messages that looked as if everyone else had seen them first. "Listen up," Dr. Withers said after perusing some pages. "Talisman Films wants to make a movie of our discovery."

"Hey, we'll all be stars," Kendra said.

Dr. Withers looked at the next message. "A company called Pyramid wants to film documentaries."

"Scratch those offers," Aaron said.

"How so?"

"We awarded those rights to Exploration Magazine. That's why they've been with us from day one."

"Bebe's book and papers along with Kenneth's photos take precedence," Chione said.

"Here, here," Bebe said.

Dr. Withers continued to read. "I can't believe half these offers."

"What else?"

"A historical novel," he said, going to the next page. "An offer to buy all our photographs."

"Ludicrous," Kenneth said.

"Someone wants to write about each of our lives," Dr. Withers said, mumbling as he read. Then he only glanced at the rest of the fax copies before passing them around.

"As much as we'd like to bring in additional funding," Chione said, "I don't care to be in a movie or a book, nor for anyone to represent me likewise."

"That's right," Clifford said. "I don't wish to be made a spectacle of either."

"As far as these offers," Aaron said, gesturing to the papers now scattered on the tabletop. "We're covered by the contracts we've already awarded." Anyone looking to cash in will conjure their plots, make their movies and write their books regardless of permission or lack of it.

"I agree," Chione said. "I suggest we limit our exposure and keep it professional."

"But to be in a real movie," Kendra said. "Think of the publicity."

Suddenly the tent flap lifted and in walked Royce with several men dragging dollies loaded with crates. His tailored khakis were crisp, yellow tone boots clean and his wide-brimmed hat sat cocked to one side over designer sunglasses. No one in the heat of a dig ever looked that perfect.

Kendra jumped up to greet her husband and threw her arms around his neck. He gave her a compliant peck on the cheek and then straightened. He carried several packages in both arms. "Gifts," he said. "From me and several families in Cairo." He sat one of the packages down and removed his sunglasses.

"The rule is that we don't accept this kind of help," Aaron said.

Royce handed Kendra one of the packages. She sat again and ripped into the box. He plopped other bundles onto the tabletop and instructed the men to open one of the larger crates.

"What do have we here?" Dr. Withers asked, standing to peer curiously into the box as Royce dug in.

"Computer supplies, film, chemicals and such," he said. "I looked at what you had before I left. You must be down to bare bones by now."

Royce's generosity took Dr. Withers by surprise. "I'll cut you a voucher," he said, raising an eyebrow. "However, you won't be able to collect till we're back in Califor—"

"I don't want reimbursement," Royce said. "You don't understand. I'm unable to contribute much here. All I do is enjoy the country, the people, and support my wife's effort."

"Which doesn't mean you must support the team."

"This is the least I can do," Royce said. "Please."

"Oh, yes," Kendra said. She held up a sparkling crystal perfume decanter and immediately broke the seal and passed the bottle back and forth under her nose.

Excited, Marlowe accepted the bottle and sniffed. "Wow," she said. "That's awfully sweet."

"Queen Nefertiti perfume," Kendra said. "I don't use it on my body. I leave the bottle sitting open in a draft and let it scent our house."

The decanter passed from hand to hand. Each person sniffed and gave a different reaction. Aaron fanned air toward himself over the bottle's opening. "It's not a bad scent when it just floats in the air," he said. "Light, sweet, provocative."

"Definitely Egyptian," Chione said, sensing the lavish gift of perfume only the beginning of things to come.

"As long as you're playing Santa on a camel in a time warp," Clifford said, "Where's mine?" He joked for the first time since returning.

"Actually," Royce said, "These four crates belong in the tech shack." He spoke a couple words in Egyptian and motioned that the first two dollies be backed out. Another was brought inside, with still others visible outside the flap. "I managed to find some very special delicacies," he said.

"It's not safe to eat local food," Bebe said.

"You can where I shop."

"Something new in our diets might be exciting," Marlowe said.

"I've rounded up some *bebaghanoug*, some *ful medames*, *farseekh*, and other local foods."

"Yum," Chione said as she leaned over the tabletop to see. "Eggplant paste is my favorite. Fava beans and dried fish too? I'm in heaven."

"All prepackaged," Royce said. "You'll also find some *tasty ta'miyya* and *falaafil* mixes. Some *tahini* too."

"Yum," Chione said again.

"And to wash it down, a couple cases of *Chateau d'Egypte rose'*, from the real good year you and Rita have difficulty finding, Clifford."

At the mention of the wine, Clifford's expression soured. "Rita," he said as his voice cracked. He and Rita would never enjoy their favorite delightful wine together again.

"You all look like you've lost your best friend," Royce said.

"We have," Aaron said, looking to Clifford whose elbows were on the table, hands clasped above his face with teary eyes cast downward. Aaron stood and reached over and put a hand on Clifford's shoulder.

"What's going on?" Royce asked.

Suddenly, Clifford bolted from the tent as tears poured out.

"Honey," Kendra said. "You had no way of knowing. I tried to reach you. I couldn't find you."

"What's happened?"

"Rita passed away."

"Wha-at?"

"Rita had heart failure and died in her sleep," Kendra said quietly. "Clifford buried her in Garden City."

"Oh, Clifford," Royce said, turning and hurrying after him. Royce's mannerisms said he would attempt to make things right for no other reason except that protocol demanded it. Quickly, he rushed back into the tent. He spotted his sunglasses, snatched them up and put them on, and left again. Maybe he could only console someone if they could not see his eyes. Chione remembered the first time she met Royce. He had smiled with his mouth, but his steely blue eyes expressed nothing. He'd probably never get crow's feet.

"Well, it's come to this," Bebe said. "We haven't located the Burial Chamber, but we've buried a friend."

"We have thieves in our midst," Aaron said. "And strangers and a spouse bearing gifts."

"We might run out of funds earlier than anticipated and find ourselves hoping for donations to sustain us," Bebe said.

"And my husband goes to Cairo for a new laptop and disappears for over a week."

"A very sad state of affairs overall," Dr. Withers said, shaking his head.

"Well, he did bring me this," Kendra said, smiling over the crystal decanter. "He does this all the time, just walks in and amazes me."

Bebe rolled her eyes and asked no one in particular, "Doesn't it make you wonder why?"

24

Kenneth enjoyed himself. He with his cameras was never seen too long in one location. No one would guess he had a back injury. The only tell-tale sign was when he came to the cook tent on the pretext of having a cool drink even though he carried a hip flask. Now he elevated his feet on another chair and moaned in relief as he rested and stretched out his spine. Then he leaned sideways and peered out the fly. "Tour groups are Randy's speed," he said with a smirk.

"I see he's living up to his reputation," Clifford said.

"How's that?"

"He's always on a break, always got a drink in a hand," Clifford said.

"Yeah, and his bone in the other," Kenneth said.

"Hey, keep it clean, you guys," Chione said. "If you need something to occupy your time, we still have artifacts to inventory."

"Then outa' here they go," Clifford said. A few minutes later, he leaned close as if to say something in secret but everyone knew Kenneth to be trustworthy, and he leaned close too. Clifford whispered, "What do you intuit from Sterling's meeting with Royce and those other people?"

"Haven't tried to intuit," Chione said. "My best guess is they want a piece of the action."

"Royce may be touting his own importance?"

"Could be. Let's not speculate, okay?"

"Okay, I'll give him the benefit of the doubt," Clifford said. The expression on his face said that he knew something was brewing; something no one would appreciate. He leaned close again and in his teasing way whispered, "How's it going with you and Aaron?"

Coming from Clifford, that was a joke. Chione smiled. "Pretty smooth, considering he knows I don't like working this closely with him."

"Smooth, huh? Too bad," Kenneth said. He flinched affectedly and shifted his back in the chair. "No pain, no gain."

"Don't you play matchmaker too," she said, punching him lightly on the shoulder.

"Would I do that?" Kenneth asked. He rose, poured the water from his flask into the makeshift sink and, surprising everyone, topped off his flask with cool Karkade and left smiling.

"I hear you two are going into the Underworld again this evening," Clifford said.

"I wish either Marlowe or I could convince Dr. Withers his expectations are creating unnecessary pressure."

"On you?"

"To perform. It's as if I'm the only one expected to come up with answers. Dr. Withers expects me to tell him every detail of my dreams and hunches." Not that she would.

"Maybe he thinks he can glean something from the details."

"Maybe, but that's about it for my complaining," Chione said. "Thanks for the ear."

"What will you do?" His concern always seemed fatherly.

"Prove myself," she said quietly.

No one spoke much as they worked. Even the local help remained somber, in empathy with Clifford's mourning, waiting for a cue from him that he was coping. Clifford did not joke much now, only made the effort to be light, which fell flat or came out sounding sarcastic without his silly grin to exaggerate his theatrical wit. Mostly, he sat with elbows folded on the table or workbench, staring unblinking through the fly.

Just before noon, Dr. Withers called another meeting and excused the rest of the help for an early lunch.

"Wonder what's so important he wants only team members present," Chione said.

"Are you beginning to feel it?" Aaron asked, taking a seat opposite her. An unsettled change of atmosphere due to things having turned negative clouded everyone's enthusiasm. What began as one of the world's most spectacular events had taken a downturn.

"You mean because of Rita's passing?" Clifford asked.

"Not Rita but the thefts, our diminishing budget, Royce's—"

"Let's not dwell on that," Chione said. "If things have gotten that low, they'll only get better, right?"

Dr. Withers made another of his hurried entrances. "Okay, everyone, listen up." Clifford scooted over. Dr. Withers sat down and tore off pages of a scratch pad filled with crosshatches. "Two of the Institute's Directors, patrons of the CIA's Archaeological Trust, will be arriving in about three weeks. With their wives."

"Why not?" Clifford asked. "They can write it off."

Bebe had arrived behind Dr. Withers. "You're also a patron of the Trust, aren't you?" she asked.

"A backer, yes. They contributed some." He cleared his throat, glanced at notes over bifocals and smiled that silly grin again. "I do like having control."

"Actually," Chione said. "Some of the patrons should have been here from day one."

"Yeah," Clifford said. "Share in the dirty work."

"Now, now," Dr. Withers said. "We'll be as pleasant to them as possible. They are, after all, the ones who helped make our Institute and this expedition possible."

"Which ones?" Aaron asked.

"Vice President and Director, Parker Philips."

Kendra groaned. "Not Carmelita too," she said, rolling her eyes. "This should prove interesting. And?"

"Vice President and Director of Academic Planning, Burton Forbes, with his wife, Gracie," Dr. Withers said. "This visit does add to our problems, however." He looked tired. "More people in addition to all the rest. We're being inundated, slowed down by tour groups and especially by other archaeologists, of all people."

The team and crews had to work around areas cordoned off for various groups. Most were respected people in the field of archaeology and everyone needed to keep that foremost in mind.

"So how many more important people are we going to allow to slow us down?" Bebe asked.

"We're obligated to a few," Dr. Withers said. He waved a pencil in the air. "The Board of Directors have asked us to hold off on removal of any more relics until Forbes and Philips arrive."

"Everything's out so far," Kendra said.

"Exactly," Dr. Withers said. "They want to be here when we crack the Burial Chamber. Also, somebody remind me to get Paki Rashad back from Cairo for the big event."

"Do the directors know we're having difficulty finding access?" Aaron asked.

"All they know is that we've emptied out all the relics so far and our time is taken up with cataloging, packing and...." He waved off the rest of the sentence. He paused and then added, "Let me get to the real reason I called this meeting. Your dear husband, Kendra," he said without smiling, "has located an evidently wealthy conglomerate from Cairo who have offered themselves as benefactors for the balance of the dig."

Before anyone could comment, Clifford said, "That could be worse than working with those danged slow college students." He shook his head sharply. "So what's in it for them?"

"Now, don't jump the gun," Dr. Withers said, studying the notes again. "Your friends, the Yago family?" he asked, again looking to Kendra.

"Who?"

"The Yagos. Know them?"

"Can't say I do."

"Well, your industrious husband has turned up this group of philanthropists willing to fund the balance of our dig. For a price."

Clifford grunted. "What philanthropists?"

"I don't know the Yagos," Kendra said. "What have you learned about them? Why are they stepping in now?"

"According to Royce, the Yagos are from Spain, but many of their international team are from various other countries. Portugal, Africa—."

"Gypsies!" Clifford said. "I know of no such group."

"Wait, let me finish," Dr. Withers said. "This group procures Egyptian artifacts which are added to the relatively small amount of relics they've already acquired."

"What for?" Bebe asked.

"Evidently the Yagos, and people of similar affluence from other countries, have united to procure artifacts in order to enhance their respective country's stature in the art world."

"Again," Clifford said. "What's in it for the Yagos?"

"Well, let's just back up a little," Dr. Withers said, motioning for Clifford's patience. "Our deal with Egypt is that we receive custody of one-half of all treasures of the tomb if we open the entire tomb. Once they've been exhibited in our neck of the woods...." He stuck a finger into the air. "And once we've recouped our expenses, maybe made a little profit, we rotate with the other half of the artifacts that Egypt holds from this dig."

"Egypt owns them all," Aaron said, recapitulating Dr. Withers' point.

"Here, here," Clifford said.

Aaron leaned forward. "And we've yet to find the Burial Chamber."

"Exactly," Dr. Withers said. "Without the Burial Chamber's holdings, we stand to receive zilch for our efforts."

"Nothing at all?"

"What amounts to nothing," Dr. Withers said. "A few small statues, if we're lucky."

This was added pressure on top of the urgency to identify the mummy entombed because the woman's life and a Pharaoh's seemed most assuredly intertwined. The prediction was that the find would make history and Chione felt no one but the CIA had the right to claim it. "What you're saying," she asked, "is that if our funds run out, someone else will acquire the dig and benefit in our place?"

"Reap all the goodies, yes."

"Would seem we almost have to work a deal with the Yagos?" Aaron asked.

Clifford grunted again. "I don't like it," he said. "How much does this do-gooder philanthropic group hope to gain for their generosity?"

The wind began to howl mournfully. The tent canvas billowed and snapped.

Chione nudged Aaron's foot under the table and motioned in Kendra's direction with her eyes. Kendra had withdrawn from the conversation and begun pouting.

"That's what I'm trying to describe," Dr. Withers said. "Let's take this slowly. I've only just heard this myself. My intention is to keep all of you apprised of our options. We'll discuss it again in a week or so if things don't turn around."

"Okay, let's hear it," Bebe said.

Dr. Withers reiterated the facts. Their intention from the beginning was to crack that rock and retrieve the artifacts to be deposited with the Madu Museum where Clifford was to remain. After they departed for California, the Restoration Society folks would do the housekeeping in the tomb. A few short weeks in duration. What they had not counted on was the delay at finding the Burial Chamber.

"You mean we hadn't planned to be here ten years like Howard Carter?" Clifford asked, an unexpected effort at being facetious.

"Carter would have been fortunate indeed to have the technology we have at our disposal," Aaron said.

Kendra chimed in. "I'll bet old Carter's rolling over in his...." Suddenly she gasped and covered her mouth. Her timing was off.

"What kind of margin do we have?" Bebe asked.

"Ten weeks more if we stretch it and no dollars beyond."

Before anyone left California, Chione received psychic messages of the team staying longer. In fact, she had not seen the team winding down to completion but, instead, having greater amounts of work ahead. Kendra once commented that had they located the Burial Chamber as easily as the other rooms, they could have been home for Christmas. Chione knew that was not the way things would be. "What's the bottom line with this Yago family?" she asked.

"They'll fund us as long as we need to stay."

Clifford grabbed the edge of the table and stiffened. "For that, we forfeit what?"

"One half of our share of the take."

"One half?" Clifford asked. He stood and took a turn pacing and thinking. "That's one-quarter of all the wealth, providing the Egyptian government and the Madu people are in agreement and still allow us our fifty percent." He continued to pace. "What artifacts that group gets custody of the world will never see again. Mark my word!"

"Why wouldn't they allow us our fifty percent?" Bebe asked.

"With new players, it's a whole new ball game," Aaron said.

"Essentially, yes," Dr. Withers said. "We'd have to re-negotiate our contract."

"And stand to lose our position for half of everything?" Bebe asked.

"Yes," Dr. Withers said. He did not look like he thought much of the idea at all. With the Yagos providing major funding, they could inherit rights over the CIA. Then, if they were inclined to share less than one quarter, the CIA would end up with practically nothing. Or lose everything if the team could not find the Burial Chamber without help.

"Then the Yago team could replace us a hundred percent and, for sure, we go home empty-handed." Dr. Withers said.

"No!" Clifford said.

Dr. Withers was to meet with the CIA's Board of Directors via a conference call if the telephone connections would fortunately hold. He said he'd have to run over to Luxor for better connections. If they thought no other alternatives existed, he would try to work with the

Yago family. Only then would he reveal their plight to the Egyptian government and try to arrange a few favors, hopefully, some that did not include the Yagos.

"We could still lose," Clifford said, shaking his head in defiance. "There must be something I can do through my contacts."

25

Chione sensed Clifford's mind working. Humor he had, but when it came right down to the crunch, if anyone could pull something off, Clifford would be the one.

"We've got to find that Burial Chamber in quick order," Bebe said.

Everyone looked to Chione. She frowned, tensed.

Aaron leaned over and peered out the fly. "Randy should have been in on this," he said.

"Damn him," Dr. Withers said. Then he sighed heavily. "Sorry folks. Guess my nerves are on edge. Where is that—?"

"Wow, sorry I'm late," Randy said, rushing into the tent. "Those kids. You just don't know how much time they—"

"Not now, Randy," Dr. Withers said. "We've got more serious issues at hand."

"Anything I should know?"

Quick glances among the rest of the group silently voiced disgust.

"Not really," Clifford said.

"What about some of those other offers?" Aaron asked. "The ones that came by fax from bigger universities? Couldn't we—"

"All we need is for word to get out that we're facing financial crisis," Clifford said, sighing out of frustration. "The money people would gobble us up. We'd be powerless."

"Our original grantors can't cough up a little more?" Bebe asked.

The wind worsened. The tent continued to billow and snap. Workers assigned to maintain the grounds scrambled. One of the yurts had partially come loose in a gust. Most certainly now, everyone would give up on trying to control the layers of dust that coated everything from the day the first wind blew. Use of any laptops would have to be done in the tech shack.

"I don't want to ask them yet," Dr. Withers said. "Now that we've collected valuable artifacts, the CIA might be able to secure a bank loan."

If they knew for sure which artifacts would be assigned to the CIA, they might be used as collateral.

"A bank loan might be too costly," Clifford said. "Considering the artifacts will eventually be returned to Egypt."

"How costly?" Bebe asked.

"Well, let's just say we got a sizeable loan," Dr. Withers said. He paused momentarily, shaking an index finger in the air. "Our little privately held institute struggles every year to collect enough donations, grants, and work-study tuition to keep our doors open. With a sizeable bank loan, we'd have to make monthly payments and maybe a huge balloon payment in a year or so. What funds would normally be spent on maintaining our facility would then be diverted to repay the loan. I don't need to explain what that means."

Chione studied Dr. Withers as he spoke, heard a ring of desperation each time he mentioned bringing someone into the endeavor. Had the others noticed? Did they understand how important this last expedition was for him, that it would solidify his private institute in the community, the country, and maybe the world?

"The Institute would suffer temporarily," Aaron said. "We'd have our exhibits to attract viewers from the paying public."

"We'd acquire grants for the maintenance of our exhibits," Clifford said. "We could even take the show on the road."

"Too expensive," Aaron said. "Unless exhibitors would be willing to pay to bring the show to their cities and states."

"Do you hear yourselves?" Dr. Withers asked. "All these things are possible, but they're all speculation about how we might be able to receive future monies to repay a loan we don't want in the first place."

"It saves having the Yagos take over," Kendra said through clenched teeth.

"If we can't open the Burial Chamber till the directors arrive," Aaron said, "I suggest you and I, Dr. Withers, work on cost analysis and projection for a bank loan. Maybe we could get Royce's expertise in on this."

"Not Royce," Kendra said adamantly. "If Royce brought the Yagos in on this, you can bet there's something in it for him too. I doubt he'd make your cost analysis come out in your favor." Kendra could not have gotten everyone's attention more had she spread a layer of ice over everyone, yet she continued to stare at the tabletop.

Finally, Aaron reached across the table and touched her arm. "Maybe we can discuss a deal with the Yagos and still come out on top," he said. "Then we can run it by the Board of Directors." He turned to Dr. Withers. "After all, you and they have final say."

They needed to take care not to lose their position. If they sought loans or public grants—now that their discovery by paranormal means had been vindicated—they could be throwing the whole ball of preservative wax up for grabs.

"An awful lot of people want a piece of us now," Aaron said, looking smug. "They even want Chione on their team."

"Fat chance," she said.

"It's like this," Dr. Withers said. "We're not out of money yet. Granted, we are cutting our budget awfully close. We've had unforeseen events occur which had not been planned for in our cost projections."

"Medical bills and trips to Cairo," Clifford said, glancing toward Randy. Then he winced and said, "Trips for a funeral."

Dr. Withers waved a hand silencing Clifford. "No one blames anyone for unexpected events. No one should feel responsible. Truth is," he said. "We're not down to the quick. You all need to know where we stand. It's important we cover our bases, so we're the ones who finish this expedition."

"I say we analyze some of those other offers you say you got," Randy said.

Clifford moaned.

"That's already been addressed," Bebe said angrily. "Maybe you should have been on time."

"Randy," Aaron said slowly. "Everyone offering financial aid wants a piece of the action in return. A huge piece."

"I haven't seen the offers," Randy said, shrugging.

"Trust our leader," Clifford said. "If he's singled out the best of the lot, we back him."

Dr. Withers had seemed more than frustrated over the last few days. Though he tried to sound positive, the Yago's offer did not do much to elevate his morale. Randy could not say anything more and stared from behind a peevish grin. Kendra again folded her arms across her chest and continued to stare at the tabletop.

After Dr. Withers and Aaron left and Randy scooted out to be with the children, Clifford said, "Randy doesn't seem like one of us anymore."

"Did he ever?" Bebe asked. "A few days ago, I heard Dr. Withers tell him to get his act together and not to open his mouth unless he could contribute something."

"Still, every time he parts his lips," Aaron said. "In goes a boot."

A couple of hours after lunch, the others went back to work. Chione and Clifford were left at the table with Kendra who picked at her meal. Suddenly, she asked, "What's all the hush-hush talk about, Clifford? Chione?"

"Just reminiscing," Clifford said quickly.

Kendra smiled weakly from across the table. "We're all here for you, Clifford," she said. She choked back tears. "I hope you're all here for me." Then she began to sob.

"Kendra?" Chione asked, scooting over to her. "What's going on?"

"I've got to leave," Clifford said. "Everything and everything's gone rotten." He picked up his water and hurried out, snapping the tent flap behind himself.

"Did you see her, Chione?" Kendra asked.

"Who?"

"That woman and those guys she came with." Kendra dabbed at her eyes.

"Who are you talking about?"

"She's beautiful," Kendra said. "Every time I see Royce, he's with her and her entourage." Kendra pulled her to stand beside the flap, and they discreetly peered out. "Look, there she is. She just parades back and forth like she's waiting for him."

A dark-haired woman impeccably groomed, and wearing designer khaki clothing much too clean for the desert, stood out at the front of the crowd. She kept an umbrella trained between her and the sun no matter which direction she paced. She constantly twirled the thing as if relieving impatience. When she turned in their direction, her smooth milky white complexion and dark hair made her stand out even more.

"You're imagining things," Chione said. "She's just another curious pedestrian."

"No, she's not. Why would she stay?"

"Because all these people never see enough. They hang around waiting for a glimpse of one last artifact, one more relic of the Ancients. It's a fever."

"Why would Royce be spending so much time with her?" She began to cry again.

"You're imagining things."

"Because she's beautiful," Kendra said, sighing heavily.

"You're great looking too, Kendra," Chione said, trying to offer comfort. "And you just happen to be his wife. His slightly jealous wife, however."

"Now I know where he's been going when he goes off on his own," she said. "He does it all the time. How is it she turned up just when he came back from Cairo?"

Kendra had worked herself up, probably imagining things. But Royce did have frequent absences from camp. "Kendra, leave it alone," Chione said.

"Why doesn't he spend time elsewhere?" she asked. She sighed again. Her lips pouted. "Why is he so attentive to her?"

"Where would you have him go? Back home alone till you finish work here? Or to stay in Cairo?"

In a short while, Dr. Withers called yet another meeting, a sign that said things may be fraying at the seams. With work almost at a standstill, being called together in the cook tent was getting to be routine. As he waited for the group to settle down, he sat with an elbow on the table, fingertips rubbing his forehead, studying notes, composing his thoughts. Finally, he said, "We're going to suspend activities this afternoon. The mummies are out of here, so there's no worry about decay. We can post additional guards at Inventory. We've got to find that Burial Chamber."

"Yes, extra guards, please," Chione said. "The harp, the lyre and the double flute we found behind the golden statue? None of that stuff's packaged yet." They were, perhaps, in the best condition of any found throughout history.

"They'll be safe," Clifford said.

"Then let's get back to the exciting part," Bebe said. "The search."

"Marlowe's coming inside," Dr. Withers said. "I don't like the feel of this wind. She needs to get out of the blowing sand."

"And the husbands?" Bebe asked.

Clifford and Kenneth volunteered to stay topside with the guards, to keep an eye on things. Bebe cast a dubious glance in Kendra's direction. Was Bebe really a busybody, or could she actually see things happening in relationships that most people shrugged off?

"What if we haven't found the Burial Chamber by the time the directors arrive?" Kendra asked.

"They know it's the next phase. We'll just say the truth, that we haven't found it," Dr. Withers said. "Geez, we've got to find it though, in the next three weeks. Something we won't do is let on that we're up against a brick wall."

"Make that a granite wall," Clifford said, smiling suddenly.

"Our visitors will spend time at the Museum first, looking over our relics."

Once inside the Pillared Hall with the area more brilliantly lighted, each member of the team chose sections of the walls to re-examine. Nothing was found. Then each person rotated places to try to find something the other person might have missed. In some places, they went so far as to touch the walls, making sure not to damage the art, but to run fingertips along grooves, similar to the ones out in the passageway that hid the entrance of the Second Chamber.

Aaron inched his way toward Chione working the south wall. He spoke in low tones. "You intuit from touching, right?"

"Sometimes," Chione said, tilting her head back, visually following a painted line upwards.

"C'mon. You get vibes off everything you touch. What about now?"

"Not everything, Aaron. Don't go spreading that around."

"Chione, every time you pick up an object or touch a relic, I watch your face. I can tell."

"I'm telling you, I'm getting nothing from this wall," she said. She wished everyone would accept that she was not his or her personal genie who had suddenly popped out of a bottle.

"Hear anything recently?"

"No."

"Jeez," he said. "Getting anything out of you is as difficult as finding the next passage."

She had to smile. How well she knew him. "What is it you really want to know?"

He smiled weakly. "Had any more dreams?"

"Have you?"

Her throwing the question back at him took him by surprise. He hesitated, a sure sign he wanted to disclose something and not sound foolish. Especially since he had one or more visions similar to her recent nocturnal visitations.

He began to move away. "I hope you find—"

"Aaron," she said, grabbing his arm. "I'm sorry. This evening, can we compare notes?"

He tried to smile. "Sure, Chione," he said. "Sure."

Dakarai and Masud had been talking with the engineers. They suggested lighting be moved about and shadows examined. Angles of the walls were measured in case the disguised block sealing the Burial Chamber might lean slightly out of alignment. The entire chamber was measured from corner to corner, ceiling to floor and wall to wall. The Egyptians had, once again, proven themselves master builders. The chamber had been hewn out of one gigantic mountain of rock. An hour passed, then another. The magnetometer and other sensors were useless since the Pillared Hall was encased in solid stone.

Next, they began the same meticulous inspection of each of the three annexes but to no avail. No hidden doorways or passages existed behind where all those artifacts and foodstuffs had been heaped. Only solid stone walls.

26

Eating a nutritious breakfast was the way Dr. Withers liked to start the group functioning each day. Too many interruptions had already occurred in the few weeks since their arrival. With everyone finally back in camp, they could resume the routine of an early morning meal and discussion of the day's agenda. Chione felt too agitated to eat much. Her appetite fluctuated. One day she would be ravenously hungry; too hot, sticky and tired to eat the next.

She glanced outside the tent. Onlookers gathered again but the group was sparser. Blowing sand kept many away. Those who dared to stay pitched lean-tos or stretched sheets of fabric on sticks to divert the gritty air. The dry earth was so stirred up, even when the wind withdrew between gusts, sand and dust hung suspended, thick as arid soup. The laborers ate breakfast inside their sleeping tents instead of out in the open, as was the habit of many. Siti and her crew of local women and girls scurried back and forth, heads and faces protected by colorful wimples, supplying occupants of each tent with necessities.

"Let's eat," Dr. Withers said.

"Thank goodness the paparazzi disappear when sand whips up," Bebe said.

"They might come inside, sit to eat," Yafeu said, meaning that he would not have been surprised if some had taken the liberty to do so. He began to serve breakfast. "I like cook this American food," he said in broken English. He danced his way around the tables like a ballerina carrying plates. Being gay in the Arabic world was forbidden. Outside the cook tent, he seemed just another Egyptian man going about his chores. Yafeu presently worked with Americans and easily adapted his ways like a polished actor. He needed no coaching at his duties. He was bold, slightly arrogant, and dared to be different. One had to understand the man was not being disrespectful of his own people, but no one ever heard him address another person in the local tradition by including a title like O Professor or O Chief Engineer.

"Have you eaten our food?" Kendra asked.

"Yes, but no taste," he said, smiling, all teeth. "I must add spice."

Aaron took advantage of Yafeu's ability to attract attention and leaned over to Chione and spoke in whispers. "Did you ever explain Hapi's mud to our illustrious leader?"

"No," she said, also whispering. "He never asked."

"You've got to put his mind at ease, don't you think?"

"If he's curious enough to ask, we'll just insist my face must have been dirty from the dust. Then I perspired and that was that."

"He won't buy it."

"He'll have to," she said. "It's all we've got."

"We?" he asked.

"Yes," she said, smiling. "Like I said, I'm in this over my head. I need backup."

"You'll explain?" Aaron asked.

"Not if he doesn't ask first. He's too preoccupied with cash flow right now."

"He'll catch up to it. Remember, I told you so."

"You know? Underneath it all, Dr. Withers is just as curious as you are," Chione said. "He just hasn't made enough time in his life to learn."

That evening Aaron cornered her again. "I saw you having a talk with the boss."

"Marlowe must have convinced him to let happen what may," she said. "I think he'd be willing to, just, so we can find the Burial Chamber."

They sat in silence. Nothing much happened during the day except in the inventory tent. Finally, the artifacts had to be covered with blue nylon tarps and battened down securely because the sand was finding its way inside the tents. Because of the worsening of the wind and grit, a mud brick hut was hurriedly being built over the hydraulic equipment atop the gaping portcullis shaft. In their haste, some of the workers included camel dung in the mud mix. It was hoped once the block wall dried the stench would lighten. The pungent odor didn't seem to bother the portcullis gatekeepers, however. The door at the original entrance to the tomb remained closed. Work was at a standstill.

With dinner finished, it was time to think about another night's sleep. Or another evening of meditation. Suddenly Chione felt compelled and reached across the table and squeezed Aaron's hand and smiled. His look asked, what was that all about? Lately, she had felt flirtatious before being able to restrain herself. Something seemed to be coaxing her to renew the friendship. Aaron kept his distance. Chione knew he was not about to offer his heart only to have it wrung out again. At least, not until she made gestures substantially more significant. He acted a bit standoffish, but she had only herself to thank for that. At contradictory times, he seemed to enjoy the exchanges.

Clifford came sauntering into the cook tent, followed by Bebe and Kenneth. Clifford unwound his head wrap, dropped it into a chair, and poured a round of coffee. Bebe removed her headscarf and primped. Kenneth sat down and propped his feet up on a nearby chair. He groaned, but it sounded more like out of habit than from any pain in his back. He picked up Bebe's scarf and brought it to his face. "You smell like an Egyptian woman," he said.

That took everyone by surprise.

Bebe turned and gave him a serious sideways look. "How would you know what an Egyptian woman smells like?"

"Like the smells inside the tomb," he said, defending himself.

No one said a word, wouldn't even look around. Ripples traipsed over Chione's arms. Kenneth smelled women's odors inside the tomb?

Then Clifford said, "The winds are going to worsen."

"Where'd you hear that?" Chione asked.

"Sterling told me. He wants us all to sleep down under tonight."

"You don't mean in the tomb?" Bebe looked aghast.

"Yep, in the Underworld," Clifford said casually. He could adjust to any change. "All of our team. Except Royce."

"Is Kendra staying out?"

"Dunno. Royce is comfortable with the locals, doesn't want to go down under."

"Isn't that kind of dangerous?" Chione asked. "With all the thefts, and everyone's belongings left out here?"

"At this point, I'd be more worried about the cats and dogs," Clifford said, casting a sideways glance in Bebe's direction. "Or the jackals." Clifford was beginning to be Clifford again.

Bebe gasped. "Jackals? I thought they wouldn't bother us?"

Clifford snickered. "That camp down there is what's attracting them out of the hills."

Bebe recovered after Kenneth reassuringly squeezed her shoulders. "Well, the only thing of value I brought," she said, "is on my finger." Kenneth kissed her cheek.

Chione touched her golden amulet through her shirtfront. "This necklace, which I won't remove, and the picture of my parents are all I brought," she said. "With the squad of Egyptian Police you brought in, Clifford, no one's going to risk getting shot for a few of our goodies."

"Had to bring 'em," Clifford said. "Somehow I don't trust that other bunch of guys in gallibayas protecting us from more of the same."

"You implying the local cops are crooked?" Bebe asked.

"Not necessarily," Clifford said. "But it is good to see a squad of uniformed officers around. Besides, the Guard unit wasn't able to control the paparazzi."

"I suppose the engineers and techs are staying topside too," Chione said. "What about Ginny??

"The rest are going to rough it," Clifford said. "Too much camera equipment to leave unattended." They're going to try to bed down in the tech shack if they can all fit."

"They're a rugged bunch anyway," Bebe said.

Kenneth commented that Dr. Withers asked the locals about building some shacks. "With the big guys coming," he said. "They'll need to get their wives out of the blowing sand."

Clifford reported that the college students were staying at a small hotel near Dier el-Bahri and would not be returning until restoration of the tomb began. "Good deal," he said, rubbing his hands together. "Those kids aren't learned enough to work at our speed." He went on to say that the media people had banded together and found various hotels in Karnak and Luxor. Some found rooms down on the flats in the Theban village.

"Those journalists have kept busy documenting anything that moved," Bebe said.

Kenneth spent time with them and related that they really knew how to build a story through their craft. They had documented the entire area. Plus, they wrote some fantastic articles, not just about the team, but of the local culture and history as well.

"Aha," Aaron said. "That's what's attracting all this attention to our dig."

"How do you figure?"

"I'm sure the journalists aren't saving up material for the trip home. Anything that happens today is front page news across the world tomorrow."

The wind came up again, billowing and snapping the tent canvas. Sand and dust blew in under the bottom edges. Hands immediately covered the tops of drinking cups. The continual, ominous howling of the wind was nerve-wracking. Aaron caught himself again doodling, drawing grids on a notepad. He ripped off the page, balled it up, and aimed for the wastebasket.

"Right now, all our work is topside," Clifford said. He kept the top of his mug covered as he sipped. "Guess we can't function in the blowing sand, though."

"How long's this storm supposed to last?" Bebe asked.

"No one knows," Clifford said. "This is highly unusual weather. Like a *Khamsin* wind."

"Doesn't that usually happen in April and May," Aaron asked.

"It's called *the wind of fifty days*," Clifford said. "Dunno why we're being hit with it in November."

"Pray it doesn't last fifty days," Aaron said as he rolled his eyes.

"Part of Randy's curse?" Kenneth asked, curling up a lip.

Later, as sleeping pallets were being lowered into the passageway, there was much confusion about who would sleep where. Finally, it was decided the women would sleep in the First Chamber. The men would remain in the passageway near the opened shaft. The usual guards would sleep in the smelly hut at the top. The ominous bell could be clanked in case anyone needed to climb out during the night to use the restroom. Slightly embarrassing, however, that in having to clang the bell, they would be announcing to everyone across the hillock that they were headed for the toilets.

"Strange," Clifford said after all had joked about the bell. "I've never seen Randy make one trip out back. Maybe that's his problem. He never has to go."

"Maybe he pisses in his footers," Kenneth said.

Chione walked away. At times, those two could be a disgusting mix.

27

Randy continued to sleep in the children's camp and that was fine. The children would be leaving in a couple of days. Living down under with Randy would present a challenge. Hopefully, the blowing sands would subside as quickly as they began.

Inside the tomb, as a warning they wished not to be bothered, Aaron said, "Chione and I will be doing our meditation thing in the Pillared Hall." The others already knew that and simply went about tending to his or her bed.

Kendra had not made it down under.

Later, as they sat facing north, Chione said, "I wonder what will happen if any of them hear the mournful sounds."

Aaron chuckled. "Guess it would be a sleepless night for some."

Aaron seemed a bit polite. She knew he did not wish her to worry about what might happen while they were entranced. Lately, she began to realize his intentions were nothing but honorable. He had always been that way. Why had she ever doubted him? She relaxed with those thoughts on her mind and soon slipped into an altered state right there in Aaron's presence. A scene appeared like the light of dawn approaching on fast forward.

Towering monolithic columns like sentries guarded a massive palace. Eucalyptus trees shaded and scented the courtyard. Date palms heavy with ripening clusters of fruit. Orchards of mango, orange, and lemon extended far. Furrowed fields supported bersim, sorghum, fuul and rice. Everywhere, an abundance of crops.

It was an Egyptian summer with crops growing in open fields. In other seasons bersim and sorghum for feeding the stock, and beans for their own consumption, would be growing in the orchards beneath the date palms. Supplies of food in different stages of growth, harvesting, and storage were everywhere. The hot sun beat down. God Aten floated high above, showering her with special blessings.

The familiar, small elegant stone house of Umi, the clothier, stood near the palace. Mud brick workers' shacks and huts stood in clusters farther away. Shops of sandal makers, weavers and jewelers bordered a busy market area.

Again, that peculiar, all-encompassing feeling washed over Chione and made her senses reel. "Where are we?" she asked, speaking in the old tongue. She looked at the man and saw Aaron!

"Akhetaten," he said in that same language. They walked side by side.

Their voices in casual conversation rang strangely sweet, rich with tones of native language. She looked at him again. His face was the same, but his voice had been astoundingly different. Then she realized he had not spoken. His thoughts had telepathically reached her mind and she had answered him the same way.

"Is this what you've seen in your visions?" he asked mentally.

"I've been calling to you," she said, lips unmoving except to smile. "There is much to be done."

"Aaron?" she said aloud. Now they were both cognizant of something phenomenal taking place.

"Remember Akhetaten?" he asked.

Chione did not feel like herself, but someone else. "Where we met? At Akhenaten's palace?" She smiled just for him. "We were so young."

Many people strode about, a few richly clad. Most were poor and near naked and bowed low as they passed.

Wispy memories faded in and out. All the buildings seemed ancient, yet familiar. Stone and marble structures of grand prominence towered nearby. She felt eager to see her family and wanted to rush, and then realized she was halfway around the world from home.

The smells and noises, animal calls, voices, and language rang familiar. The more she concentrated on perceiving details, the more they faded. When she relaxed, they came in with clarity and again, she felt herself being drawn into something for which she had no understanding or rationale. Strangely, she was filled with a sense of returning home after a pathetically long absence.

Chione had not felt her feet trodding the inlaid stone path as they moved along. Instead, she floated, like in a dream, and Aaron was with her. That made it his dream too. A rush of elation, as well as frustration, engulfed her as she lost track of the vision. She wanted to be home. The moment the visuals faded, she realized she was having a lucid dream, consciousness and rationale intermingling. She struggled to stay calm and not disrupt the flow of events. "This is Akhetaten—our home!" her mind screamed.

"We have important matters to attend," his deep voice said.

When she tried to focus on the lips through which that wonderful voice flowed, the image of his face faded in and out. Vertigo overtook her. She felt drunk. "More," she said. Then someone nudged her shoulder.

"Chione," the voice said softly. It was not that same low voice but another that also rang true in her heart.

"Home," she said aloud.

"Chione," the whispering voice demanded. "Chione!"

She opened her eyes and saw Aaron in the dimmed light of the Pillared Hall. "Akhetaten," she said.

"Chione," he said quietly. "You're making too much noise. Someone will come to find out what's going on."

"I-I spoke?"

"Sh-h," he said again. "Sound echoes off these stone walls."

She glanced around, suddenly cognizant of where they sat. Aaron's wonderful face and reassuring smile were the only things that kept her from crying out for Akhetaten. "I-I guess I was dreaming."

He studied her. "You're disoriented," he said. He seemed so attentive.

"Were you dreaming too? Was I in your dream?"

"Yes, you were, and no, I wasn't dreaming."

"Was I sleeping?"

"Can you usually sit up unsupported while you sleep?"

"I'm sure I dreamed you and I were at Akhetaten, in Tell el-Amarna," she said, excited. "The city wasn't in ruins. What I saw of it was...." She was lost for words. "You were with me, Aaron. We were headed toward a great palace."

Aaron's mouth hung agape as she related details that he corroborated. "I never dreamed tapping into other planes of existence could be so real."

"It gets better."

"This is an example of what you've experienced all along?"

She cast her gaze downward and swallowed hard. "And more. I don't have to try to receive information. It's suddenly being heaped on me."

"When did all this begin?"

"When we reached the site on day one. It's as if some special energy exists around this dig and I've tapped into it. Or... it into me."

"Evidently me too, Chione."

"It's awesome." She was overwhelmed and swiped at tears. "I can't contain it any longer. I'm sometimes frightened, and yet so compelled—"

"Listen, there's no reason for you to be alone in this."

"Aaron, I can't control what I receive. It happens in a rush. How will you cope?"

"Trust me. I'm already tapping into your experiences."

She felt the longing in his heart and knew that was what kept them attached. Even when she told him she wished no more dependencies. Ego's last stand. Deep in her heart, she knew they were meant for each other, and his patience and fate kept throwing them together.

She could not push him away any longer and would not try to. "We were together," she said, marveling. "You're a part of it all."

"You mean you've seen me in other visions?"

"What did you perceive just now, Aaron? Do you know who you were?"

"Not who I was, but that you and I were together and headed toward this behemoth ancient structure." She waited as he tried to mentally rebuild the experience to glean all he could. "I felt we were home," he said. "Then I remembered California and that really threw me."

"Me too! Me too!"

His smile encouraged. They already had too much to think about and all she wanted to do was sit quietly and absorb everything.

Perhaps Aaron really did not realize who he was in the vision. He seemed only to think he was himself together with her, witnessing a scene that took place thirty-five hundred years earlier. He had not yet realized he could become someone else and thought he had merely peeked into another place and time. He needed to discover this on his own.

She concentrated on the vision they had just shared. Curiously, she found herself wondering who she might have been. Within moments she felt herself floating again. An ethereal spiral rose majestically above her, opening at the top into bright light. The air spun with a continual snakelike hiss and enveloped her until suddenly she was yanked upwards with great velocity and lost consciousness.

They splashed in a shallow reflecting pool. Aaron laughed playfully. She quickly pulled loose a handful of lotus pads and whipped them down over his head with a spray of water. They laughed gleefully. She ran away, splashing, daring him to catch her. He grabbed her and they fell together. Then, looking past him, she was surprised to see a woman, regally costumed, approaching, attended by handmaidens. The woman watched them, seemed saddened, and then led the servants away.

When Chione next looked to Aaron, he had become someone else. The face resembled Aaron's but he had become another person who looked fa-

miliar. *Gone were the sturdy khaki pants and shirt, replaced by a pleated white linen tunic soaked with green silty water and stuck to his bronzed skin. He dabbed at the black kohl around his eyes. She did the same to hers and found it streaked down her cheeks. She quickly washed her face in the water.*

He was sensually aroused and ran his hands down her curvaceous body and pulled her against himself. "I will have you now," he said.

"Oba," she said softly.

He quickly laid her backward in the water, holding her head up with a hand. His other hand lifted her leg and she raised them both. He was about to take her at that moment, right there in the pond, and it filled her with wantonness.

They kissed passionately. By the time the kiss ended, the scene had changed. It was a new day, a new time. They were naked and lying under a blanket on a woven reed pallet covered by a thick soft mat. More lattice panels of red mashrabia wood covered the walls. Rich colorful tapestries hung everywhere. A flask of uro and two marble goblets wait on a low carved table. The rich scent of incense hung in the air on trails of smoke.

"Umayma," he said, whispering, and then sighed heavily.

"Come to me," she said in an urgent provocative tone.

"I cannot, after all, Umayma," he said. "We must protect Yahya. You're my only hope." He turned away quickly. "Protect Yahya."

Her longing for this man through eons welled up. She reached for him again but found him gone.

"Oba!" she cried, still reaching for him.

"Chione!" that other voice insisted.

Again, she felt a strong nudge. She opened her eyes to find herself lying on the sitting mat beside Aaron, propped on an elbow close to her. The insufferably hot air in the Hall brought to mind another time when she had meditated and came out of it feeling lustful. She rolled to him and pulled him into her arms.

"Chione!" he said, exasperated. "It's me, Aaron."

Chione withdrew quickly when she realized what had happened. "I'm sorry, Aaron, I'm sorry," she said, sitting up. "I was really dreaming that time, didn't know I'd laid down."

Aaron smiled, sat up, evidently not angered. "You used to meditate lying down too."

"You mean we did it again?"

"Just went with the flow. Is that how it happens to you too? You intend to meditate and it yanks you into a scene somewhere?"

"Aaron, it happens if I simply clear my mind. It happens on a lesser scale while I'm concentrating deeply, like when I'm working."

"Like we saw you do in Inventory with that little box that had a piece missing off the back?" he asked, as he strained to see her in the dim light. "You zone out to some other place while you're working?"

"Not often while I work. But I get flashes of scenes. The visions usually never lasted unless during meditating, daydreaming, or in a similar state."

"Well, I flashed on something, just now."

"What was on your mind a moment ago?" she asked.

"I was trying to sort out all that I received in that first presentation."

"Concentrating deeply, you were ripe to be swept away."

"Is that how it works?"

Without realizing it, she placed a hand on his knee. He noticed but had not moved. "That's how it's been happening," she said, withdrawing her hand. "It's like some other power wants us to view these scenes."

"Do you think all these visions have something to do with the lives of people associated with this burial?"

Chione smiled. "Now you're getting it."

"Because we're both open to extrasensory input? Simple as that?"

This was mind-boggling. Aaron was finally learning how much he had opened himself up for when he became enchanted with her abilities. Maybe he did have potential to develop. Maybe he had some garbage, some blockage, to clear out of his psyche before knowledge came through with ease and clarity. Judging from what he was now receiving, had he somehow cleared his psyche in absentia? Was he seeing an aspect of his inner self that was closed all these years? On the other hand, was he likely to become possessed by something he had no power to control?

Chione was undaunted, eager for experience, driven to learn all she could. She evidently had many more experiences than he did and always returned from them rational and coherent. The scientist in Aaron felt enticed to find an explanation to the peculiar occurrences. She wondered how he rationalized the dream and vision sequences he recently experienced.

Chione needed time to think things through and hoped by merely concentrating upon them, she would not be swept away again. She needed to comprehend what was happening before it happened again. More than that, she had to know the meaning of the scenes that were so natural she could have lived them. She no longer merely watched, but now participated. How much could she endure without becoming swallowed by the paranormal?

She returned from that last scene filled with lust and desire for the man who began as Aaron. He became someone else for whom she felt the same burning intensity? Then just now, when they returned from their supernatural excursion, how was it that she and Aaron found themselves lying side-by-side, similar to the two people they experienced in the vision?

Her mind reeled. Too many questions needed answers. The Pillared Hall seemed suddenly cold. She wanted to cuddle up with Aaron, keep warm, but that would be impossible. "It's late," she said, reaching for her boots. She hesitated, felt awkward. She wanted to give him an endearing peck on the cheek, say good night, and show appreciation in some simple way. He would misinterpret her motivation. She rose to her feet. "I'll see you in the morning," she said nicely.

He smiled that same encouraging smile as she turned to leave. "Sure. Good night, *Umayma,*" he called after her as she padded across the stone floor in her socks.

She trained her flashlight beam on the floor of the passage. When she climbed the last flight of stairs heading toward the First Chamber, she clicked off the beam and made her way toward the dim light near where the others had bedded down. Aaron's pallet had been placed next to Kenneth's just outside the doorway to the First Chamber. On the other side of Dr. Withers, Clifford snored.

As she entered the First Chamber, she heard reeds creak. A quick look back told her Aaron had laid down and stretched out. In the dim light, Kenneth raised up. "Hey, you two learn anything?" he asked not too quietly.

Normally, she would detest hearing someone pry into her visions. This time she felt at ease, even playful. By now, the team members could not help themselves. They were all being affected in one way or another, especially Kenneth, who seemed thankful he and Bebe had drawn close again. He smiled all the time and touched her lovingly when not around the locals. Chione listened from just inside the First Chamber.

"You awake?" Aaron asked quietly.

"Can't sleep," Kenneth said. "Not much back support on these woven things."

"Softer than stone though."

Chione wondered if any of hers and Aaron's conversations seeped up the passageway. If Kenneth had difficulty lying on the woven cot, how had he spent his time? He would not have lain in discomfort all that time. Chione shuddered at the thought anyone might have crept close while she and Aaron tapped into that other existence.

"Aaron," Kenneth said, keeping his voice low. "How do those vision things work?"

"You're asking me? You'd better talk to Chione."

"You get 'em too, don't you?" Kenneth's curiosity was never more evident. What a time to start a conversation that could take too long to explain, if one could.

"Sometimes," Aaron said.

"What did you get tonight?"

"Some names. Remind me in the morning to look at your wife's dictionary."

"Got it right here," Kenneth said, reaching under his cot. "Earlier, none of us could sleep so we got out some reference materials and studied for a while. What I really wanted to interpret were some words I heard a couple locals saying. They acted awfully suspicious. If I can translate those words, we might learn who we can or can't trust."

"Oh, the thefts you're referring to?"

"Yeah, I don't trust some of those workers out there," he said. "I learned in Nam how to tell by a look in the eye if a guy planned to shake your hand or flip out a knife. He didn't have to blink to give a clue."

"You think you can read something in their actions?"

"I'm on to something, but these guys are harder to read because their eyes are always smiling."

Aaron sat up as Kenneth produced the dictionary. One of them brought out a tiny pocket light and Dr. Withers rolled over away from the beam. Kenneth held the light close while Aaron accepted the dictionary and began flipping pages.

"What exactly are you looking for?"

Aaron flipped more pages. "Yahya."

"Where'd that come from?"

"Heard it in meditation."

Kenneth would not believe let alone understand what she and Aaron had just experienced. In any event, the episode was too personal to divulge and Aaron should have waited until morning. As it was, their peers thought she and Aaron had rekindled their relationship and were trying to be discreet by telling everyone they were meditating together.

"Ah, here it is," Aaron said. "Yahya means *gift of Aten*."

"How was that word used?"

" 'We must protect Yahya'."

"Run that by me again?"

Aaron flipped through the pages. "Wait a sec," he said. "*Oba*."

"Strange words," Kenneth said.

"Yeah, here it is," Aaron said. "King, Oba means king." He flipped more pages. "One more. Umayma."

"I haven't heard those words among the locals," Kenneth said.

Chione strained to hear. She hoped Marlowe and Bebe behind her in the room would not wake and catch her eavesdropping.

"Little mother," Aaron said. "Little mother?"

"Make any sense?"

"Like pieces of a puzzle."

Aaron lay back and stared up into darkness. Chione knew his active mind would keep him awake late into the night. "Umayma... Oba... Yahya," he repeated as Kenneth also lay back. With Aaron repeating the Egyptian words like a mantra, Chione wondered if he would be pulled into another trance.

28

The sandstorm thickened the air and left only a few feet of visibility.

"Face masks, scarves, and protective goggles are now standard attire," Dr. Withers said in an authoritative voice.

The following four nights, the team slept down under. No one came to disturb Chione during meditation in the Pillared Hall. With so much to do to keep the encampment safe, the last few nights Aaron had not joined her.

Most of the laborers' tents had been dismantled and taken away. It was anybody's guess where they bedded down, but they always showed up each morning. Masud suggested that many caves could be found up in the cliffs behind the site and that the locals knew of them from past digs. Many of the workers had no fear of the dead and might sleep in opened tombs if they found any.

The team's yurts had been collapsed on top of personal belongings and battened down with heavy boards, boulders, and anything else weighty enough. The whole campsite looked forlorn, devoid of the hum of busy voices, chanting, and onlookers; replaced by the eerie howling wind and blasts of arid sand.

Because of the dust, Clifford suggested any film be developed in Luxor across the Nile. Since he knew his way around, he took the film. Upon returning, he announced finding a reputable shop near the train station. In exchange for fast developing service, he promised the shop owner and two clerks and their families a tour of the tomb.

Yafeu and Irwin did their best to keep sand out of the food. Old portable electric grills and burners were rounded up because the wind kept blowing out the pilot light and burners on the propane range. Even the pyramids that kept potatoes, vegetables and other edibles fresh on storage shelves were now covered with cloths. All prepared food was wrapped airtight before being transported out of the cook tent and then down under.

Once at dinner, after having announced finding sand in his food, Clifford said, "If we stayed long enough, our teeth would wear down like the Ancients who got used to chewing on the grit."

"Enough of that could tear up your gut as it passed through," Kenneth said.

Inside the inventory tent, the team still wore face coverings. Each time the tent canvas billowed and snapped, dust and sand gusted in on everything. Many artifacts had to be cleaned a second time before being packaged. Some of the local help fashioned screens of large swatches of fabric and stood close to deflect particles from both the precious relics and those packaging them.

Chione was not bothered much by the elements and took it all in stride. While still in California, she had seen visions of more to come. The dig would go on until those visions manifested into reality despite morale being low. Recently, she experienced other dreams, portraying the team's further progress. She would wait out the sandstorm and irritating dryness it produced and would do what she could to foster higher morale. Marlowe and Bebe had to learn how to cope. Kendra already knew. The hot sand got under clothing and scratched and stuck to sweaty skin. Even if Marlowe and Bebe had been known to get down in the dirt for a find, neither they nor Kendra were the type to tolerate gritty skin and scalp very long. The portable showers worked overtime.

Then, as usual, Siti came through again. In addition to other tasks, she took it upon herself to maintain the team's laundry, enabling all to have fresh clothes. It beat having to wear the same khakis three or four days in a row. Tarik's only set of ragged clothing was laundered, too, but wasn't holding together well. Chione decided to let him keep a set of her kakhi's and grow into them since she seemed to be growing out of them.

"He is orphan, you know?" Siti asked when returning fresh clothes to Chione, Marlowe, and Bebe. "Sometimes sleeps behind rocks."

They waited till Siti departed. "That's why his clothes are so ragged," Marlowe said.

"We need to do something for him," Chione said. "He's been devoted to all of us and our work from the beginning."

Marlowe looked to be conjuring something. "We should find him a home. How do you think he would fare in the U.S.?" She didn't wait for a reply. "He's a brilliant child, works diligently, and most of all, he's honest."

Later Clifford made an announcement none wanted to hear. "No word yet when the sandstorm might end. The meteorologists say it's a freak occurrence."

Randy and the chaperones had packed the children into the old bus and moved their camp a few miles away between Valley of the Kings and the Nile. In the interim, all tours were being diverted to Randy so tourists' vacations would not be wasted.

"Randy says the sandstorm's not affecting other areas," Aaron said. "It's blowing in way off the Libyan Desert to the west and culminating here in Valley of the Queens."

"Wonder why it's affecting only this area in Thebes?" Clifford asked.

"You know what Randy would say about that," Aaron said.

Nerves were on edge. Dr. Withers sat in the cook tent each night till way after dark, drinking Karkade to calm his nerves. The light inside reflected his shadow hunched over a notepad as he racked his brain to come up with a way to save their project. He scrutinized fax messages hoping for answers. From time to time, others joined him. Now that the Yagos and other gawkers were not around, Royce's insistent shadow became an all too common sight alongside Dr. Withers' likeness.

Later, down under, Bebe excitedly pulled her aside in a hush-hush. "Chione, you're not going to believe this."

"Try me."

"I had a vivid dream the first night we slept in here," Bebe said, utterly pleased about something. "I dreamed someone was with me—don't know who—but I woke knowing I'd never have my surgery."

"What?"

"That was it. And I haven't had menopausal problems since."

The treatment room echoed in Chione's mind. Bebe had slept in Tauret's treatment room. So had she and Marlowe. Chione was flabbergasted. "Who do you think was with you in your dream?"

"Never saw a face. It was a woman though," Bebe said. "So why are you smiling like that?"

"Think about it, Bebe," Chione said, whispering. "You did a spell for better health. You're sleeping in a room full of spells used by a woman who evidently treated people with related problems."

"Do you think it was her?"

Chione shrugged but looked hopeful. "Who's to say?"

"Did she come to me?" Bebe asked. Her eyes flashed as she became enrapt with the possibilities. "Is that what that woman did? She helped me?"

"You asked for help, in her way," Chione said. "Watch your condition and see what happens."

Bebe showed signs of teetering between belief and denial. Time would tell a lot of things.

The next morning, after re-braiding her hair and covering all but her eyes with a headscarf, Chione climbed out of the shaft to see Clifford jumping into the back of a jeep. He and Aaron were about to drive away with the Bolis.

"Hey, you two!" she said, yelling down to them. "Wait for me!" She readjusted her headgear and goggles and scrambled down the hillside, hoisting herself into the back of the open jeep next to Clifford on the sand covered seats. "Where are we going?"

"All hell broke loose," Clifford said as the jeep lunged forward.

Everyone wore goggles and hats or headscarves. The driver strained to see ahead through the blowing sand as they bumped along the road crudely set down over rough terrain.

"Meaning?"

"You haven't heard?" Aaron asked, twisting around in the front seat. "Someone found two bodies in the beggars' camp. Dr. Withers and some of the Bolis took off on foot."

The jeep bumped hard into something. They were all thrown forward.

"Jeez!" Clifford yelled as he swung from the roll bar.

Chione was thrown up front and Aaron managed to catch her and keep her from smashing against the windshield.

The officer cursed in Arabic under his breath. "Sorry!" he said, straining to see ahead. "So sorry." Egyptians were really committed about not touching a woman. After seeming to want to help, he sat looking straight ahead until they were seated again and Aaron gave the sign to get going.

They must have been off the road. The driver backed and nearly got stuck in the sand. He pointed the vehicle in a slightly different direction and stepped on the accelerator.

"Two bodies?" Chione asked after settling back into her seat. "That doesn't sound good."

Clifford wrapped his arm around her as if helping to keep her in the seat. "On top of that," he said, "Marlowe's headaches are becoming severe. Sterling wants to send her home, but she refuses to go."

"There is some good news, though," Aaron said, twisting again in his seat and smiling behind his eyewear. He raised his voice to be heard over the howl of the wind. "Our directors decided if Randy could be of no use here, they want him working at the Museum."

"Blessed be to Al-lah!" Clifford yelled.

The driver threw a quick glance back at Clifford. His eyes laughed. He braked to a stop as a thicker cloud of dust came up from behind and enveloped them.

They needed to wait for a better time to discuss all the changes taking place.

Chione never visited the beggars' camp. Tents of all types, from sleeping to temple sizes, made up a village of billowing colorful tapestry and canvas tentatively held to earth by ropes and stakes. Some of the coverings had been appliquéd by hand in bright, multicolored Egyptian designs, now muted with dust. Where one tent left off and another began was difficult to determine if not for color and pattern.

An officer on the scene remained with the jeep. They made their way deeper into the proliferation of tents, careful not to trip over tie-downs and stakes. No thoroughfares or footpaths had been established. One simply picked one's way through the conglomeration that nearly blocked the only access road into the area. The wind brought every scent from fresh to foul to the nostrils in a rush.

"Love the incense," Clifford said, pressing his face cloth close.

With Yafeu's and Siti's cooking, the incense, and Kendra's Queen Nefertiti, their area smelled somewhat similar. At least they didn't have open sewers and murders in their camp.

The pleasantries vanished as a gust of wind tainted the air with the horrific stench of urine.

The officer made a motion, and they thankfully ducked inside one tent. They stopped short, bumping into one another. To their amazement, in a sumptuously draped entry foyer, the air thick with incense, scantily clad women lounged about. A makeshift dance floor lay to one side decorated with plastic flowers and tapestries and stands for musical instruments. At such an early hour, it was difficult to tell if the two men wearing only undershorts instead of gallibayas were coming or going.

Quickly, the officer turned and guided Chione by the shoulders back toward the entrance. Too late, however. She knew what kind of establishment that one was. His embarrassment was evident behind a masked smile. He danced two quick steps to the left then two to the right, trying to keep the hilarity of the situation subdued. Still smiling, he clasped his hands, bowed his head and begged in accented English, "Forgive, forgive." His squinting eyes told that he might burst out laughing. He turned and led them out.

After a few moments, it became evident the officer was lost. He asked directions. They walked farther. Finally, he called out in Arabic and another officer stuck his head out of a tent just ahead.

Chione heard Dr. Withers's voice but upon entry did not see him until he turned around. He was wearing a gallibaya! With his tanned face and head coverings, he looked stunningly Egyptian.

Royce and more local police were with him. Royce reacted, too, surprised at seeing her enter. One body lay sprawled across a bed. His legs dangled to the floor. No one recognized him. He had been shot in the forehead, possibly at close range. Blood had splattered over much of the inside corner of the tent from when the bullet exited out the back of his head. No blood came from the forehead wound and the tent canvas had a hole in it. Another man lay face down on the woven floor mat between the cots with the top of his head toward the exit. An officer lifted the man's shoulder from the floor exposing his face. He lay in a pool of blood that had spread from beneath his chest. Aaron and Dr. Withers bent down.

"Recognize him?" Dr. Withers asked.

"Can't say I do," Aaron said.

Pulling away from the officers who tried to block her way, Chione bent down for a look. "I know him. That's Usi."

Dr. Withers straightened. "How do you know him?"

"He worked with us for a while in Inventory."

"Let me see," Clifford said. They lifted the man's shoulder again. "I believe you're right, Chione. Damn it anyway, he was good help."

"Which one's Dakarai's cousin?" Dr. Withers asked of the Bolis.

Two of the officers conversed in Arabic and then one pointed to the man on the floor.

"Then where's Dakarai?" Aaron asked.

The officer shrugged and looked doubtful.

"We can do nothing more here," Dr. Withers said. He turned to the officers. "We make ourselves available to you at any time."

They crowded into the jeep for the ride back up the hill. Somehow Royce managed to wriggle himself into the front seat, showing no respect for Dr. Withers. Dr. Withers looked off into the distance, not that he could see much through the sandy haze. He and Clifford positioned themselves on the tool boxes sitting on each side over the rear wheel housing. Aaron motioned for Dr. Withers to take a seat beside Chione.

"Are the killings included in the negative incidents you saw in your visions, Chione?" Royce called out above the wind.

"No," she said as simply as she could, considering the inability to hear much or speak above the worsening howl. "I didn't see any of this."

"Then the negative occurrences you report seeing are yet to happen?" he asked. "What other incidents are likely to occur?" He seemed so formal when the wind and sand alone made everyone else drop pretenses.

Chione stared at him. She did not wish to answer. Things had a way of working out. Besides, she had only received hunches about certain danger. She might disclose bits and pieces, but only to Dr. Withers, if it helped members of the team to stay safe.

Dr. Withers sat quietly, hanging onto the roll bar and shaking his head. Chione reached over and wrapped her arm around his back. The jeep bounced over a rock, jostling them into the air. "We do finish the dig," she said when they had settled down.

Dr. Withers smiled again. His mood changed quickly. "You mean you've seen us finish our job here?"

"Of course," she said and smiled beneath her face coverings. "What do you think I've been working on after hours in the Hall?"

"How does this happen?" Royce asked, leaning toward her from the front seat. "Do we have help from a new team?"

Clifford's expression as Royce spoke was one of utter disgust. In fact, of late, his demeanor showed total lack of respect for Royce. She remembered Clifford's loyalty to Dr. Withers. Like Clifford told Randy weeks earlier, Dr. Withers had donated a huge inheritance, along with funds from other directors, in order to establish the CIA. His lifelong dream of a privately held institute had become reality. Reputable people had pooh-poohed Dr. Withers' nonconformist attitude, commenting that his private institute did not stand a chance. Yet, this tomb validated his effort. Dr. Withers would let nothing rob him of it. Not Randy's careless antics, nor lack of funding, nor jackals at the gate. Chione began to wonder if Kendra's suspicions of Royce's interest in the Yago woman might be valid. She did not answer Royce, who then sat back and took a turn staring off into the haze.

Back at camp, Kenneth appeared as if having been created from the blowing sand. The fabric used for his head covering was wrapped tightly around his cameras. The neck of his undershirt was pulled up over his nose. He wore goggles and had toilet paper stuck into his ears. "Sterling," he said above the howl of the wind. "I've got something."

"First, get inside. We've got a bit of a problem here." Dr. Withers started to walk away, then turned back. "Why aren't you wearing a gallibaya?" He did not wait for Kenneth's reply but walked swiftly away.

The others headed toward the cook tent with Kenneth in pursuit. Now Chione remembered something and slowly waved a hand in front of her face trying to clear her view. She looked around to see Aaron watching her. She wiped the air again in front of her face. "Aaron, the haze!" she said. "The haze I saw in a vision. This sandstorm is the haze that blocked everything from view."

"A sandstorm?"

"Yes, happening at a time when everything looks bleak and right now, we're threatened with having to abandon the site. I was right! I was right!"

They carefully hurried to the cook tent, not able to see it but knowing the general direction to take.

Inside, Dr. Withers asked, "So what about this problem, Kenneth?"

"A short while ago," he said. "I saw Dakarai running toward the necropolis."

"Running? That's strange considering no one can see far enough ahead to make it worth the risk."

"I thought so too. That's why I followed him."

"You sure it was Dakarai?" Aaron asked. As an archaeologist, Aaron always sought tangible evidence.

"Yeah, his blue gallibaya flapped in the wind."

"A lot of laborers wear those blue things," Bebe said.

"But they don't hide their face when you try to get a look at them. Besides, Dakarai is one of the tallest Egyptians around here."

"Maybe he covered his face from the sand."

"Not likely," Kenneth said. "He was running at full tilt barely able to keep his face protected. When he saw me, he covered up quick and turned away. Believe me, in my gut—"

"Okay, but I told you to stay out of—"

"There was no one else to follow him. I mean, why would he be running so fast and hiding his face?"

"Okay," Dr. Withers said. "What did you learn?"

"He disappeared, vanished."

"You lost him in the haze?"

"No, actually I had sight of him off and on as he ducked around the mastabas trying to hide." Kenneth was excited, knew he was onto something. "He disappeared. And get this. I lost him just about where I saw that hole with a box in it."

"Where Chione felt we were being watched?" Dr. Withers asked. "That is all too coincidental."

Chione thought so too. Something about that area of the necropolis kept trying to come to mind. She had thought about returning there herself to lay hands on the mastabas to see what she might receive through her sixth sense.

"You remember, don't you?" Kenneth asked. "Many of those mastabas were built with compartments above ground so offerings could be left."

Dr. Withers took a quick breath. "That must be why you felt we were being watched, Chione. Whoever took our goodies must have stashed them in some of those empty spaces. Whoever you felt was around might have been hiding in those empty cubicles."

"I'm sure no one's leaving offerings in this ancient burial site," Chione said. "The compartments would be perfect for storage." That still did not answer the gnawing feeling she had about the area.

"Dakarai couldn't just disappear," Clifford said. "He ducked into one of those."

"Same thing I thought," Kenneth said. "I suggest we round up some of the Bolis and go investi—"

Dr. Withers quickly raised a hand. "Ju-ust hold on there. The Bolis, yes. Us, no. That's not what we're here for. The Egyptian police won't need our help and you stay out of the necropolis for now, you hear?"

Later over breakfast down under, Dr. Withers said, "Hear me, all of you. We may be onto something. No one's to leak a word about Dakarai being suspect. Got that?"

After lunch, Chione watched the last load of crates being hoisted onto a dilapidated truck for delivery to a barge for the Nile crossing. Vehicles waited on the opposite bank to transport the precious cargo to the airport in Luxor for the flight to Cairo.

Tarik, whose many duties included being a messenger, handed her a fax message. He stood and waited like the curious child he was, turning his ear toward her. He so wanted to be part of the team. He never once put out his hand for baksheesh, and he honestly worked hard to show his intent. "Yes," she said, reading the message. "Yes!"

"One of us has good news," Clifford said.

"Mom and Dad, they're in Cairo," she said as she waved the paper in the air and danced with glee.

"Was that planned?" Dr. Withers asked with a teasing smile.

"Oh, no sir," Chione said. "After Dad retired, they mentioned a vacation in the Holy Land for next year."

"Just as well they come now," he said.

"Really?" Chione asked. "They're asking permission to spend a few days with us. Oh, please, Dr. Withers. They won't be in the way."

"Ask permission?" He smiled his crooked smile. "With all the tourists, dignitaries and study groups who've passed through? They, of all people, don't need permission."

"But to stay in camp with us? They'll bring their own food."

"If they don't mind sleeping down under for a while. After this storm passes, they can use Randy's yurt."

"Thank you, Dr. Withers," Chione said, jumping with excitement. "Thank you, thank you." She gave him a huge unexpected hug then wrapped her arm around Tarik, and they walked away while she reread the fax.

Shortly after that, Dakarai showed up in camp carrying something. Chione watched him look around till he spotted her. He walked over and surprisingly handed her the framed photo of her mom and dad.

Dr. Withers and Clifford overheard and joined them; evidently not what Dakarai counted on, judging from his expression of dismay. Dr. Withers' gaze was intense as if he meant to get to the bottom of something. "Where'd you come up with that?" he asked.

Dakarai smiled meekly, pressed his hands together at the fingertips and said, "Among mastabas. I chase someone. They drop it." He sighed and relaxed into his lie.

"Who could it have been?" Clifford asked. Chione nearly laughed at Clifford's feigned nonchalance.

"You still have thief," Dakarai said. His smile went sour.

"Who did you chase?" Dr. Withers asked.

"I cannot see," Dakarai said. "I lose him in necropolis."

"If someone dropped this," Chione said, showing the intact picture and frame. "Why isn't the glass broken?"

Again, Dakarai fidgeted. "Maybe put down," he said, bending low and sideways, motioning as if to quickly lower something to the ground.

Then Dr. Withers asked, "Do you know about your cousin, Usi?"

"Yes, Usi is cousin." Whether his reply was out of innocence or feigned, it now sounded like avoidance.

"Have you heard about him this morning?"

"No," Dakarai said. Still, he couldn't hide his lie. "About Usi?"

"He was shot," Dr. Withers said as they watched Dakarai's reaction.

"Shot?" Dakarai asked. "Where he is now?" Dakarai's calm acceptance of the information was a dead give-away.

"You'd better get down to the camp," Clifford said.

"Yes, I go." Dakarai turned abruptly and folded into the blowing grit, hurrying, like he wanted to get out of a tight situation.

Chione waited a moment till she knew he was out of earshot. "No remorse," she said.

"You noticed too?"

"My guess," Dr. Withers said. "Is that Usi and maybe some others stole for Dakarai, who used his contacts to get rid of the loot."

Chione remembered having placed the wrapped picture and frame inside her suitcase. "Someone's been under my yurt. Maybe everyone's."

"All right, you two," Dr. Withers said. "We can't let word of this get beyond our group. If we have a snitch among the workers, we'll lose the element of surprise in identifying who it is." He waved a hand decisively. "We'll check our belongings, then pass this information to the Bolis."

"Better report it to Cairo too," Clifford said. "And I'd keep the information away from the Guard."

"Why did Dakarai incriminate himself by bringing this back?" Chione asked. "To stay in our good graces? How would he know whose tent it came out of?"

"If he wasn't in on the taking," Clifford said.

"Dumb," Dr. Withers said as he began to walk away. "Dumb if he thinks we'd buy into his lies. His little scheme just backfired."

29

After the few laborers disappeared at the end of the workday, the team examined belongings. No one was foolish enough to bring anything of great value other than jewelry kept on his or her person. Some combs and brushes were missing. All of Rita's belongings, which Clifford locked inside a travel trunk were untouched. The trunk had been dragged under the collapsed yurt and, too cumbersome to carry, evidently abandoned when it could not be opened quickly. The business tents inside the circle had not been accessed, only the collapsed yurts on the periphery.

"Whoever breached security did it on their bellies," Clifford said. "Slithered like serpents crawling under rocks."

"Pros," Dr. Withers said, scratching his head thoughtfully through the headgear.

Beggars would have stolen a scrap of stale bread. They would have taken anything movable.

"Not so much as a loose notepad has been taken," Bebe said. "Professional thieves can't use those?"

"Maybe Aaron doodled on too many of 'em," Clifford said, evoking laughter.

Whoever raided the camp looked only for things with immediate saleable value. "We'll let the Bolis handle it," Dr. Withers said. "Let's stay focused on our work."

The next morning Randy was in camp before breakfast preparing to check out. His arm was no longer in a sling, but he still did not use it much. "I'll be bussing it back to Cairo with the children," he said. "Save the team some dollars by not taking a flight."

Deliberately ignoring the gesture of pseudo-altruism, Dr. Withers said, "Once in Cairo, get over to Vimble's clinic for a check up on that shoulder."

A little later, Randy approached her looking around to make sure they were alone. "What is it, Randy?" Chione asked as they stepped inside the now empty inventory tent.

Bare pallets lay haphazard on the ground. The packing materials and tools were stored safely so thieves could not get them. Only paraffin tubs and sundry other items remained. The inventory tent, usually bustling with activity, camaraderie, and dialect, seemed forlorn.

"I just wanted to say goodbye. I'll see you again sometime, back in California maybe."

"Is it permanent? You're to stay in Cairo?"

"For a while. I wanted to say something else though." He paused briefly. "Chione, the children, according to the translators, they wanted to say goodbye to you."

"To me?"

"Yes. Some cried when they asked me to tell you."

"Cried?" That did seem odd. "Do you know why?"

"No, I don't. Except some of the kids refer to you as Ari. I was told Ari meant guardian. Why would they call you that?"

"A lot of things you'll never understand, Randy. You're too fixed in your thinking about what life is and isn't. Your skepticism makes the paranormal too mysterious and scares the pants off you."

He thought for a moment and then said, "You know, Chione, there was a time I'd have shined you on after comments like that."

"Why be different today?" she asked, not expecting anything else.

"I've been evaluating things. Your dreams did come true. And all the strange things that keep happening—?"

"The occurrences you pass off to a curse?"

"Curse or not, something's going on." Even a curse implied something different, and he could not deny it.

"If you believe in them."

"I didn't think I did, that is, something's making things happen. Not everyone has dreams like yours."

"What are you saying?"

"I want you to know I'm awfully sorry to have taunted you so badly."

"You're apologizing?" She could not believe her ears.

"I've changed, Chione. Something's happened over here. Look at me. In the month we've been in this oven of a desert, I must have lost between twenty, thirty pounds." His clothing hung on his body. His face was thinner and tanned and his hair clean and shiny. His eyes were clear, and they sparkled as if he had been re-made. "Does that bother you?"

"No, I hope to lose more. I never knew what to do about my weight. Now it's being taken care of."

"Like a blessing? Or a curse?"

He smiled wryly. "Something else," he said. "I've never been part of this group or close to any of you. While you're all making these magnificent discoveries, I'm relegated to something else and not a part of it."

"Well, your shoulder, Randy."

"It's as if it was meant to happen to keep me from getting too involved here."

"I wouldn't carry it that far," she said. When a person in denial found some validity in anything she did, they usually swayed in her direction and got carried away with exaggerated belief. She did not wish to see that happen to Randy.

"Don't you see? I didn't get to work with the mummies when they were brought out. Didn't get to see any of the relics unless I poked my nose in here while they were being packed. For some reason, I was supposed to work with the kids and the tour groups. Chione, listen."

"I am listening, but I've got to get going."

"No wait, don't you see? There's a reason why I wasn't supposed to get involved. Now I'm being sent to Cairo."

"Well, your work waits for you at the Madu." She knew Randy well. Playing the metaphysical guru and predicting why he was supposed to be where and when was not like him. He was puffing up his ego again, yet, she was curious enough to want to listen, even though history hinted that she should walk away.

"You know me, how I work, right?"

"You can be exceptional."

"Well, thank you," he said, looking surprised. "But listen. When I learned I was going to the Madu, this great surge of self-actualization came over me like there was more to come. Don't ask me how I knew that. You understand. I know you do."

Randy's excitement seemed to escalate over the news he had to relate. He was swept up in a current Chione recognized. "Go on," she said.

"I phoned Cairo, did some snooping. Do you know that the Museum has their own program to establish the DNA blood prints of all the mummies? They're trying to establish who among the living might be related to the Ancients."

Chione felt cold shivers go up her spine, a premonition so strong she had to listen. "Why is that of interest you?"

"I specialize in genetics and biochemistry, remember? I have medical research training. I can fit into their DNA program working with the Museum's Microbiologist. I want in. I already have this theory—"

"Go for it. Apply."

"Listen," he said, still caught up in his thoughts. "My theory is that when they do the genealogy of the American presidents, they find each one related to past presidents. If past Presidents produce the current ones, well, maybe it's possible that these genius Egyptian kids—born with knowledge of Ancient Egypt—don't you see? Maybe they're descendants of the Pharaoh's families."

Another chill transited Chione's body. "Your thesis is tenable but, again, based on metaphysical thinking," she said. "Quite unlike you,

Randy." She felt dizzy again but had to concentrate because of the chill that lingered.

"They DNA printed members of the Egyptian government and came up with next to nothing. With all the millions of people in Egypt, there has to be a new starting point, or they'll scrap the project."

What better place to resume the program than with those who have innate knowledge of history, the Pharaohs and the dynasties? Still, she said, "Wow, that's stretching it, don't you think?"

"Maybe. We could also DNA print the Hamitic peoples. The Copts are believed to be the closest blood relatives."

"Descendants of ancient Egyptians?"

"Rather than give up on the DNA program, they should first investigate every angle, wouldn't you say? Starting with my kids?"

"I don't know how intelligent those kids are," Chione said. Nor could she believe Randy had acquiesced to any part of past life theory.

"I can't explain it, but don't you see? I'm onto something like it's been handed to me," he said. "Just like I was pulled away from the group effort. Spending time with the kids? Chione, I'm really getting to know Egypt and her history. When I started studying with the children, something just came up and enveloped me. Now I can't get enough."

"Is that part of the curse?" she asked, smiling, so he would know that she teased.

"More like a needs recognition."

"Then you should apply for the program."

"It's not that easy." He looked down at his boots, evidently preparing himself to do something humbling. He looked up, straight into her eyes. "Could you help me a little?"

"Get into that program? What could I—"

"Maybe not you, Chione. Can you influence Dr. Withers to give me a recommendation?"

If Randy thought she had any influence, it would certainly not be used to contrive. "Why don't you present it to him yourself?"

"I'm sure he's given up on me. He doesn't see the broader changes happening here," Randy said. "I've been pushed in this other direction and my fate lies elsewhere."

If only Randy knew the changes the other team members were experiencing, dressing and eating like Egyptians. Yet, his rationale seemed totally based in metaphysical concepts. "Do you hear yourself?"

He pleaded for her to hear him out. "I haven't been able to guide my own life or decide what I should do," he said. "Now I've been pointed in a direction without any effort on my part. There certainly are other forces at work."

She could only smile. Randy was softening, allowing that he could not be the manipulator of his or anyone else's universe. He was seeing the light, but why had he come to her after all their conflicts? "Speak with Dr. Withers."

"I need your help." His tone begged. "I belong in this program. I didn't like Egypt when I first arrived. Those kids did something to me. If I can stay in Cairo with the DNA program, I can see the children."

"That's quite a change."

"I want to say something else," he said suddenly. "Sort of from a man's point of view."

She already knew he would have more to say. "Give it your best."

"My mom nags me to get married," Randy said. "She drives me nuts. She wants grandchildren. I don't want marriage. I want my career and, believe it or not, I'm happy to be away from my mother's nagging. Meeting these kids—they're my family now. I got attached to them as if they were my own."

Chione felt a twinge of caution. Randy was about to invade her personal life. "Well, thanks for confiding in me, Randy. I think your mother will understand eventually."

"That's not all, Chione. Don't you see? I heard the rumors about why you broke off with Aaron." Chione stiffened, about to cut him short, but he went on. "I sympathize with your situation. But let me say this just once. Think twice about Aaron."

"That's none of your—"

"I got used to these kids and I don't want to leave them. They're my family now. They accept me and love me and it feels better than great. You can't tell me Aaron couldn't live without having his own—"

"That's none of your business, Randy!"

Randy did not flinch. "You're right. But you should know that I've accepted these kids with all my heart. To have your love, Aaron would do the same."

Chione trembled. Nothing Randy ever said had gotten so deeply into her. "It's my life," she said.

"I know. I had to say that because I'm only now beginning to see how special you are."

"Don't patronize me," she said. "Maybe you ought to go see Dr. Withers while you have a chance." As soon as the biting words spilled out, Chione regretted having said them. Here was Randy pouring out his heart. She marveled at how much he had matured. She sensed his loneliness and realized that on his own, he chose a wonderful direction for his life.

The look on his face said if she chose not to help, he would understand. He smiled sadly, sighed, and turned to leave. "Guess I'd better see the boss."

"Wait, Randy," she said. He turned back slowly. "You should break the news to him first. I'll see what I can do afterwards."

"Oh, Chione," he said, sighing relief. "If there's ever anything I can do for you, just ask. I swear I'll give it my best. I'll never say no."

"It means that much?"

"I wish you knew," he said, smiling timidly. "The times, they are a changin'." Then he walked back and hugged her.

That was the closest she had been to Randy since they had to bump elbows working together in California. Since that time, she had not wished to be near him at all. As they embraced, a vision appeared and in a split-second vanished. Something about blood. She thought of the gash that he sustained on his arm when he fell into the Second Chamber. She felt his pain and pulled away. "Good luck to you, Randy," she said, meaning it.

"One more thing," he said. "Don't tell anyone about this conversation, okay?" He curled up a lip. "I wouldn't want to spoil my image."

Chione looked tenderly at him for the first time. "You know, Randy," she said. "Maybe you should bring your mother to Egypt for a vacation, and to meet your new family."

She held the tent flap and watched him walk away into the haze. He definitely was thinner; shoulders taller and broader, with a posture more positive. Yes, the times they were a changin'. Then she saw the vision again.

Blood, fresh and red.

The kinesthetic feel of the scene was more of great expectation than fright.

More blood, spots of blood.

30

Helen and Jibade Ini-Herit arrived with a small group of Egyptian friends. As an American housewife traveling in a Muslim ruled country, Helen accepted the cultural norms and wore Egyptian women's clothing covering all of her body and a colorful wimple concealing her hair. Their group brought an abundant supply of local foodstuffs, even their own cooking utensils.

Aaron had met her parents only a few times. On those occasions, Chione watched him and Jibade bond. Their friendship helped Aaron understand the reason she took so readily to this foster father. The look in Jibade's eyes told of deeper understanding. That was why her parents never interfered in her relationship with Aaron when it existed, nor when it ended.

The sandstorm scared off the paparazzi with their expensive photographic equipment. The blowing sand prevented anyone from spending free time outside. Chione and Aaron spoke in low tones at the far end of the dining tables.

"Something's brought them to Egypt a year early," Aaron said. "Jibade tunes in to you, Chione. Could he have sensed our difficulties?"

Did Jibade, in fact, have something to offer to help her break through any mental blockages to finding the Burial Chamber? Certainly, he was deeply spiritual, spending time with the local men during prayer breaks. His penetrating eyes said he well understood the paranormal.

"I feel drawn to him for support," Chione said. "This time, Aaron, feelings of dependency have nothing to do with it."

"I'm glad to hear you say that," he said, smiling warmly. "We're all growing."

After lunch, Dr. Withers kept the team together briefly. On the tabletop, he scattered newspapers gathered and sent by colleagues in California. Magnificent photos and articles in the San Francisco Sentinel, Stockton Journal, and the London papers reported what their journalists experienced firsthand. Other major world papers speculated as to Chione's psychic abilities, of which they proved to know nothing. The articles were, perhaps unintentionally, maligning. In other papers, photos and some news written by those without authorized representation at the tomb site were good but lacked depth and conciseness.

Various tabloids and rag mags published exploiting pictures questionably portraying members of the team. Chione perused a few and became angered. "Just look at this!" She held up a cover showing a photo of herself subtitled, "Daughter of the Nile." Another touted "Reincarnation in Egypt."

Aaron snatched the papers from her hands. "I suggest we ignore these. They're still laughing at us."

Dr. Withers waved a hand as if he could not be bothered. "Listen up. I've done a background check on the Yago clan. They're not widely known; however, they have a commendable reputation as artifacts procurers."

After hearing preliminary details of a very shaky prospective deal with the Yago family, Clifford said, "Gypsies!" Then he took off for Cairo.

While awaiting the arrival of the Directors, and with time on their hands, everyone took the opportunity to get out of the wind. Visiting archaeologists and dignitaries ventured to view other tombs and sites. Marlowe packed up her headache pills and accompanied Radcliffe Stroud, Hadden Bourne, Leigh Stockard and Gram Berkley on a photo shoot nearby. Amenhotep III's royal residence, the Palace of Malkatta with its man-made lake, Birket Habu, the intended subjects.

Thomas Banning returned briefly to England. Ginny McLain and her staff of technicians would find plenty to occupy their days.

Bebe and Kenneth left before the others woke in order to catch one of the local taxis. If not early, all were commissioned. Driven by locals, Kendra and Royce rode off in a jeep not speaking to one another. Their lack of conversation was common of late. It seemed Kendra was taken over by her suspicions in trying to keep track of her husband, who seemed to have an agenda all his own.

Too many people needed vehicles. Hopefully, no more would be brought into the area. The glut of foot and vehicle traffic had become unbearable.

Chione and her parents took quick excursions through some of the other tombs in Valley of the Queens and Dier el-Bahri. Though closed to the public, Jibade bribed workers who allowed them access to Queen Tyi's tomb in Valley of the Kings. The next day Aaron accompanied them on a city tour across the Nile. The ever-present stench of urine in the old poverty sections of Luxor reminded them of the beggars' camp below the tomb site.

After a few more days, the sandstorm let up. Quaashie and Naeem supervised laborers digging the camp from under drifts of sand. As yurts were re-erected, the Ini-Herit's group pitched their own tents near Chione's and blended in.

The improved climate meant the Directors would reschedule travel itineraries and arrive soon. Though Chione's dreams predicted work progressing at full tilt, Dr. Withers might have to stall to cover up activity being halted. His quiet look of desperation begged for a clue to continuance, which her dreams had not pinpointed. Nor had seismologists discovered new rock formations.

Jibade went off with the locals. Helen and Marlowe disappeared with Siti to the kitchen for cooking lessons of authentic foods. Chione felt more content and surmised that her parents' visit was the cause of the dramatic feelings of euphoria. Her health and mood swings alternated between cases of sensitive nerves, to elation, to a constant upset stomach, and then, even hunger.

She needed to compare notes with Aaron. "Hey there," she said, having found him.

"When does it begin again?" Aaron asked, his expression too serious. "We desperately need to get on with—"

"Certainly, your dreams haven't stopped, have they?" she asked. "You've been in...." Suddenly, her face began to heat.

"You've had the same dreams, haven't you?"

Chione glanced away. "I don't know what dreams you've had."

"Chione," he said, waiting momentarily for her attention. "Tauret and Tut were close, maybe even—"

She gasped. "You did... how much... you're having the same—"

"I am, aren't I?"

"We must both be receiving a lot of their sensual information right now," she said, trying to hide embarrassment. If he tapped into the physical aspects of dreams she experienced as Tauret, he would have seen himself as Pharaoh. Tauret and her King most certainly shared a bed of lust. The thought made her face heat again. She avoided looking into Aaron's eyes. Still, the experiences were, after all, psychic in nature and not the real thing. "This can't be forced, but we'd better get serious in the Pillared Hall again."

"If we can't come up with something on the Burial Chamber—"

"We will," she said. "Don't you trust that yet?"

Aaron's anxiety to succeed sometimes got in his way. Not waiting for sunset or the evening meal, they went early and sat in the Pillared Hall. Concentration was broken by the others clamoring up and down the ladder in the shaft removing belongings and cots.

As the noise quieted, they tried again. She did not notice a slip in consciousness.

Tauret, petite and elegantly clothed, stood in front of her, eyes heavily outlined with kohl, pupils black as onyx gleaming.

Tauret's image was even more vivid, her glow, otherworldly.

Hair cropped below the ear line, framed clear olive skin. So real, yet ghostly. Tauret motioned her to follow. She floated and took Tauret's hand and felt an electric energy!

Chione's heart beat wildly. Then....

...a gentle sinking feeling...

...like floating down...

...into a room as bright as yellow sunshine. Statues, jars, vases, elegant tables heaped with jewels, clothing in piles.

She was receiving Tauret's telepathic vision. Chione began peering into a coffin but was frustrated by a blurred image with only one area coming into focus. Tauret disappeared from in front of her as another scene opened out.

Tauret laid quietly, arms crossed over her chest. Over her heart, an unusually large carved lapis lazuli scarab.

Then Chione heard....

"Once my body is discovered...."

Tauret's soft, heavily accented voice, expectant and ghostly, reverberated through the eons.

"Remove the amulet from beneath the scarab. No other eyes must see. Wear the amulet, a gift from Almighty Pharaoh."

Chione thought that at any moment she would faint.

"Do not remove it from around your neck until you understand the meaning of the token. Speak of it to no one who is not Pharaoh."

Again, Chione saw Tauret's face, so much like her own; in Tauret's eyes, a hint of desperation accompanied by a feeling of waiting and a need to hurry. *I promise!* Chione said in a mental message. Then suddenly, she snapped back inside her physical body.

"What is it?" Aaron asked. "Too much noise tonight?"

"How long have I been out?"

"Out? You haven't left. You only now closed your eyes."

"You won't believe what I just saw."

"Just now? In the blink of an eye? How much did you get?"

"Let me sit here, please. Let me absorb."

They sat. The next time she opened her eyes she found him slumped. Then he quickly roused. When he saw that her eyes were open, he rubbed his own and stretched. "I have a feeling I wasn't with you."

"Where were you?" She still tingled with the effects of her vision.

"Suspended somewhere." He rubbed the back of his neck. "Listening to a voice saying that all the children haven't yet reincarnated."

"So, it's true," Chione said quietly. "The spell was meant for those children." She could barely contain herself, like she was still inside her vision, or about to go back into it; all the while experiencing Aaron's as well.

Aaron beamed. "Tell me, did I add a piece of the puzzle or what?" He sounded happy to supply something she did not already know.

"We were right," she said. "Those gifted children who piled up like the stack of mummies, if they are reincarnates of the little ones in the Second Chamber, the children are being reborn."

"Do you believe the person in the Burial Chamber is going to reincarnate too?" he asked. "Aren't we already stretching things a bit?"

"Can't say. The particular feeling I'm left with is a dire urgency to find the sarcophagus."

"Urgency?"

"Other than for obvious reasons, I'm not sure." Her intuition told her they must find that chamber soon. Perhaps this was the best time to tell him. She wanted to share her theory with someone and felt she would not be able to withhold much longer. Aaron was the only person in whom she could confide. "Do you remember?" she asked cautiously. "The golden statue in the Second Annex?"

"How can anyone forget?"

"Tauret was pregnant."

He looked straight into her eyes, his expression one of expectation, then comprehension and surprise. "Could it be…?"

"That statue wasn't an Amarnian figure with rounded hips and full thighs."

"She was designed to look pregnant?"

"That's what I believe."

"Well, if all the children are reincarnating," Aaron said. "What about Tauret's child?"

Now Chione wanted to tell him everything. Suddenly she felt herself being pulled into another trance. She had intended to tell Aaron about Tauret's message but found she could not speak. Tauret warned her never to reveal the message. She was being pulled into an altered state to keep from blurting it out! Tauret's face appeared again, the face of a woman who could influence a Pharaoh and seal their liaison with her spells. What power she had possessed. Even now, as Chione studied the image, the patient eyes spoke all. Here was a woman much sought after for wisdom. She was also a woman feared for her authority and not to be crossed. Chione felt Tauret's strength and feared her. Then she realized that the strength was not too foreign from how she perceived her own.

The image faded and Chione's thoughts drifted to Queen Tyi. Jibade felt a strong connection with her tomb. That was why he bribed a caretaker to allow them inside. Ever since she visited that Queen's tomb, Chione's emotions had been stirred and a great shift occurred in her psychic sensibility. She was thankful no one else accompanied them. Jibade bypassed studying the walls and opted to sit on the floor of the Queen's empty Burial Chamber. Chione felt a presence surround them. It was a familiar vibration, thought without visual images, and left her mother, Jibade, and her with feelings of deep peace. The glow lingered. That connection could be responsible for her now having dreams and visions with deeper, more distinctive qualities.

Aaron's gentle voice penetrated into her reverie. "What was it inside Tyi's tomb that affected you?"

She roused. Had he been reading her thoughts at that very moment? "I told you. It's in a state of repair. Not much to see."

"I get it. It's not what you saw. It's what you perceived. What does all that mean?"

"Aaron, you need to deepen your own perception. You'd understand much more."

"I'm trying, Chione, but tell me anyway."

"It's this way," she said. "When you're trying to tune into something, you need to immerse yourself in information about it. That's what I did in Queen Tyi's tomb, immersed myself in the surroundings of the Ancients."

"Why did you pick Tyi's tomb for a meditation?"

"Jibade chose it. Tyi's likeness was found in this tomb, after all."

He hesitated, with an expression she had come to know that meant he had something on his mind.

They sat cross-legged facing each other. "Chione, everyone knows you're getting more than you let on," he said. "Once in a while you say something no one else could possibly know." He smiled and took her hands. "Listen, when we first went through the passageway and read the walls, you told us you'd have to gather more information, but you never disclosed your findings."

"So how do I tell them Tauret was pregnant?"

"It would help everyone to be prepared for what we stand to find in the coffin."

"I'm not ready to disclose the pregnancy," Chione said. "I had thought of it only as speculation."

"It's not something we should keep from the others. They have a right to know. Plus, all the signs are there."

"Mostly in our visions."

"You can't find anything about it in the glyphs?" he asked. "You've got to say something."

"I can't reveal everything, Aaron. Some of it's too sensual."

"Not that part. Just tell what the glyphs say."

"Which amounts to a lot of metaphysical implications."

"You think anyone in this group's not up to hearing about the paranormal, after all we've learned from you?" He glanced at his watch. "C'mon. It's early. The others are still up."

"You mean tell them now?" She leaned away from him, back into the darkness, needing time to think.

"Why not?" Then he smiled. "Can you hear the music drifting in?"

"It's those laborers Jibade met."

"Let's join them." He stood and offered a hand. "The music will put everyone in a more receptive mood."

31

For the first time in nearly three weeks, the evening was mild. Clifford was in Cairo and Royce off elsewhere. The team, with Marlowe and Kenneth, remained in camp. The bloodthirsty paparazzi had not yet returned. For a while, no one needed to be concerned about the media's spying zoom lenses, which made camera-happy tourists seem docile.

The balmy late-year breezes caressed. No more unpredictable gritty wind came at them from all directions. The workers built a campfire, around which the team gathered. Some of the laborers were invited, delighted to play their instruments.

"Tonight, you eat *Koushari*," Yafeu said. "Make by Irwin, American cook. He have few news people to cook for."

"Aha," Dr. Withers said. "Now we get to see what kind of progress Irwin has made." He accepted a bowl and passed it to Marlowe.

Irwin joined them carrying more bowls of the tasty mix of macaroni, rice, chickpeas, and lentils. "I'm serving sauce on the side for those of you who can't take the heat," he said. He always carried a handful of chopsticks, hoping someone would give them a try.

"That's me," Bebe said, laughing. "Never could eat spicy food."

"We again have several types of *aysh* for the bread eaters," Irwin said as he studied the group curiously. "Doesn't anyone eat meat anymore? That's my specialty."

"No meat," Yafeu said quickly and with an exaggerated accent. "Maybe it's camel."

Siti and Yafeu served American decaf coffee and Egyptian teas. Many had adopted the drinking of hibiscus Karkade. Yansun, from aniseed, was also served since some had complained of becoming hoarse from the dry winds. Tantalizing scents of the beverages wafted in the air and pleased the senses. Around the campfire, a douceur, the gentle sweetness of the local people, fostered friendships.

The musicians knew how to set a mood. Chione sipped hot Karkade and watched purple shadows creep across desert sands. She felt mellow, deeply at peace. She had to tell the group of her findings, that she knew. This could be the best time, but she felt no rush. Each of them seemed to want to savor the moment.

The musicians began to play a tune called *Cairo*; a local hit Chione had heard them play before. Alone at home in California, she sang that very song in accompaniment with Egyptian musicians on DVD. As the musicians strummed, in front of her very eyes, their instruments changed shape. Discreetly, she did a double take and saw the musicians dressed as Ancients. The scent of Queen Nefertiti perfume wafted by. Chione felt her consciousness shift, felt compelled to stand and began to croon the torchy ballad of a person home sick for their beloved Cairo. She poured her heart into the lyrics. Not until she finished the song did she realize how entranced she had been.

As the scene shifted back to the present, "You sing like an Egyptian," one musician finally said. "With American accent!"

"I didn't know you could sing," Bebe said. "In Egyptian?"

Everyone spoke at once. Except for Kendra, who looked around from time to time, clearly wishing to find her husband. Helen and Jibade sat proudly. Helen had tears in her eyes. The musicians were energized. The oud player strummed a tune in the background. Everyone quieted and looked to her, evidently waiting for her to sing again. The mood was most conducive to disclosing a bit of information, having captured their attention inadvertently.

"Actually, Aaron and I aren't meditating this evening," Chione said. "We need to discuss some of the messages of the glyphs." The others ate in silence, leisurely, yet attentive. Music continued softly. "The overall tone of this burial is as we already know. Tauret was a priestess, involved in magic and spells, mostly having to do with women's problems though men seem included. It would seem she caused women to become pregnant when they couldn't normally conceive."

"We've verified that," Bebe said. "She extensively used pyramids in her practice too."

Chione looked to Aaron whose expression questioned. She was not about to disclose anything other than what was shown on the walls and hoped he would not let anything slip. "Something else I'm pretty sure of," she said, continuing cautiously. "About the golden statue."

"An Amarnian type figure," Bebe said. "From Akhenaten's era."

"Yes, that one," she said. "I don't believe that much gold would be consigned to a commoner."

"Nor all the other golden relics and jewels," Dr. Withers said.

"Tauret was in high favor with Pharaoh," Chione said. That was the message gleaned from the art on the chair alone. "My belief is that Tutankhamon planned to marry her."

Everyone seemed surprised but concurred.

"Maybe so," Dr. Withers said. "That would explain why he was leading her to sit in his presence."

"Yes, that chair was to be her throne," Chione said. "The story shown in the art on the backrest was the crafter's way of saying they were soon to be married."

"Tauret was to become a minor queen?" Kendra asked. "Why would Pharaoh marry a commoner?"

Bebe took a bite from Kenneth's fork, and then fanned her mouth to tame the flavor. "Don't forget," she said, still fanning, "Tauret's parents were courtiers." She gulped a couple swallows of her drink. "What we don't know is whether they gained favor before or after Pharaoh took a liking to Tauret."

"Do you find anything to verify your theory?" Dr. Withers asked.

"Many of the glyph phrases are common," Chione said. "Not a lot of solid facts, except that even this woman's beliefs make history."

"What do you think she was trying to say?"

"Twice we found references to Pharaoh wanting children," Chione said as Bebe gestured and nodded in agreement. "Since his Queen Ankhesenpa bore two stillborns, it was accepted practice that he would attempt to have children with someone else." Everyone stopped eating. All eyes were upon her. They could not learn enough. The entire team was into this way beyond professional motive and personal curiosity. "Tauret's thoughts, written as they were, say she was dreaming of giving Pharaoh a son. Much like young girls today dream of having a baby with some guy they're in love with." Chione fidgeted and could not look up. The idea hit too close to home. She wished she could give Aaron a son. She sighed and withdrew a small writing tablet from her pocket.

"Tut would take a minor queen," Dr. Withers said. "Stands to reason."

"If Tauret was near the young age of Tutankhamon," Kendra said. "Why did she die? Of a broken heart?"

Marlowe touched the side of her head as if her headache might be pounding. "It is said King Tut may have been murdered."

"Where does it say that Tauret died around the time Tut did?" Kendra asked. "If that can be proven, maybe it was suicide, over his demise."

"Nothing like that shows up on the walls yet," Bebe said.

"If she committed suicide," Aaron said. "No one's found hieroglyphs anywhere in Egypt documenting someone having taken their own life."

"You know something," Bebe said thoughtfully. "I have to say it again. This burial took place in rapid order, in a hurry, just like at Tut's tomb. Why?"

"What were the signs in Tut's tomb?" Kenneth asked. He ripped off a shred of aysh and used it to scrape around the inside of his bowl.

"The most convincing," Bebe said, "was that his quartzite sarcophagus seemed carved for someone else. The granite lid didn't match or fit and all the shrines were haphazard, not placed facing appropriate directions."

"The coffinettes found inside the canopic jars," Kendra said. "They show inscriptions of having been made for Smenkhkare."

"Maybe suicide was a disgrace in those days," Bebe said. "Maybe no one cared for her afterward, if that's what she did. If she was involved with Tut, and they murdered him for worshipping the Aten, no one would care about a concubine who believed the same religion, whether or not she was in the process of converting."

That was food for thought. Even the musicians seemed astonished. They had worked alongside the team making discoveries and heard their speculations.

Again, everyone spoke at once. This was an exciting theory, albeit speculative. Chione knew the group's interest had wandered away from what she was trying to convey. Conversation focused on the fact that the First Chamber had been neat and orderly. They could not detect the initial state of the Second Chamber due to the collapse. The Pillared Hall looked planned, but in the three annexes, everything looked thrown in. Complete wall etchings existed inside the Pillared Hall although some were not painted. Some of the glyphs in the passageway were in the process of being reworked, as well as glyphs on some of the art pieces in the Pillared Hall. The Aten was being restored to Amon, yet not completed.

"The way we can assume there was a hurry is to remember the spells Bebe and I logged," Chione said. She hesitated, waiting for someone else to put the pieces together and comment.

"You mean," Jibade said, breaking his silence. "That the spells have cloaked meanings?"

"They could have," Chione said. "We'll learn more once we find the Burial chamber." The sun was sinking fast. She turned the notebook toward the flickering firelight in order to find the page she wanted.

"Have you found any other rubrics, evidence to lead you to this way of thinking?" Jibade asked.

"Here's a new one," Chione said, studying her notes.

Spend not one night below

the Underworld lives
intruders must go.

"Oh, my," Bebe said. "When did you find that one?"

"A few days back. I was trying to decipher a pattern out of all the writings before mentioning it."

"Was that verse warning us not to sleep in the tomb, which we've already done?" Marlowe asked.

"Evidently not," Chione said. "Since nothing bad happened to any of us."

"Any other messages?"

"Try this one," she said.

Mourn not those
in the Afterlife,
for they live
without any strife.

Dr. Withers put his fork down and poked a familiar finger in the air. They waited for him to finish chewing and pull his thoughts together. Then he asked, "Could you be wrong, maybe a little off in your translations?"

"Not unless Champollion's method of deciphering is faulty," Chione said.

"Ah, yes, Jean-Francois Champollion," Dr. Withers said. "Can't negate what he proved about interpreting hieroglyphs."

"What do all the spells mean?" Kenneth asked, chewing while he spoke. Bebe jabbed him in the ribs.

"Everything points to belief in not just the Afterlife," Aaron said cautiously. "But toward reincarnation as well." Chione was glad Aaron was the one who offered that information.

"Now, c'mon, Aaron," Kenneth said. "That's stretching it a bit, don't you think?"

"Everything about this tomb is far from ordinary," Marlowe said.

With the irregularity of the spells, the magic, the pyramids, why couldn't anything else that went along with it be entertained, at least till they learned more. "I believe that's why the god Khentimentiu shows up a lot," Chione said. "He's the god of the dead's destiny."

"Yes," Kendra said. "What was that other spell about Khentimentiu?" Aaron quoted it.

Down this corridor no living walk.
No sounds in these halls creak.
Only Anubis inside doth stalk
till Khentimentiu speak.

"See there? What does it mean if Anubis is hanging around the hall? God of embalming? Guardian of hidden and secret things? His job was supposed to be finished after mummification." Kendra said. "Then Khentimentiu, god of the dead's destiny, is to speak. Why?" She looked around but did not wait for a reply. "To tell us of an unfinished destiny for the mummy? Is that why Anubis is hanging around? Because someone is to live again—reincarnate—before they go into the Underworld once and for all?" That was a mouthful for Kendra. The theory did have some mystique involved, after all, and Kendra did not seem afraid to examine it.

"That's re-e-ally stretching it," Dr. Withers said.

"This will take some figuring out," Aaron said.

The belief system of the Ancients of that time period needed to be examined with an open mind if they were to understand.

"The spells mean something," Kendra said. "How about that other one?"

Beware, two who would enter
the spell is cast to last
till all of time has passed.

"Which two would enter?" Kendra asked. "This refers to future life here."

"You're going too far afield with this," Dr. Withers said.

That was all Chione intended to tell them for now. Their thoughts were focused in the right direction but in no way was she going to disclose her dreams of being Tauret and making love to Pharaoh. Especially since everyone knew Aaron had dreamed of himself as King Tut. As real as visions were for her, the rest of the group was not ready to hear of royal trysts. Somehow everything would be revealed to the rest of them at the proper time, perhaps with the help of the ancient gods.

Later, as everyone parted for a good night's rest, Aaron approached her looking a little perturbed. "I thought you were going to tell them Tauret was pregnant."

"The way the conversation went, they'd heard enough," she said. "Don't mention Tauret's pregnancy, Aaron. That's not something I want known until I'm sure. We found nothing in the glyphs about her condition."

"Why not tell? Surely we can trust the team."

"Because, Aaron, I believe Tauret and Tut had to keep their affair subdued for a while. So until I get a message from Tauret to divulge her secrets, I don't think I'll be shocking anybody with unproven speculation."

"Okay," he said, sighing. "That can wait a bit more." Turning to leave, he looked back and smiled gently. "You were spectacular. I didn't know you could sing."

"I didn't either," she said quietly.

He stopped in his tracks, turned back again. "You've never sung like that before?"

"Not like that."

"You mean you were entranced right in front of everyone, taking on Tauret's characteristics, and no one noticed?"

"No one would understand. A lot of things must go unsaid."

Later, Chione lay on her cot, crossed her arms over her chest, and mentally recited Tauret's admonishment and her own promise. Her last thought before falling asleep was to wonder why Tauret had shown her a scarab placed on top of the mummy on the outside of the wrappings. Tradition dictated amulets and other valuables be embedded between layers of wrappings and inside the mummy's body cavity.

32

Chione and Aaron peered at the crowd from behind the double fly of the cook tent. "From the day the paparazzi got wind of Rita's demise," Chione said, "reporters from around the world have taken it upon themselves to plague the site." Now that the sand had stopped blowing, the curious returned in droves.

"Too many visitors was the reason Dr. Withers refused to take time off like the rest of us," Aaron said, shaking his head. "He's the one the dignitaries want to talk to. It's left him little time to scrutinize incoming offers. He wants to review all of them in order to avoid being backed into a corner."

"Before committing to the pressures of the Yagos?"

The directors inadvertently put a hold on further work until their arrival. A faxed message said they would remain in Cairo until the most recent shipment of artifacts was uncrated at the Madu. Dr. Withers seemed, at times, ready to pull out his hair. Endless days of biding time took a toll while engineers continued taking soundings on the hillock. Each negative report drove home Chione's warnings of failure with the usage of sensors. Dr. Withers grew fatigued pretending everything was going according to plan. Yet, how long could he hide not having found the burial chamber once the directors arrived?

As if needing to stir up some activity, he ordered sleeping rooms be completed for the directors. In a flurry of activity not seen in weeks, a crude flat-roofed mud-brick structure, two rooms with a common wall, went up before nightfall. No windows were built in, just one front and one back doorway in each room for ventilation. Those would be covered with swatches of heavy cloth for privacy. Two single woven cots would be placed inside, one against each side wall in the tiny cubicles. The shacks would have time to bake dry in the penetrating sun before the intended occupants arrived.

Messages came in from all over the world asking when the Burial Chamber would be opened. Chione, too, felt frustrated. Neither could she, capable in ways transcending conventional methods, come up with the location.

"I've let everybody down," she said to Aaron. The grand opportunity to prove herself and the legitimacy of her abilities was at stake.

"Never mind that you were instrumental in how we've progressed so far," Aaron said testily.

Not finding the Burial Chamber left them open to ridicule. "The pressure's on," Chione said. "I'm feeling every bit of it." Yet she knew she needed to stay in control. Anxiety disturbed her concentration.

That evening as she and Aaron prepared for their quiet time in the Pillared Hall, Chione asked, "Do you mind if my parents sit with us?"

"Why?" he asked, showing much surprise.

"Because I want Jibade present."

"What can he contribute that we can't learn by ourselves?"

"I think four of us would be stronger together."

Aaron looked frustrated and she understood. Here he was, finally able to share with her again and now she asks to invite others into their precious time together. She felt empathy for Aaron and longed to show him she was actually having strong feelings for him again, but now was not the time for personal interests. Any emotion other than focusing on the Burial Chamber would prove too disconcerting.

"Maybe you and he should sit alone," Aaron said. "You did well at Queen Tyi's."

"Aaron, in case you hadn't noticed, you're a part of this and there's no turning back."

"Perhaps not." He shrugged, looked dubious. "Maybe all you need is a strong opposite. Surely Jibade is more adept than I."

If Chione had not known how successful Aaron was in his career and the rest of his life, he would have seemed meek at that moment. He had built a great career and was confident in all aspects of his endeavors. In his mind, the only thing he lacked was her presence. His readiness to relinquish his place beside her at a crucial moment, despite balking momentarily, was actually another example of his manhood. He would do just that, step aside, so as not to be an obstacle.

She smiled sincerely. "You need to be here. Trust me." He would because she knew how much he wished their lives could be forever entwined.

"All right," he said, standing.

She stood too. "I'll go invite them."

"I'll go."

"No, I can go," she said, rushing ahead of him. The moment began to sound like a game. They both laughed. He had hold of her arm and pulled her back. She turned quickly to face him, and they bumped smack together looking into each other's eyes.

Both his hands were on her arms. He pushed her away slightly, still staring hard, momentarily stunned at their closeness. "I-I prefer to be the one climbing out of the shaft in the dark," he said finally. He did not let go immediately, just stood looking into her eyes.

Helen did not come into the tomb, did not wish to climb down in the semi-darkness. Chione sat in her usual place. Aaron hesitated. Chione motioned for them to sit, and they did. Then Jibade stood again and motioned. "Sit there," he said to Aaron while pointing beside her, so they would form a triangle.

"Why?" Aaron asked.

"This time you both have the opportunity to face north," he said. "I'll be your battery for the energy."

He evidently knew much more than Chione realized. Once they sat in place, Jibade closed his eyes and began to chant a prayer in Arabic as a hint of incense wafted.

Soon, Aaron slumped. Then Jibade quieted and a great peace came over her as a scene opened out inside her mind.

Lush scenes of Ancient Egypt. Being fitted for leather sandals with jeweled straps, a jeweler sealing a lock of Pharaoh's hair inside the back of an amulet, a trek to an oasis.

On and on the scenes paraded, each one beckoning, drawing her in.

Mixing potions, casting spells. Surrounded by thankful women swollen with child. Pyramid forms standing over herbs used in prescriptions. A familiar hand touching hers—

Quite unexpectedly, Chione emerged out of the trance. How disappointing! Her heart ached for more. She yearned to re-enter that ancient time. Nothing happened. *Please*, she begged silently, *we're so close*. Still, nothing. Her mind began to wander over the glorious scenes she had just witnessed; life in Ancient Egypt and curiously, pyramids being used as she presently utilized them to preserve food and other items. Yet, where was the man who had been present in the other dreams and visions? What made her snap back to consciousness?

She concentrated on the hand that had touched hers and began to float back into that same room...

...on the woven reed bed behind the mashrabia panels, intoxicated with incense and uro. His kilt and nemes cast aside. His black hair sun bleached with fine streaks of red. His lips, his body pressed urgently.

"I see you unclothed as another sees you, my King."

"Yet, you do for me what the other cannot."

Floating out of the trance, Chione sighed loudly and flinched with disappointment when she realized what had happened. She glanced at Aaron, then Jibade. They remained just as she left them. She wondered if she should attempt to go back into the trance now that she was out again. Like before, she came out of that same scene unexpectedly, knowing the two on the pallet would make love. Why was she being shown such a scenario that was, perhaps, of a lifetime left unfinished? Why did she feel such burning desire to complete what had been taking place? Could the scene ultimately offer clues to the location of the Burial Chamber? If she returned to the scene, would she be intruding on royal privacy? The decision was not hers to make.

His body was heavy on her, buttocks hard as diorite in her hands.
"Your passion is great in spite of the child," he said.
"Take me, my King. Give me your true flail!"
"But the child in your womb...."
"Easy then, O Pharaoh most powerful, slayer of enemies, benevolent protector. I give you an heir when others cannot. Oba, take my breath, pleasure me your body."
"Yes, Umayma. I cannot resist. I will have you now."
And so, he did. As she touched and teased and enticed, he took her again and again until they were sated.

Chione was suddenly back on the mat in the Pillared Hall, disoriented, breath labored. She had felt it all. Tauret and Pharaoh had loved, and she felt the ecstasy that Tauret experienced. She had never felt such sensational intensity of anything in her life. Was that what making love felt like? Was that why many sought sexual gratification above all else? She felt numb, yet awed. Sitting on the mat in the dimly lit Pillared Hall, she wanted more. Flames of passion licked through her. Why, when making love as Tauret, had she seen that other face instead of seeing Aaron?

Both Aaron and Jibade roused quickly. She reached for Aaron, who looked like Pharaoh. She withdrew from his look of utter surprise and caution. Had he just had the same experience? Had they...? She reached for her father, then clung quickly again to Aaron.

"Yes!" Aaron said in that ancient voice.

She pushed away from him. The look of Pharaoh burned in his eyes.

"What is happening, my daughter?"

Jibade's voice seeped in and calmed her disorientation. Aaron reached for her. Panic welled up, and she quickly scooted away on her buttocks and gestured that they wait till she got her bearings. She took a few moments. Finally, Jibade bade her to come close again. "What did you perceive?"

Instead, she looked to Aaron. "W-what did you g-get?"

He looked away quickly. "Pictures, just pictures. Lots of scenes." He looked up as if pathetically struggling with emotions. "And you?"

"Me, too," she said, lying though she burned with want. She could barely resist throwing herself into his arms.

"Tell us," Jibade said.

"Lots of scenes, the Ancients," she said, finding it difficult to speak. "More pieces... pieces of the puzzle."

"You must have experienced something different," Aaron said. "Anything stay with you?"

"I-I came out of it too fast," was all she dared say.

They talked a while as she struggled for some semblance of normalcy. Later she hugged Jibade a good long hug. "Good night, Father," she said. "Thank you for being a beacon in my life."

Aaron prepared to leave as well and touched her arm. "You were upset about something," he said. "Let me hold you for just a moment."

Pharaoh's eyes. Her first impulse was to melt against him. *Buttocks hard as diorite in my hands.* She controlled herself and pulled away. "I-I'm okay."

"No fair," he said with a teasing whine. "Jibade got to!"

They had to laugh. She went into his arms, loving arms that held her snugly. Surely, he must have sizzled in that same vision. Now she burned for him again. Her arms went around his neck. She nuzzled her face in close and detected... the scent of Pharaoh!

The next day, Dr. Withers reported Marlowe's headaches were getting the best of her. Siti insisted Marlowe ingest helva with fenogreek and other local herbs to settle her stomach.

"The local people ingest the ancient remedies when they contract *Bilharzia*," Chione said.

"That's potentially a life-threatening disease of the tropics," Dr. Withers said as if he could not believe that might happen to his wife.

"Caused by infestation of schistosomes from the local waters," Aaron said.

"I spoke to Vimble," Dr. Withers said, rubbing his chin thoughtfully. "Marlowe has no other symptoms of infection, like dizziness, drowsiness, abdominal pain or backaches. Can't you do something, Chione?" He looked like a man about to be pushed over the edge. "She'll listen to you, Girl. Vimble said she should be tested for parasites anyway. If need be, he can prescribe *Praziquantel* or something like that."

Marlowe had a mind of her own. She claimed not to have eaten or drunk anything from the local foodstuffs not prepared by Yafeu or Irwin. She, like everyone else, had eaten some of Royce's food. Yet, the headaches began long before that. Chione suspected something else. Marlowe remained quiet, not moving about much and barking at her dear husband every time he caringly suggested she return home to see her doctor. With Marlowe's preoccupation with the paranormal being intensified by the effects of the tomb, would she be able to break away and return home to save her life?

Later alone with stacks of paperwork inside the tech shack, Chione watched through the window as Marlowe approached. As usual, in recent days, she loosened the tight hair bun at the back of her head. Her black hair hung loose around her shoulders, to keep the hair from pulling at the headache, she said. With shiny hair billowing loose, she looked younger, freer, with something new in the way she walked. The closer she came; the more Chione sensed her excitement. She looked around before entering. That meant she wanted to talk about things the others would not understand. When she stepped inside, she looked outside again, and then closed the door. Then she spoke excitedly but in whispers. "It's happened."

"What?" Chione asked.

"I've had a vision just like some of yours!" She put a hand over her heart, reveling in the truth.

"No kidding."

"It's about my headaches, that is, these are not my headaches." To know for sure was to have experienced an extrasensory moment that told her something undeniable; something she would not have been able to reason out with only her conscious mind.

"Tell me what you received," Chione said, interest peaked.

"My headaches, you know? They just slam into the side of my head." She made a motion with her hand nearly slapping her temple. "Earlier today, something told me my headaches are from being hit."

"You were hit? By whom?"

"Not me, Chione. I've never been hit. I think I saw it, but I'm not sure. You know, in a kind of vision, while I was resting."

"Maybe you're hoping too hard for answers."

"The only thing I know is that I'm getting these headaches as a result of a blow. It's not a blow to me. I've never been hit, not even as a child."

"What are you saying?" Chione asked. "You're seeing someone else who was hit? Or it's going to happen to someone?"

"I saw a fleeting moment of someone with jet black hair, crying, I think," Marlowe said. "I just know the headaches are the result of someone being hit."

Chione saw herself...

...sitting in the royal chair, gifted from Pharaoh.

She remembered the first time they were in the Pillared Hall. Aaron and Dr. Withers thought she had fainted again as her head flopped over suddenly. She fell out of the chair as if she had been someone else who had been pushed. Who might she have been? Goosebumps traipsed down her arms.

Marlowe looked puzzled and then smiled suddenly. "You want to know something?"

"Tell me."

"Ever since I realized this earlier today, I haven't—oh, Chione!" she said as the revelation hit her. "I haven't had a headache since."

"You sure?"

"Do you think someone or something was trying to give us a message through me?"

In a few moments, Marlowe went from weariness to the optimist she had always been.

By late that evening, Marlowe had not had another headache. Her husband was relieved, to say the least. So relieved, he hurriedly faxed a glowing recommendation for Randy to Cairo. Chione did not have to cajole, request or encourage any effort from Dr. Withers. After all, what could the recommendation do but tell the truth? In the past, Randy's work performance had been exemplary. All people have shortcomings. Randy had his own peculiar idiosyncrasies that grated on people's nerves and, at times, interfered with his job performance.

Quietly, so the others would not hear, Chione asked, "Dr. Withers, can I run something by you about Randy?"

"Of course."

"Before he left, Randy thanked me for what he thinks he learned from me."

Dr. Withers' expression showed a deep relief. "That's encouraging," he said. "I was hoping I hadn't overdone my praise of the man in order to be rid of him."

33

With work at a standstill, Masud occupied himself leading tours. He was a blessing in disguise since the team members avoided association with anyone asking too many questions about the stalled progress. Masud played his sense of innocence well, through feigned broken-English, deflecting much of the nagging curiosity of those waiting impatiently for a glimpse of the grand prize. He had a keen sense of what needed attention and just set about doing what he found to do.

Between tours, Masud approached Chione when she was alone and asked if he might speak about Dakarai. "I have bad feelings for this man. Too many times our people watch him."

"You have suspicions about Dakarai?" Chione needed to be careful not to divulge past encounters with the man. "What kind?"

"Well, look now," Masud said avoiding eye contact. "Do you see him? Does he show for work?"

"You're upset because he's mostly absent from the site?"

"Always like this," he said. "At other work sites too. He disappears."

"What's your concern?"

"That he has other business with wrong people." His gaze wandered around the ground at their feet.

"How can you be sure?"

"Our office does not hear from him for days or weeks," Masud said as he opened out his hands. "He is not here. Please, what does he do?"

"Tell me, Masud," Chione said. "How do I know I can trust you? How do I know you're not fishing?"

"Fishing, like in the Nile?"

He looked puzzled. Was this more practiced innocence? "Not exactly. Listen. How do I know you're not trying to get information out of me?" She faked preoccupation with some papers. Something about Masud and the conversation cautioned.

"You do not. You will trust me?"

"First, you should have faith."

"Trust to Allah?" he asked. "Sometimes this takes long. Then more artifacts disappear before Allah finds him."

Chione saw...

...a dimly lit chamber with boxes stacked around.

That threatening feeling came again. "You think he's involved with the taking of our artifacts?"

"That's what you must learn."

"Me? How?"

"With your mind, O Little One." Now his hands were clasped, but he still kept his gaze lowered. "You see pictures."

"Oh, Masud, I've never seen anything involving Dakarai."

"Nothing?" He sounded sorely disappointed. "I hope to see an end to this."

"You mean if you can catch Dakarai, or the thieves, we'd have no more missing artifacts?"

"Yes, O Little One." He pushed his clasped hands toward her. "Please. Talk to Allah. Ask if Dakarai—"

"I can't do that, Masud."

"Excuse, please," he said, and then began backing away. He had made a fool of himself. He bowed his head and then turned to leave.

"Wait," she said, glancing in his direction. "Masud, believe me. The situation will take care of itself. We've got ample guards now."

"Safe here. What about future? What happens when Dakarai take from other places?"

"Seriously, Masud, if Dakarai's the one, he along with all the others working with him will be caught."

Quickly, he came close again. "Do you know if they look for him?" Suddenly his willingness to resume the questioning seemed too probing. Chione had no way of knowing if Masud might be involved with Dakarai. In the beginning, both men had worked side by side. Until Dakarai's lengthy absences began, one would have thought the two were inseparable and Masud involved in everything with Dakarai. That may not have been the case, but she could not take the chance. "I don't know anything. But I do have faith in higher powers."

"You will tell if he is caught?" Masud asked.

Truly now, he was fishing and his motives were unclear. He would get no more information out of her. He backed away apologizing.

Chione wished he had not sought her out. If Dakarai was caught perpetrating the thefts, and if Masud were implicated in any way, then Masud would have to accept whatever fate had concocted for both of them. She wanted no part of it.

Later, completing the telling of the Masud episode to Dr. Withers, she said, "Those are my suspicions."

"Fine, looks like we have a lot to be thankful for."

"Sir?"

"Tomorrow's Thanksgiving, or have you forgotten?" he asked. "Everything's playing itself out. We have a lot to be thankful for."

"Oh," Chione said, embarrassed at having forgotten. "Our American holiday."

He reached for her hand like a father might. "Seriously, the Bolis are conducting their own investigation."

About the only person who knew anything was Kenneth, who could not withhold fascination with the necropolis and mastabas. The only thing everyone wished was to have the artifacts returned, not for their own delight and satisfaction, but for posterity.

Two days later, Parker and Carmelita Philips and Burton and Gracie Forbes arrived about midday. They wore appropriate khaki clothing for such a trek, albeit designer made, settling into the dusty surroundings quite easily. Except for Carmelita, who complained her sleeping room was no better than a tent and why did Dr. Withers build such meager quarters.

Carmelita was much younger than her husband, and both were younger than the Forbeses, who looked to be in their early sixties. The Forbeses adjusted the easiest. Having met Helen and Siti, Gracie Forbes decided she would learn to cook local fare. She was surprised to learn the impeccable Marlowe Withers spent much time in the kitchen as well.

The team members previously met the directors at the university. Only Dr. Withers socialized with them and maybe Clifford and Rita had once or twice. To the rest, these were people who evidently lived well on their own turf.

Another meal table was added and lunch served except to Kenneth and Royce who, lately, was elsewhere. After Gracie sampled the food, she said, "What a wonderful dinner party this would make, with Egyptian decorations and music, belly dancers and all. Yafeu, would you consider a trip to California?"

Burton responded the way Dr. Withers might have with Marlowe in the same situation. He simply smiled lovingly as if his wife could do no wrong.

Carmelita, with her long blood-red nails, and pancake makeup threatening to streak from perspiration, did not fare as well. "We should have made preparations for our arrival," she said. "That shack will never do. We need air conditioning. The smell of the mud walls is horrible." She fanned herself and looked around expecting pity. Her attitude was patronizing, self-serving. She picked at her food, complained about everything, and gossiped about people no one else at the table knew or cared to hear about. Just when it looked as if she might open her mouth to say something more, a hard-stomping sound came from under the table, boot on boot. Carmelita flinched. Her husband had nipped the urge in the bud.

After lunch, the new arrivals went for a tour of the tomb. Dr. Withers, Aaron, and Chione led the way. When Carmelita learned she would have to climb down the portcullis shaft on a makeshift wooden ladder she refused. She eased close to the edge like a frightened cat and looked into the deep, gaping shaft, then backed away nervously.

"We could lower you in a swing," Dr. Withers said. Chione knew her boss well. His offer was one of patient compliance. Had Clifford been present with his unique humor, he might have suggested they throw the catty complainer over the side and assume she would land on all fours.

"Can't we just walk in somewhere?" Carmelita asked, whining.

"That part of the tomb was never completed," Aaron said. "There's a passage, but you'll have to crawl through."

"That sounds easier," she said, looking to her husband for assurance. He only scrunched up his mouth and hand gestured, signifying they would enter through the smaller passageway.

"I'll bring them along," Chione said. She had a hunch Dr. Withers and Aaron wanted to speak with the Forbeses and Carmelita was in the way. She would guide Parker and Carmelita through the axial corridor slowly to allow the others time to say a few words. The way Carmelita was so picky she would probably take her time anyway, so as not to get too dirty. She was in for a surprise.

When Carmelita saw the size of the opening through which she would have to pass, she balked again.

Parker sighed heavily and said, "Look, Carmel, no one here's responsible for these ancient passages. Do you want to see the inside or not?"

Carmelita looked disgruntled but signaled they should enter.

"Okay, this is what you do," Chione said, lowering herself on all fours and backing into the opening.

"Ba-ackwards?" Carmelita asked in that same high-pitched whine.

"You can't go head first," Chione said, her own patience tested. "It's too steep. Look." She leaned to the side as far as possible. "The floor has rungs to step on. It'll be easy."

"I can't do this," Carmelita said. "I can't—"

"Just get on your knees!" Parker said.

Chione wondered how Parker could tolerate this woman's game playing. He looked like an easy-going cowboy off some dude ranch. Maybe that was his problem. Finally, Carmelita got down on all fours and began following Chione who kept her flashlight trained upward for Carmelita's sake. Parker eagerly followed his wife who grunted and whimpered.

Not half-way down the long passage, Carmelita whined again. "It's too dark. I might slip."

"You're doing just fine," Parker said, directing his voice downward toward his wife.

"You should have gone first, Parker. What if I slip?"

"You won't slip," Chione said. "Just move slowly and place your feet firmly on each rung."

A few feet farther and Carmelita whined yet again. "Stop, stop, I can't do this. It's too narrow."

Chione looked up. Using the heel of her hand so as not to break her nails, Carmelita pushed against her husband's boots to signal him to climb upward.

"Carmel!"

"Go out," she said. "Go out." So, they began to climb upward to go out.

"I'll see you inside," Chione said, "I'm going down." Let Parker deal with her. Chione was not about to let Carmelita become a problem.

As Chione approached the others inside the tomb, she pulled her braided hair out of her shirt where she had tucked it so it would not drag in the dust. "To think I had to get this gritty again," she said, whispering to Aaron. "For her."

"Where are they?" he asked quietly.

Just then they heard Parker's voice coaxing his wife down the portcullis ladder. "I'm right below you," he said.

"Ay, Dios!" Carmelita said.

"Just take it easy. I'm right below you," Parker said again.

Chione put her hand across her mouth to keep from openly laughing.

Aaron beamed a broad smile and shook his head. "I'll take them through the first chambers," he said quietly. "If Carmelita will allow herself to reach the bottom." Then he headed back up the passageway.

In time, Aaron and the Philipses caught up to the group in the Pillared Hall. After a cursory examination of the annexes and reliefs, Carmelita asked, "You still haven't opened the burial suite for us to see?"

"It's not been located yet," Aaron said.

"They'll need to do some excavating topside," Burton said. His voice expressed practiced patience, probably more for Parker's sake.

"We will get to see it before we leave, won't we?" Carmelita asked. Her superficial interest was evidence she understood viewing the tomb was merely part of another vacation. She had no inkling of the importance of the work at hand. Nor would she be able to understand the dire situation of locating the most important chamber of all.

Everyone headed topside scrambling up the portcullis shaft. Dr. Withers stayed at the bottom while Parker again coaxed his wife to make the return trip. Dr. Withers had to call up for a rope to attach around Carmelita's waist should she lose her footing. Some of the men in gallibayas performing duties atop the shaft spoke in Egyptian, which Chione pretended not to hear. Their eyes flashed as they tried hard not to laugh out loud.

Burton shook his head and walked away.

"Don't mind Carmelita," Gracie said to her and Aaron. "She needs a lot of attention."

"Really?" Chione asked, not wanting to say anything derogatory.

"She's *nouveau riche*," Gracie said with a French accent.

"Pardon me?" Aaron asked.

"You know, the *new rich*," Gracie said. "People who aren't born with it. They marry into it." She smiled. "They complain about everything. They've never had anything. When they get it, they pick it apart. That's the new rich. They put on airs because they don't know how to act like they've always had it."

"I see," Chione said, being nice.

"She married Parker just after he inherited big," Gracie said. "But I guess it's me who's gossiping now." She smiled cautiously. "Just wanted to warn you. Carmelita's nice enough, but she can wreak a lot of havoc." Then Gracie became serious again. "Help Burton and me prevent Carmelita from ruining things, won't you?"

What could Carmelita possibly do to ruin anything other than grate on people's nerves? She was only a visiting Director's wife. Surely, she would have no say over what might happen or when. She might, however, be able to influence Parker's decisions and that could lead to a split in management decision-making. In any event, they would soon find out when they met again in the morning to hash over the details of the Yago family offer.

After dinner, Carmelita again made a nasty issue of her accommodations. Despite footers, no one seemed surprised to hear her frantic screams when she found a huge yellow scorpion in her bed.

34

Dr. Withers slipped off to take a nap and others scattered, taking advantage of the slowdown in project activities. Tarik approached and seemed beside himself. Always friendly, Chione welcomed the camaraderie of this young boy, though she did not understand why. She had never felt close to any child. They stepped into the deserted inventory tent and sat at a workbench.

"Jibade make Aaron wear Egyptian clothes," Tarik said, smirking and hunching his shoulders. "Gallibaya, turban."

"Why would my dad make him do that?"

"To hide. Jibade say, because of media." The boy seemed to have much to say and could not relate everything at once. "They go see Amunet, below." He gestured in the direction of the beggars' camp.

"Amunet?"

"A magic woman. That how you say?"

"He wore a cover-up to see a mystic?" The idea of Aaron going down there did not surprise Chione. His need to find the burial chamber seemed frantic. If a mystic could help, he would see her.

"Jibade say no one to see Aaron," Tarik said, then tapped his cheek. "Sun make Aaron skin dark. Look like Pharaoh." He was cuter when he was being devious. "Jibade tell Aaron visit woman. Aaron, he go. Jibade wise. He hide Aaron in Egyptian clothes." Tarik giggled.

"Well, that's interesting, but I really must get busy now."

"Please wait, Ma'am," Tarik said quickly. "Maybe Aaron sick."

"Aaron ill?"

"I hear him say—"

"Wait a minute. You eavesdropped?"

"Eav…eaves…." Tarik struggled with the word.

"You listened, Tarik?" She was about to scold him but curiosity made her hold her tongue. Maybe she enjoyed Tarik being devious because it helped her loosen up. "And?"

"Aaron tell Jibade he see something."

"Aaron saw something." Chione realized that neither was it the right moment to give Tarik a grammar lesson. "What did he see? Where?"

"Aaron tell Jibade about picture in head."

The moment Tarik mentioned pictures in Aaron's mind, Chione saw a vision of…

…a young boy, with hair cut in the sidelocks of youth, wearing only a child's pleated kilt, scantily clad for the heat of the day.

"Wow!" she said.

"You see picture too," Tarik said. He was excited. "I know about picture."

"You?"

"Yes, Ma'am." He looked pleased. "I follow Aaron and Jibade and hear."

"You understand about mind pictures?" She stood and looked outside the tent to make sure no one else heard. "You what? You followed them?"

As their conversation progressed, Chione gleaned that Jibade told Aaron that a message awaited him if he would visit the psychic reader.

With the increased frequency of his paranormal episodes, perhaps Aaron trusting Jibade would shed some light on the often at times frightening aspects of phenomena. Aaron recently admitted to repeating Tauret's spells like chanting a mantra, as absentmindedly as when he doodled those crosshatches. He was succumbing to the phenomena without a clue of understanding.

Chione's interest peaked. "What else?"

Tarik spilled everything. He told of magicians, sorcerers and psychic readers setting up reading tents at the lower end of camp to capture the attention of tourists. Jibade took Aaron to see a woman purported to be a legitimate reader.

"Real woman. Tell future, always true."

"How do you know that, Tarik. You can't poss—"

Tarik pulled down the lower lid of one eye and said, "I see."

As Tarik related more of what he witnessed, he said Jibade asked Aaron to listen with an open mind. Jibade dragged Aaron by the elbow into the tent. Chione had to smile. Aaron would have mixed feelings about going, even if he trusted her father. "What happened when they came out?"

"Wait," Tarik said. He hesitated and squirmed on the bench. "I hear more."

"That's right, you little—you eavesdropper."

"I go behind tent, hear voices. Then go on ground, put head inside tent, and hear." He must have read the admonishing look on her face. "No one say no."

Tarik related that the woman was an American costumed as Middle Eastern. She was tall and thin, wore much jewelry, colorful clothing, and thick makeup. The way he described the curtained and veiled room sounded like a theatrical scene from an Agatha Christie movie.

Jibade introduced Aaron as the man who dreams. Then the seer lit some candles.

"What happened?" she asked.

"She goddess of mystery," he said and giggled again. "She have many crystal. She say Aaron to say name and birthday. She say 'inside mashrabia paneled room'."

Chione gasped. "I know the room."

Seeming to remember more about Amunet, Tarik asked, "All American woman wear much bracelets?"

Chione shrugged. "Some do." Her mind was on Aaron's reading. "Tell me more."

"Amunet say about woman on cot, soft pillows." He hesitated then raised his eyebrows and said, "I know what they talk."

"Tarik!"

"Aaron grab head." Tarik grabbed his head at the temples, imitating what he had seen Aaron do.

The moment Tarik mentioned Aaron grabbing his head visions she had long before seen traipsed through her mind.

Making love on a woven cot among soft tapestry pillows. Another love scene in the desert. Another, floating on a barge on the Nile.

Her head reeled. "Oh, Aaron," she said.

"Amunet tell Aaron he together again with woman."

"That he has reincarnated? With which woman?"

"The one he call Umayma."

Chione ran her fingers through her hair then held her head. She was receiving too much information too fast. Again, she had a sense of urgency like she had so much to learn and so little time. So little time till what?

Aaron was fascinated with the fact that after many incarnations and great growth, when the soul neared perfection, it used the physical body only for coming and going between ethereal and earthly planes. Perhaps being told by someone else, Aaron would see that he had reached a highly evolved state, having completed many incarnations, which allowed him to float in and out of psychic experiences. His energy was becoming pure.

"What else, Tarik?"

"Woman say he know life as Pharaoh. How Aaron do that?"

"I can't explain now." She actually wanted to spend time with this child who seemed to be teetering on the edge of the Sacred Mysteries. "Anything else?"

"Woman say need purity for connection to Ancients." Tarik stood to leave then changed his mind. "Wait, wait. Woman say, 'The spell been cast'."

"What spell?" Chione asked. "Did she say what spell?"

"No, I no understand. Woman say Aaron make big de... cee..., wait. Decis...."

"Decision?"

"Yes, de-ci-sion. Aaron make big de-ci-sion, change history."

35

During breakfast the next morning, Bebe sat beside Kendra consoling her. Chione knew exactly why. Royce spent little time at the site. Kendra thought the Yagos returned to Cairo. Instead, when the onlookers and everyone else cleared out during the sandstorm, the Yagos set up tents down the hill near the beggars' camp. Royce probably spent much of his time with them. Though the wind had not calmed completely, the Yagos returned to their favored spot on the other side of the restraining wall. Waiting to pounce. Surely Kendra felt her husband was undermining her life and career.

Bebe consoling Kendra was nearly comedy. Did she honestly know where Kenneth spent his time? Rumor had it that he, too, visited the camp, but not to see the Yagos. Between the two husbands and now Carmelita, their little village could well become what Clifford referred to as the Peyton Place of Thebes. Chione meant to ask him what he meant by Peyton Place.

After breakfast, the team scattered to tend to minor chores. Sunlight was brilliant again. Then Chione saw Aaron, standing high on the hillock, looking out over the site.

Pharaoh surveying his Kingdom. Pharaoh wearing khaki.

He saw her and pointed behind her. She turned to see Dr. Withers rushing up with Burton and Parker and motioning for all to join them.

She felt ready for a session in the cook tent. Being outside meant always being photographed. It was beginning to unnerve her.

"Okay, listen up," Dr. Withers said as cool drinks were being served. He pulled at his mustache, shifting gears.

Chione watched from her vantage point at the far end of the table, and wondered if Dr. Withers would be able to think without the fetish on his upper lip.

"First of all, I want you, Aaron," Dr. Withers said, holding up a notepad for all to see. "To stop doodling on every piece of scratch paper in camp." Aaron's crosshatching covered the page to the far corners. They laughed as Dr. Withers ripped off the page and threw it onto the table, and then ripped off yet another also marked. "To get down to business, we've got two predicaments here." He sat forward and peered over his bifocals. "We're going to make some decisions today, and we're going to move forward. Burton and Parker and I have already discussed our situation."

Burton and Parker nodded and waited.

No one said a word. They did not know how much detail had been supplied to the Directors, so it was best to let their leader have his say.

Aaron still doodled crosshatch lines. Chione leaned over and quickly inserted an X in one of the spaces. Aaron positioned the mugs side by side to make sure no one watched their play, and then drew in a circle. The game ended quickly.

Chione had been feeling powerfully bonded to Aaron and for a moment, mentally questioned why. Then he drew another crosshatch. Quickly she put her X in the same open square she favored on the side of the grid. Her leg was against his under the table. Body heat came through his khaki trousers. He had not moved his leg away. He would not. She pretended not to notice and left hers against his, wanting it there. Then she saw them...

...*on a woven mat, his long bronzed muscular legs wrapped around her.*

305

"Aaron," Dr. Withers was saying. "You talk for a while. Tell us your idea."

She and Aaron looked up and tried to pay more attention.

"We plan to bore holes around the periphery of the Pillared Hall," Aaron said. "We'll have to clear more rubble off the hillock though. If we can drill down to core rock, some deep delicate holes could tell us when we've gone through into a new chamber."

"Excellent idea," Burton said. The others agreed.

If the drilling could be done right away, they might find the chamber and would not need additional financing.

"We'll follow through on Aaron's plan," Dr. Withers said. "We'll go ahead and hammer out details with the Yagos. We just won't sign anything yet."

"Has anyone checked into receiving an endowment?" Parker asked. "How about the E.P.E.A.?"

"Endowment for the Preservation of Egyptian Antiquities?" Aaron asked. "They're a small start-up group out of Connecticut. They require all artifacts be turned over to them for exhibition. I doubt our Institute would be graced, even temporarily, with any of the artifacts. No thanks."

"Well, then," Parker said. "Any others?"

"Examined all possibilities," Dr. Withers said. "Most would be a bigger sacrifice than the Yagos expect us to make." He sat back in his chair but kept two fingers in the air signaling he had more to say.

"What about the bank loans you and Aaron—?"

"Scratch those," Dr. Withers said, flagging a hand. "Interest rates are exorbitant. Plus, banks don't particularly want artifacts as collateral, especially since we don't yet know which ones we're to receive."

"It's too risky," Aaron said. "Too high a price to pay. The Institute would have to jack up fees for work-study students, launch an all-out campaign for additional grants and donations—"

"A possibility," Burton said. "But I'm not much for relying on speculation."

"My sentiments exactly," Dr. Withers said.

Bebe hesitated, and then said, "I hate to suggest this, but what about a small loan with the Institute's property as collateral?"

Dr. Withers and Forbes and Phillips looked at one another. Then Forbes shook his head. "We've agreed not to jeopardize the CIA's home base," he said. They, too, had an investment in the Institute.

"This won't be the last discovery for the CIA," Phillips said. "We can get through this."

"Originally I wanted to keep our find to ourselves," Dr. Withers said.

Bebe chuckled. "You don't have to worry about keeping it to ourselves."

"How's that?"

"The crap the tabloids print has surely further weakened financial interest in us."

Dr. Withers looked around at the group. "Have I been too selfish?" he asked. "Are we being too selfish? After all, this find does belong to the world."

"Exactly," Kendra said quickly. "Not in someone's personal museum. We have every right to protect what we're doing. Our intentions have always been honorable."

"So, the most attractive offer," Dr. Withers said, eyeing the others, "is one which potentially costs less in the long run. It's the Yago family's offer."

Several people grunted. Kendra's expression soured. Dr. Withers took in the reactions.

"Potentially cost less?" Kendra asked. Her voice elevated in anger. "Considering my husband won't discuss this with me, what's hidden here?"

Dr. Withers waved a hand. "We have yet to work out a deal," he said. "I've held off negotiations as long as possible. We'll find our Burial Chamber. Aaron's idea is how we resume."

"What about you, Chione," Parker asked quickly as he turned toward her. "Carmelita knows about your abilities. Her aunt was somewhat psychic, told people all kinds of things."

Chione cringed. How could he compare her with a common psychic? When would people learn the difference? She had to temper her response, keep peace within the group, and bite her tongue again. She already needed to avoid Carmelita who was into everybody's business. "I don't tell people things," she said quietly. "I've just had some dreams, and they've brought us this far."

"Carmelita says it never stops. You must have gotten more."

"Is Carmelita a seer?" Chione asked pointedly.

"No," Parker said. "She knows, from her aunt."

Expressions on the faces of the others said they were not into hearing Carmelita's name again. Aaron talked more about the technical difficulties and expense of drilling. Chione sat quietly drawing crosshatches. Every time someone else spoke, Aaron leaned over and drew circles to block her X. When she did not start a new game, he drew a new crosshatch and playfully drew circles around the area where Chione always put her first X.

Then Chione caught the look on Kendra's face as she stared out the tent flaps. Chione peered outside. Nearby, Royce waited with the Yagos, so jovial, so friendly, part of that group, not this one. He was waiting to be called into the meeting. After all, this was why they had gathered, to strike a mutually advantageous deal. Give up some of their right to the dig, their blood and sweat in order to keep going. Poor Kendra looked as if she had already given up more than that.

"When we find the Burial Chamber," Dr. Withers was saying, "I want Randy back here to be a part of it."

"He is still a part of us," Bebe said. "He didn't get to see the other chambers opened."

"He is a part of our group...," Dr. Withers said. He looked as if he might say more on Randy's behalf but stopped himself.

"Where's Clifford," Burton asked.

"In Cairo," Dr. Withers said. "Taking Rita's death pretty hard."

Chione glanced out the flaps again and there stood Carmelita, laughing and talking with the Yago woman. Judging by their body language, they must have been talking in Spanish. Royce was not sharing in the conversation and spoke with the brothers.

Chione looked at the paper on the tabletop in front of Aaron, further hidden behind his pile of folders and other paper work. He enlarged the tick-tack-toe grid, elongated two lines and added another cross bar. A double game. Doodling. She drew additional lines angular to the crosshatching, distorting the grid so it no longer looked like a tick-tack-toe game. Still, Aaron invited her X by darkening the lines around the same open square she favored. She discreetly moved her arm over and, instead, drew small squares around where each line intersected. Six of them. Doodling.

"These are the tentative details worked out thus far," Dr. Withers was saying. "Pending approval by the Egyptian officials, of course. In exchange for funding, till our task is completed, we will bequeath to the Yago family a proportionate share of the artifacts equal to the amount of funds they match against ours."

Kendra gasped. "If the Yagos receive any of the artifacts, Egypt will never see them again."

The others looked as if they had been told the team would lose everything. Should the Yagos end up funding more than the CIA, they would end up with the larger share and all without having lifted a finger.

"The deal has yet to be approved by the Egyptian government," Dr. Withers said, surely trying to dispel their reactions. "The Yago family agrees not to seek control of the dig at least until such time as we abandon the site." He paused, staring at the papers in front of himself on the tabletop.

Perhaps a more thorough search for funding might have been undertaken had Royce not informed the Yago family of the team's dilemma and made it all too easy to arrange a deal. Clearly now he looked like a man on a mission of his own, someone who had more to gain from his patronizing scheme than to endear himself in his wife's good graces.

"We won't abandon the site," Aaron said. "Yet, if we take too long to find the Burial Chamber, the Yagos end up having contributed more and therefore own us?"

"Would seem that way."

"Say we abandon the site now," Aaron said. "To whom would our share of the artifacts be disbursed?"

"All depends to whom the Egyptian government issues the next permit." Dr. Withers stood and paced. He swatted the notepad nervously against his palm and shook his head.

Aaron breathed a sigh of frustration. He scratched another random line across the tick-tack-toe grid. He had not moved his leg away from hers. Chione's heart beat wildly. She again reached over and put a large X inside the heavily outlined side square in the now elongated grid. "Double game," she said, whispering.

"So, we and the Yago family," Aaron said, motioning toward the outside of the tent, "have not solidified anything in the form of an agreement?"

"Right," Dr. Withers said. "That's what we're here for today. To allow the Yago family to make their case and have an open discussion. Then we'll vote in a couple of days, if the hole boring proves fruitless."

"Even then we'd still have to secure approval from Cairo," Burton said.

Dr. Withers announced it was time to take a short break before meeting the Yagos. Some in the group got up to stretch. Yafeu and Irwin replaced the pots with fresh hot coffee and shoved a few more bottles of water, juice and sodas into the rusting old refrigerator.

The moment was at hand. Chione felt angry and frustrated with herself for not being able to identify the location of the Burial Chamber. She felt angry with the Yagos for being so compliant. They were no different than any of the local panhandlers with their hands out crying, "Baksheesh! Baksheesh!" Except, most of the locals needed whatever they received. The Yagos need was pure greed. But for intention, perhaps the CIA team was no different. Chione reached over and cut a couple more lines across the grid. Doodling. Relieved tension.

In a few minutes, as the group reconvened, the Yagos were brought in and introduced. Royce led the introductions of Ms. Elbertina Yago and brothers Emilio, Claudio and Rogelio; the latter smallish with shiny skin and an expression looking much like a child trying to be a man. Claudio carried a thin brown leather valise. Elbertina, of course, primped after having stood in the wind for too long. She looked like royalty, the brothers pale and nondescript in her shadow. While the spouses stayed away from most business meetings, Carmelita made herself at home with her newfound friend. She smiled as if she was part of that family, babbled in Spanish and repeated each word spoken to assure Elbertina thoroughly understood.

Like a dutiful servant, before Carmelita sat, she brought a cold soda to Elbertina, who refused it. Realizing she had made a mistake, Carmelita hid the can on the seat beside herself. Someone like Elbertina surely would not press her lips against the pop-top opening of a common aluminum can.

Parker, clearly embarrassed by his wife's actions, kept a poker face and chose to say nothing.

Royce stood flicking invisible dust from his clothing.

While they were getting settled, Aaron leaned over and whispered, "Carmelita and Royce should marry into the Yago family."

Chione almost burst out laughing then reminded herself not to be catty.

Royce introduced the team to the Yagos. When it came time to introduce his wife, he gave her name only as Kendra. Then he remained standing beside Elbertina's chair.

Kendra's suffering was clearly etched on her face.

"Now we'll hear from the Yago family representative," Dr. Withers said.

Carmelita quickly repeated Dr. Withers' last sentence. "I'll be interpreter," she said to the group, smiling.

"Elbertina is fluent in English," Royce said dryly.

Slightly embarrassed, Carmelita, who had inched her chair closer to Elbertina sat back, suddenly quiet.

Clearly, Carmelita was a hindrance Royce had not counted on. Chione began to understand. Carmelita was a nuisance distracting Royce from maneuvering smoothly as he walked a tightrope. He would need to keep his cool or risk exposing his motives.

Kendra watched Royce with the keenness of an animal stalking prey. Royce avoided meeting her stare. When had he begun calling that woman Elbertina instead of Ms. Yago? Kendra's expression seemed contemptuous.

One of the brothers removed some papers from the valise and placed them in front of Elbertina. She reviewed and organized the pages while everyone waited.

Aaron doodled, drew connecting lines between the others on the grid. Now the game looked more like a tall box with a checkered bottom.

Finally, Elbertina began to speak. "First of all," she said in a gentle feminine voice laced with a proper Spanish accent. "My brothers and I wish to thank—"

Suddenly, the noise volume outside increased dramatically and captured everyone's attention. Men with gruff Egyptian voices yelled what seemed to be orders. Chione could not decipher the words from among all the other noise. The uproar approached the cook tent. Elbertina looked annoyed with the interruption. Her eyelid twitched. Dr. Withers looked puzzled. Aaron was already on his feet at the tent flaps. An officer of the Bolis, covered with dust, greeted him and quickly stepped inside followed by another officer. Laborers dragged in a couple of crates on sledges. Everything was covered with dust. Kenneth pushed his way in, all smiles and out of breath, his face, hair, and clothes laden with thick dry grit. With all of them came a hint of rancor, not unlike that first encountered upon opening of the sealed chambers.

"You couldn't have come bearing gifts," Bebe said, teasing her husband, but watching Royce's reaction to the comment.

Royce caught her implication. His eyes flickered from Bebe to Kendra and back to Bebe. Then he looked away.

"Better than that," Kenneth said, seeming beside himself.

Two men opened the lid of a crate labeled with the stencil markings C-23.

"Our toys?" Chione asked, rushing to kneel beside the container.

Kendra came to her side. "Wow! Not our relics," she said as she poked through the box. "But priceless."

Dr. Withers came to peer into the crate. "What have you found, Sirs?"

Four carved wooden busts were neatly packed inside the box, as if ready to be shipped.

"Our C-23 box," Chione said. "But nothing we brought out of this tomb."

"As we suspected," the officer said. He turned and nodded to Kenneth.

"Didn't see your C-22 box anywhere," Kenneth said. "But I made my own discovery," He seemed unable to stand still. "No offense, Chione." He waggled his shoulders. "I found mine wide awake with both eyes open."

Raucous laughter broke the tension. She had gotten to know Kenneth, and they had shared a chuckle or two. He must have found something magnificent to compare it to what her dreams led them to discover. Not that she was being immodest. She smiled and then stood and waited while Kenneth strutted.

"For heaven's sake, man," Dr. Withers said. "We haven't got all day."

"Oh, yes you do," Kenneth said. "If you want to stay in Egypt, you have reason to stay as long as you want. I hope you enjoy your work."

"Kenneth!" Bebe said.

One of the officers folded arms across his chest and smiled broadly; fully aware Kenneth was building up to a grand announcement.

Aaron bent down to take a closer look at the contents of the crate.

"Dr. Withers," Kenneth said finally. "I'm proud to have much more to contribute than my meager services of photography." No one said a word. "We found these and other boxes among the mastabas."

Elbertina gasped as the brothers exchanged whispered comments.

"Hidden in the compartments?" Dr. Withers asked.

"Underneath, actually."

"Kenneth, why are you hesitating?" Bebe asked.

No longer seeming to have a care in the world, Kenneth blew his wife a kiss followed by a most promising smile. "We found a passage inside one of the mastabas."

For some reason, the faces of the Yago brothers went pale. Eyes widening, Elbertina stared straight ahead. An eyelid twitched again. Chione watched but detected nothing more. Except Royce's shirtfront heaved as he took in a subdued breath of surprise. He lowered his gaze to the floor and closed his eyes tightly for a moment as if experiencing great pain.

Had Kendra seen her husband's reaction? "A passage to what?" Chione asked.

Kenneth looked like he wanted to belt out the words, but they would not roll off his tongue. Finally, he threw his shoulders back, stood taller, and blurted, "Another tomb!"

36

All spoke at once and crowded around Kenneth and the opened crate.

"It was down the far row, twenty-eight to thirty mastabas into the necropolis, right?" Chione asked.

"Come to think of it," Kenneth said. "Right where I saw boxes the first time."

"So that's how Chione knew we were being watched," Aaron said.

Another unrecognized box was opened exposing a stash of exquisitely carved stone scarabs and other amulets, along with two small steles, and myriad smaller items. Joy permeated the conversation with Kenneth being frantically congratulated. Dr. Withers raised a hand for attention but the pandemonium continued. Suddenly Aaron stuck fingers into his mouth and blew a shrill tone that cut through the din.

The Yagos looked numbed. They should have been happy. Providing a permit could be secured for the new find, the Institute would require additional financial aid. Not that Chione rooted for the Yagos. The way she saw it, the Yagos should pounce on this opportunity. Instead, they looked defeated.

"This new tomb," Kenneth said. "I was with these men." He thumbed to the officers. "We found a mastaba with the entry slightly ajar. We pushed. It opened. The sidewall inside stood agape. Then the Bolis rushed past me through that opening. I went in after them." He dusted the front of his shirt. "They surprised some Egyptian guys sealing up the crates."

"What guys?" Aaron asked.

One of the officers standing at the fly held up his hands with wrists together as if handcuffed. He motioned with his head signaling they had someone in custody outside.

"Two guys," Kenneth said. "Guess they're involved in tomb robbing."

"You followed the Bolis through the opened wall?" Bebe asked.

"You bet I did, Honey," he said. "And slid down the ladder to the bottom." He gestured to the dirt on his clothing.

"What about your bad back?"

He shrugged, excited, ignoring her question. "Guess what I saw? Crates of stuff laying everywhere… in a very large chamber."

One of Chione's visions repeated. She saw…

…a very large empty chamber.

"Boxes like these?" Kendra asked.

Chione wondered if anyone had heard Kenneth say a very large chamber. Or was too much happening to be absorbed at once?

"I thought those particular crates were yours," he said. "They were separate from the others and I remembered the C-23 label."

"The crate is ours," Chione said. "But not what's inside."

"Could these artifacts be from that other tomb?" Bebe asked, finally coming over to look into the crates.

"Could be," Kenneth said quickly. "Maybe not."

"What do you mean 'maybe not'?"

"We heard other voices and went into a passageway to look and found another opened mastaba above in the ceiling and a ladder—"

"A passageway?" Dr. Withers asked. He looked to be reeling in disbelief.

"Other guys may have escaped," Kenneth said. "Looks like they were using the tomb to stash their spoils from other sites."

The Yagos had not moved. In fact, they seemed trying hard not to react.

"What else did you see?" Chione asked.

"Except for piles of boxes, that chamber is empty."

"Can we visit that tomb?" Dr. Withers asked of the officers.

"After we investigate," one officer said.

"Hey, get this," Kenneth said. "The officers advised that you file for a permit immediately. If you want to claim the find, do it now. Don't wait till you see it."

"Better get your claim to Cairo before word of this action spreads," Burton said after silently observing. "This is big, Sterling."

"My thoughts exactly," Dr. Withers said, repeatedly pulling on his mustache, first one side then the other.

Parker shook his head. "This exceeds our wildest expectations. Yet another discovery on the back of the first."

"I think we should claim it," Carmelita said unexpectedly.

Elbertina's look of astonishment asked why. She leaned away from Carmelita.

"You mean your government won't want to claim this one?" Dr. Withers asked of the Bolis.

The officer waved him off. "Too many tombs," he said. "Every country in the world has permission on our soil. Egypt cannot afford to finance so many excavations."

"Won't you allow us to see inside the tomb, so we'll know what we're filing for?" Dr. Withers asked. "We could be securing a permit on an empty hole in the ground."

"There's still the artwork," Aaron said.

"And the history," Bebe said.

"These and other containers would be your treasures," the officer said, gesturing to the boxes on the floor. "If artifacts can be proven stolen from other tombs, probably a great reward awaits you."

"The tomb won't be empty," Kenneth said. "If you'll take my word. I doubt the tomb's been totally looted."

"How could you tell, Kenneth?"

"Listen, after they secured the two guys they caught, the officers and I went back into the passageway. You'll never guess what we saw."

"Kenneth...?"

"Footprints, two sets in the dust going down the passageway and back. We walked it with our lights and found more doors."

"And?" Bebe asked.

"None of the seals are broken."

Several people gasped, then again, all talked at once. Except for the Yagos.

"Wait a minute," Dr. Withers said in a more demanding voice. "What makes you think they couldn't have gotten in through another mastaba?"

"Well," Kenneth said, motioning to the man standing beside him. "This officer thinks they would've broken open all the doors if they had and just raped the place and left."

"Few footprints," the officer said. "Maybe still intact. You claim it?"

Chione glanced out the flap again. "Dr. Withers?" she said, motioning for him to see. "Looks like some reporters may have the story already."

Outside, reporters mingled, interviewing people, and filming and taping conversations with the handcuffed men in the jeep.

"Damned!" Dr. Withers said.

The three Yago brothers glanced quickly at one another with expressions of utter disappointment. Somehow, Chione knew their dismay went much deeper.

"Mastabas are under guard, secure," the officer said. "You send claim first."

"Rashad," Dr. Withers said. "We've got to get Paki Rashad back here on the double." He turned, smiled politely at Elbertina and gestured toward the family. "Then we'll have to hammer out a new deal to—"

"Hey-y!" a familiar voice said coming through the fly and taking everyone by surprise. Clifford strolled in wearing a summer weight business suit. The jacket hung on his finger over his shoulder and his shirtsleeves were rolled up. He smiled, made his way around the crates, shook hands and received well wishes and hugs. He looked ghastly, exhausted, but sounded upbeat.

"Jeez, old buddy," Dr. Withers said, hugging Clifford and patting him solidly on the back.

"What's with the two in handcuffs in the jeep?" He threw his jacket over the back of a chair, then noticed the opened crates and the Yago family members and paused. "What gives?"

"We were in the process of polishing details of our agreement with the Yago family," Dr. Withers said. He managed a tight smile at Elbertina.

Clifford's jaw dropped. "Am I too late? Have we signed anything?"

"Not yet," Aaron said.

Clifford sagged with relief. "Good," he said. "Good." He picked up his jacket again and pulled out papers from the inside pocket. He opened them out and handed them to Dr. Withers.

"What's this?" Dr. Withers asked, cocking his head. He looked at the papers through bifocals while everyone waited. Then suddenly he said, "Three hundred thou! Where—"

"Already deposited in the CIA's Egyptian Archaeological Trust," Clifford said. "We don't need to be making any deals and giving away the fruits of our labors."

Elbertina finally wilted. Slowly, she rose from her seat. The brothers came to attention. She said something in Spanish to Carmelita, then bent down and placed an obligatory peck on her cheek. She motioned to her brothers with her eyes. One of them scampered around to clear the way, so she could pass through the group. They left quietly. Royce followed.

Carmelita looked bewildered. So did Kendra.

"There's more where that came from," Clifford said proudly. "Soon as the deal's done."

"Where'd you get your hands on this kind of dough?"

"My winery in Napa."

"You must have mortgaged that business to the hilt, old buddy," Dr. Withers said. "Why'd you go and—"

"No mortgage," Clifford said. "I sold it."

Dead silence filled the cook tent.

"You sold your winery?" Dr. Withers asked quietly. He looked ready to cry.

"To the Alessandro brothers who own the neighboring facility. I just got back."

"For us? You sacrificed your holdings for us? After the way you struggled to get that property?" Dr. Withers did a double take. "You what? Just got back... from where?"

"California," Clifford said quietly. "I talked to my attorney on the phone from Cairo and took off. He made all the arrangements and all I had to do, just about, was sign the papers."

"You couldn't have gotten the best deal on such short notice."

"Even with the short notice, the sale was reasonable. I knew the value. What do I need that property for now?" His voice expressed confidence. "My Rita's here. My life's here. When the deal's done and my other mortgages are paid off, there'll be over a million in operating capital."

No one said a word. Kendra began to cry with quick little whiffs. Still stooping down, she clutched the edge of one of the crates. She was at her breaking point. The good news saving them from the likes of the Yagos and her contemptible husband's scheming put her over the edge.

As if needing the support, Dr. Withers eased himself onto the bench beside a table. "How do we repay this?"

"We can discuss it later," Clifford said, shrugging. "I do want to stay in Egypt though." He smiled one of his most facetious grins. "Just keep me on the payroll till we work something out, okay?"

Dr. Withers pulled at his mustache harder than ever. "I can't... we... Clifford...?"

"Something else," Clifford said. "That ragged old Victorian across from the south corner of your property, the leased crop fields?"

"That Victorian? What about it?"

"It was for sale. I put a deposit."

"That rundown structure?" Aaron asked. "Fourteen rooms someone converted to a ballroom. It's probably dry rotted. Why?"

Clifford may have gone totally over the edge, but he stood firm. "Can be remodeled," he said. He turned back to Dr. Withers. "You should reclaim the lease on the south end crop fields for direct access to the ballroom. It's big enough and can be completely restored as a show-place for our artifacts."

Dr. Withers knew what he held in his grip. Clifford Rawlings had just handed him the funds to the Institute's future. Dr. Withers's eyes got glassy. He looked around at everyone. "We can finance that other tomb now!" he said. He jumped up, excited again, and then hurriedly gathered up his papers.

"You want to repeat that?" Clifford asked. "What other tomb?"

Dr. Withers was already at the fly. He stopped, opened his mouth but the words would not form. Clearly, he was overwhelmed by Clifford's act of benevolence, but not about to turn it down. He removed his bifocals. "Aaron," he said, gesturing with the glasses. "Aaron." He turned, motioned for Kenneth and the officers to follow, and then disappeared outside.

"I'd better get Randy and Rashad back here on the double," Aaron said.

Clifford sighed wearily and poured a cup of coffee.

"Hey, Clifford, bring that karkade over here, would you," Aaron said.

Chione joined them as Clifford sat the cups down.

Kendra and Bebe who huddled at the other end of the tables talking in low tones. Everyone else had cleared out.

"Somebody clue me?" Clifford asked.

"Kenneth and the Bolis caught a couple of thieves," Aaron said. "In the process, they discovered another tomb under the necropolis."

"You wouldn't be kidding."

"That's why Dr. Withers rushed off," Chione said. "He went to fax our claim before anyone else gets to it."

"Have you seen it?"

"Not yet," Chione said. "But it must be deeper than this one."

"Buried beneath the necropolis," Aaron said. "Who would have thought?"

"Good," Clifford said. "We'll be here for a long time." Then he turned to Chione. "How's my Rita?"

She touched the amulet through her shirt. "Down under," she said. "Safe and sound—" *Down under,* a ghost-like voice echoed inside her head. *Safe and sound.*

Then another vision...

...a withered body

...laying like Rita on her deathbed. The vision shook her to the core.

"How are you holding up, Clifford?" Aaron asked.

"Rita would want me to keep working," he said, smiling sadly. "Staying busy helps ease the pain."

"If we can do anything...."

Clifford swallowed hard, smiled again ruefully. Then he asked, "What's this?" as he pulled a pad of paper across the tabletop toward himself.

"Aaron's doodles," Chione said.

"Looks like the Pillared Hall," Clifford said.

"It's just doodling."

"Some doodle," Clifford said. "Looks as if we're looking down into the Pillared Hall from above."

They studied the lines and turned the pad first in one direction and then another. Sure enough, the double-layered tick-tack-toe grid with its little squares and other lines looked like a floor plan of the Pillared Hall and its six columns, as if viewing an architect's three-dimensional blueprint from above.

"You've got a good imagination," Aaron said.

"No, really," Clifford said, taking a sip of coffee. "See here. Remember the Pillared Hall has shallow grooves in the floor. The floor looks like a big checkerboard."

Chione felt herself...

...floating down into that bright yellow room.

Anxiety ran rampant through her nervous system.

"Look here," Clifford said. "These small squares where the major lines join are the six pillars. And what's this?" He pointed to the open square on the side that Aaron had darkened as a signal to Chione to fill in her X. "What is this X in the side square?"

"A tick-tack-toe grid, a double game." Then she felt compelled to reach over and touch the X mark. "That's my mark," she said as another vision swept her mind.

Down under—safe and sound.

She bolted as if having received a shock from touching the X. Then she could not resist and touched again.

A body. Like Rita's.

"But not Rita!" she said.

"What?"

"Not Rita," Chione said softly.

"What about my Rita?"

Chione gingerly touched the X mark again, saw Aaron out of the corner of her eye signal for Clifford's patience.

Tauret motioned her to follow, floated downward, against the north wall, into the bright yellow room.

Then, her own words spoken to Randy back in California repeated from memory. *The pyramid will not be found near the surface.* "I-I've got it!" Chione said, though whispering, only vaguely aware of Kendra and Bebe leaving.

"Tell us," Aaron said.

"Wait," she whispered, not wanting to break the spell. With shaking hands, she touched the X again.

Down under, safe and sound.

Chione stood suddenly, jerking the table and spilling the drinks. She did not have time to explain to Clifford. "Come on!" she said quietly. "But no one else."

They left the tent as calmly as possible walking toward the portcullis shaft, not wishing to draw attention. Having traversed the shaft many times, Aaron used a rope to repel to the bottom, occasionally bouncing off the rungs of the wooden ladder. Chione did the same.

"Jeez, you guys," Clifford called down as he descended the ladder. "You gotta' show me how to do that."

They all but ran to the Pillared Hall. Chione got down on hands and knees, put her face to the floor and ran a fingertip over a groove.

"What in the name of—"

"Sh-h-h!" she said. She made her way along the floor following the groove, not caring the least that her rump stuck up in the air. She blew the dust from the groove as she crawled along. Breathing fast in anticipation and excitement, she inadvertently sucked up the smell of the floor into her nostrils, dust and all. She choked but kept going. She crept along quickly, like an animal rooting something out of the ground. She put her face right up to where one of the pillars met the floor, then ran a fingernail along the groove and screamed. "I've found it! I've found it!" She jumped up and grabbed their hands and shook them in the air in triumph. "I've found it! I've found it!" she said again. Her excitement echoed off the walls, and rumbled through the empty chamber till the sounds ran together then dissipated.

Clifford looked toward the pillar she had just examined. He tried to see around it. He shrugged. "The only thing left to find is the entrance to the burial chamber."

"You're standing on it!"

37

All three dropped to their knees and routed along the grooves Chione directed them to follow.

Clifford checked a few other areas across the Hall then returned to the first. " 'By Jove, I think she's got it,' " he said. He blew dust from a groove, spat, and rubbed a small area clean. "My word, those ancient stone carvers did miraculous work."

Aaron studied his doodling. He followed one groove away from the north wall to the center pillar, then over to where Chione knelt near the first pillar closest to the doorway.

"The same area you darkened on the tic-tac-toe game," she said. "And where I put my X."

"But wait," Clifford said. "Let's check the floor, all of it. If there are seams anywhere else in the grid, maybe that's the way it was made." He chose a section to examine at a far corner.

"Or," Aaron said. "Maybe the whole floor will have to come up."

"This entire tomb is non-conforming," Clifford said, on his knees again. Soon he reported, "No cracks in these grooves over here."

"None here either," Chione said from across the Hall.

"Nor here," Aaron said. He waved his page of doodles motioning them to follow. Near the doorway looking back into the Pillared Hall, they compared the drawing.

Grooves carved into the floor looked just like the crosshatching of the double tic-tac-toe game grid. Squares that Chione had drawn

The Ka

on the paper where lines intersected were in the exact locations as where the pillars stood over the intersecting grooves in the floor. The opened square on the grid containing Chione's X marked the same open square on the floor along the north wall; same area where they sat in meditation; same area from which Tauret always appeared.

"Here's our access," Chione said, pointing to the floor.

"How'd this happen?" Clifford asked.

"What?"

"The doodling similarity," he said. "Or are you getting as good at this as Chione?"

"Who would have guessed? I thought I'd been doodling out of nervousness," Aaron said. "Chione's the one who made a tic-tac-toe game of it. She always put her X in that particular square."

"The two of you did it together?"

"I guess we did," she said.

"Now you're both tuning into the same message, or how's that go?" Clifford asked. "The message is being sent through both of you at once?"

"Something like that," Chione said. "Whatever the message, we both received the clues."

"Oh, no," Clifford said, animated with hands clutching at his hair. "Now, both of you are... that way!"

They exited the portcullis shaft and stood looking out over the site. What an industrious place their camp had become in only a few moments. Life pulsated in the middle of the desolate craggy hills with whippets of sand and temperatures again beginning to soar.

"There's the boss," Aaron said. "Over with that group of men near the shacks."

They watched as Dr. Withers pointed along the ground. Laborers followed, scratching lines in the sand with sticks while other men drove stakes.

"Looks like we're building more sleeping rooms," Clifford said.

"Yes!" Aaron said, pumping a fist into the air. "He must have gotten the go ahead on the other tomb."

326

They started down the hill but Clifford grabbed their arms. "Look," he said, motioning with his chin. "Over there."

The four Yagos stood huddled far back on the other side of the restraining wall. They spoke head to head with another man whose gestures were animated and his face partially hidden behind a loose turban. Elbertina closed her umbrella and provided a clear view of Dakarai hunched into the center of the group, evidently highly agitated. No casual conversation there. Elbertina's closed umbrella jabbed the ground several times. Her other hand suddenly upthrusted was surely a gesture of great anger.

Dakarai suddenly looked up the hill and saw them, then forced a smile and waved. He said something to the Yagos, and then approached. "Good afternoon," he said, calling to them up the hill, all smiles. "I hear you made great discovery."

"Guess we did," Clifford said.

"That Kenneth," Dakarai said, reaching them. "He should become archaeologist too."

"Haven't seen you around much, Dakarai," Aaron said.

"I work at other site."

"Another site?"

"The Norwegians over at Dier el-Medina," he said. "They don't have such good luck."

"I hadn't heard they were wanting to make discoveries," Aaron said. "They're refurbishing existing tombs."

Dakarai smiled sheepishly. Then he beamed, too quickly, and shrugged nervously. "The Yagos. They still like to help. You do business with them?"

"We considered it," Aaron said. "But we won't be needing extra funds now."

What business was it of Dakarai's? Snooping could give away his position, his involvement with the Yagos. In recent days, Chione had seen Dakarai with that group too many times. Casual conversation, onlookers might think. Dakarai always acted somewhat afraid of her though, cautious of giving away clues to activities inconsistent with his position.

They followed long-legged Clifford downhill, heading toward Dr. Withers. When Dakarai noticed where they were going, too quickly he said, "I must attend to my men." Then he disappeared into the throng.

The crowds had thickened in the days since the sandstorm passed and would, again, swell in droves once word of the new tomb and finding the Burial Chamber got out.

The tent camp below had already erupted into a festering eyesore. Trucks now had to make regular trips to haul away garbage left over after the beggars and animals picked through it. Gradually the addition of more and more tents along the road edged closer to the site. Fortunately, some wise souls in the camp had the foresight to run the open sewers downwind from both their own camp and the dig site. Yet, quite romantic, music drifted up at night and took the bite out of solitude in the desolate region.

Out of the proliferage, the scourge of mangy cats and dogs increased. From where had they emerged? They devoured the scraps thrown their way. Yafeu and Irwin paid local boys each day to take the leftovers and other kitchen leavings farther from camp to keep the animals at a distance. Surely, some remnants were given to the many beggars. They would feast on the meat bones, potato peels, vegetable cuttings, fruit rinds, and other leavings. No one knew how the families in the distant village of Thebes managed to survive. Other than a few rundown hotels, no other area in the nine square miles that encompassed Valley of the Kings and Valley of the Queens could offer enough full-time employment for the locals.

Uninvited reporters and media teams swarmed about. Other than the few makeshift hotels that were hastily put up across the greater necropolis and a handful of better ones in Karnak and Luxor, where did they stay? Each was intent on catching that one news item of the day that would sell a few thousand additional copies of their hometown newspapers.

Jeeps and antiquated vehicles were strewn along the side of the narrow-rutted road, the area looking much like a junkyard. Yet each rickety contraption was ready for use at a moment's notice. Even a faded white Mercedes limousine was parked nearby, it's body full of dents and wear and rusting in spots. Camels for hire were plodded about, their owners looking for paying riders. The animals were kept decoratively shaved and tattooed on their haunches and tails showing ownership. Tarik had said a camel would pee on its own legs to cool down. Every time the winds shifted, it brought with it the odors of urine, camel dung, and human excrement. Hopefully enough to keep the tourists at bay, Dr. Withers had said. As had been the case since the first day, many tourists who bussed in took advantage of the opportunity to experience a brief camel trek. Chione wondered if the stench might change their minds.

Halfway down the hill, Clifford stopped. "Look at Carmelita," he said as he stifled a laugh.

Down along the road, Carmelita inspected the limo as if shopping to buy a car and getting the pick of the lot.

Aaron could not keep from chuckling. "Look! Look at Parker."

There was Parker, hurrying down the road after his wife, motioning for her to return.

"We got it," Dr. Withers yelled as they approached. "We got our permit." He snapped his fingers. "Just like that. It's you, Clifford. You and your involvement with people in high places. It's all worked in our favor."

"Actually, no," Clifford said. "Remember, Randy thinks Chione's put a hex on us all."

"Randy believes in hexes?" Burton asked. "I'd heard digging in Egypt did funny things to the mind."

"By the way," Clifford said. "Where is that little trouble maker?"

"Transferred to the Madu," Chione said. Now she resented the thought of team members demeaning Randy as they had in the past. They did not know about the changes that had come over the man; changes they were all experiencing, too personal to notice in themselves, perhaps since all had begun wearing gallibayas and other Egyptian clothing, and preferring Egyptian food and drink.

"Rashad will be here tomorrow with our new permit," Dr. Withers said. Still, he sounded resigned, frustrated. "The engineers will begin boring holes in that other—"

"Sterling," Clifford said. "I think these kids have something they want to say."

Dr. Withers waited and pulled his head wrap farther down over his eyes.

Chione motioned for Aaron to begin.

"It's your find," Aaron said.

"If one of you doesn't say something," Clifford said, hugging himself, "I'm going to burst."

"Sir," she said. "I think we've found access to the Burial Chamber."

Dr. Withers' expression did not change, nor did his stare. Then he looked from her to Aaron. He looked at Clifford, glanced at Burton. He remained still and looked past them out over the valley.

"Sterling?"

He glanced at the ground, out over the valley again, then to all of them. Finally, he leaned forward and said, "Did I hear you right?"

"Yes, sir."

Dr. Withers looked at all of them again, almost as if having an inner debate as to the legitimacy of the news. Then he walked unhurried, yet without sauntering, in the direction of the portcullis shaft.

38

The cook tent served as the place the team could be away from prying eyes. They could laugh and joke, and touch and hug one another without offending anyone. They were protected from people taking pictures. After team members observed the floor for themselves, and after the evening meal, Dr. Withers said, "Aaron's already sent word to borrow hydraulics from the Norwegians again." He stood, raised his glass and waited for everyone to come to attention and raise theirs. "We've a lot to be thankful for. Once again, I want to cut to the core. Here's to Chione."

"Here, here," Clifford said, lifting his mug.

They toasted, sipped.

"It was Aaron's grid," Chione said, raising her voice over the cheers.

"Here, here," someone said as they toasted Aaron.

"Here's to Clifford," Kendra said, thankfulness ringing in every word.

"Don't forget my husband," Bebe said, toasting him. He leaned over and wrapped an arm around her shoulder. Lately, all the stress of Bebe's life seemed to have left her face.

Kendra watched Bebe and Kenneth with a look of longing. Royce was not present.

The pressure was off. Round and round they went with joyous thunder. The Directors and their wives got involved. No one denied the biggest day of discovery was at hand.

Over breakfast the next morning, probably the final leisurely meal they would have for a while, Dr. Withers took a last bite then laid his fork across the plate. Yafeu's arm came from behind and took the plate and utensils away. Bebe slid her plate to her husband who ate the last bit of food quickly as if he thought it might be suddenly taken away.

Egyptian voices rang out nearby. Masud, Quaashie and Naeem and other locals greeted Paki Rashad, who entered the cook tent with his photographer. In a few minutes, they were served meals. After Rashad had eaten, he and Dr. Withers became involved in a social conversation. Chione wondered why Dr. Withers hesitated leading them down to the mastabas.

Finally, Dr. Withers led Rashad out of the cook tent seemingly on the pretense of explaining something, and they headed toward the tech shack. It was strange how Dr. Withers could allow himself to get sidetracked from seeing the new tomb. Rashad had arrived and everyone was ready. Then she knew. Dr. Withers was secretly delaying in the hope Randy would return to camp soon. Dr. Withers was truly a fair man.

Later, when they could wait no longer, as they trod the winding well-worn path to the mastabas, Randy appeared on a camel coming up the road toward them. The lanky animal plodded along as Randy sat perfectly relaxed, undulating in sync with its gait, in no particular hurry and completely in charge.

"Randy?" Bebe asked. "On a camel?"

"Hey, everyone," he said, yelling and waving. They waited until he caught up.

A smiling young Egyptian walked alongside and took the reins. "You learn well, O Professor," he said, looking up at Randy and then bowed slightly. "Tss, tss!" he said to the camel as he tugged on the reins. The camel dropped to its knees to allow Randy to dismount. The young man led the animal away. Marlowe had moved aside, having previously learned the hard way what it meant when a tall camel bent down and wrapped its slobbering lips and tongue around her hair bun.

Clearly, Randy's metamorphosis was ongoing. He was thinner and wore fitted clothes. "I'm getting the hang of it," he said, smiling and shaking hands offered more eagerly. If Clifford stared any harder, he would have trouble pushing his eyeballs back into their sockets.

Randy looked at the entourage. "What's going on here, Chione? Some spell commanding everyone to Exodus?" he asked, making light and winking. The others saw the wink and now looked upon a changed man.

"We haven't had a chance to tell you this part," Dr. Withers said. He shook Randy's hand. "Kenneth, along with the Bolis, discovered another tomb."

Randy's mouth dropped open.

"Under the necropolis," Clifford said.

"Did you see any of this, Chione?" Randy asked.

Randy's question seemed like one the others might ask. In the past, Randy might have made derogatory insinuations. Now his acceptance seemed the norm and surprised everyone.

"I'm not sure," she said.

"What do you mean 'not sure'?" Dr. Withers asked.

She had to smile, knowing she was about to shock them again. "Back when we opened the Pillared Hall," she said, motioning up the hill toward Tauret's tomb. "I expected a larger room and four larger pillars."

"What?" Kendra asked.

"I remember," Aaron said quickly. "Someone asked if that was the chamber you saw in your dreams."

"That was me," Clifford said. "And you, Chione, said, 'No, but it'll do.' I never thought to ask want you meant."

"So, in this new tomb," Kendra said, "Chione tells us we'll see a large empty room and four larger pillars?"

"Four massive pillars," Kenneth said. "I never got the chance to tell what I observed."

"That's okay, Kenneth," Clifford said, grinning. "Chione beat you to it months ago."

The Bolis reported that the remaining packed boxes had been left the way they were found. The first inspection group consisted of Dr. Withers, Paki Rashad, Burton, Parker, the photographers and some of the Bolis. When they returned, Dr. Withers seemed overwhelmed. He kept shaking his head. Finally, he sat down on the ground and leaned back against a mastaba. Marlowe went to his side, produced a paper fan from her pocket and lovingly cooled her husband.

"...a lot to be thankful for," he said finally.

"It's that good?" Clifford asked.

He motioned for them to go and see for themselves. Remaining members of the team scampered, accompanied by more of the Bolis who were just as eager.

Chione led the way just behind an officer. They crouched to enter the mastaba, then passed through the opened sidewall and dropped onto a ledge.

They found themselves above a deep chamber. Chunks of the solid rock ceiling and wall, which had encased the chamber, had fallen inside to the floor and shattered. Footprints showed further crushing and scattering of the pieces. Chione flashed her light. Someone had braced up the mastaba. The one beside it helped prevent both from falling into the tomb. A lot of sand had also been cleared. The area was well-supported with beams and covered by sand and rubble above ground. It was a great hiding place. The gaping hole into which she peered was big enough to glimpse the grandeur as the Bolis inside flashed lights about.

They eased down the shaky ladder. At the bottom, Kendra squeezed Chione's hand. "I don't think I'd be afraid to see the things you see."

"Have you heard?" Bebe asked. "Marlowe's had some strange dreams."

"I heard," Chione said, hoping to drop the subject.

Bebe lowered her voice. "Marlowe dreamed you had a baby."

A scene burst into her mind.

A beautiful woman sleeping with movement of life inside her swollen belly.

Chione nearly dropped her light.

"Marlowe didn't want Chione to know," Kendra said, nearly hissing at Bebe.

"Why not?" Chione asked feeling numbed.

"Bebe, how could you?"

"It's all right, Kendra," Chione said. "Now that it's out, why didn't Marlowe want me to know?"

"Because you put so much stock in your dreams, she didn't want to give you false hope."

Chione smiled sadly. "Marlowe's having wish-fulfilling dreams," she said, managing a weak smile. "While I'm busy dreaming other things."

Bebe took her hand and clasped it in both of hers. "Guess I'd better learn to curb my tongue. I'm so sorry."

Bebe's disclosure of Marlowe's special dreams was no surprise. Marlowe had already related some of her dream scenes, and they were of paranormal quality. Marlowe was getting her wish. She wanted to be more like her, if it opened up slowly, so she could adjust. Like Aaron, what she needed to do was wish with all her heart for what she wanted.

Four massive pillars at least eight feet in diameter supported the center of the expansive chamber. Again, painted reliefs as only the Egyptians could create, covered walls depicting grandeur. Beyond the pillars, over in the corner, Randy stood studying some glyphs with his mouth agape.

Chione was in awe making her way around the immense dimly lit chamber. Magnificent history spoke from the etchings. Her heart quickened. She wanted to read and learn who had been laid to rest in the burial chamber of this opulent tomb, yet the unfinished tasks at the first tomb took priority. Tauret's tomb would not allow her to focus her attention elsewhere until the mission of that discovery could be satisfied.

Aaron backed into her. "Oh! Sorry, sorry. We need more light in here. Let's peek down the passageway."

They passed where Randy stood. She glanced over and immediately recognized what had captured his interest. A couple of cartouches! Two she had already seen. Her heart beat wildly. She stepped into the passageway with Aaron. He flashed his light and began to walk down the passageway.

"Oh, please, let's not," Chione said. "Let's leave this tomb exactly as it is until we finish with the other one. Please?"

They re-entered the main chamber and prepared to exit. While Aaron held the ladder, Clifford went up first, so he might help the others when they reached the top.

Randy was suddenly at her side. "You saw them, Chione," he said. "Do you concur that the cartouches belong to the people I think they belong to?"

"Meskhenet and Umi," she said, whispering. "You agree?"

"I'm fairly certain, but you've studied their cartouches more than anyone else."

"This is Tauret's parents' tomb," she said. "They were buried in this valley because they were courtiers. No wonder Tauret was buried nearby."

"So when will you tell the others?"

Chione thought a moment and then smiled warmly as Randy waited. "I'm not going to tell them."

"Until the team's ready to begin work in here?"

"No, Randy, it's your find. You make the announcement. Maybe tonight over dinner?"

"Me?" he asked. "Me?"

"Why not, Randy? You found them first."

"I guess I did. Yeah, I'll break the news." He was evidently pleased he could contribute that much. "I can do that. Thanks, Chione."

She waited till everyone was preoccupied at the ladder then scurried into the passageway. She climbed another ladder and exited out through the second opened mastaba. Outside in daylight and unnoticed by the others, she crept back into the first mastaba, coming up behind Clifford who stood on the ledge looking down into the tomb, waiting to help the others ascend and climb out. Chione leaned close behind him and whimpered with a most unearthly sound. Clifford bolted and let out a ghastly cry, turned and saw her and almost fell backwards through the hole! The hollow chamber filled with laughter.

Burton and Parker stayed inside waiting for their wives. Dr. Withers went back in with Marlowe, Helen, and Jibade. Chione walked away. She did not care to hear the muffled echo of Carmelita hesitating on the ladder, creating attention to her pseudo-importance.

39

The hydraulic jacks and capstans arrived mid-morning with the Norwegians to operate the equipment. By noon, the inventory tent was neatly arranged with shipping and other supplies at the ready. News of Meskhenet and Umi's cartouches in the second tomb enhanced the vigor of the team.

"That about does it for the inventory records," Kendra said to her and Bebe. "Thanks for the help, you two." Her mood was flat. She was withdrawn, remained pensive, always seeming preoccupied.

"Let's see what's up down under," Bebe said.

Inside the passageway, sweaty laborers grouped close to the circulation fans. She, Bebe, and Kendra greeted Quaashie and Naeem, indeed, two valuable aides and greatly trusted. Dozens of workers milled around studying the beautiful walls. Suddenly Chione saw...

...a woman wearing a long white cloak.

Smelled...

...the sweet perfume from the melting beeswax cone atop her head.

And heard...

...her sandals padding on smoothed stone.

Chione sighed as she heard the sounds her boots made on the granite. She longed to return to the vision to fully experience the captivating woman and live her time and culture. Once Chione acknowledged Tauret in the visions, Tauret's life began to seem as real as her own. She was seized with an idea. Perhaps she could better contact her, experience more of her life by being more like her. "Yes," Chione said under her breath, but how she might go about it still eluded her.

The designated block of granite in the Pillared Hall floor had already been hoisted.

"Oh, no," Chione said. "Did they have to gouge holes?" A small square hole had been cut into the floor at the north wall along both sides where the slab once laid.

"No other way," Aaron said. "The space between the slabs wasn't wide enough to get a razor into."

"Those Egyptians," Clifford said, walking over. "To think we still build our modern houses where the wind blows through the cracks."

To get leverage, the engineers made the holes big enough to get a grip on the slab from underneath. Once they raised it a bit, they slid it away from the pillars and stood it on end. Chips of stone filled a large cavity beneath.

Aaron turned to Chione and gestured to the slab being lowered onto soft padding placed on the floor at the back of the chamber. "I can't tell you what this means for us," he said. He hugged her briefly, then evidently remembering that they should not be emotional or touch in plain sight of the workers, stepped away.

If only he knew what it meant to her. Her intuition hinted that all her dreams and visions were about to be explained, from the simplest to the most incomprehensible. All the pieces of the puzzle were jostling into position. She looked at Aaron and knew that he, too, experienced the same anxiety.

Off to the side, Dr. Withers watched, blatantly smiling, with Clifford now at his side whispering something through an equally mischievous grin. Had they never seen her and Aaron hug?

Laborers began filling containers and wooden trays with the rubble and scurried in and out of the Hall. She and Aaron moved aside and watched the lines of men work the bucket brigade. After a while, Chione peeked into the passageway. Two lines of muscular laborers moved along, some paused to partake of the current of air as they passed the fans. One line of workers took rubble to be hoisted out through the portcullis; the other passed back the empty containers to be filled again.

Suddenly the men in the pit excitedly called to Dr. Withers to join them and the team followed. The smooth wall of the pit, beginning between the two pillars, slanted downward toward the north wall. More than a foot in on the angular slant, they had uncovered a niche big enough where one might place a foot. One man reached down with gloved hands and quickly brushed aside more chips. Another niche appeared a foot deeper.

Aaron closed his eyes and threw his head back, as if the tension was more than he could bear. Clifford gave a hand to Dr. Withers to steady him as he placed the toe of his boot on each rung and bounced from the knee, getting the feel of the footholds. Then he let Clifford help him out. "Yes," he said, giving two thumbs up.

Randy simply waited, took it all in, reserved yet eager. After a usual cursory inspection, Paki Rashad went to stand beside him, his quiet demeanor intact. Though no one spoke, the atmosphere was electrified.

After more than an hour of emptying the pit, the slanted floor was found to be a ramp with a row of footholds on each side. The ramp led downward, under the north wall and beyond. No glyphs presented on the walls or ceiling, only stone chipped smooth.

Then Quaashie appeared from his post in the passageway. "Excuse, min fadlukum, excuse," he said, bowing his head several times as he spoke. "They call you to lunch." He tapped his wristwatch.

"My word," Dr. Withers said as he glanced at his. "It's almost four in the afternoon."

They went topside for a meal and rest. Sweaty laborers, relieved, did the same. Out in sunlight, other men and women sifted through the rubble brought out of the pit. No artifacts were found. After about an hour, the team returned to work.

Bebe and Kendra sat on the floor with legs dangling into the slope. Chione stood nearby, too anxious to sit. As the rubble was being removed from deeper inside the passage, the workers became excited again.

Bebe leaned way down to peer inside. "Look," she said as she pointed into the passage. "A withered board."

The long board was fastened against the north end of the deep passage at the ceiling. Another board was exposed below that, then another, and another as more rubble fell away and was removed. Finally, the level floor was revealed.

"About eight feet tall by six wide," Aaron said. Boards covered the entire back end of the pit. "Certainly, those boards alone didn't hold back tons of rubble."

Dr. Withers joined Aaron at the bottom. "Shine that light over here."

They got up close looking into the spaces between the dry splitting timbers. Dr. Withers leaned back, cocked his head and looked again through bifocals. "A wall," he said for all to hear. "Another wall."

"Well, the passage leads somewhere," Clifford said. "They didn't dig this cavity to pass the time."

"Come down here and get your close-ups," Dr. Withers said to the photographers. "Then we can take the boards down."

Ginny and another photographer tediously eased down the footholds with aides carrying peripheral gear. Suddenly a piece of granite broke loose from the slanted ceiling, almost knocking Ginny down. It crashed to the floor, shattered and sent up a billow of dust. She stood frozen, looking up at them with eyes widened.

"Wait!" Paki Rashad said. "Come out, come out!"

The photographers scampered. "I thought I was about to enter the afterlife," Ginny said as her lips quivered. Her aide relieved her of the camera as she sat on the floor and put her head down to steady herself.

"No one goes down there again till we shore up the ceiling," Dr. Withers said. He looked at his watch. "It's late, but we'd better do it tonight. We've worked too hard to come back in the morning and find everything in a state of collapse."

Too excited to sleep much, the team rose early the next morning.

"I'll bet I make it down under before you," Chione said.

"Just eat your breakfast, young lady," Clifford said in a fatherly way. "We're going to need a lot of energy today."

Chione went back for seconds. When excited, she could eat, and she had been excited a lot lately. She had even put on a few pounds, her khaki pants fitting snuggly.

Unexpectedly early, two tall, muscular Norwegians dressed in work clothes and carrying hard hats strutted into the cook tent and helped themselves to coffee but declined breakfast.

"Today is big day," one of them said.

"You seen anything like this before?" Clifford asked.

One of them shook his floppy sun-bleached head. "We make repair, never discovery."

"Glad you're here," Dr. Withers said as he stood and offered his hand. "We're about to open what we hope will be the Burial Chamber."

"Terji here," the taller Norwegian said, shaking Dr. Withers' hand.

"I'm Finn," the shorter man said and eagerly began shaking hands all around.

The team was introduced and Kendra beamed and offered to scoot over, so they could sit beside her.

Finn sucked air through his teeth. "You make good find," he said to everyone. "This good."

Inside the Hall, after the photographers finished and the film was developed, the boards against the back wall of the pit were removed one by one. Care had to be taken in the now confined space to avoid banging into the support scaffolding. As each board was taken down, what greeted them was a huge opening sealed again with mud plaster containing cartouche imprints of varying sizes. Laborers speaking in Arabic could not hide their elation as their ever-sparkling eyes flashed.

Aaron studied the wall, pointing as he counted. "Thirty-three imprints," he said loud enough for all to hear. "Five different patterns."

"Get down here, Chione," Dr. Withers said. "See if you can decipher."

She eased down the footholds to the bottom and studied the marks. "Tauret's," she said, calling up to the others. "Meskhenet and Umi's. Some are Tutankhamon's and this other one, I'm not sure."

Then the photographers went down. The wall would have to be removed which meant possible destruction of the imprints.

"We'll go no farther," Dr. Withers said. "Until such time as these photos are developed, and we're sure we have a legible record."

By lunchtime, the photographers had produced the photos. Several copies of each were still to be made. Two would be for the Madu Museum's records, two for Bebe, plus extras.

Though care was taken to preserve as much as possible, as the hard mud plaster was chipped away, the cartouches broke into pieces. Behind, a wall of granite blocks appeared revealing the structural soundness of the tomb.

More photographs. More developing. Finally, the first huge block at the center top was removed and exposed the sparkling gleam of a gold filigree gate.

Dr. Withers could wait no longer. Two men steadied the ladder as he climbed, clicked on his flashlight and peered into the chamber. The second his light flashed through the gate and hit the opposite wall inside, Chione, eagerly perched halfway down the incline, saw a flash of yellow brilliance and...

...a very solemn Tauret standing in the next sunny chamber, waiting.

Dr. Withers turned slightly on the ladder. He looked to be reeling in disbelief.

"Well, what do you see?" Clifford asked impatiently.

Dr. Withers smiled slowly. "Loot," he said. "History, ol' buddy." He glanced at everyone. "Artifacts that'll change history."

"Is it the Burial Chamber?" Chione asked.

"It's a glorious Offering Chamber," he said, starting down the ladder. "Howard Carter ain't got nothin' on us." He was giddy and almost lost his footing. Once stable on the solid floor, he said, "I'll bet my boots I know exactly how Carter felt looking into Tut's chamber that first time."

"That can only mean good stuff," Clifford said.

"Things you'd never dream of," he said. "Unless you're Chione. It's loaded with artifacts!" He signaled the workers to hurry and remove the rest of the barricade. The heavy blocks were dragged up the incline on sledges, probably much the same way they had been lowered. But the team's sledges were dragged on rubber wheels to avoid adding new marks to the ramp.

After removal of the first block earlier, air seeped out of the chamber. Chione again smelled the perfume that haunted her from the start of the discovery. Now the scent became stronger, more distinct, as if freshly applied. No one else seemed to notice.

The gate was fashioned of wood carved into lotus blossoms and covered with solid gold overlay. Light flashing through the gate and into the room revealed abundant treasures. More photos needed to be taken before removal of the gate. More waiting.

Hand mirrors were brought in to provide a glance at the inside wall where the gate was attached.

Aaron eased a mirror between the filigree and positioned it, so he could see the way the gate was attached on the inside. "It's stuck into holes. Plastered in place."

Rashad took a turn and poked his hand and a mirror through the filigree. Then he conversed with Dr. Withers who said, "We don't need to poke a camera through the spaces to photograph how the gate's installed. We'd risk damaging the gate. Remove it."

While watching in a mirror held by a laborer, Quaashie reached through the gate and gingerly scraped away the plaster with a hand tool, loosening its grip in the hollows around the mounting studs. A little pressure applied, a little shaking, and the gate broke free.

Lights were set up at the doorway. After Rashad, Dr. Withers and the photographers made their inspection, the room was opened for viewing.

Chione stepped inside. The first objects beyond personal artifacts to catch her eye were the two standing golden statues of an elegant woman in full priestess attire. They faced each other about eight feet apart in front of another plaster-laden wall to the left.

"Who does she represent?" Bebe asked.

"Probably our mummy," Chione said. "Guarding the entrance to her Burial Chamber." She could not help but smile. The intense look of resolve on the faces of the statues seemed to have captured everyone's attention. Dr. Withers and Bebe glanced from the statues to her face and back to the statues. Was there a likeness between her and the priestess? Still, as with the golden statue in the Second Annex, no one paid attention to the convex abdomens, except Aaron. Chione breathed in eagerly accepting that the fragrance had possibly been Tauret's favorite perfume. She watched Aaron's nostrils flare as he secretly sniffed the air. Then Bebe seemed cognizant of it and sniffed, but the others still had not noticed. Was the perfume actually floating in the air or was it a manifestation of the paranormal? The fragrance was so heady, surely the others would notice. The hypnotic effect of the scent made her mind reel.

"The same cartouche imprints," Bebe said.

Aaron stood beside her and Bebe as they examined the plaster covered wall with its border of hieroglyphs. "Finally," he said. "Here is our point of embarkation into the Underworld."

Yet, they turned attention back to the present chamber. "About twelve by fourteen feet is my guess," Aaron said. "Another pyramid above." As in the other chambers, beams of a pyramid carved as part of the ceiling rose above them. More Egyptian blue. More yellow stars.

Brilliant yellow coated the four walls from shoulder height to ceiling and pyramid edge. Below that were endless painted reliefs and hieroglyphs.

"Again, not your traditional messages," Chione said, studying them.

"Not your traditional walls either," Bebe said.

"This form of decor is called *dado*," Clifford said. "The walls were covered with gypsum plaster then painted yellow."

"Look at all this loot," Kendra said. "None of it looks decayed."

"It's the pyramid's effect," Dr. Withers said.

He was not joking, nor smiling. He simply made a comment as if talking about the weather. Chione wondered whatever possessed him to say such a thing and why the others did not crack a joke in response. Were they finally accepting all the metaphysical implications?

The contents of the room included Tauret's personal belongings. Tall sealed jars and bronze vases stood about. Many glass objects and jewelry lay on tables and in piles on the floor.

Randy, with a professional air about him, stood away from the activity and talked in low tones with Rashad and the Norwegians. Rashad treated Randy respectfully, perhaps the first professional colleague to have done so. The burial site affected each of them in different ways. Certainly, she was not the only one undergoing metamorphosis.

"Look at these jeweled sandals," Chione said, feeling compelled to stick a foot into one as she saw…

…sandaled feet padding on smoothed stone.

"No!" Clifford said, yanking her away. "That could fall apart at the slightest touch. You know that."

"No touching the family jewels," Dr. Withers said sternly. "In fact, don't even make the air move over any of these fragile items."

Around the room, all sorts of clothing had been heaped in piles for…

…a woman who had earned the right to much finery.

Long pleated cloaks, gowns, many and varied pairs of sandals and gold jewelry lay everywhere as Chione remembered…

…amethyst earrings to wear in Pharaoh's court. A carnelian studded collar with feldspar and malachite for the rituals. A collection of blue anhydrites, gifts from Oba.

Wigs and hair adornments lay on a dressing table along with perfume bottles, jars of kohl, and other items for applying makeup. Chione breathed again.

Scents for all occasions, and one, Pharaoh's favorite.

"Whatever Tauret owned was evidently dumped in here," Kendra said.

"Dumped like in the other chambers," Bebe said.

Chione heard their comments but was unable to contribute. She floated in and out of ancient scenes, pulled far away from the voices around her.

"Chione?" Aaron asked. "Chione, what's up?"

"What's the matter?" Bebe asked, appearing in front of her.

Chione wilted against Aaron. "I-I guess it's just stuffy in here," she said weakly. Her knees threatened to buckle.

"She's right," Dr. Withers said. "Let's leave this chamber. We won't be going through that next passage till this room is cleared."

The decision was right. Besides, Chione felt her energy draining.

Aaron volunteered to take the Norwegians on a tour of the tomb and Kendra invited herself along. Chione no longer felt concern about Kendra shadowing Aaron.

Due to most items being fragile, many days would be required for the preservation and removal of the Offering Chamber contents. The Norwegians returned to Dier el-Bahri. The Forbeses and the Philipses took off sightseeing at Elephantine, Philae, Abu Simbel and regions to the south. Surprisingly, they invited Randy and Tarik.

Bebe announced that the unidentified cartouche imprint on the doorway of the Offering Chamber belonged to Queen Tyi.

"Bebe, Chione," Dr. Withers said. "Get busy. I want to know what Queen Tyi has to do with all this."

He needed to have patience. Chione knew it would take time to sort out.

40

A message arrived stating Egyptian high government officials and other dignitaries from England and South Africa were scheduled for tours.

Dr. Withers looked frustrated. "Look how long it took them to recognize that we're real," he said over dinner.

"As far as I'm concerned," Clifford said, "I wished they still believed we're just hocus-pocus."

Dr. Withers sighed, shook his head. "No chance of that anymore. Their being here will further validate us anyway."

Progress clearing the Offering Chamber slowed. Luckily, like the other chambers, with the exception of the Pillared Hall, and being that deep into the ground and sealed, little dirt and dust was found. Items thought to be most fragile were treated with more melted paraffin to help them retain their shapes. Kendra assured the procedure was only a precautionary measure to prevent damage. No one could deny that pyramids preserved everything, at least till they were brought out into the air and sunlight.

Chione asked Aaron to move their sitting mats into the First Chamber. Something was drawing her to him, perhaps because the dreams had not let up. She patted the mat for him to sit. "I want to bounce something off you."

He sat facing her. "So, bounce."

"Can you feel this room, Aaron? Can you sense anything in here?"

"I hadn't tried to," he said. "We're always so busy."

"It's mystical in here. More so than the other rooms, like Tauret's purpose is here."

"Is that what you perceive?"

Though emptied of the artifacts that Tauret herself had touched and used, the room vibrated with her presence. "Can't you feel the power in here... in this room of potions and magic, representing how Tauret cast spells to help women conceive or give birth?"

"I had a strange feeling the first time I came into this room, but I thought that was only my reaction of first entry."

Suddenly that perfume wafted past her nostrils. Chione felt a strange sensation and looked around the chamber.

The people on the walls came to life and went about their duties.

...as if Chione sat gazing at a movie on a screen. In one mural...

Tauret swirled her incense burner over the head of a man and chanted spells.

In the other mural...

Tauret was in the process of removing Hapi's mud from the woman with the blackened face.

Chione was peeping into their lives, unbeknownst to the Ancients. Vaguely, she heard their archaic dialogue. Her head reeled, but she welcomed the shift in consciousness as normal, even desired a greater intensity of it. She studied Aaron curiously. "You agree that Tauret was pregnant, don't you? And that Tut was the father?"

"Would seem that way."

"He was ready to take a minor queen," Chione said. "Ankhesenpa bore two stillborns. Maybe Tauret would have to conceive before Pharaoh would marry her. He wanted an heir."

"History never mentioned—"

"History never had a chance. The King was deposed because of religious beliefs."

"And left behind a woman carrying his child."

"Who was also killed for those same beliefs," she said. History of the High Priestess could only be written now, as her tomb was being unearthed.

"We need to see that mummy."

Chione hesitated a moment, then said, "I was inside her coffin again."

"Again?" Suddenly he was up on his knees in front of her, almost begging. "Tell me, tell me."

"That's all, Aaron. Darkness... as I'm lying and waiting."

Aaron's shoulders slumped. "Of course, I wouldn't see that," he said as he sat down again. "I don't experience Tauret's life."

"You once called me the same name the King called Tauret."

He smiled weakly. "You mean Umayma?"

"Yes, Oba," she said. Her voice had changed again as she saw...

Pharaoh sitting opposite her. A great strength filled her.

Then she saw Aaron's face again.

"Tauret," he said softly in that strange other voice.

"Oba," she whispered, giving in to the moment. "My Oba."

Aaron shook his head. "Chione?" he asked, reaching for her. "What's happening to us?"

She melted against him. Aaron's smell. She was in Aaron's arms and wanted to be there. Aaron was holding her. She pressed her lips against his before he could say anything. She wanted him. Forever. His arms tightened around her, and they were lying locked together on the meditation mat. His mouth opened, his tongue probed. She could do nothing but respond. His excitement was rigid between them. She pressed against him. His hand slid sensually over her hips. His face was close, and he breathed heavily and looked into her eyes. Then he pulled away quickly. "Is this for real?"

"Oba," she whispered, pressing her lips against his again.

Aaron struggled uncomfortably to sit up and took deep breaths. "I'm sorry, Chione, sorry. No excuse." He scooted away and drew his knees up and crossed his arms on top and sat very still trying hard to regain composure while his breath calmed. "This isn't right. You're feeling too much like Tauret and—and I'm feeling like Tut. Maybe there is a spell."

"Are you fighting it?"

The flicker of an eyelid said he did not intend to answer that question. "What else have you seen, Chione? What other clues?"

"I-I saw Tauret lots of times. She approaches me then merges into me."

He remained quiet a while. Finally, he said, "Chione, I don't want what I'm about to say to sound like a lot of gibberish, okay?"

At this point, anything would sound plausible. "Okay."

He paused again and then said, "We're being led into something."

"Led?" She took his hand again.

"Admit it. You've changed since we've been here."

"In what way?"

"You're more accepting of me." He reached to touch her face then stopped.

"Accepting? C'mon, you think I'm being coerced?"

"No, that's not what I meant. What I see happening is that by us seeming to be Tauret and Tut, we've drawn closer."

The thought warmed her. "You mean we're drawing closer because Tauret and Tut were supposed to be together? And we're feeling the same about each other because we're experiencing their lives?"

Aaron leaned over and kissed her gently. Suddenly she went into in his arms again. She could not move away. She wanted more. They were passionate again, as Chione and Aaron. Then he pulled away all too quickly.

She did not think it wrong. "Aaron, I'm me. I'm Chione."

He rose quickly and almost forced her up by an arm before she could resist. "Let's get out of here before we lose control."

On the way out, just as Aaron clicked off the dim lighting, Chione looked up at a mural hoping to see Tauret again. What greeted her was the face of the woman in the mural after having Hapi's mud removed. The face resembled Bebe with her new hairdo!

"Wait a minute," she said suddenly. She clicked on the lighting and looked again. The murals were just as they had found them. Chione hesitated as she felt the magic of the room shift into limbo again. She clicked off the light. Surely if anyone knew the truth about all she saw, she would be labeled a real nut case.

Finishing touches were applied the next morning to the mud brick buildings. Built like those for the Directors, the blocks of sleeping rooms had been completed in one long row and dried in the scorching heat. The new tenements were immediately occupied. One unit was left available for visiting dignitaries. The reporters were relegated to tents since they often times stayed in other locations, dependent upon their schedules. One wise person ordered a lean-to build at the end of the structure, out of the wind. That was for Tarik.

A mud brick dining room had also been built to replace the large tent. However, the same appliances and furniture still stood on the hard-packed dirt floor. The new, larger dining room was virtually the same as the former one. The only exception was that instead of tent canvas that flapped and spread dust when the wind blew, they now had walls with a couple of windows and curtains to help keep the grit out of their food. Yafeu had a sign painted in English that said "Fine Dining." Even the locals chuckled over that.

Days passed before the Offering Chamber was finally emptied. Preservation and packing of artifacts would soon be completed and another shipment sent to Cairo. This time, two Egyptian police officers would accompany the crates from the site all the way to the Museum.

The expected dignitaries arrived and departed after several hours, taking only a cursory view of both tombs. They didn't even have a meal. What was the point?

Chione and Bebe finally had a chance to decipher some of the hieroglyphs in the Offering Chamber. After they finished their meal, they disclosed a few of the more mysterious messages they gleaned.

"Listen, everyone," Chione said. "We found one reference to Queen Tyi inside there." She had their attention. "As far as we can make out, a very young Tauret worked briefly for, and was favored by an aging Queen Tyi, who bequeathed her to Tut and Ankhesenpa's household."

"Now we have something concrete," Clifford said.

"On the right side of the wall leading to the Burial Chamber, behind one of the statues, Bebe and I found this spell."

Look not far
no life to find
in a jar.

"Must mean canopic jars," Kendra said.

"If there's nothing to find in the canopic jars," Clifford said. "Where'd they stash her innards?"

"By the way," Aaron said. "Anybody see the containers?"

"None so far," Kendra said. "Must be in the Burial Chamber."

"Or in another room beyond," Bebe said. "Like Tut's Treasury, which Carter's team accessed behind his Burial Chamber."

"Oh, I can't stand it," Dr. Withers said with feigned exaggeration. "Another hidden cache?"

"Here's another phrase," Bebe said. "From the opposite side of the doorway."

The seed planted will bloom
but not before passing through doom.

"Doom?" Kenneth asked. "That one's obscure." He was the only one finishing his meal. Kenneth could eat.

"Chione, surely you have something to say about that verse," Marlowe said.

Dr. Withers could not wait. "C'mon, out with it."

Again, she hesitated, but they were asking for it. She smiled. "I believe that second verse implies something or someone must die before living again."

"Not reincarnation again," Kenneth said. Bebe gave him a quick elbow to the ribs that made him spill his drink.

"Could be another reference to resurrection in the Afterlife," Clifford said. "Any other phrases?"

"That's all right now."

"You know what I haven't found an answer for?" Bebe asked, looking around the group. "I'm still stuck on the fact that the deeper we go; the more haphazard things look. I really need to know why the artifacts were hurriedly dumped." No closets for the clothes were found, nor any trunks or containers of any kind. It appeared that many of Tauret's cloaks were carried over someone's arm and simply allowed to slip off in heaps. They retained the shape of having been bent over an arm. "If I wanted, I could have stuck my own arm into the heaps of clothes and walked away with them."

"Very interesting observation," Dr. Withers said.

Even her jewelry and other tiny items were left in piles here and there on the floor.

"Don't forget the jars of figs," Chione said.

"Figs?"

"A symbol of the womb," Bebe said. "Rebirth was expected."

"Clifford," Dr. Withers said. "After all your years in and around tombs, what's your best guess?"

"Simple," he said. "They were in a hurry." Everyone laughed. Clifford had a way of making a statement. The meal was resumed.

"You really think that's all it was?" Dr. Withers watched Kenneth drag a shred of aysh around his plate. Then he did the same to gather up the last of the delicious sauce.

"That's not the point," Clifford said. "It's why they were in such a hurry that sticks in my mind."

True, no one could know till all of the chambers were opened, maybe not even then. It took years of analyzing and interpreting.

Translations especially remained subject to various theories from many different historians.

"We will document, document, document, to the best of our ability," Dr. Withers said. He stood and prompted everyone to hurriedly finish the meal. "Let's get back to Inventory and wrap up. Then finally," he said, throwing a fist, "the Burial Chamber!"

41

The day of reward, at one time almost relinquished to others, arrived. The Directors and Randy returned late after dinner the prior evening. Two physicians were expected, sent by the Egyptian government to view the mummy. Dr. Jasper Kent, a British medical research scientist, and Dr. Salib Asim, an Egyptian forensic pathologist specializing in mummies.

Cartouche imprints, two Eyes of Horus, one on each upper corner of the second quadrus of plaster of what was hoped to be the burial chamber wall, and a section of the lotus border, were marked for cutting. They had been photographed and verified.

"I suggest, O Teacher?" Naeem asked cautiously to Dr. Withers. "We find plastered quadrus with blocks behind." He gestured first toward the doorway that had led to the Offering Chamber, then to the new wall. "Same to this one for Burial Chamber."

"I agree, O Teacher," Quaashie said politely. "Plaster covers whole wall. Support blocks will be behind."

"Good thinking, men," Dr. Withers said.

Both Quaashie and Naeem's broad range of experience, knowledge, and dedication continued to prove invaluable.

Most of the cartouches were crowded toward the center of the wall. The Eyes of Horus, though, looked to have been drawn too deep. If the artist's finger penetrated the wet plaster all the way to the stone behind, lifting those in one piece might prove impossible. Because they chipped at the imprints on the Offering Chamber doorway with hand instruments, only two were salvaged whole.

"We'll cut and break away the smoothed plaster from around the imprints first," Dr. Withers said. "To get it out of our way." He stooped to pick up a small electric circular saw. "Quaashie," he said, offering the tool. "Please do the honors."

Quaashie's eyes flashed wildly. "Deepest gratitude, O Teacher," he said, nodding several times. Someone handed him and Naeem each a set of goggles and Quaashie pulled a handkerchief from the jeans pocket under his gallibaya. He tied it over his nose and mouth. Naeem rewrapped a portion of his turban around his face below the goggles. Both Dr. Withers and Masud lowered goggles and pulled up facemasks.

The empty Offering Chamber was overcrowded with team members and others waiting impatiently. Dr. Withers, Rashad, and Masud stood up close to Quaashie and Naeem.

The rest stood back, to give them room. Forbes and Philips stood with them, all shifting places each time the photographers jockeyed for a different view. Marlowe chose to stay out of the proceedings and only viewed new findings at a more convenient time with her husband.

Randy watched quietly from the doorway. The next time Chione looked his way, he was shaking hands with two men, probably the doctors. One of the men sucked a pipe, though it emitted no smoke. Each time Chione glanced in that direction, he was saying something that made Randy and the Egyptian bend over with laughter.

Masud stepped back from the wall to join the waiting group and dropped his facemask. "Photographing the men," he said. "Good record of how they work."

"They seem highly skilled," Chione said. The drone of the electric saw was similar to a hum she sometimes heard accompanying her visions. She felt distracted. Then came another vision, a vivid image of...

...a motherly woman in a dimly lit room, weeping, offering garlands, expressing heart-wrenching, indomitable sadness as she leaned over another in repose.

Chione was stunned. She must have wavered. Someone placed a hand momentarily on her shoulder. It was the first time she had seen anyone other than Tauret and Pharaoh as clearly in her visions.

As suspected, plaster was applied over granite blocks. Plaster around the outer edges that did not bear imprints was first separated from the center portion by sawing grooves to segregate the sections to be saved. The edge plaster was chipped or pulled loose. Quaashie was able to lay the round saw blade flat against the blocks and free the valuable imprints from behind. Cheers went up as each historic piece came loose into waiting hands.

Rashad stepped away from the wall. Dr. Withers stayed beside Naeem to help catch the chunks when they were freed. Powdered plaster coated their clothing.

"Usually Dr. Withers only watch," Masud said.

The culmination of a lifetime of hopes and dreams for Dr. Withers was at hand. The plaster wall was more than half removed when, between the starting and stopping of the handsaw, Chione heard unusual noises in the passageway. Randy, still at the entrance, turned and went up the incline into the Pillared Hall. The noise of the handsaw drowned out all sound again.

Randy appeared with Kenneth who pushed his way into the room and yelled to gain Dr. Withers attention. His voice was lost to the high-pitched mechanical hum. He pushed his way up front, the look on his face grim. Chione looked to Randy who shrugged.

Kenneth did not tap Dr. Withers on the shoulder as he normally might. He took hold of both of Dr. Withers shoulders and leaned close and said something into his ear. Startled, Dr. Withers turned quickly. He signaled for the saw to be turned off. Kenneth again whispered something. Dr. Withers looked utterly aghast as he swatted nervously at his clothing to remove powdery dust. He and Kenneth stepped outside the Offering Chamber and Randy scooted in.

"What's going on?" Clifford asked.

"Got me," Randy said.

From the conversation at the doorway, the words desert...
Dakarai... Yago floated in. Then Dr. Withers motioned and called,
"Kendra!" After he and Kendra spoke, Dr. Withers stepped back inside.
"Sorry to do this, folks," he said. "On the day we've all been waiting for."
His disappointment was evident. "There's been a tragedy." He waited
as if he did not know how to break the news.

Kendra's expression was one heightened expectation.

Clifford stepped forward. "You don't have to soften it, Sterling.
We're big kids."

Dr. Withers seemed lost for words. Finally, he said, "Masud, come
over here."

Masud acted like a little boy about to be scolded. "Yes, sir?" he said
obediently.

"Masud," Dr. Withers said, placing a hand on the man's shoulder.
"I'm afraid I have some bad news for you." He looked around the group.
"Bad news for us all. The Bolis have found two bodies in the desert."
Shock rippled through the group. "They believe one man is one of the
Yagos. The other is Dakarai."

"How?" someone asked. "Why?"

"Someone in a hot air balloon spotted the bodies," Kenneth said.
"The Bolis believe they were assassinated."

Chione looked at Masud who stood staring at nothing. His eyes
bulged. "What it means?" he asked. He seemed frightened.

"We'll have to delay again," Dr. Withers said. He shook his head and
signaled. "Everybody out. Leave everything as is."

They waited high on the hillock while Dr. Withers and Aaron went
down. The two bodies were being temporarily brought back to camp.
In the absence of the rest of the Yago clan, identification had to be
made of the suspected Yago brother. Dakarai they knew.

"Shot in the back of the head," Kenneth said. He stood close to Bebe
who lovingly rubbed his back. Perhaps hearing of a shooting brought
back painful memories for Kenneth. "I knew Dakarai was involved in
something."

"What else have you learned about this?" Clifford asked.

"Seems they were forced to kneel, then shot. Their hands were tied behind their backs."

"No!" Chione said, feeling numb. Surely everyone felt the same. Their benign little expedition had turned treacherous at someone else's hands.

A squad of Bolis appeared on horseback plodding up the hill through the rocky terrain. Each of two horses being led carried a body thrown over its back, one wearing a blue gallibaya. The dead men's hands were still tied. People from the beggars' camp lined the road. Tourists and other spectators pressed closer, gawking and snapping pictures. Dark skinned and near naked children ran beside the horses. The hungry media got more news to sell their papers. Ginny was right down there too.

"You'd think they'd put those bodies in crates or something," Clifford said. "The whole world doesn't need to see."

The photographers and anyone with a camera zoomed in on the only action of the moment.

"Look at Sterling," Clifford said. "So many problems to sort out."

"Be thankful it hasn't happened to one of us," Kenneth said.

"Yeah," Chione said. "Our grave robbing is legal."

Kendra and Royce passed below, both gesturing frantically, evidently arguing. Royce joined the group meeting the horses and Kendra headed toward the shacks.

"Kendra!" Chione said through cupped hands.

She looked up the hill, took a couple of steps, stopped to wipe her eyes and then headed up toward them.

Kenneth suddenly said, "I want some pictures of Royce. Cold blue eyes can't hide all lies." He took off down the hill before Bebe could stop him.

Kenneth arrived as the horses halted. Masud gestured to one body, presumably Dakarai's, and then nodded. Royce walked over and half squatted, changed position and bent down again, trying to view the man's face. Then he straightened and also nodded and said something. From his position next to Ginny, Kenneth made it look like he was merely filming the entire event. Ginny would capture what they needed to record. Kenneth was focused on Royce.

Kendra arrived. Her eyes were red. "Damned husband of mine," she said.

"What happened?" Bebe asked.

Kendra sighed heavily. "You may as well know. My husband doesn't come back to camp till late at night, if at all." She gestured toward their shacks.

"Where does he go?"

"I'm sure he's with the Yago woman."

"You don't know," Clifford said.

"Where else would he be and knowing what he now knows?"

"Which is?"

"He heard from some of the Bolis that the Yagos might have been kidnapped. All of them."

"Wha-at?" Clifford asked. "Why?"

"The Bolis claim Dakarai, through his connections, led the Yagos to treasure found in the desert. They make off with as much as they can and Dakarai gets a cut. Wealthy patrons get black-market artifacts as Dakarai maintains his contacts and credibility at the Madu."

"How is it the Bolis happened to tell your husband that much?" Clifford asked. "Why Royce?"

"Maybe because he showed concern the Yagos," Kendra said. "Instead of himself."

Clifford pulled a handkerchief from his pocket and handed it to Kendra. "Why would they be kidnapped?"

"The Bolis think they discovered the other tomb before we discovered Tauret's," Kendra said. "Whoever plundered that tomb stopped when we arrived or worked at night."

"They must be the ones who stole our crates of toys," Bebe said. "As if they didn't have enough."

"So why were you crying?" Chione asked. Kendra had watched Royce perform his choreographed dance alongside the Yagos. By now she should be past the point of tears.

"Royce is leaving. He's going to help the Bolis find the Yagos. He's involved with Elbertina, I know he is. He goes off on his own when we're in Egypt. She's the reason."

"He's going away with the Bolis?" Clifford asked.

"No, he probably knows where to look for her. He'll go on his own." She began to cry again. "He said not to expect him back."

Clifford put an arm around her and let her sob. "These things are never easy. Royce will be back."

"No," Kendra said. "He feels responsible for Elbertina and her family and said not to expect to see him again till everything is set right. He's packing his things and leaving."

Bebe shook her head and looked doubtful.

"Elbertina's devastated, I'm sure. She was probably forced to watch her brother being shot," Clifford said. Kendra stepped away from him and he waved a hand signaling she should keep his handkerchief. "Why don't you try to go with your husband? Maybe you should stay beside Royce through this."

"I don't want to, Clifford. You haven't heard it all," she said, sniffling. "Royce was with the Yagos in Cairo, came back with them bearing gifts of bribery. My dashing husband has been my beloved infidel all along."

"I'm sorry to hear that," Clifford said.

"About five years ago, some Spanish dignitaries arrived in San Francisco," Kendra said as if needing to confess. "Royce was conveniently away on a business trip all that time. I'm certain he already knew the Yagos. There were other times here in Egypt and other places we've visited. It's taken me a long time to face it. I even found his old computer, the one he said was stolen."

"I saw the computer," Chione said. "Isn't that new?"

"No."

"Aren't you carrying this a bit far?" Clifford asked kindly.

"No, that's the same laptop. It's been cleaned to look new," she said. "When he first bought it, I accidentally closed a pen inside and made a tiny chip on the back edge." She blew her nose. "I never told him.

Mr. Perfect would never forgive me. The laptop he brought back to camp has a nick in the same place."

"Are you saying he faked the missing laptop just to go to Cairo?" Bebe asked. "Or he must have gotten the laptop back from the thieves somehow."

"That's right," Kendra said. "It proves he's on friendly terms with whoever took it."

"The desert does change a person's life," Bebe said.

Chione was surprised to hear a statement like that from Bebe. Like everyone else, Bebe dealt with her own nemesis.

"Hey, look," Clifford said. "Sterling's motioning everyone to the mess hall."

Guards were posted outside and told to keep others some distance away, especially the media. Inside, Dr. Withers expression was grave. "Let's put our learned heads together again."

Kendra related everything she knew.

"Agrees with what the Bolis told me," Dr. Withers said.

"Would seem tied to the killings of Dakarai's cousin, Usi, and his bunkmate too," Clifford said.

"Understand, Kendra," Dr. Withers said. "Your husband's affiliation with the Yagos—especially knowing they wanted to pick up artifacts from our endeavor—increases the likelihood Royce knew what they were up to."

"I can't believe my husband would stoop so low." She began to whimper again. "He's got lots of money." She sighed. "But maybe black-marketing artifacts is how he gets it."

The Bolis suspected Elbertina and the brothers were kidnapped because they failed their mission, which was robbing the tomb under the necropolis. Had they been successful in taking over the CIA's venture, their patrons would reap some huge rewards.

"The Yagos must have embarrassed a lot of people," Bebe said. "But why kill them?"

"To make them pay," Clifford said. "That's why they were kid-napped. Could get a hell of a ransom from the wealthy Yago clan. Save a lot of face."

Kendra looked numb and stared straight ahead.

"Evidently one brother was expendable," Dr. Withers said.

"Rogelio, the younger one," Aaron said.

"Now I'm going to say something." Dr. Withers shot a finger into the air. "And I don't want any contradictions." They waited. "Kendra, if your husband's involved, you might be at risk here."

"No way."

"Let me finish. If Royce is involved—that's if—if someone wanted to get at him, they could do it through you."

"Are you saying because they killed one Yago brother, my life's now at risk?"

"One Yago?" Clifford asked. "One Yago and three Egyptians."

Chione felt Kendra reach for her hand under the table.

"Everything depends on Royce's involvement," Dr. Withers said. "He's going out and stirring things up, making himself look dirty."

"That's my point," Kendra said. "His place is here with me, not chas-ing after Elbertina."

"You sure?" Bebe asked. "Why else would he?" The point was well taken.

"Fact is," Dr. Withers said, "I'm putting guards on duty around our sleeping quarters at night."

"That's ridiculous," Kendra said. If anything irritated her more, it was having restrictions placed upon her.

"No, it's not. We've had four murders here, people. The Egyptian police will have someone on duty covering both the front and back doors and I'll hear nothing more about it."

"But, Dr. Withers—"

"That's all folks," Dr. Withers said. "And Kendra? I suggest you keep the lid on your Queen Nefertiti perfume so your cubicle is less con-spicuous."

After a quick snack, and heading toward the portcullis shaft to resume work, Chione looked up the hillock to see Dr. Withers arrive first. He looked out toward the necropolis and danced his little dance of excitation with fists clenched at his sides, happily bouncing up and down.

"He seems determined not to allow the murders to discourage him," Aaron said.

"He's not even bothered by this smothering heat," Bebe said, taking a sip of Karkade from her hip flask.

"Was supposed to be cooling down this time of year," Clifford said. "Moving into the best season."

"Why do you suppose it's different this year?" Kendra asked.

"Don't say we've been cursed," a voice said, coming up behind. They laughed as Randy joined them.

Inside, Dr. Withers donned goggles and his facemask and held the circular saw waiting for Quaashie. Once the rest of the imprints and mud plaster had been removed and carried away, Dr. Withers announced, "I don't understand why the entire wall needed to be opened just to get a sarcophagus through. We'll remove a couple of the center columns of blocks first, see what's beyond."

Terji and Finn arrived, having responded to a fax. The team was fairly certain of entering the Burial Chamber.

The top two blocks were removed with workers yet unable to get a good look inside the next chamber. The curious odor that oozed from that room seemed much akin to the smell that billowed from the mummy room when Randy was rescued.

Dr. Withers could wait no longer. Again, he climbed a ladder and stuck his flashlight and head as far into the darkness as possible. Suddenly, he gagged and coughed. His exclamations echoed from the next chamber. He stretched farther inside, casting his light about. He kicked at the wall blocks as he struggled to hoist himself farther into the opening.

Clifford flashed one of his ridiculous grins. "Sterling," he said, calling out loud enough to be heard in the next chamber. "Access would be less arduous if you'll allow the blocks to be removed."

Dr. Withers pulled himself out of the opening and half turned the ladder, then blew out a breath. He choked and fanned himself.

"Good or bad?" Clifford asked.

"A little of both."

"Oh, no," Chione said. "Tell us the chamber hasn't been breached."

"Nothing like that."

He was off the ladder now, holding his flashlight in one hand and motioning with the other, unable to speak. He went to sit on one of the removed blocks. "If I keep getting these kinds of shocks," he said, patting his chest firmly, "I'll need my own sarcophagus."

"That doesn't sound good," Bebe said.

Dr. Withers sighed heavily. "It's good and it's bad."

"So, what did you see?" Bebe asked impatiently.

"A strange but beautiful sarcophagus," he said as he fanned fresher air against his face. "Golden statues... and two bodies."

42

Terji and Finn tried desperately to understand the mixed rush of exclamations as everyone in the chamber spoke at once.

"Why would that be strange?" Chione asked. No one heard.

Dr. Withers called for attention. "Here's what I'm going to do.
Rashad and Aaron are going to stay inside here with me and the cameras. The rest of you will leave until the blocks are removed." Everyone
protested. They wanted to be in on the expose'. "Because of the exposed bodies," Dr. Withers said. "We're going to be hanging a shield to
keep the dust off everything inside. You won't see anything anyway."

An air of impatience permeated the Pillared Hall. Voices and equipment noises echoed out, distorted. Lighting and shadows flickered.
Perfume wafted up from below. Chione breathed in deeply, all the
while watching to see if any others had detected it.

"It's taking forever," Bebe said as they watched another huge block
of granite being drawn up the incline.

Then no more blocks came out. According to the way reflections
moved about in the Offering Chamber, the lighting equipment was
being repositioned into the Burial Chamber.

It was difficult to decipher the overall mood of the workers. One
person down there laughed. Another spat out an Egyptian oath. The
rest just talked, excited and loud, while Dr. Withers tried to maintain
some order. Aaron came to the incline and motioning for the doctors
to go down. The photographers exited.

It took another twenty minutes before Aaron motioned for the rest of the team. "Face masks and gloves," he said.

Chione caught the look in his eyes as his brows pinched together. An uneasy feeling crept over her.

Bebe and Kendra eagerly went first and stopped abruptly at the doorway. Tall Clifford squeezed through, creating a gap through which Chione saw the tilted beams of a black stone pyramid, the middle of the massive black sarcophagus, and the torso of a withered body lying on top. Dr. Withers's hand pointed downward to an area into which gangly Clifford nearly stepped. Clifford turned and bolted from the Chamber, white as a ghost. Another shriveled body sat on the floor slumped against the sarcophagus just inside the doorway. Chione pushed the others into the room as Dr. Withers followed Clifford out. Foul air moved with them and forced Chione to hesitate outside the doorway because she felt nauseous.

"I had one of those déjà vu experiences," Clifford said. "When I saw the body on the floor, I felt I was the one sealed up in there. The oxygen was depleted. All I could do was sit down and wait to die." Even now, he struggled to breathe. "I must have tapped into a moment of that guy's life."

Dr. Withers and Clifford spoke a while longer as Clifford relaxed. Chione did not need to hear any more to understand. She turned her attention back inside the room. The golden goddesses standing at the corners of the sarcophagus waited.

"Aw, Ga-wd!" Terji said, crowding in behind her.

Chione saw the full view of the female on top of the sarcophagus. The vision she saw while standing in the Offering Chamber of the bereaved woman offering garlands repeated. The woman in her vision and the shriveled body on the sarcophagus were one and the same.

Randy gasped so loud it caught the attention of everyone. Ignoring the golden goddesses, and being careful not to step on anything that might lie on the floor, he walked around the sarcophagus conspicuously examining the woman's body.

Dr. Withers and Clifford re-entered the Chamber.

"What is it, Randy?" Dr. Withers asked.

Randy looked up and said, "Forgive me, Clifford, for what I'm about to say." He quickly glanced at everyone. "I don't want any of you thinking I'm making a joke of Clifford or Rita, okay?"

"Let's have it," Clifford said, not quite recuperated but trying to carry on.

"Look here," Randy said. "See the way her one leg's bent up? See her crossed arms? Her hands are turned backwards, and she had been holding a child's rattle." The toy lay loose on the woman's shriveled chest. Her hands, like the rest of her body, had dehydrated and shrunk and released her grip on the toy. Randy spoke and gestured professionally like a physician lecturing a class. "Now look at her face." The woman's mouth hung agape, held in place by taut, dehydrated skin.

"What are you getting at?" Clifford asked.

"Well, again Clifford, forgive me. But, minus the toy, this is the identical position your Rita lay in when she passed away."

Clifford's eyes bulged as he went in for a closer look. "Rita? Why Rita? Who can these people be?"

No one spoke. It left a lot to the imagination.

What remained of the woman lay on the far side on top of the sarcophagus under the slanted black pyramid beams. Her head and neck rested on a tiny carved wooden bench used as a pillow by the Ancients. Her long curly red hair lay sprawled around her head. The skin and bones of her feet remained in preserved sandals. Wearing a long-pleated dress of the finest linen gauze, she seemed wonderfully preserved, naturally mummified. Her white dress and cloak had yellowed slightly. Historical accounts of fashion proved true. The clothing she wore left her nearly naked, in those days, a way of handling the oppressive heat. One breast was exposed. The woman had drawn her garment partially over her body. With one leg slightly bent and raised at the knee, her pubic hair showed underneath. She wore nothing else. Her many gleaming jewels spoke of one dressed for the auspicious occasion of being entombed.

Remains of the man sat on the floor slumped against the gloriously carved sarcophagus. His carved pillow bench verified that he had not made it to the top to lie under the pyramid beside the woman, as they might have planned. Nor had his body fared as well. With legs outstretched, his sandals had broken apart and fallen off. The leather strips lay haphazard.

"See here," Dr. Asim said, pointing. "His toenails have fallen out."

The man's legs seemed elongated, grotesque, stretched out like that inside withered skin. One of his arms had come loose at the shoulder socket with skin stretched to coarse tethers as the arm hung limp in the sleeve of his disintegrating garment.

Four golden tutelary goddesses wearing scorpions on their heads stood at each corner looking down at the huge black sarcophagus, arms outstretched encirculating beams of the pyramid.

"Look at their faces!" Burton said. He cringed, put a hand over his mouth, and then spoke in a whisper. "They look like they might speak."

Clifford silently studied the position of the woman. Seeming to remember, he produced a small compass and half-turned with it. "Shrines, sarcophagus, and coffin usually face east and west. Chione's alter ego, here," he said, tapping the lid, "sleeps with her head to true north."

Chione smiled. "Remember the goddesses found in King Tut's Treasury?" she asked, motioning to the golden statues quietly gleaming under the lights. "The one on the southwest corner is Isis. Nephthys is on the northwest."

"So Neith is on the southeast," Bebe said. "Selket's on the northeast."

"They're all facing inward," Clifford said. "Whatever's in this black box must have needed extra protection."

Clifford moved close to one of the Goddesses and blew dust from one of the arms. He leaned forward, and as if to test for true gold, opened his mouth, and prepared to chomp down.

"Clifford!" Dr. Withers said. "Leave your bite impressions at the dentist's office!"

Making people laugh was Clifford's way of carrying on despite having difficulties being in the room.

The laughter subsided. Dr. Withers looked as if he needed to make his a personal connection despite his rule of not touching anything. He hesitated and then rubbed a finger leaving a mark in the dust on the lustrous stone. "Black diorite," he said, bending closer to inspect. "Looks like the lid and the pyramid are one piece."

The lid was actually the floor of the pyramid structure, square at the bottom, creating an overhang on both sides of the rectangular sarcophagus.

"What do you make of that lid?" Clifford asked. In all his years as an Egyptologist, surely the odd shape was out of the norm.

"You've heard of nonconformists, haven't you?" Dr. Withers asked with a wry smile.

"Black represented rebirth," Chione said.

The sarcophagus was etched around the edges with a border of beautiful lotus blossoms and lotus buds, known as iniuts. A mural on one side showed Tauret in meditation inside her pyramid and surrounded by tools of her trade.

"Look at this," Bebe said as she bent down to study the carvings. "The Aten."

Sure enough, opened hands on the ends of the rays of the Aten reached down.

"Why the Aten?" Clifford asked. "We already know she was converting to Amon."

"The Aten symbol helps confirm my theory," Bebe said. "Look around you, people. Except for those few items in the corner, this chamber's empty."

"Which suggests?" Parker asked after having inspected intently but not commenting.

"They were in a hurry," Bebe said. "They didn't even have time to make her a new sarcophagus depicting Amon."

"Yes, yes," Dr. Withers said, nodding.

The opposite side of the sarcophagus contained a scene with several children lovingly attentive to Tauret. On each end, to the north and south, Tauret's full cartouche showed, written with the symbol of Aten.

"What was the rush?" Bebe asked again. "Once a person died, the mummification process averaged seventy days. They had plenty of time to make changes."

"Agreed," Burton said. "Once she was dead, why not take the time to correct things?"

"Same with Tut's sarcophagus and coffinettes," Aaron said. "In addition to coffinettes possibly belonging to Smenkhkare, his sarcophagus was thrown together from parts of different sarcophagi, the base meant for Nefertiti."

"Particularly since Tutankhamon was Pharaoh, why didn't they take the time to make things right?" Parker asked. "Why the sense of abandonment in his burial as well?

"See what I'm getting at?" Bebe asked. "Why were these two people—Tut and Tauret—whose lives were connected, buried in such haste?"

"With a little luck," Dr. Withers said, "we'll be able to offer some new theories before we vacate this hillside."

"Like Chione first mentioned," Bebe said. "Maybe even change history."

Chione looked up. "Another pyramid ceiling." She flashed her light upwards. Then she saw it. The others did too.

"Would you look up there," Dr. Withers said, teasing and acting as if he had not seen the ceiling when the photographers went through.

Chione studied the glyphs up inside the point of the pyramid ceiling. She turned circles, with her head tipped backwards. "It's the Egyptian Zodiac."

"Who's going to interpret the symbols?" Parker asked, being facetious, but friendly.

Up inside the tip of the ceiling pyramid, was a full astrological calendar, carved and painted in glorious color. The rest of the ceiling was painted black. The walls were solid black, nothing more. Chione took a better look and exclaimed, "Hey, everyone, get a load of these walls!"

Again, they directed flashlight beams. Hieroglyphs seemed crudely scratched into the black paint on the remaining three walls.

"Not your everyday glyphs," Clifford said, exaggerating.

"Scratched in after the walls were painted?" Aaron asked.

"Too crude," Randy said. "Like they were done in the dark."

"Randy," Clifford said quickly. "You just turned the lights on."

"I beg your pardon?"

"These glyphs, Randy, everyone? One of these two people," Clifford said, motioning to the bodies, "scratched these into the wall in the dark."

"Probably the man," Dr. Kent said. He had been leaning over the male body. With gloved hands, he carefully lifted the edge of the man's garment revealing a pouch out of which poked handles of small tools.

"Chione... Bebe," Dr. Withers said. "I want those glyphs interpreted as soon as possible. These two people had something important enough to say that they gave their lives for it. Put your expertise together and don't quit till you understand the meaning of every last mark."

They took a closer look at the walls. Scratches and gouges were everywhere, as high as the person might have reached.

The doctors examined the man's body. Randy stooped next to Dr. Asim. "Look here," he said, with gloved fingers carefully pulling aside the rumples of the man's cloak over his chest. "A cartouche."

"It's Father," Chione said, blurting, for a moment not realizing what she had said. She and Clifford stared at one another. The others thought she had made a joke and laughed. She knelt to read the small turquoise cartouche that hung around the man's neck on a leather strap. "I mean this is Umi, Tauret's father."

"Then the woman is Meskhenet," Kendra said.

"If so," Dr. Withers said. "That second tomb containing their cartouches stands empty of its intended occupants."

"So why—how would they end up in here?" Burton asked.

Chione stood. "One thing I'm sure we'll find scribbled on these walls is that Meskhenet and Umi chose to die with their daughter."

"It's all here," Clifford said. "What Umi had to say will make people listen."

What motivated Clifford to make such a statement, given he was not that adept at translating the glyphs?

Silence filled the room with respect and reverence. The presence of Tauret's parents raised more questions and heightened the mystery.

"Why?" Randy finally asked.

"We'll learn it from the walls," Clifford said. "But, hey, where are the canopic jars—"

"Over there," Dr. Withers said as he swung his light.

In the far corner stood the elaborately decorated alabaster canopic jars, translucent and dazzling. Their lids, each bearing a different carved head of one of the four sons of Horus, sat haphazard and loose on the floor. One lid lay upside down. Other jars sat nearby. Aaron and Clifford went to inspect. "Two are empty," Aaron said, flashing his light to peer inside. "Why do you suppose that is?"

"Ask the goddesses," Chione said.

"Can't," Clifford said. "Judging by the way these jars have been handled, they must have fled."

"What's under this diorite pyramid better be perfectly preserved," Dr. Withers said. "In as good a condition as Chione's lunch."

"I couldn't tolerate another thing going wrong," Kendra said.

"As archaeologists," Clifford said, reminding. "We can't change a thing, can we?"

The entrance wall of the Burial Chamber was opened completely and hefty support beams had been installed with the capable aid of the Norwegian crew. Simultaneously, runners brought freshly developed photos in for approval. Dr. Withers decided it was time to move to the next task.

Chione exited the tomb to help prepare Inventory for arrival of the statues. The four golden goddesses covered with padding and cloth exited the tomb to a chorus of exaggerated responses from onlookers.

The breeze blew at the coverings exposing a glimpse of a long graceful golden arm and hand. The Egyptian police kept at bay the daring that tried to sneak close in order to snap a chance photo. The media were held back as well, but their equipment could zoom in on a grain of sand at two hundred feet.

Drs. Kent and Asim examined the bodies of Meskhenet and Umi and released them for shipment to the Madu. Each of the withered remains was treated with preservative, wrapped in thick layers of gauze and placed on a separate tray. Because of Umi's sitting position, they taped him upright on the tray with legs outstretched over sideboards.

Aaron arrived out of the shaft to await the bodies. Bebe came next up the ladder and met Kenneth, and they stood among the workers awaiting the arrival of the parents. Soon, Masud joined them from down the hill.

As the bodies were hoisted out, wailing began from a group of women among the throng of onlookers; plaintiff wails like none yet heard. The wailing escalated to a full-blown chorus. Some wailed, nearly screeched, while others cried. Dogs howled mournfully. The onlookers seemed confused by it all.

"Word gets around just too fast," Aaron said. "Some of the workmen must act as a voice for the locals, keeping them posted about our findings."

"Why the sudden swell of locals too?" Chione asked. "The crowd seems in a state of unrest, a lot of men milling around." Another foreboding chill transited her body. She closed her eyes tightly, then opened them wide and could only wonder what had come over her.

The tray bearing Meskhenet began to appear at the top of the shaft, rising in slow motion as the laborers cranked the lift winch gently so as not to tip the tray. A hush fell over the crowd. Immediately after Meskhenet came Umi. The crowd went wild again, yelling and applauding upon seeing each major artifact.

The wailing and screeching resumed, as laborers hoisted the two trays to their shoulders for the trip down to the inventory tent, a hot air balloon passed too low overhead dragging an ominous dark shadow over the portcullis area. The balloon and its occupants drifted slowly. Like the mourners on the riverbanks in 1898, who honored a cache of royal mummies being transported by Victor Loret, the archaeologist who found them, gunshots rang out. More wailing and more gunshots. Some in the crowd screamed and pointed upward as the hot air balloon flapped limp and began to deflate, finally plummeting to the rocky earth in the distance.

"This is not happening!" Masud said, taking a step sideways to better see. More gunshots. Masud groaned and doubled over clutching his chest. Kenneth screamed, dove for Bebe and knocked her sideways to the ground, covering her with his body. More wailing. More gunshots. Masud flew backwards from the second impact and landed where Bebe moments before stood. His chest was covered with blood. The workmen dropped the trays and everyone lay prone with no place to go. Chione lay flat and covered her head with her arms and hands. They were in plain view, like targets in a shooting gallery.

Chione moved her arm slightly to watch downhill as police on foot and horseback pushed and shoved their way through the throng of people pressing in for a better view. Only three to five seconds had passed but her heart used up a year's worth of beats. No more gunshots. Chione crawled over to Masud. Aaron was on his knees beside him.

Dr. Withers and Clifford finally exited the shaft seeing everyone on the ground.

"What's hap—?" Seeing Masud, Dr. Withers dropped to his knees to help.

Kenneth and Bebe stood slowly and peered cautiously around. Kenneth kept himself between his wife and the crowd.

The two doctors came out of the shaft and were dragged over to Masud. A police officer arrived, breathless, having run up the hill. "A stray bullet?" he asked.

"What a horrible accident," Clifford said.

"Never mind," Masud said. His breath gurgled. "No accident." Blood bubbled from his mouth.

"Masud?" Dr. Withers asked. "Why you?"

"Not for me… for Kenneth."

"You weren't near Kenneth," Aaron said. "You were beside Bebe."

"Yes," Masud said, gurgling, barely able to hold his eyes open. "Best way… hurt… Kenneth… shoot his wife."

"Wha-at?" Kenneth asked, keeping Bebe behind him.

"Someone… doesn't… like… Kenneth," Masud said as his breath faltered. He gurgled and choked. "Praise be… to Allah!" Then he went limp and his breath stopped as the doctors tried frantically to revive him. Workers gathered around waiting to help.

When Dr. Kent pushed on Masud's chest applying CPR, blood squirted out of his mouth and nose. The blood did not flow unless his chest was compressed. Finally, they knew Masud would breathe no more. Dr. Kent sat back on his heels and shook his head. His gloved hands dripped blood that had gushed up through the bullet holes in Masud's chest.

"Someone's trying to pay you back, Kenneth," Clifford said. "For having found that other tomb."

"How would Masud know who the bullets were meant for?" Chione asked.

"You think he had something to do with those… those—" Dr. Withers could only sigh heavily.

"I'm not insinuating anything," Chione said. "But how would Masud know they wanted to get to Kenneth?"

"Did he mention Bebe and Kenneth to keep suspicion off himself?" Dr. Withers asked.

"Maybe not," the police officer said. "With his dying breath, he prays to Allah."

"More likely," Clifford said. "The bullets were meant for Masud, to keep him quiet because of his involvement with Dakarai."

"Who was in the balloon?" Kenneth asked. "Why'd they shoot that thing down?"

"Shot down what balloon?" Dr. Withers asked, looking to the sky.

"Yeah, what balloon?" Clifford asked.

"The air balloon," the officer said, pointing down toward the valley. A group of people and more Bolis had gathered around the colorful deflated balloon spread over the rocky terrain. "Maybe pay back men who found two victims in desert."

Maybe Masud had told the truth, but with his death went the secret as to his involvement with Dakarai. Maybe someone did mean to kill him.

Kendra lay curled into a knot in the dirt whimpering. Chione went to her side.

"I can't bear the thought that my husband is involved," she said, uncurling and wrapping herself in Chione's arms. "Chione don't you know? Can't you tell?"

"You know I can't, Kendra unless it comes to me. I haven't received anything about Royce."

"I've got to get myself together," she said, drying her eyes. "Got to make some decisions."

By late the next afternoon, the few artifacts in the Burial Chamber had been removed and packed. Two of the polished canopic jars were found to contain a good supply of ancient natron, a salt compound of sodium carbonate and sodium chloride used for dehydration in the mummification process. A sizeable quantity of cowry shells, representing a desire of the wearer to have children, was found on the floor around the jars. Two faience vases contained more glass beads, a rare commodity in those days. Scattered children's toys were gathered.

Shabti statues, meant to jump to the command of Osiris if the dead preferred not to work, were not found in figure form nor scratched on the walls; in fact, nothing substantial to signify progression into the Afterlife.

"So why didn't they use up the natron?" Clifford asked. "Where are this woman's innards if not in the canopic jars?"

Meskhenet, Umi, the goddesses and the artifacts were sent on their way to Cairo under heavy guard that afternoon. A fax from the Madu Museum put Quaashie and Naeem temporarily in charge of the Egyptian laborers.

"With the help of the Norwegians," Dr. Withers said. "The lid of the sarcophagus will be lifted in the morning."

The elusive climax of the exposition of this tomb was finally at hand. Remembering the opening of Tutankhamon's sarcophagus, no one chanced a second guess at what they might find in Tauret's, or in what condition.

"All I want is to see Tauret's face," Chione said. Mentally, she reminded herself of the promise made to Tauret. The memory of the interactive vision sent another chill through her body. She felt an eerie sense of apprehension and duty since making the promise to wear Tauret's amulet until she understood its meaning. For some reason, Tauret had chosen her, called to her through the centuries and made her feel this was her life too. She had to follow through.

43

Terji and Finn helped with the hydraulics when needed from day one and were again on hand. Nothing could keep them away. They thrilled at having been in on the unveiling of portions of the find and looked forward to viewing the mummy.

The burial chamber entry wall stood open with jacks and capstans in place. Dr. Withers gave the signal. The Norwegians and a handful of laborers went to work. Sealed in place, the sarcophagus lid squeaked and groaned in rebellion, like suction about to burst.

Before long, Dr. Withers gave another order for the men to cease. "We're going to have to loosen that seal. I wonder what they used."

"We'll take samples, of course," Aaron said.

Chione and the others watched from the Offering Chamber. With all the equipment plus the photographers and their paraphernalia inside, the Burial Chamber was congested. Clifford repositioned a ventilation fan.

A shiv was carefully inserted between the lid and sarcophagus body to puncture the seal as hydraulics applied lift tension. As the parts came loose, a rubbery tearing squeal emitted.

A potent perfume filled the rooms, the odor Chione smelled all along but which few seemed to detect. Surely the fragrance was a figment of Tauret's spell over them, undetected by most. Then, as Chione discreetly watched, everyone began sniffing. Everyone smelled it!

Chione and the others inched forward. The lid was being lifted. The hydraulics creaked and groaned carrying the weight of the diorite lid with its symmetrical pyramid.

Dr. Withers remained crouched under the lid overhang. "Would you look at that," he said, peeking into the widening space. Chione went up on tiptoes and stretched to see past the others. A second sarcophagus came into view.

Aaron kept a sharp lookout to assure the lid did not sway and hit the walls. The Norwegians seemed experts at their equipment. Raised high, the pyramid lid accentuated the peaked ceiling.

The photographers picked their way through equipment circling the sarcophagus to film from various angles. Paki Rashad took silent visual inventory.

"Can we see, Dr. Withers?" Chione asked. "Let us come in."

The photographers finished, gathered their equipment and retreated to the Offering Chamber. As the photographers crowded past, Drs. Kent and Asim stepped inside. Then Chione and the rest crowded in.

"It's pink granite," Kendra said, running gloved fingers between the sarcophagi. "This one's carved too."

The second sarcophagus was slightly smaller than the diorite rectangle by a couple of inches all the way around. Both Rashad and Aaron shined lights between the two. Rashad looked at the others and pointed inside.

Everyone tried to see. "Well, I'll be," Dr. Withers said. "They left the papyrus ropes inside after lowering the second sarcophagus."

Bebe took a turn at a close-up. "Inside his sarcophagi, Tutankhamon had three coffins and that gold mask. We've yet to see a coffin here."

Since the room was too small and the lids and pieces should not be stacked, the black diorite lid would have to be removed from the chamber before anything else could be examined.

"Trouble is," Dr. Withers said. "Do we want to ship everything to the Madu or let the Restoration folks decide what stays?"

"If something stays," Rashad said. "It will be the diorite base of the outer sarcophagus until we hear differently. All else can go." He motioned upwards.

The rest of the day would be spent transporting the diorite pyramid lid to the portcullis shaft. Terji estimated the lid weighed well over a ton. It had to be inched between the scaffolding and up the inclined passage outside the Offering Chamber, maneuvered between the pillars in the main hall, then up numerous stair steps and high up over the balustrade in the passageway. The laborers sweat like never before and worked in rotation. The tanned Norwegian hulks peeled off their shirts, drank lots of water, and flexed their muscles. Those unable to help were asked to clear out.

To everyone's astonishment, Kenneth, Jr. and several girlfriends showed up at the site. Bebe had taken it upon herself to notify her estranged son the news of his father's discovery of the second tomb. Bebe once admitted she was the only one to maintain the connection in their family. Kenny was a ski instructor in Switzerland and only sporadically answered their emails over the years.

Kenny seemed cool toward his father and mother, shaking hands or giving a quick peck on the cheek. Yet, when he saw Terji and Finn, two blonde Norwegian hulks laboring alongside the brown-skinned Egyptians, he must have felt some sort of kinship. Kenny was tall, blonde and as suntanned as the Norwegians. He sought and was given permission to work with the Norwegians in moving the pyramid lid.

By late afternoon, the pyramid made its entry back into sunlight, appearing peak first out of the shaft.

"What a sight to behold," Jibade said.

"Mom, Dad, wasn't this worth staying for?"

"It's a dream come true," Helen said. Chione looked at her mother and wondered if she realized the meaning of what she said.

Like an audience attending a play, a hush fell over the crowd. The men at pulleys relaxed the ropes, allowing other laborers to maneuver the peaked form onto a dolly for transport to Inventory. Dozens of men lined up ready to pull the dolly with long ropes. The pyramid lid was wrapped for concealment and for protection against nicks and dings, but its shape was undeniable. Cameras clicked away as the concealed structure rolled past and was eventually swallowed into the inventory tent.

"Some snapshots will make it into various papers," Jibade said.

"That will only whet the public's interest," Chione said. "It'll make them want to see more when the exhibit goes on tour."

Dinnertime was an hour away. Waiting for films to be developed, everyone was too high-strung to take advantage of the moment to relax. The Norwegians sent Tarik and a driver with a printed message telling their crew at Dier el-Medina they would stay another night. Tarik's enthusiasm to do anything to help had endeared him to everyone.

Several of the team headed out for a walk. Kenny and his friends came along. Some of the Egyptian police accompanied them. They found themselves alongside the mastabas again, the only other area interesting to an archaeologist in close proximity. Except that the purple hills and shimmering distant sands were beautiful to behold.

"Strange how the Khamsin blew away all the sand down here," Kendra said.

"Look at Terji and Finn," Randy said. "They're curious about everything."

The Norwegians wandered off down the hill. One called to the other farther down. They seemed to be inspecting the ground, then moved their arms in different directions measuring something. Suddenly Finn called out and motioned them to come down.

By the time they made their way to Finn's location, he was on his knees digging in the dirt with a broken rock. Terji measured off an invisible straight line toward Finn.

"Found something?" Randy asked.

Finn was excited. He shot them a glance but continued to dig most frantically. The groove exposed some stones. He moved back a couple feet and scratched away more loose rubble. More stones appeared.

"Aha!" he said finally, quite beside himself. "There is wall here." He stood and pointed along the area he had unearthed. "A wall, you see?" They looked. Finn dropped to his knees and dug some more. Terji joined him and dug at right angles. Sure enough, a straight line of solid blocks began to appear in each direction, too squared in position to be happenstance.

"Oh, my," Bebe said.

"A wall?" Kenny asked as he walked alongside the marked area. He dropped to his knees, dug with his bare hands and became excited. He seemed adept at not disturbing the blocks as he swiped away loose earth. "Mom, look," he said as if seeking Bebe's recognition and approval. He had exposed another block sitting at an angle to the others.

Finn came to his feet again. "We make good find," he said, beaming.

"How did you know?" Bebe asked.

Terji swept an arm toward the mastabas. "Burials of commoners had to live somewhere while working graves."

Terji and Finn marked off more space with the heels of their boots.

Randy bent down and examined a cornerstone. "You know, they might be right about a village being here. The people had to live somewhere."

The Norwegians walked the area and returned with Kenny on their heels. Finn took a notepad from his pocket and drew. Together, they plotted out a small village and showed the crude drawing.

"What makes you so sure a village stood here?" Bebe asked.

"The sand blows away," Finn said. "We see same blocks near Dier el-Medina."

"Yah," Terji said. "This our kind work. We never make discovery before. Only dig, rebuild after someone find."

"We make big discovery?" Finn asked, smiling proudly.

Chione saw it coming. The Norwegians might wish to claim the village as their find. Dr. Withers and the rest of the Directors would make the decision if anyone else would be allowed to work the site. "You've found something we've already got a permit for," she said.

"No," Terji said, disappointed. "You know this village?"

"Not specifically," Chione said. "We have a permit for the entire area."

The Norwegians looked deflated. Terji shrugged. "We make discovery for you?"

"You probably have," Randy said.

Finn smiled again. "Maybe you need men like us for rebuild."

"Yah," Terji said. "Maybe we work together some more?"

"You'd have to run that by our boss," Randy said.

"So how does a newcomer break into working on this dig?" Kenny asked, surprising everyone.

Bebe leaned over and whispered in Chione's ear, "Kenny told me that last year his girlfriend dragged him to a psychic. The reader told him that he had been an Egyptian priest in a past lifetime at the temples at Karnak. He was told that he worked with the hidden mysteries." She rolled her eyes and shrugged in disbelief.

The next morning, Kenny treated his parents like human beings. He showed new respect for what his mother did for a living, and for the fact that his father's life evolved well past the war years. It also seemed that two blonde men working among dark-haired, dark-skinned Egyptians had given him a much-needed attitude adjustment. He departed having nearly begged his parents to get him approved to return and work.

Chione watched the interaction between Bebe and Kenneth and their son. She could not help herself. Perhaps the spell Bebe drank did more for her life than just cure her menopausal malaise.

Dr. Withers was in the best of spirits. News of finding remains of a village sent his emotions soaring. Over breakfast, he said, "Listen up, everyone." They came to attention. "There's one thing I never want to hear around here again." Who would have said something to offend their respected leader? He smiled suddenly. "The one thing I don't want to hear is... when do I plan to retire!"

With the second tomb and now the village, Dr. Withers would not quit, despite his career faltering between past sites. He had caught a second wind.

Clifford, too, would have work to last for years, not having to return to California except to finalize the sale of his properties.

Lifting off the lid of the second sarcophagus would take little effort. No seal was found. The lid would merely be hoisted and moved out. No one was kept out of the chamber as long as the photographers were not deterred. Although no one knew what to expect, the next thing anyone saw would most likely be a coffin. Marlowe decided that would be too good to miss and rejoined the group.

Sure enough, as the pink granite lid was hoisted, an exquisitely carved wooden coffin as clean as if it had been positioned yesterday came into view.

The laborers were ecstatic. In eagerness to see, one man almost let go of his rope causing the heavy lid to droop and bang against Clifford's shoulder. He yelped. Terji grunted and gripped the granite lid as it came precariously close to banging against the diorite sarcophagus. Naeem took over and the laborer politely bowed, relieving himself of his honored duties, and swiftly exited the chamber. Terji and Finn stared wide-eyed.

Chione was nearly in tears. Most likely, the entire coffin was the carved likeness of the woman whose mummy was housed inside. "Oh, Tauret," she said. Her knees felt weak.

Aaron came to her side. She glanced at the others who also watched her. Clifford's expression said he understood more than he let on.

"Time to clear out again," Dr. Withers said unexpectedly. He waved his hands shooing them. "Let's get this lid out. There'll be time enough for viewing."

Once back inside, Chione studied the elegant sculptured face of the coffin. The black onyx eyes were large, round and heavily outlined with kohl in the style prevalent during the Eighteenth Dynasty. The eyes seemed lifelike and looked straight up into the Egyptian Zodiac, as if they might at any moment blink. Her nose was straight, with sensuous lips full above a proud chin. Carved and painted around the face was a common Egyptian style haircut cropped below the ears. The cut was the same seen on the golden statue in the Second Annex and on the two statues guarding access to the Burial Chamber. All exposed skin on the face, body and limbs glowed in a painted translucent flesh tone.

"I can see why ol' Tut would want to use his crook and flail on her," Clifford said.

"Look at her jewels," Marlowe said.

Jewelry was inlaid in the carved hair and ears. The suggestion of a cloak was decorated with patterned rows of cloisonné inlay of every kind of jewel available. Her arms lay across her chest with hands opened flat. She looked at peace, but Chione knew differently. The coffin was only a crafted artisan's likeness of the priestess, incapable of feeling emotion the priestess had taken to her grave.

Clifford bent into the sarcophagus for a closer look. "It's sycamore fig," he said, breaking the silence. "The type of wood used to make royal coffins."

"Adds credence to Chione's theory about Pharaoh planning marriage with this woman," Dr. Withers said.

"Look." Rashad pointed and bent in for closer inspection. "These seams do not appear sealed."

Clifford rubbed a gloved fingertip around the area where Rashad pointed. "No sign of goo."

"Oh, no," Bebe said. "If air got in through those seams, I'd hate to think what condition the mummy is in."

"Given the diorite sarcophagus was sealed and probably preserved everything under it," Aaron said, "I'd not lose faith here."

Clifford carefully stuck his hand down inside the sarcophagus and under the coffin. "It's resting on supports."

More time was taken to assure the photographers were absolutely finished and that film developed well. The photos would be the only record of the coffin in its original placement and condition. Things would never be the same once the coffin was opened.

As everyone spoke and examined, Parker came to her side. "Chione, the resemblance between you and the priestess is uncanny."

Chione gasped. "Oh, please," she said, whispering. "Don't repeat that."

Parker was not the only person onto something. The others had heard. "My sentiments exactly," Dr. Withers said. "Now, Chione? Why do you suppose you and this coffin image look like twins?"

The fact that she might resemble Tauret did not bother her. She just did not want everyone making more of it. She could not stand to be teased the way they reminded Aaron about resembling King Tut. She crinkled up her nose, showing non-importance.

Clifford brushed close to get her attention and quietly spoke behind his hand. "Remember one of the spells from the First Chamber, 'Beware. Two who would enter....'"

Later, Ginny's news was not good. "Films of the coffin developed hazy, despite what we thought was ample lighting." She shook her head. "Must have been the reflections off all those jewels."

"Shots of Umi's scratchings on those black walls are indiscernible too," Aaron said.

The photographers set about focusing on every individual feature and glyph, adjusting lighting to create shadows of details or lines barely etched. With the second set of photographs completed, Clifford would again expedite the batch over to Luxor. The photo shop's more specialized equipment would best bring up any vague images. With Clifford went an offer of extra pay if the local shop could do the job in record time since the next day was *Victory Day*, a local holiday. Money talked among all people who eked out a living. If the film could be developed in record time, they deserved the extra pay.

Victory Day was spent catching up on inventory chores and paper work. The locals who stayed in camp spent time in quiet celebration. Many laborers had left. Even the beggars' area seemed abandoned with all the rickety cars and animals gone.

The near solitude was welcomed. Dr. Withers gathered the team. "Since Christmas is less than two days away, you should all be deciding how you want to spend the holiday."

"I don't think we'll be going anywhere," Burton said. "The four of us will be leaving after we open the coffin."

"Duty calls," Parker said. "Someone's got to run the Institute. With that new tomb, I don't think any of you will see California any time soon."

Early the afternoon of Christmas Eve, the photos came back strikingly clear.

"This is the best Christmas gift we could hope for," Dr. Withers said, as they stood huddled over the images spread on the table. He paused momentarily. "We could postpone now and celebrate. Get past Christmas before we open her up."

"You wouldn't dare," Clifford said.

44

Quaashie and Naeem stood guard and waited inside the Burial Chamber in case a stealthy worker tried to squeeze through.

Inside the Pillared Hall, Dr. Withers counted. "We've got too many people here. Who's going to volunteer for second round viewing?" Nearly everyone objected. "Sorry folks. I count twenty-three heads."

"Let's just pick 'em," Aaron said eagerly.

"Good idea. First of all, I know my wife will mind me." He grinned playfully. Marlowe lightly punched his shoulder and stepped aside. "I hate to slight anyone," Dr. Withers said. "But we all know the rules. Paki Rashad has right of first inspection. In fact, so do Drs. Asim and Kent. That's four of us, plus the two photographers and their equipment."

"I'll wait and go with Kenneth," Bebe said.

Kendra stepped back beside Bebe. The two Norwegians stepped back. So did Chione's parents. Then Burton and Parker decided to wait and share the viewing with their wives.

"But... but," Carmelita said in her practiced whined. She detested having to spend time with the other wives in the kitchen and made an issue of finally getting to see something new. "We're officials of the Institute. We don't get to see first?"

"Sh-h!" Parker said, jabbing her in the arm.

"Okay, we'll view later," Carmelita said. "We're lucky to be here. Who'd guess any of us would have the opportunity—"

"Sh-h!" Parker said again.

"One thing I do want," Dr. Withers said, "is for Chione to be present for the unveiling."

"I can wait," she said quickly. She never approved of Dr. Withers showing favoritism. Neither would she protest too loudly and miss the chance to go in first.

"No, I insist," he said. He spoke to the group. "Without Chione's prompting, I may not have followed through on this venture."

"I agree," Aaron said. "Chione should go first."

"Then you three are left," Dr. Withers said, looking from Aaron to Clifford to Randy.

Randy stepped back, his actions no longer a surprise to anyone.

Clifford looked from her then back to Aaron. He almost smiled. "Aaron should go," he said. "After all, he is your understudy and I'd rather he be the one to help open the coffin." First, the irony of his words made him look sad, and then he smiled like he had just pulled something off. "I'll wait. After all, the lady isn't going anywhere."

The first group entered.

"Listen up," Dr. Withers said, poking the air. "What's inside may be yet another coffin. If not, we're down to the nitty-gritty. Who's going to volunteer to carefully lift the lid of this priceless sycamore fig while the rest of us get first peek?"

No one volunteered. Then Quaashie spoke. "May we, O Teacher? Naeem together with me?"

Dr. Withers waited for objections. No one wanted to tend to the lid once it was removed. They wanted to view inside the coffin without distraction.

"Okay," Dr. Withers said. "When in Egypt, the Egyptians have the honor."

Dr. Withers first placed a hand on each side of the lid near the hips attempting to rock the lid slightly to test the give. Quaashie went to the head and Naeem the feet. They bent into the sarcophagus ends and with gloved hands found places to safely get a grip. Both Aaron and

Dr. Withers waited, ready with small shims, in case the lid might be tight and have to be gently pried.

The videographers moved about with cameras perched on their shoulders, catching each minute step of the process.

Quaashie and Naeem exchanged quick instructions in Egyptian. After a little coaxing, a little pulling, and acting as if the task might prove impossible, Naeem looked up and said, "Okay, tired now. Need a break."

Response was frantic. Quaashie could not contain himself, backed away and doubled over in a fit of laughter.

"That's something I'd expect out of Clifford," Dr. Withers said, laughing with the others.

Adding to the moment of drama, Quaashie and Naeem lifted slowly. As the lid rose, a blue white light began to gain in intensity from inside the coffin. Glowing silver-white streaks radiated directly at her and Aaron from the interior, permeating them both. Chione welcomed it in through every pore. Aaron put up opened hands as if to shield his eyes from the brightness. More energy shimmered in the air around them.

The others continued to chatter away, sounding oblivious to detecting the light. She and Aaron would be the only ones to perceive such a transmission. Yet, the real purpose the chosen group came to Egypt in the first place was still unknown.

A new sweet heady perfume, unlike any other scent, drifted to Chione's nostrils, a familiar, provocative scent. Again, no one noticed. Aaron inconspicuously breathed in a slow, deep breath and moaned as if reliving memories. If only she could capture the fragrance and reproduce it for posterity. Or to later use to entice Aaron!

Mixed exclamations from the others filtered into the reverie as Dr. Withers said, in an elevated voice, "Well, so much for finding a mummy."

The light was blinding. She and Aaron stood staring at one another as the rays permeated them.

Suddenly, Chione felt faint and reached for Aaron's arm. He put his arm around her shoulder. "Don't hyperventilate and faint at the crucial moment," he said, whispering.

She poked him in the ribs as the energy began to dissipate and let go of its hold.

"Chione! Aaron!" Dr. Withers said sounding thoroughly irritated. "You with us?"

No longer smiling, Quaashie and Naeem dutifully lifted the coffin lid over the heads of the others. They carried it into the Offering Chamber to lay it gently on padding on the floor by the back wall.

Chione and Aaron leaned in for a closer look and froze. Ginny maneuvered around with her camera.

"Is this a bloomin' joke?" Dr. Kent asked, evidently not impressed. He held his empty smoking pipe behind himself and bent in closer. "I'd say she's bloody real!"

Tauret lay poised in regal posture. Her skin glowed like fine polished stone.

"Could the figure be the epitome of a master artisan's work?" Dr. Asim asked. "Perhaps a lifelike replica of Tauret."

"Is it bloody possible this is polished stone and yet another carved coffin?" Dr. Kent straightened and chomped down hard on his pipe stem. At times, it was difficult to determine when he was being jovial and when he was disbelieving.

Rashad bent deep for a closer look at the face. His head twisted and turned as he examined. Finally, he straightened. "She's not been mummified!" he said, emotional and completely out of context with his unassuming demeanor.

"Mummified?" Dr. Withers asked. "She's preserved. Under that pyramid." He pointed upwards. "That's what kept her intact."

Rashad stared unblinking as he clung to the edge of the black sarcophagus.

"Does anyone have an explanation for the condition of this... this... woman?" Dr. Kent asked, close to anger.

"Truly, it's someone's joke," Dr. Asim said.

Dr. Kent sucked frantically on his pipe. "You had a death here in camp, did you not? Is this that woman?"

"Just a minute," Dr. Withers said. "Who do you think we are?"

"Where are the remains of the woman who died?" Dr. Kent asked. "The body here is fresh, just been laid to rest. How do you explain that?" Now they were seeing the critical professional side of Dr. Kent's British personality.

Calmer than the others, Aaron only smiled. "The pyramid, Doctors. We've had first-hand experience that pyramids preserve anything under them."

Dr. Asim nodded. "It's been speculated that's one reason our pyramids were built."

"The theory seems to hold true," Dr. Withers said. "Laying sealed and undisturbed thousands of years under that diorite point and under the pyramid ceiling?" He gestured upward again. "She's been preserved. Besides, Clifford's wife was in her mid-sixties."

"Where is her body?" Dr. Kent asked again.

"Buried with love in Garden City," Chione said. "Nearly two months ago."

Chione waited for Aaron to comment. His arm was too tight around her shoulders. She pulled away.

Rashad kept shaking his head. Surely, in all his years of inspections he had never seen anything like this.

Chione looked over the body again. There it was! The huge scarab amulet lay over Tauret's heart just below her folded arms. Exquisitely carved lapis lazuli trimmed with pure gleaming gold. The combination of gold and lapis, a symbol of eternal life and resurrection, ensured the protection of the sun. Beside the scarab lay a swatch of wavy hair bound by a finely braided gold rope. Chione's heart danced. Yet, with so many people around, how would she be able to retrieve what Tauret instructed her to remove from underneath the beetle?

Tauret wore thick black kohl. On closer examination, her translucent skin showed signs of decay. Almost imperceptible light graying blotches occupied one cheek, the backs of her long graceful fingers, and her shins.

Chione felt suddenly overwhelmed with a fear of having arrived too late. But for what?

"How are you holding up?" Aaron asked quietly.

His words came to her as if through a tunnel. She had to concentrate for a moment before realizing it was Aaron who spoke and that the words had not come to her through paranormal means. "It's warn in here," she said.

"Want a breather?" he asked. "Go topside?"

"Not on your life."

Chione looked at Tauret then back to Aaron. "Is that the face you've seen in dreams?" she asked, whispering as the others spoke among themselves.

"The very same," Aaron said. His expression was full of love.

Several flower garlands had been placed between the coffin wall and the top of Tauret's head. The blossoms had dried, perfectly preserved, and still contained splashes of color. Chione gripped the side of the sarcophagus as another vision overtook her.

A motherly woman in a darkened room, holding flowers and a blue faience perfume decanter; splashing the body in a last ritual, weeping for Tauret.

The greatly distraught woman, seen in a previous vision arranging the body's clothing, had performed a last ritual. "Meskhenet," she whispered. She felt a gnawing sadness at seeing the flowers, which represented a deep connection to lost ancient times through gifts of caring.

Jeweled ornaments decorated Tauret's cropped Egyptian hairstyle. More jewels lay on each side of her head.

"Look at those earrings," Ginny said from behind the lens as she zoomed in. "I can't associate her style with Ancient Egypt."

The head and partial body of a golden cobra protruded aggressively and zigzagged outward from one earlobe. The snake's tail curved from the other earlobe, suggesting it had wrapped its body around the back of Tauret's head.

"Our lady was definitely a nonconformist," Dr. Withers said.

Her jeweled collar and many necklaces told of riches bestowed on a much-favored person. Among other gems, red jasper and green feldspar cloisonné reflected light magnificently. Her arms were covered with bangles and beads from wrists to armpits. She wore multiple jeweled rings.

"She wears a lot of silver," Aaron said.

"Then she was special to someone," Dr. Asim said. "Silver was the rarest of metals in those days."

"There's enough finery here to make any woman livid with envy," Dr. Withers said. "Look at that scarab."

Chione's heart fluttered again at the thought that someone might lift the chunk of lapis before she could. Then she remembered that no one would touch so much as a hair on this woman's head until such time as preparation for removal was completed.

Tauret's white pleated skirt and cloak had turned grayish. Under her folded arms, a jeweled collar and necklace covered her bare chest. The skirt was fastened to the cloak below her breasts, which lay bare, the nipples still clinging to their color.

"Meskhenet and Umi saw to it that their daughter's burial wishes were carried out," Aaron whispered into her ear.

"You saw that vision too?" Chione said quietly though astonished.

"In the Offering Chamber. I put my hand on your shoulder. I saw a vision that you must have had at that moment."

The sandals on Tauret's feet were also jeweled. Who would expect anything less? The leather had not disintegrated. The footwear looked as if one could put them on and walk away. Around the body lay handfuls of polished cowry shells. On both sides of her waist lay tiny toys. Among all the souvenirs meant to follow her into the afterlife, the wide neck of a bottle protruded upright from the curve at the side of her waist.

"Look," Chione said as she pointed. "Look!" She knew exactly why a bottle was included. She bent down and sniffed hoping to smell a fragrance more than three thousand years old. The scent was the same that billowed out of the coffin when it was first opened, more delicate than the heady perfume many had smelled throughout the tomb. "It's the perfume bottle Meskhenet used to perform the last ritual."

"How do you know that?" Dr. Kent asked. He had stepped back while the others marveled. He paced, sucked his cold pipe and looked to be suffering from anxiety.

Aaron bent down too and used his flashlight. Soon, he straightened but motioned for Chione to take another look, which she could not refuse. She got as close as possible to the bottle opening and breathed in.

"Use your light," Aaron said.

She clicked on her flashlight and peered through the wide-mouth opening. To her amazement, at the bottom lay tiny remnants of, perhaps, herbs or flowers used to make the perfume. The mark of a thick liquid having evaporated stained the bottom.

"So how would you bloomin' know what the bottle was used for?" Dr. Kent asked.

"You're just going to have to trust her," Dr. Withers said.

"Sir," Chione said to Dr. Withers. "I want this bottle preserved in every sense of the word. I want it capped somehow so the particles inside are not disturbed."

"Fine, Chione," he said. "That part's up to you."

She was already immersed in yet another feeling, a great desire to merge with Tauret. She thought Tauret would stand at any moment, and they would become one. She felt herself shaking uncontrollably and felt...

...herself lying inside the coffin under the protection of the Zodiac, waiting for that one indefinite interval in time.

Chione sighed heavily.

Trained to control their emotions and to catch fleeting moments, the photographers said nothing and kept shooting. Perhaps their cameras absorbing the scene acted as a buffer preventing anyone from expressing overwhelming feelings.

"I've seen enough for the moment," Dr. Kent said with tones of disbelief. He left the chamber followed by Dr. Asim and Rashad with his photographer.

"I'd better prepare the next group," Aaron said.

Chione stayed in the room unable to make her legs take her out. Ginny eyed her curiously but, thankfully, did not aim her camera.

The spouses came with the rest of the team. No one said much, as if upon entering the Burial Chamber they found themselves in such awe, no words would complement the moment.

Except for Clifford who said, "Someone wake Tauret so we can get on with our work."

Kendra could not produce a smile to share with anyone.

Randy bent close, then straightened, his eyes wide. He walked to the opposite side of the sarcophagus and again examined the body. "Hey, the Priestess was pregnant. Look at the shape of her stomach."

The thin cloak garment had settled over Tauret's body. Over the stomach area, the garment served to accentuate the uneven mound inside her belly. In fact, her body was thin, hipbones pushing up against skin and delicate fabric. If she normally had a protruding stomach, one would believe it would become smooth and flattened as she lay on her back. Such was not the case.

"Strange we didn't notice that," Dr. Withers said.

"Now we know why they didn't put her innards in the canopic jars," Clifford said.

"Let's examine her," Randy said, gesturing over the unusual shape of one side of the abdomen. "Here lie the fetus's buttocks and legs. The head, of course, is deeper into the pelvis."

Ginny zoomed in again.

"Someone get one of those doctors back in here," Dr. Withers said.

Aaron returned with Dr. Kent. He looked to be reeling in disbelief but had no choice but to go along with the scenario, perhaps crack another sardonic joke to get through it. He bent over the body, visually examined it from different angles, and moved to the other side of the sarcophagus. Finally, he straightened, chomped down on his empty pipe and said, "If she was pregnant—and it bloody well looks it—she was past the middle of the second trimester. Nearly six months preggars, she was!"

Marlowe moaned and bent close to Tauret's head. She straightened and held the side of her own head. "I knew it! I knew it!" she said, running from the room in a panic.

Dr. Withers followed. So did Ginny and the others. Through the doorway, Chione watched as Marlowe collapsed into her husband's arms in the Offering Chamber. Everyone crowded around her. Dr. Withers sat her down on the floor. She held her head.

Chione found herself completely alone with Tauret. She may never have another chance. Quickly, she reached for the lapis lazuli scarab, pausing only a moment to steady her trembling hands. She grasped and lifted the amulet, not knowing what to expect.

Suddenly a gleaming golden chain fell from the back of the scarab. Chione turned the lapis scarab slightly to see a squared hollow. Inside the hollow lay another scarab made of gold! The scarab was the object Tauret told her to remove. Just as she was about to bring the larger scarab to her to retrieve the one underneath, the golden scarab fell out and lay gleaming under the lights. Quickly she picked it up and replaced the lapis scarab in its original position on Tauret's body. Chione examined the golden scarab. It had a little compartment and lock in the back and seemed to be an exact duplicate of the one she already wore, the one her parents had purchased from a scruffy street vendor in Cairo years before.

A pang of guilt ran through her as she thought about secretly taking something. But Tauret made her promise to take it. Invited into an otherworldly existence both voluntarily and involuntarily, she felt compelled to obey. With hands that no longer trembled, she lifted the chain over her head and felt the scarab fall into place inside her shirt. Just as the beetle came to rest over her heart, blinding radiance obliterated everything else and expectation filled her. A powerful brilliance beamed from the center of her being where the scarab came to rest. She saw nothing but light.

The energy filled the room and began to shimmer like a million tiny stars bursting. Then Pharaoh materialized before her, not the Boy King, but...

...Tutankhamon, the man, in all his glory and regalia.

Their eyes met. What a magnificent presence! His sensual touch on her arm made every cell of her body tingle. The golden scarab amulet pulsated like a throbbing heart. The King stood emoting an eternity of thankfulness for her bearing his heir. He reached right through her shirt and grasped the golden scarab into his fist.

Chione felt her love intensifying, burning. She longed to be Tauret, who teased her Pharaoh by feigning obedience. She wanted to take him again to her bed. She sent him a mental message.

I am your servant, O Great King, now and forever, forever, for... ev... er....

The promise had long ago been made. Chione did not know when. She, as Tauret, loved Pharaoh with all her heart and remembered their lovemaking and knew this was her destiny.

Pharaoh's likeness began to fade. She longed to follow him. *They will take me too!* she said silently from somewhere deep within. *Wait for me, while I cast a spell for your heir!* The priestess knew life on earth for the two of them was about to end, yet, vowed the child would live, even as she ached to die with her King and share his afterlife. *They will take me too!* she said, screaming it from her heart.

Chione heard the others as if they were far away. Or was she the one detached from them?

From the Offering Chamber, Dr. Withers voice said, "Show me. Just show me where you saw that."

As the sparkling energy dissipated, Aaron materialized in front of her looking deep into her eyes... standing right where Pharaoh had stood!

Chione did not understand why she was to wear the scarab. She became Tauret whom Pharaoh had loved and Pharaoh just thanked her for carrying his child.

Her head reeled. Was this scarab any different than the one she already wore? Perhaps the gift from her parents was solid gold too. Could it have been looted from a tomb somewhere? Why did Tauret want her to wear the scarab gifted from Pharaoh? And why had she seen the vision of Tutankhamon immediately upon wearing it?

Marlowe's crying dissipated the reverie as the others returned. She held the side of her head. "There," Marlowe said, pointing as they reached the sarcophagus. Everyone crowded around.

Dr. Withers bent low near the side of Tauret's head. "Someone bring a light over here."

Marlowe crept around the coffin and came to lean on Chione's shoulder. "Chione, they killed her!" Marlowe said quietly as she whimpered. "She's the woman I dreamed about with black hair... murdered!"

"What are you saying?" Chione asked.

"My headaches. They killed her just like they murdered the King."

"Aaron," Dr. Withers said. "Get your young eyes down here. Tell me what you see." While Aaron examined, Dr. Withers turned to the others. "Rashad, you and the good doctors better have a look."

When Aaron straightened and stepped out of the way, his sympathetic expression confirmed something tragic had happened to Tauret.

Dr. Asim bent down. "Under the jewelry," he said finally. "Would seem to be something matted in her dark hair. Is it blood then?"

Dr. Kent turned to Marlowe. "What makes you think someone's done her in?"

The question put Marlowe on the spot. She would not know how to respond. She could not say the headaches stopped when she realized they were not her headaches, and that the pain belonged to someone who had been struck. She had not even shared the speculation with her husband till moments ago.

"She had a recurring dream," Chione said quickly, covering for Marlowe. "Similar to the one I had that led us to this tomb. The dream was of someone being struck on the side of the head."

"That's a lot of trot," Dr. Kent said. "How do dreams tie to Tutankhamon's demise?"

"Remember Tutankhamon?" Rashad asked, turning to Dr. Kent. "You've seen his mummy and the X-rays of the hole in—"

"Yes, yes. But you seem to be implying this person might have been murdered in the same way?" That what we find here confirms Tut having been done in? His cheeks puffed as he blew out a disbelieving breath. "A lot of trot!"

"Not since the reliefs and glyphs in this tomb tie this woman to that King and his family," Chione said.

"Murdered?" Dr. Kent asked again, sucking air through his pipe. "I find that hard to swallow."

Chione knew better than to press her luck and say more. If he could not entertain the clues written thousands of years ago, he certainly was not open to anything paranormal that she might add.

45

An eerie calm pervaded that evening. Darkness began settling. Christmas Eve was upon them. Everyone was free to come and go as they pleased.

Aaron's preoccupation with watching her had generalized to watching everyone else. Chione hoped he was learning a lot about human nature in the process, specifically, how the individual team members adjusted to the paranormal. His attention momentarily elsewhere helped her relax despite feeling woozy.

Laborers gathered more dry branches and sticks for the crackling bonfire; from where was anyone's guess. Musicians strummed. They seemed to have accepted some of the team's American ways of showing feelings. Dr. Withers and Marlowe sat wrapped in separate blankets, swaying to the dreamy rhythms. They smiled lovingly at one another; looks meant only for each other.

Chione tried not to watch. "Not a lot of conversation tonight," she said. No one seemed in a hurry to talk. They smiled, stared at the fire, and savored their drinks.

"I heard Dr. Kent requested a DVD of the glyph and mural analyses," Dr. Withers said finally.

"Plus a lot of the photos," Chione said. "He'll have to burn the midnight oil to get through that mass of information."

"I hope you gave him copies we can part with. He's leaving in the morning."

"So soon?" Aaron asked.

"Wants to spend what's left of the holiday with his family at home in Heliopolis."

"Can't say I blame him," Chione said. "I ran duplicates."

"Did you hear what he did late yesterday?" Aaron asked.

"Something we should know?"

Aaron could not keep from smiling. "Dr. Kent spent a bit of time down at the beggars' camp. He came back wearing a gallibaya and a colorful headwrap."

Dr. Withers looked smug. "Another one returning to the fold."

Jibade tried his hand at a few musical instruments. He was quite good. Bebe and Kenneth went for a walk to enjoy the pastel dusk. When Chione next saw them, they were sitting by themselves by the end of the mud shacks. Off in the distance, Clifford squatted with a group of locals, all boisterously playing a betting game on the ground, the way many of the local men passed free time.

"Poor Kendra," Chione said, whispering to Aaron. "She doesn't have time for friendship anymore."

"I hope Bebe's been able to console her," he said. "You'd think Royce would send word to his wife."

"Kendra doesn't think she'll hear from him again."

"We're being deserted," Randy said, joining them and placing a couple of small branches on the fire. He rolled out his mat and lowered himself to the ground. His new groomed appearance still took everyone by surprise.

"No one left but the die-hards," Dr. Withers said.

Carmelita's high-pitched whine drifted toward them from time to time.

"Something wrong over there?" Dr. Withers asked through a crooked smile.

Randy stifled a laugh. "Carmelita's purchased too much stuff and can't get her suitcases closed."

The two Norwegians returned to their own jobsite, disappointed they could not lay claim to the ruins of the village they discovered.

"I've given some thought to that village down there," Dr. Withers said.

"Something else we should know?"

"Not now. Wait till we regroup. After I've been in contact with California."

What could the professor have in mind? Chione really did not want to concern herself now. Christmas Eve was a time for putting aside work and its cares, a time for rejoicing.

Chione hummed and sang softly along with the musicians. She had heard all their songs enough to know them by heart. Occasionally, she pressed the front of her shirt, feeling the pendants hanging inside. Then she remembered that Aaron no longer doodled. He had not brought a notepad to the fireside even though he always carried one.

Aaron leaned close and whispered, "You've never been one for public displays, yet you've been singing a lot lately."

"I feel so compelled."

"What happens to you?"

"Singing sort of alters consciousness, I guess. It's deeply peaceful. I sometimes wonder if I'm the one doing the singing."

Jibade interrupted softly. "We'll be leaving after Christmas."

"Oh, no," Chione said. "Don't you want to share the rest?"

"We're wearing out our welcome," Helen said.

"We're going back to Cairo," Jibade said. "We'll stay with friends through Ramadan, and tour a week through the Holy Land before going home."

Christmas morning, Chione did not eat much at breakfast nor did she have any energy. Must have been the heat. She napped most of the day, coming out for the group's Christmas dinner and gathering around the fire. She did sing though. Aaron studied her curiously.

The next day would be another Arabic Sabbath, which meant a slower workday, allowing time enough to open the coffin again. Removal of the remains would happen after more film processing and when more workers were available.

In the morning, while waiting for the last batch of the film from several days earlier to be returned, the team members said their goodbyes.

"We're experiencing a mass exodus, folks," Clifford said.

Reporters and crews from Exploration Magazine, the Stockton newspapers, and the London News-Herald departed. In the initial agreements, they conceded rights to filming of the tomb's occupant to the San Francisco Sentinel, who now had the pictures they needed. The others would receive secondary rights photos to publish at a later date. Aaron drove a hard bargain the others were forced to abide by in order to get the privileges they did.

"We're having trouble saying goodbye," Helen said. "We feel like a part of the group."

"That means we've stayed too long," Jibade said.

A little later, Chione asked, "What's Carmelita doing now?"

"She's insisting they ride in that rusted-out Mercedes limo," Aaron said, shaking his head in disbelief.

"Parker ought to throw her on a camel and let her hump her way home," Clifford said.

Just then, Rashad arrived in a jeep and the San Francisco Sentinel crew hailed the driver to take them away for the last time.

"They're going too?" Chione asked.

"Yeah, you'd think our priestess scared everyone off," Clifford said. "They'll all be back when we've opened the parents' tomb."

Ginny rushed over with photos in hand. "Get a load of these."

Close up photos showed the lapis lazuli scarab in full glorious detail. Several photos exposed different angles.

"Nice work you do," Aaron said.

"You don't see it?" Ginny asked. She was in a huff. "The impression, do you see it? Did someone move the scarab between the time I took the first photos and the next set?"

Fright rolled through Chione's nervous system. How would she explain what she did, and why she did it?

"I doubt it," Aaron said. He looked closer. Ginny pointed again. They compared sets of pictures. "Hey, you're right."

"Look at this second set," Ginny said. "Looks like that impression in Tauret's cloak is where the scarab had rested. It's been moved."

"Who would have touched anything?" Clifford asked.

"Someone must have jarred the coffin," Aaron said, passing it off with a wave of his hand.

Later, and again inside the tomb, they would lift the lid for the second and last time to view the priestess before preparing her body for transport. Given the fact Tauret was not mummified, it was decided to ship her remains to the Museum inside the sycamore fig coffin. After measuring, they learned her coffin could be lifted catty-corner through the portcullis shaft in order that she not be tilted and instead remained lying prone. A specially prepared sledge was built and lay waiting on the floor in the Offering Chamber. Finally, the team and several helpers gathered in anticipation.

The sun had been strong since Christmas and Chione still felt woozy. She entered the Burial Chamber behind the others to hear Dr. withers asking where she was. Then he saw her. "What's with you?" he asked.

"Oh, don't mind me." She felt unsteady.

Quaashie and Naeem did the honors again. Tauret lay in all her glory. Yet, somehow, vibrancy of the first viewing was no longer present. No energy burst forth from the coffin like the day before Christmas. Her perfume was barely perceptible. Chione directed Aaron's attention to the aging spot on Tauret's cheek that now seemed darker. Chione felt pangs of sorrow. Finding Tauret, moving her, could well be the end of the continuance she intended for herself in the Afterlife. Chione felt great remorse. Her mind raced and her head spun much like she always felt before merging with Tauret. Then she was suddenly aware that she was...

...*pregnant Tauret, majestically standing not two feet from Aaron, with a very full womb inside her belly. She reached for Aaron's hand and placed it on her stomach. But only a wife or concubine would dare reach out first for the hand of Pharaoh!*

She realized he was not Aaron. The man who stood before her was Pharaoh!

Chione viewed what happened from the eyes of both herself and Tauret. Aaron became Pharaoh. In a few seconds, she became herself again. "Aaron?" she asked quietly.

He, too, seemed lost in the moment and jolted back to reality as he saw his hand pressed against her stomach. He gasped and quickly withdrew it. His eyes widened. He looked at her belly. "You'll never guess what I just saw," he said, whispering in disbelief.

"Wouldn't I?" she asked.

"Hey, Aaron... Chione...." Dr. Withers' voice seemed coming from a distance. "You with us?"

"Look at the area around the scarab," Ginny was saying. "I'm sure the scarab's been moved."

The scarab definitely left an impression in the soft pleats of Tauret's cloak where it rested for centuries. Now it sat at angles with the indentation. "I still don't think anyone would have touched it," Aaron said. "We're professionals."

Rashad and Dr. Withers were discussing how best to lift out the coffin. Aaron turned to say something to them but seemed having difficulty. Again, he looked at her stomach. "Tauret's energy is gone," he said, again quietly.

"Tauret knew what she was doing," Chione said, though she, too, felt unsure. "Trust her."

"Chione," Dr. Withers called impatiently.

Clifford called to Aaron. Chione did not wish to be distracted. They had plenty of time to move the priestess. Right now, she wanted to explore the possibilities with Aaron, tell him what she had just seen and learn what he might have felt. Somehow, she knew all would be okay despite any delay. "Yes, sir?" she said, responding to Dr. Withers' growing impatience.

"We're counting on your opinion here, okay?"

"Yes, sir."

"Our priestess was preserved under that diorite pyramid. What happens when she's not under that peak?"

"She's still under a pyramid," Chione said, pointing to the ceiling.

"But no longer sealed," Randy said. "When you did those experiments back in California, once you removed anything from under a pyramid, it wilted, disintegrated, if we didn't eat it right away."

"Exactly," Dr. Withers said. "My concern here is that if we don't keep our lady under a pyramid to transport her, we'll lose her somehow."

"We could put the diorite lid over the transport box," Chione said. "But first, Dr. Asim should examine the remains to see how durable they are."

Dr. Asim shook his head. "I must admit, I am now perplexed. How does one begin to examine such a specimen?"

"We'll need to know if the body will hold together during transport," Clifford said.

"You've got to feel her," Kendra said. "We pick up mummies all the time. There's no other way."

Bebe moaned and turned away. "How can anyone touch her?"

"We could spray her," Clifford said with a silly grin. "Stabilize her with fixative, then cart her off."

No one in archaeological history ever dealt with a situation as this.

"It could only happen to us," Randy said. Everyone looked his way. "We were meant to handle this situation, because of who we are." It was something to think about as everyone paused a moment to reflect on Randy's profound metaphysical statement.

Just then Ginny said, "Oh-oh!" She took her eye away from the camera, looked and then focused quickly again as she zoomed in on Tauret's stomach.

"What do you see?" Kenneth asked, pointing his camera in the same direction.

Dr. Asim saw it and gasped. Dr. Withers and Rashad saw it. So did all the others. Tauret's stomach, and even the cloth over it, began to disintegrate and collapse!

46

Chione cradled her belly as she focused on the disintegration, not wanting to give up what she had just received.

The settling accentuated the distinct form of the baby Tauret carried. Its legs were crossed in the normal fetal position with buttocks and shoulders forming soft mounds inside Tauret's abdomen. Dr. Asim pointed to its tiny elbows and arms. As more of Tauret's clothing and body disintegrated into dust, the form of the baby's head protruded. The fetal remains lingered as the surrounding area gave way. At that moment, no doubt existed. Tauret had surely been with child.

"Get that, Ginny," Aaron said, pointing. "Kenneth!"

As if clinging to life, the mound the baby made remained firm while they filmed. Then finally, it shivered and collapsed.

Chione held her stomach while she watched.

The darkened gray blotches in Tauret's exposed skin collapsed leaving little irregular gaping holes in her cheeks and hands. Her legs began to crumble.

"No," Marlowe said. "No, this isn't happening!"

They could only watch as the photographers documented the progression of the disintegration. Tauret's body continued caving in, a little here and a little there. The weight of her jewelry pulled at her form and ripped small tears in her pleated clothing as it, too, turned to powder with no longer a body inside to hold it in place. The toy rattle on her chest shifted and fell with the rest. Its tinkle had a hollow sound that seemed to echo through the eons.

"No-o," Marlowe said. She reached in quickly and touched the area of Tauret's head that held the mat of dried blood in the hair, the part of Tauret with which she had connected.

No one spoke. They simply stood watching, having no choice but to accept the horror and disappointment.

Next, Tauret's feet collapsed. One sandal flopped forward. The other flopped backward, exposing a wear pattern on the bottom, marked by Tauret's own foot and toes thousands of years before. Toenails flaked off like scales and disappeared into her powdery remains.

Jewelry clinked as pieces fell together in her dust. In slow motion, her fingernails dropped one or two at a time, into the heap of matter.

Kendra was in tears, emotions already weakened by her own plight. Bebe had to help her stand but neither could prevent themselves from watching.

Little by little, Tauret's face fragmented and slowly caved in. Her skull collapsed into a mound of powder. Her white teeth lay like scattered pearls half-hidden in fine sand. Her black hair settled into a mat, the caked blood discernible only as a blotch of dust upon the silky heap. Finally, Tauret lay in total disintegration.

"It's over," Marlowe said, whimpering.

"Not yet," Randy said, capturing everyone's attention.

"Over," Kendra said.

Randy was not through. He pointed to the mound of powder that had been Tauret's head. "Her teeth. Tauret was either much pampered, with only the best of foods, or she was simply too young to have worn down her teeth."

"Her teeth?" Ginny asked.

"The Ancients had dental caries. The way they baked their bread left a lot of sand in the finished product. Eating those gritty loaves is said to have worn down even the teeth of royals."

"What are you getting at, man?" Dr. Withers asked.

Once again, Randy pointed to a few of Tauret's teeth lying haphazardly. "Everyone, please notice," he said. "Tauret's teeth are whole. They even shine."

No one had dry eyes. Dr. Withers cradled his wife's shoulders and swiped at his own eyes with a handkerchief.

Emotional control from everyone seemed vacated.

"You were right, Randy," Clifford said. "No one else was meant to see this."

Aaron turned to her and Chione looked at him through bleary eyes. The priestess being pregnant meant a lot to her. For a few brief moments, Chione felt the presence of Tauret stronger than ever. Chione wanted to savor the moment of being pregnant. Perhaps with the disintegration, this was the last time either she or Aaron would feel the presence of the priestess and her beloved King and their child.

Because Chione felt undeniably close to Tauret, when her remains were ready to be shipped to Cairo, Dr. Withers insisted she accompany Aaron and the coffin to the Madu. Chione did not resist. She would get to spend time alone with Aaron. Dr. Withers also reminded her to think about getting a checkup with Dr. Vimble. "Your eating habits have changed," he said, staring at her curiously. "You look a little peaked."

After checking into the hotel in Cairo, she and Aaron found their way to Rita's gravesite in Garden City. Fresh dirt still lay in a mound on top. They sat for a while, holding hands in quiet reverence. The headstone contained information in both English and Egyptian, with half the headstone that contained Clifford's name waiting for statistics.

"Clifford...," Chione said, choking up.

"Yeah," Aaron said. "One day this is where he...." Neither could he finish what he wanted to say.

They headed off to the Madu Museum.

Randy wore a white medical jacket and showed them through the internal workings of the research laboratory. "Sorry I can't take you where the actual DNA tests are being conducted, sterile conditions and all." He unlocked a door on the second floor and flipped on the light revealing a pleasing air-conditioned office with modern furnishings and tasteful art. A large rectangular photo of Randy and all the children, taken at the dig site, hung on a side wall. The window overlooked a nice garden with greenery, benches and a fountain. The swatch of hair bound with gold rope, which had lain on Tauret's body beside the lapis scarab, now lay in a Plexiglas case on Randy's desk. "I'll let you know to whom this belonged as soon as I can perform comparisons. Hope it matches someone we have on file."

"What are the chances?" Aaron asked.

Randy thought for a moment. "From what you've told me about the tomb, about Queen Tyi being in there? A swatch of her hair was found in Tut's coffin. Now we find she's part of Tauret's burial. It's my guess, this is either Queen Tyi's or Pharaoh's hair."

"My thought too," Aaron said.

"You'll let us know about our own DNA tests?" Chione asked. "Aaron's and mine?"

"Remember," Randy said. "Tell no one I did this freebie just so you two curious kids could see your own prints, okay?" He smiled mischievously. "Exciting times, aren't they?" He handed her a thick binder. "This will help you understand what goes on here."

Chione took one of the two chairs and opened the cover and flipped through pages and saw...

...spots of blood.

Pictures showed spots of blood being DNA printed. The same spots she saw in a vision when she hugged Randy in the inventory tent. No wonder she did not feel intimidated when the paranormal scene first occurred. Pieces of past visions traipsed end to end through her mind. She leaned back, closed her eyes, and pressed a hand against her chest.

"Too much excitement?" Randy asked, sincerely attentive.

"I'm all right," she said, handing the binder to Aaron. "I will go to the garden for some air, though." She stood, about to leave, but first embraced Randy.

"Remember my promise," he said. "Should you ever—ever—need anything."

She felt woozy and reached for the doorknob when she remembered. "There is one thing," she said as she retrieved a wrapped item from her bag. Slowly, she removed the bubble wrap from around the blue faience perfume decanter. "They've already lifted prints off this. I'm so thrilled. They're probably from Meskhenet."

Randy accepted the decanter. "They lifted prints off everything, didn't they? I'll bet we have our own archive of fingerprints of the Ancients." He really was excited. "Did you know that if they can come up with whose fingerprints are on which artifacts, they can build some sort of history as to the level of each participant's social standing and involvement with the burial?" That was Randy's forte'. He investigated clues that might go overlooked. "Why did you bring this? Some tests you want me to run?"

"I have a favor to ask," she said. "Sort of."

"Name it," he said, passing the bottle beneath his nose and sniffing.

"I want to know if the particles and residue stuck at the bottom can be duplicated."

Randy turned toward the light of the window, brought the bottle to his eye and looked into the interior. He sniffed at the opening again. "This fragrance isn't the same scent I detected at times in the tomb," he said as he turned back to face them.

She and Aaron exchanged surprised glances. Could Randy have been privy to the sweet scent they thought was made available only to themselves? During all the weeks of work, no one mentioned different fragrances. "You smelled a different scent?" Chione asked.

"This scent is the one I detected only in the Burial Chamber," Randy said, "Peculiar, though. I'll bet if this could be recreated, it would be a magical scent." His eyes got really big. "Hey, wouldn't that make history if one of the priestess's magic potions could be remade?"

She glanced quickly at Aaron who seemed to recognize that Randy had caught on. "You wouldn't fall under her spell, would you, Randy?" Chione asked, teasing.

He sniffed again, and then pulled the fragrance deep into his lungs like he could not get enough. "I'm not sure I wouldn't. Once you sniff this, it calls you back for more."

Both she and Aaron understood. Every member of the team put his or her nose to the bottle. Each said the fragrance was nearly non-existent. They at least detected it! Now here was Randy innocently confirming he smelled that fragrance in the Burial Chamber. He not only perceived a scent from the blue faience decanter but also knew it was a different fragrance from the one in the tomb overall. Had he been privy to the power of the priestess's potions? Had Tauret influenced Randy's metamorphosis? Tauret was the one who sent them to him. Her spells brought together those needed to participate as her plans and schemes played out. They watched Randy still sniffing the bottle.

"You sure it's not the same fragrance as in the tomb?" Aaron asked.

"Smells familiar, from the Burial Chamber, but from somewhere else too... can't remember, like an old memory or something." He sniffed again, then again.

Aaron looked at her and nodded his approval, ready to take the next step.

"You want to be a part of our venture?" Chione asked.

"You mean you want to know if this perfume can be made again?"

"Yes, I believe—that is, Aaron and I believe—only those who detect this scent will be allowed to participate in its recreation."

"You think I qualify?"

"You've already proved it," Aaron said. "By showing you actually detect the scent."

Randy stood motionless with his facial expressions going through changes. He paced back and forth behind his desk, sniffing, thinking and then sniffing again. They quietly watched as he inhaled his in-doctrination. Finally, he asked, "You mean start a perfume business? We three?"

"Not so much a business," Chione said. "Dr. Withers gave me cus-tody of that bottle. As I said, Aaron and I believe only certain people will be invited into this project."

Randy smiled cautiously. "I think I know you, Chione," he said, hesitating. "Correct me if I'm wrong. You believe if this potion can be recreated, the spell that goes along with it might help enlighten us, perhaps, to further understand details of Tauret's life?"

Chione did not want to give away the entire scheme, not just yet. It seemed Randy was being mysteriously initiated. Could yet another of Tauret's spells be at work on him? "Not everyone will understand," she said. "Only those who are called upon to be a part of this venture will be directly affected."

"We believe whoever is meant to be excluded will be," Aaron said, "through no action from any of us."

"Sort of like Tauret's will?"

"Sort of," Chione said, smiling hopefully. "Can you trust the gods?"

"It's kind of devious," he said. "But I'll do it. In fact, I met a chemist I'll bet we can trust." He looked surprised. "Hey—he's been to the tomb. This chemist and his scientist friends went out on one of those tours. Recently, right here in this office, he told me he experienced the strangest déjà vu like he had been in that tomb before." Randy held the bottle high. "I guess the next step is to stick this under his nose and see what happens."

47

Aaron found her in the garden below Randy's office window. They went back to their hotel and took a dip in the pool. The swim truly was diversion and restorative at the same time. Chione felt ready for some quiet time from all the activity and throngs of people. She needed to think. Upstairs in the hotel, the same mysterious energy from inside the coffin illuminated their room.

"It's curious how Dr. Withers insisted we accompany the remains," Aaron said.

"He's still trying to throw us together."

Aaron half frowned, half laughed. "It's worked. Look at us."

The nice room was at Aaron's expense. He would not take advantage of Clifford's generosity of funding the team's expenses. Elegant modern furnishings with a four-poster bed and a huge chaise decorated room. Lamp bases and vases, figurines, drapes, and wall art were the only Egyptian items but added the right ambiance.

"We only claimed to be married so you could share this hotel room."

"No way was I going to let you stay alone," Aaron said. "Not with the questionable attitude that waiter out by the pool showed you earlier. He even looked angry at you needing to eat during Ramadan."

"Aaron, I swam in knee shorts and a long baggy tee shirt, with my bra on."

"And made too much eye contact with him," he said. "In this country, they think that's a come on. That story we heard? About that friendly

417

French woman getting raped and killed by a driver?" Aaron paced. "It's not enough they rape, Chione. In this country, a woman having been raped is considered spoiled for anyone else. It's obligatory practice here to kill the victim afterwards."

"You told me all that already. Hope you don't mind sleeping on the chaise."

Momentarily, she wondered about the plight of Elbertina Yago. Visions strung end-to-end paraded again in livid color; in particular, the Priestess's dance before she and Pharaoh made love; later, Aaron as doting Pharaoh thanking her for bearing his child.

She remembered the spell performed alone in the yurt the night Bebe left materials behind. As all the clues crashed together, she grabbed her purse and dashed into the bathroom. She removed a Home Pregnancy Test kit purchased earlier and followed the instructions and nearly fell off the toilet seat. She tried to remember how it could have happened. In the Pillared Hall, maybe? Could she and Aaron have made love while entranced? Maybe the test malfunctioned. She began to tremble. She sought reassurance by looking into the mirror to see her reflection and saw... Tauret...!

Nervously, she rubbed a sore spot inside her blouse and felt something strange. Unbuttoning exposed a chafed patch of skin where the amulet dangled. She lifted the scarab and looked at the back and saw a tiny dark spot that felt prickly, and which had rubbed her skin raw. She needed to fix it but promised not to remove the scarab...

...till in your belly the child you feel.

She barely made it to the toilet seat again. Her body trembled. Truth she denied suddenly gripped her. She performed one of Tauret's spells so that she might have a child. She drank from Tut's bowl. Tauret passed the child she carried, Pharaoh's heir, to her to be born!

...till in your belly the child you feel.

"I'm pregnant!" she said, too loud. She began to whimper. Waves of shock rolled over her.

Aaron knocked at the door. "Chione? Something wrong?"

She was glad she was not alone at that moment. "I-I'll be out in a minute," she said as her voice cracked.

Suddenly her mood swung in the opposite direction. Waves of elation washed over her. "I'm having a baby!" she said. Her gynecologist said she would never conceive. Yet, the little stick from the kit showed a plus sign.

She needed to calm down, to think. Aaron never touched her. Being sneaky was not his way. She was given visions that brought the team to Egypt to play out their parts. Tauret had chosen her from the beginning. The powerful priestess's...

...spell is cast, to last, till all of time has passed.

She felt lightheaded. If she was going to faint—

"Chione?"

"Aaron," she said weakly.

He opened the door cautiously and then flung it wide as she collapsed into his arms. He carried her to the bed and lowered her gently.

She saw them...

...inside the mashrabia-paneled room.

She tried to close her blouse.

"What's that nasty looking spot?" he asked. "Is that why you're sick?"

"From... the pendant."

He reached for the chain around her neck. "Let's take it off and—"

"No!" she said, jumping across the bed. "I promised."

Aaron jolted backwards in surprise. "I've never seen you so unnerved, Chione. I only want to fix it."

She clutched her blouse closed and lay back and lifted the pendant for him to examine.

"Something's sticking out," he said, rubbing the back. "It's a hair. Rita's hair is what's scratching you."

Of course, she knew that could not be. "I'll fix it later."

"How did you put Rita's rings and hair in here?" he asked, still fumbling with it. "The back is sealed."

Her own pendant opened easily. Her heart raced. Whose hair was sealed in the back of Tauret's pendant? "Leave it for now."

"Wait, Chione." He refused to turn loose. "The back is sealed and there's a tiny cartouche stamped on it."

Chione's head reeled as she saw...

...a jeweler sealing a lock of Pharaoh's hair inside the back of an amulet.

Another piece of the puzzle slammed into place. Everything she suspected manifested in wave after overwhelming wave of images and thoughts. She could not withhold Tauret's secrets from Aaron any longer. She lived fragments of Tauret's life. Aaron experienced portions of Pharaoh's life. Now was the time to reveal Tauret's secret. "Do you believe in reincarnation?" she asked as she slipped the pendant away from him.

"I'm not sure," he said, looking surprised by the question. "From all we've been through, I'm beginning to believe in past life memory."

"Because you've experienced being Pharaoh?"

"Of course, and because I'm still me, not having gone whacko—yet."

His willingness to laugh at himself helped her relax. "How often do you see me as Tauret?"

His expression said he would rather not admit the truth. "Quite often," he said after hesitating. "Especially after you styled your hair like hers."

"Do you share Tut's feelings for her?"

"Where are you going with this?" He went to the dresser and lit one of her incense cones. He looked perfectly natural doing so.

"Many times, I see you as Pharaoh. I feel Tauret's feelings. All these emotions, they're new to me. If the Ancients believed they thought with their hearts, then these emotions must be Tauret's."

"Are you saying the emotions you feel are not for me?" He sat beside her on the bed.

"That's just it. I do feel them, even when you're not Pharaoh." She reached for him....

...inside the mashrabia paneled room.

"For me? You feel them for me?"

"We're us, Aaron."

A groan escaped his throat. They rolled together. Their passions flared. "Umayma," he said in that other voice.

"Oba," she said, whispering, feeling like Tauret.

Sparkling energy burst around them and flickered in the air. Just as he called her Umayma again, suddenly he pulled away. "Wait! Umayma means little mother. Chione, Tauret was pregnant." He stood then and paced. "We can't be doing this. We're captivated by these people's lives. We can't act them out, carry on from where they were cut short."

"I want to. I need to."

"Wha-at?"

"You'd better sit down again. I've got something to tell you."

Their eyes met. He sat but looked ready to spring again. "I don't want play-acting someone else's lives to bring us together."

She sat up cross-legged and buttoned her blouse. "Unless we're living out our own?" The lights went on behind Aaron's eyes and then dimmed again. "Remember the confirmation we found among Umi's scratchings?"

"Yeah, he wrote of an order given by Aye that anyone who worshipped the Aten was to be done away with," Aaron said. "Blood relatives of Akhenaten were to be extinguished. Umi and Meskhenet worshipped the Amon, but chose to die with their daughter, who was killed for carrying the heir of an Aten worshiper before the religious conversion began."

"Umi confirmed Tauret cast a spell that Tutankhamon's baby would one day be born, if it took 'till all of time has passed'. She wasn't mummified with her innards ripped out. It was her last wish and Meskhenet and Umi sacrificed their lives to make sure the spell wasn't broken."

"No one among the Ancients ever put that much value into living," he said. "They lived to die and all their lives prepared for burial."

"But Tauret was a nonconformist. She wanted to give her child a life, a purpose that it, too, could carry into the Afterlife. It would have to live first." She moved closer to him on the bed.

"How does that affect us?"

"When I stood beside Tauret's opened coffin," she said. "Pharaoh stood in front of me, touching this scarab that hangs around my neck."

"That chain, the scarab with Rita's stuff in it?"

She held the scarab in her fist. "This isn't Rita's. I gave my necklace to Clifford."

"Where did that one come from?" He could no longer push away the reality of the situation.

"From under the lapis scarab over Tauret's heart. She made me promise to take it."

Aaron's mouth flew open. "You moved it? You're the one!"

"It's a gift from Pharaoh. The day before Christmas I put the necklace on when all of you were out of the Burial Chamber. Pharaoh appeared in a burst of shimmering energy. I thought I was Tauret. He thanked me for carrying his heir." She felt relieved at having disclosed her extraordinary secrets and surprised she was not pulled into a trance in order to keep from divulging all she knew. *Tell no one who is not Pharaoh.* The mysterious bond that developed between her and Aaron seemed cemented. Aaron looked even more like Pharaoh. The sparkling energy around them persisted.

He stood, paced again and then turned to face her. "It's not the scarab that's made you sick." He paused again, thinking, his gaze penetrating.

She turned the amulet over. "The hair sealed inside this beetle is thirty-five hundred years old."

"A gift from Pharaoh?" he asked from the foot of the bed. "Pharaoh's hair is in that scarab?" He shook his head. The intensity of his expression said he had just come to grips with what she was trying to relate. "Pharaoh gave you a gift? Were you Tauret or were you Chione?"

"I was myself," she said quietly.

"Why would he give you, Chione, an amulet?"

"For carrying his baby." She hesitated as their eyes met, then slowly said, "I'm pregnant, Aaron."

He grabbed hold of the bedpost as he wrestled with the words. "You're carrying Pharaoh's... the spells... are true? You're carrying Pharaoh's baby... for Tauret?"

"I just tested in the bathroom."

"Could the test be wrong? We have a job to do at the tomb site." He seemed to have slipped into a self-protective state. "How are you going to justify this to the others?"

She shook her head. "I don't have all the answers," she said. "But if slipping in and out of trances with Tauret and Tut is the only way I can have a child, I'll take it." She sighed, worried. "I'll manage somehow."

Aaron still paced and studied her. "You mean it? You'd accept it and go on?"

"I have no choice, Aaron. I'm pregnant." Regardless of the dilemma, she felt elation.

He went to the window and looked out. The sun had set. Ramadan had ended for the day. Lights flickered on from the street below and cast an eerie glow into the room. People boisterously greeted one another. By now their language sounded second nature.

"I have an idea," he said after a while.

"You're not obligated in any way."

"But I am. I've just made my decision."

"I didn't know you had one to make."

"Yes, I do." He sat down and took her hands. "Jibade took me to get a psychic reading."

She already knew.

"I went because he's your father. He dragged me down to that camp."

"When did you go?" she asked, playing innocent.

"Doesn't matter," he said, waving a hand. "That woman told me I'd have to make a crucial decision the moment I learned the meaning of the spells."

Tarik earlier having quoted to her in confidence what was said, she could only hear Aaron out. "And?"

"She insisted when the spell would be brought to light, I had to make a decision immediately and that I would know when the time was at hand."

"What did you glean from a message like that?"

"The time is at hand, Chione. If you're really pregnant, the spell is being carried out. The time has arrived for me to make that decision." He spoke as a person who meant to carry through.

"You understand what the psychic implied?"

"Oh, yes," he said, nodding. "And my decision is not to abandon you. I have a plan."

"A plan?"

"Listen, despite experiencing ourselves as Tauret and Tut, you and I have discovered new feelings for one another, haven't we?" He looked as if his heart might break should he hear anything but an agreement.

"Yes, strangely, we have." At that moment she had great difficulty deciphering whether she was herself or Tauret. She decided the only way to deal with it would be to leave her feelings alone and see what developed. It was a matter of faith.

Truth was, they would have to explain this pregnancy to everyone and that presented a huge dilemma. She and Aaron were experiencing Tauret's and Pharaoh's lives for the sake of the child. The child was as much hers and Aaron's. Something else that mattered was that she and Aaron had never consummated a relationship. Despite knowing their peers thought differently, she had always told the truth.

Aaron tapped fingertips together thinking, the way he always did when demanding answers from within. Then he said, "Chione, I need to get a little personal. Do you mind?"

"Well... no." They could keep secrets no longer.

"Once in the Pillared Hall, you told me you've never made love with anyone."

His candor startled her. "So?"

"The spell," he said, excited again. "The psychic said a certain level of purity had to be maintained in order for the spell to be carried out. You were meant to live without a man or a child in your life."

All that was happening was meant to be. They were beginning to see the reality of it. "Remember?" Chione asked as another revelation hit. "Tauret was a virgin when Pharaoh took her!" Surely Aaron knew she had gotten that from one of her visions.

"How does this sound?" he asked. "Aaron Kheperu Ashby."

She was nearly speechless. Did he really love her that much? He was claiming the child as his. "Your name?"

He prefaced what he was about to say by looking humble. "If only for the sake of the baby. Marry me, Chione."

She did not know what to say. "For the sake of the baby?"

Aaron went on to explain that if she carried Pharaoh's child, they needed to make the truth known. "We could get on with the deeper aspects of the spell, the hidden mystery that's coming to light here."

"Marriage?"

He looked saddened. "Not in the fullest sense as man and wife. Not if you don't want that much. But think of the child."

"I am thinking of the child."

One thing he said was right. What worried her as soon as she saw the results of the pregnancy test was how she would explain the situation. She would not tolerate people thinking she had become pregnant from hers and Aaron's supposed *tête-à-têtes* in the Pillared Hall. Then refuse to marry him? Yet, only the right decision could be made for this unique child, regardless of what their colleagues wanted to believe.

Perhaps if they were reliving moments of Tauret and Pharaoh's lives, marriage would provide a safe haven. As Tauret and Tut, how would they manage life apart? She began to yearn again for Aaron because of Tauret's love for Pharaoh. Now she was deeply in love with Aaron.

He touched her shoulder and let his hand run down her sleeve. "My decision is that I want to protect you and this special child."

"Is marriage the answer?"

"Chione, I've always loved you."

"Are you willing to accept that we're two unique people given the chance to live two exciting lives simultaneously?" The concept was mind-boggling, but the dichotomy seemed strangely natural. "Marrying would bring Tauret and Tut together finally."

"Are you saying that you as Chione, care for me only when you're Tauret?" He seemed on the verge of complete dismay.

"Oh, no! I-I want you in my life, Aaron."

"Then all I need to hear is that you'll marry me."

She smiled warmly. She loved his face and his pure heart. "What do you think of the name Nefertauret Ashby?"

Aaron looked proud. "Beautiful Tauret," he said, but shook his head. "Save it for the next one. We already know this one's a boy."

48

They broke the news to Jibade. He accepted it like one who had already read the book and waited for the others to catch up at the ending. Helen's reaction was calm because Jibade first prepared her by taking her on a sightseeing tour during which time he explained. Helen always felt a deep connection to Egypt. She had, after all, given her daughter an Egyptian name. Maybe Jibade's preparing her had nothing to do with her acceptance. Now she clung to Chione and Aaron like a mother hen protecting her brood. Her attitude clearly reflected that she had grieved over Chione's disparaging first news of being unable to bear children. Now it seemed she intended to do whatever necessary for the adopted daughter she loved as her own.

During the week following New Year's, Helen and Jibade's host family located a minister willing to perform a simple marriage ceremony during Ramadan. After sunset, one of the biggest celebrations of the season took place among the small group of Egyptian friends.

They arrived back at their hotel room very late. Chione went to light an incense cone and said, "I'm not feeling sick anymore."

"I'm glad about that." Aaron opened the window a little to allow the draft to spread the fragrance through the room.

Early morning greetings among jovial friends drifted through the opened window from the street below. Aaron looked at the chaise where he would sleep and frowned.

"I want to be in Egypt when the baby arrives," she said. She held her hands on her belly. She had begun to feel tiny movements.

"That sounds right," Aaron said. He didn't look a bit comfortable on the chaise. He sat gripping the edge and leaning slightly forward.

"I wonder if Randy found enough cells for DNA prints for the Madu's archives," she said.

"I have a feeling Randy is being guided like the rest of us." He stared at the floor and did not speak for a few moments. Finally, he asked, "What's to become of us? Is there another reason this special child is to be born?"

"I don't know," Chione said. "How will Pharaoh's son fare in today's world and modern society? Shouldn't he be allowed to grow up in Egypt?"

Aaron stood and went to look out the window. "More than that, what kind of life might Tauret have willed for the boy through spells in order that he later take something of value into the Afterlife?"

Chione paced, deep in thought. "Why were we chosen specifically? Why did millenniums have to pass? Tauret couldn't have known how much life would have changed in all that time."

"I wondered too," Aaron said, leaning against the windowsill. "Do you think that people in Tauret's time knew something about the paranormal that the rest of humanity is only now catching up to?"

"I'll need to re-examine the hieroglyphs for secreted formulae," Chione said, joining him to look out over the view. Aaron seemed to melt when she wrapped an arm around his waist. "Umi wrote that Ankhesenpa was insanely jealous of Tauret and may have been responsible for both Tauret's and Tut's deaths. Suspecting danger, Tauret cast a spell that Ankhesenpa's reprehensible deeds turn back on herself."

Voices floated up from the street below. Not a lot of business noise typical of industrious Cairo. Daytime was fairly quiet during the month-long fast.

"Did you find a spell like that in her writings?" Aaron slipped an arm around her shoulders.

"No, but it's already known that Ankhesenpa's plan after Tut's demise backfired."

Ankhesenpa had asked a Hittite prince to marry her and become Pharaoh so that she could retain her own royal status.

"That's right," Aaron said. "Historians suspect Aye had the prince killed when he arrived in Egypt. Ankhesenpa had no choice other than to marry Aye, her grandfather."

"After which she and her younger sisters were not heard from again."

"Makes you wonder what kind of life Tauret might have willed for her son," he said. "I remember something else. Back in California, you said history might be changed. If we're the only two to know about our child, history will not have been changed as far as anyone else is concerned."

"It's already been. The hieroglyphs clearly add Tauret as part of Tutankhamon's history. Plus, the child hasn't yet been born." She placed a hand on her belly again and smiled. "He may have a few surprises for us all."

"Have we missed some of Tauret's messages?" He looked tired and began to unbutton his shirt.

"I'm sure a lot more is encrypted in the hieroglyphs, especially Umi's." One thing was certain. If anyone else tried to decipher the glyphs, only the people whom Tauret wished to know her secrets would receive the true messages.

"Get our historian involved," Aaron said. "Bebe's participation will help authenticate the findings, no matter how peculiar they turn out to be."

Chione checked the incense cone and went to sit on the edge of the bed. "We're married now," she said.

"Uh-huh," he said, sounding uncertain.

Evidently, Aaron was having difficulty accepting she was finally his wife. She patted the bed again, inviting.

Aaron approached slowly and sat, keeping his distance. He was a man of integrity. They married for the sake of the child, despite him wanting marriage for reasons of love. Now he would suffer that love, rather than pounce upon the mattress like a newlywed. He would not be the one making any first moves.

Her love for him clutched at her heart. She wanted him more than ever.

"We've been up all night. Let's talk after you rest."

The sparkling energy began to surround them again. Chione felt her consciousness slipping. She crawled on her knees across the bed reaching Aaron and kissing him. He returned the kiss but still held himself in check. "I'm not tired," she said suggestively. They kissed again, passionately. Though Aaron still withheld, she sensed him beginning to succumb to a tide welling up like an approaching Khamsin wind. She took his hand and gently placed it on her belly.

"Umayma," he said in that other voice.

She was seeing Pharaoh again. The shimmering energy continued to envelop them, permeating their bodies. "Oba," she said, realizing her voice had also changed. This time they were not in the mashrabia room. They were in their hotel on a grand four-poster bed. They were Chione and Aaron and he was still reserved.

She kissed him again; remembering the intense desires Tauret had felt for Pharaoh. She wanted that same feeling with Aaron.

Then, in Pharaoh's voice, he said, "Your passion is great in spite of the child."

The vision came again.

His body heavy on me, buttocks hard as diorite in my hands.

Chione lay back on the bed and pulled Aaron over her. He groaned as his resistance fled. She intended the seduction to complete the scenes taken from her so many times—scenes that left her insane with want. She needed to know Aaron the way Tauret knew Pharaoh.

Chione took Aaron's face in her hands and found his lips. He moaned and succumbed. She pushed her hands deep into his trousers and clutched at his buttocks.

Hard as diorite in my hands.

"Take me, my King," she said in Tauret's voice. "Give me your true flail!"

"But the child in your womb," Pharaoh said.

"Easy then," she said in a lusty whisper. "But pleasure me!"

Aaron's breathing became labored. She sensed him struggling with the reservation of Aaron and the desperation of Pharaoh. The rush of shimmering energy came again. Whispering, he said, "Yes, Umayma, I cannot resist. I will have you!"

He tore at her clothing. Suddenly they were naked...

... in the mashrabia room, on the woven reed bed among soft tapestries.

"Chione," Aaron said. His voice rasped.

"Aaron, take my breath," she said, kissing him hungrily, eager for what was to come. "Pleasure me your body."

And so, he did, without hesitation and with the strength of Pharaoh, as incense filled the room and a bubble of energy glowed around them, shifting consciousness and sealing their fate.

Chione felt the sting like Tauret had felt, and the burning, as Aaron, not Pharaoh, ravaged her with abandon.

After their energy was spent, she lay still beside Aaron. He touched her face, her hair. Finally, she felt complete. She would let nothing take away all that they had gained. She looked into Aaron's eyes and knew that he felt the same and would stand by her.

During Ramadan, the suqs opened for a couple hours of business each day after dark. While visiting Chione's parents' host home, Aaron and Jibade returned late from shopping. Aaron announced he purchased a stack of red lattice mashrabia panels. Jibade would see them safely back to California.

Aaron had also brought a gift for her, the Egyptian harp in a storefront window she had lovingly admired. As Chione touched the harp, she felt the now familiar energy surround her. Her consciousness slipped and she began to play and sing. Other than having carried the harp found in Tauret's tomb, she had never touched one in her life. They needed to begin their journey back to Thebes. They would tour some of the countryside along the way and soak up as much of the culture as possible. Chione wondered if the ancient couple had a way of learning about modern-day Egypt through them.

49

Back at camp, settling in for another evening around the fire, Chione asked, "So where's Kendra?"

Marlowe spread a mat on the ground beside her husband. Dr. Withers wore his gallibaya and looked more Egyptian than ever. The fire's glow reached out into the night to comfort those around it. Siti, who smelled like an overdose of Queen Nefertiti perfume, poked the embers, threw on a few cut branches, and headed for the kitchen.

"She hasn't returned from California," Dr. Withers said.

"Kendra went home?"

Dr. Withers first looked at his wife, then to the others. "She's filing for divorce."

The news was not shocking. Other team members saw it coming. Chione felt regret for not being more supportive of Kendra.

"She's being a little impetuous, don't you think?" Clifford asked.

"Just after New Year's, she received a fax from Royce," Marlowe said. "Didn't say where he was though."

"And?" Aaron asked, leaning forward.

"He probably wouldn't be returning to California. Maybe only to sell his accountancy firm."

"Was that all he said?" Chione asked.

"Not much more."

Bebe and Kenneth walked up hand in hand, too involved to remember that the Egyptians did not approve of affections being displayed in public. Earlier, Marlowe said the drapes to their sleeping cubicle remained closed most of the time and people avoided going near. Seeking privacy meant only one thing. Chione had seen Bebe and Kenneth once when they sat alone on the retaining wall talking. Bebe talked, Kenneth listened. Then, all of a sudden, he turned away from Bebe as scarlet Karkade jettisoned from his mouth. He choked. He stood and paced and gestured with his hands. Bebe motioned for him to sit down. They talked some more, then Kenneth's hand found its way, again, to his wife's buttocks as he tried to kiss her. Surely at that moment, Bebe had disclosed to Kenneth the truth about the spell she drank in hopes of curing her menopausal malaise.

"Kendra knows exactly what she's doing," Bebe said. "These past few weeks, she's been getting herself poised. Now she's going in for the kill."

"I'm glad you were there for her, Bebe," Chione said.

Marlowe patted the ground offering Bebe to sit beside her. Kenneth squeezed in. Surely, Bebe's spell had worked, and she was now able to give her husband more personal attention.

"The San Francisco Sentinel reporters have returned," Aaron said. "Guess they didn't want to miss much."

Dr. Withers strained to see past the shacks. He raised an arm and was about to call for Ginny as she walked into view. To everyone's amazement, she wore a long Egyptian skirt and blouse with a sheesh covering her hair. Just as he opened his mouth to call out, one of the Sentinel photographers came along and gave Ginny's hand a quick squeeze before they headed for a walk down the road. "When in Egypt," Dr. Withers said. "Fall in love."

Chione and Aaron exchanged quick glances. Ginny floated away as her skirt billowed softly. Every team member had natural and intense curiosities. Of course, they would be interested in a woman who dressed and worked like a man, but who seemed feminine and wore provocative perfume, and who just happened to be their very own adept photographer.

"I'd hate to think of how many pictures she's taken catching us unaware," Clifford said. He reclined and stretched out his long legs toward the fire and laid back on his elbows. "Bebe, how's your manuscript coming along?"

"Make that plural. One for the dig overall; another a coffee table photo display of the major artifacts; maybe, smaller publications for each of the Chambers, since each contained a unique set of relics." She counted on her fingers as if having thought it all out ahead of time. "Another to document our lives out here in the desert, including the Egyptians who've been a part of this."

"Some of the workers allowed us to photograph them," Kenneth said. "We could also document our photographic safaris, the two camel treks Bebe and I took. The possibilities are endless."

"Oh, yes," Dr. Withers said as he rocked backwards and looked toward the purple hills. Then he came forward again. "Excuse me while I bask in our glory. Lathrop, California may have a bigger dot on the map now, but the CIA has made its own mark."

"Here, here," Clifford said. They raised cups.

Siti came with a refill and left the pitcher.

"Where's Irwin," Kenneth asked. He filled his cup, sipped, and savored the Karkade.

"Went home," Dr. Withers said. "Didn't like the climate or being this remote."

"He couldn't convert the Egyptians to using chopsticks," Clifford said as he drew back the corners of his mouth.

Several musicians strolled up with their instruments and made themselves comfortable.

"Most of the gawkers cleared out because of Ramadan," Dr. Withers said.

"There's nothing much to see till we crack that new tomb," Clifford said. "Enjoy the calm while you can."

Moments of quiet and slow movement would allow savoring of the experience and sentiment of the past few months. The transient beggars' camp dwindled to a dozen or so small tents. Catering to tourists and laborers provided lucrative employment for the tent dwellers. Setting up business in transient locations meant they made their livelihoods on the run.

"The Restoration crew has started work in Tauret's tomb," Clifford said. "More workers equate to more tents down the hill real soon."

"I've got a plan," Dr. Withers said, grabbing their attention after some silence as they listened to the music. "Except for Kendra and Randy, we're all present. We need to act on this."

Chione breathed a sigh of relief. She still had not come up with a way to break the news about herself and Aaron. Their story needed to be told because the pregnancy could not be kept secret for long. Her breasts had already begun to enlarge. Her stomach was fuller. Her menses had never been regular. Because of that, she guessed the night she drank her spell and soon experienced the complete love scene between Tauret and Tut, meant she was about three months pregnant.

"What's cookin'?" Bebe asked.

"You know the ruins the Norwegians found?" Dr. Withers asked. He stretched his legs out straight and cross his ankles.

"Terji and Finn found it together," Chione said.

"Kenny found one of the walls," Bebe said proudly. She looked stunning in her Egyptian clothes and dangling earrings, a gift from Kenneth from his visit to the tent camp.

"Well, here we are with two tombs on our hands," Dr. Withers said. They waited as he absent-mindedly stroked his mustache, shifting gears. "We've got a lot of research to wrap up." He gestured over his shoulder toward Tauret's tomb. "With the artifacts and all. Now we've got a second tomb."

"You've been inside again?" Bebe asked.

"No, ma'am," he said. "I had Quaashie and Naeem seal it tight before Paki Rashad left."

"C'mon," Kenneth said. "Tell us you didn't sneak back in."

Dr. Withers looked quizzically at Kenneth. "I rather like us working as a team." He did, however, make a thorough examination of all the mastabas above the area. "I'm hoping the rest of the chambers haven't been breached, via one of Randy's entrances."

"We'll walk it again," Aaron said.

"Yes, we will."

"Wait," Kenneth said suddenly. They had learned to be patient when he had something to say. "We need to find the real entrance to that tomb, like the hole our guy fell into with Tauret's tomb."

"We'll test for weak spots in the ground," Aaron said.

Kenneth chuckled. "Maybe the seismologists will get to earn their pay."

"Kenneth, you sure you don't want to take a few courses at the Institute?" Dr. Withers asked. "You'd make a great archaeologist."

That was a fine compliment. Kenneth looked utterly surprised at the acceptance shown him. "You mean all I've done won't be accepted until I have my degree?" Surely, he imitated Randy in jest.

After another moment, Dr. Withers said, "Here's what I propose now, because of the massive amount of work we've got on our hands. Judging by the size of the main hall, that's a huge tomb under the mastabas. We've got less than four months before the Egyptian sun dictates that we leave this arid land."

"Do you think we can clear that tomb as quickly?" Bebe asked. "Considering the main chamber was plundered?"

"We worked at breakneck speed on Tauret's tomb," Clifford said. "A handful of people have worked here during the summers. Why can't we?" If the team left and returned in a cooler climate, Clifford would stay and oversee any work carried on in the team's absence. Even though the main hall stood empty, it was impossible to guess how many additional chambers and annexes would be found or how many artifacts.

"Then we can slow up a bit," Bebe said. Chione was surprised to hear that Bebe would stay.

"You've had nearly all of Ramadan to recover," Dr. Withers said, teasing.

"Don't forget," Aaron said. "Unlike our predecessors, we have modern technology and procedures to speed up the work."

"We just might be able to get in and out of this second tomb before we get fried," Kenneth said.

"Look, here's my point," Dr. Withers said as he stuck his famous two fingers into the air. "Those Norwegians were sorely dismayed at making a grand discovery and not being able to claim it. I've already run this by our Board of Directors, and they concur but leave the final decision to us." He looked around the group, as was his habit, reading faces, anticipating each person's reaction. "I suggest we bring the Norwegians in on the village find. Let them claim the discovery inside our permitted area. They become partners in our village endeavor and receive the glory they deserve."

"You mean let them do what they usually do?" Bebe asked. "Restore that village?"

"I'm certainly not totally giving up a find that will help the CIA's credibility. But those two guys stuck by us."

"They're not afraid of work," Aaron said.

"They deserve the credit," Dr. Withers said. "Besides...." He made quick eye contact around the group like he always did before releasing one of his ideas. "They can pump additional capital into their part of the obligation."

The group sat quietly mulling over the suggestion. A gentle breeze began. The musicians took up the lapse in conversation.

"Let's hear your thoughts," Dr. Withers said finally. No one spoke. "Okay, let's have a show of hands. All those in favor of bringing the Norwegians into the village project, raise."

Five hands shot up. "That's all of us present," Chione said. "How about Kendra and Randy? Or are we a quorum?"

"We can run it by them. More importantly," Dr. Withers said, smiling his sideways smile, "maybe we ought to run it by the Norwegians."

"Hey, you two," Clifford said, turning to her and Aaron. "In Cairo, did you get a chance to peek in on Randy's new digs?"

"We did," Chione said. "But first we visited Rita." Chione tried not to imagine Clifford lying in the ground beside his wife.

Clifford smiled sweetly and pressed a hand to his chest.

"Tell us about Randy," Marlowe said.

"Cushy, cushy research lab," Aaron said. "He's not getting any sand in his boots."

"Does he like his work?" Dr. Withers asked.

"Sir," Chione said. "He's finally where he belongs. They need him. He's found a place where his training can be utilized."

"We've seen that young man go through some drastic changes," Bebe said.

"He's not the only one," Marlowe said. Coming from her, that was a strong hint.

Nerves danced in Chione's stomach. Was now the time to shock them all? How would she begin? "I understand Quaashie and Naeem are permanently in charge in place of Dakarai and Masud," she said, changing her mind.

"Personally," Dr. Withers said, "We'll get a lot more work out of those two giddy souls." Masud was always overworked pulling the weight of two because Dakarai was seldom present.

"Who arranged that for Quaashie and Naeem?" Clifford asked. "The same person who made arrangements for Randy?"

Dr. Withers sighed and looked smug. "Power's a wonderful tool in the right hands," he said, affectedly feigning innocence as the background music swelled.

They laughed, talked jovially. Then again Marlowe insisted, "Chione, Aaron? Tell us about your adventures in Cairo."

She mentally thanked Marlowe for the lead in. "It's a long story," she said, smiling and looking into Aaron's eyes.

"Speak up," Dr. Withers said. "You think out here in the middle of this stretch of sand, where no one can keep secrets, we're going to let you two have yours?"

Chione wondered how much they knew.

"We had a great trip," Aaron said. "Spent a lot of time with Chione's parents and their host family."

"Have any of you ever eaten dinner with a local family after the sun sets during Ramadan?" Chione asked.

"Many times," Clifford said. "Everyone counts down to sunset, then the food flies."

"Literally," Chione said. "I had no idea. Meat bones, vegetables, whatever's in the main dish. A feast for twelve is consumed in about ten minutes. Food literally flies through the air as people dive in."

"Humph!" Kenneth said.

"It's tradition," Clifford said. "Different culture."

"Humph," Kenneth said again.

"Ought to try it, Kenneth," Clifford said. "No different than the way you dive into a dish!" That brought a round of laughter.

On the way back, Chione and Aaron toured Khufu's humble digs, as Aaron jokingly called them, at the pyramids at Giza. They took a camel trek through the countryside for a firsthand view of the fellahin and their farms. "Really soaked up Egypt," Chione said. Camels were introduced in Egypt within the last six hundred years. If Tauret and Pharaoh were experiencing modern-day Egypt through them, Chione wondered what they thought of riding the strange beasts.

"What are you two not telling," Marlowe asked. "You, Chione, you come back from Cairo with Tauret's hairstyle and smelling of some strange perfume. Even that white Egyptian dress you wore your first day back resembled the clothes we found in the Offering Chamber."

Marlowe had detected the scent! Chione was in a quandary as to how Marlowe might smell any fragrance without her having applied any, unless—

"What gives?" Kenneth asked.

Chione's face got hot. She hoped shadows stretched long by the setting sun might hide her blush.

Aaron looked at her and smiled deviously. "Should we drop it on them?"

"If you're not talking," Marlowe said, "I'm going to drop something on you."

"Pray, tell us," Dr. Withers said quickly, flashing that idiot grin of his.

Marlowe laughed with the others. "When Gracie first heard of the sorcerers and magicians down the hill," she said, innocently capturing the limelight. "We slipped down there to get a reading."

"You didn't," Kenneth said.

"We did," Marlowe said. "Gracie was more interested than I. Gracie's motto was, 'When in Egypt....' "

Chione nudged Aaron. What if Marlowe had gotten the kind of reading Aaron had received? What if Marlowe was about to spill the fava beans?

"You and Gracie make a team," Clifford said. "Carmelita go with you?"

Marlowe adamantly shook her head. She long ago admitted she could not stand Carmelita. "The medium told me to expect the unexpected," Marlowe said.

"Some reading," Kenneth said.

"Wait," Marlowe said. Her expression turned serious. "She told me a message in the tomb about two people relate to two in our group."

"Run that by me again," Dr. Withers said.

By this time, Chione knew if she did not speak, Marlowe would inadvertently usurp the surprise she and Aaron had primed themselves to deliver.

"Remember one of the first spells in the tomb?" Chione asked, realizing Marlowe had provided a perfect set up. "Remember, it said, 'Beware! Two who would enter.'"

"That's right," Marlowe said. "The medium told me we're a group of people who are only carrying out spells cast a long time ago."

"I hope you're not going to say we're reincarnated," Kenneth said.

"Sounds like someone's kept the people down the hill informed of what we've translated from the glyphs," Bebe said, passing it off. She looked disappointed, then smiled unexpectedly, probably remembering how she had been helped. She owed it to Tauret to try to believe.

Marlowe frowned. "Regardless, the medium said two people mentioned in the spells are in this group and that shocking events would irrevocably proceed once the tomb was opened."

All listened intently. Chione recognized how deeply each person's interest had been captured by the paranormal. As a cohesive group, they shared an exceptional experience that changed personal views of a reality beyond life and death. They were more accepting of the beliefs of the Ancients. Still, that gave no clue to them accepting the special child she carried. Perhaps she and Aaron might be the wiser letting everyone think the child was his and hers.

"What else?" Clifford asked. He sipped tea as if the conversation was as ordinary as talking about the weather.

"Two people will live out the spells," Marlowe said. "We're in for some surprises. The medium said that anyone—anywhere—who doubted the spells would be hit harder with the truth later on."

Chione felt a surge of happiness at hearing Marlowe's last statement. It just about said people had better listen, wise up.

Aaron took her hands. He, too, recognized the opportunity and nudged her to speak. Chione felt a surge of happiness.

Dr. Withers's secreted expression of great relief at seeing them clinging to one another encouraged. "What's this mean, you two?"

Chione beamed, looked at Aaron then back to the group. "We got married."

50

Shock rippled around the campfire. Mouths hung open. Before anyone recovered enough to say anything, Clifford pounded the ground
with a fist and said, "I knew it! I told you guys. Ol' Tut was having a
clandestine affair!"

A quick sudden strumming of the oud player punctuated Clifford's
words. Everyone expressed congratulations, along with disappointment at not having been present for the ceremony. Marlowe suggested
planning a wedding party. Siti arrived with more tea. Chione accepted
the Karkade and felt herself slipping into an altered state, but this one
was different. She felt in control, utterly empowered. She looked to
Bebe who understood. Whether or not the others accepted, she meant
to go on. This was her life, and she was not about to allow anyone to
denigrate it. From this day forth, she would not fear the reactions of
her colleagues.

The sky darkened and the breeze cooled. Night was truly upon
them. Light from the fire cast shadows across their faces. Chione was
sure no one would leave at that moment. Even so, she signaled Aaron
that she did not want to disclose more just yet.

During the next weeks, the team seemed more resigned, afraid to
talk or ask questions for fear of stirring up something best left alone.
Chione's pregnancy began to show. Her breasts grew larger. Now everyone looked at her curiously, wondering. She could only rub her
stomach lovingly and give thanks that she had conceived. She did

not care how. She and Aaron were inextricably a part of Tauret and Pharaoh's lives and that pleased her. Yet, what pleased her more was the commitment she and Aaron shared.

One evening after dinner, Dr. Withers pulled her aside and asked, "So have you seen a doctor about your condition?" When she told him she had not, he insisted she and Aaron get themselves immediately back to Cairo to see Dr. Vimble. He looked like he might shake a finger at her. Instead, he thrust his famous pointer into the air. "I don't want you working another day, till you get back from that checkup. Maybe not even then." He, like everyone else, thought she and Aaron had been fooling around all along and that saddened her momentarily.

The next day, Dr. Withers disclosed that he had to return to California with Clifford to finalize papers. Marlowe would accompany them. Bebe and Kenneth opted to stay in camp and wait for their son and help get him indoctrinated into the village work at hand. The entire dig site would be closed, with Rashad's men left to guard the gates, until all were reunited.

Later, when she and Aaron were alone and standing in the doorway of their sleeping room, he wrapped his arms around her, and they stood looking out over the valley. "We've got to tell them, Chione. Everything you've told them from day one has proven itself out. They'll believe us now."

She lived with a supernatural ability and knew nothing else. She could only be rational and considerate of people's pessimism. Yet, she resented the team feeling sorry for her not being able to conceive, then sneaking peeks at her belly when they thought she had. She had only herself to blame. "We're the only ones who know the truth about this child," she said. "And maybe Bebe." Perhaps Chione was being overly cautious. Soon enough she would give birth. She was not about to allow uncertainty to diminish the glory that belonged to her and Aaron and their special child. They needed to do something to validate what happened to them. Their colleagues were on the verge of accepting, but it might take something special to sway their thinking fully toward belief.

Aaron seemed pleased. "Marlowe and Bebe have already been initiated. Kendra will go along with anything that draws attention. What about Clifford?"

She thought for a moment and felt empathy with Clifford. "He and Rita always treated me like a daughter," she said, turning in Aaron's arms. "If anything, he'd accept because he believes in what actually happens."

"Yeah, but right now he could be believing that you and I have, you know, been having a clandestine affair." Aaron rolled his eyes.

They shared a moment of silence. Aaron passed his hand lovingly over her stomach. She turned in his arms and said, "I'm glad Randy's with us." She loved to see the intensity in Aaron's eyes.

Then there was Dr. Withers to consider. He was more concerned about holding the team together; though not cognizant of help from the Ancients, a team he thought he had hand-picked. His interest was incited because of his love for Marlowe, who knew well how to maintain balance between the paranormal and social constraints required by her husband's career.

"A higher power has brought us all together," Chione said. "For the sake of the child." She was the person who needed to be the strongest in order to keep the team from falling into irreversible realms of disbelief. She and Aaron had to do something to help their rational peers feel okay with what they would soon disclose.

They stayed in Cairo nearly three weeks, timing their arrival with the return of the Witherses and Clifford. Chione felt awed about the new information she and Aaron had just days before learned about their child. It would be difficult at best choosing the right moment to disclose information that shocked even her. She was filled with a new sense that a power had been bestowed on her and Aaron that would provide guidance to them all.

Dinnertime was a good time to introduce a topic other than work. They entered the dining room to a hearty welcome. Dinner was being served, and they sat down for the meal. Everyone except Kenneth wore Egyptian clothing. Bebe and Kenneth took quick glances at her stomach. Proudly, Chione rubbed her belly and smiled. She wore another long, loose Egyptian dress. She would need to find larger sized khakis if she expected to continue working. With the way they all dressed, and the food being served, there seemed little, if any, American influence among them, other than Kenneth's stubborn naivete.

No one said a word. They still believed she and Aaron had been having an affair. She and Aaron were about to wipe out that dogma. Their peers, whose lives were entwined, not only with one another but also with Tauret and her Pharaoh, teetered on the brink of a new consciousness.

Aaron swallowed a bite of food. "Randy was able to salvage Tauret's teeth. It's opened up a lot of possibilities."

"Like what?"

"He believes he and the scientists can rebuild her bite. From the way the teeth fit together, they'll be able to recreate her likeness using holographic technology and our photo images."

"Yes," Clifford said. "The Old World and the new unite."

"What else?" Dr. Withers asked. It seemed he expected to hear a lot more.

"He's also been able to extract DNA from the teeth."

"If there's anything today that can prove a point," Dr. Withers said between bites. "It's DNA. You want proof positive? Turn to the DNA."

"If only they could clone her," Clifford said, deep in thought. "Bring her back to life. She feels like one of us, like family."

"The Madu Museum has its own archives of DNA prints from many of the Ancients," Chione said. "They're trying to prove who in these modern times are descendants." She looked at Aaron who beamed.

"Hey, wait a minute," Dr. Withers said, interrupting. "I gotta tell you something, all of you." They waited. He took a sip of water and even as he held his cup, that pointer finger that always shot into the air still stood straight up away from the cup. "Marlowe took me down to that camp to get a reading," he said as if it had been a most natural occurrence.

"I'm not hearing this," Kenneth said.

"Well, I wouldn't have believed what that reader said… if she hadn't first told me something I already knew."

"Like?" Kenneth asked, but his expression said he did not really want to know. Bebe shoved her plate over, so he could finish her food. It seemed she always did this as a way of telling him to shut up.

"This woman, this seer, told me things I never told anyone. She actually looked into my mind and saw my secrets."

Kenneth swallowed. "Like what? We need some proof here." Always the skeptic, he would be the one who might hinder the others from believing.

Suddenly Dr. Withers looked proud like he thoroughly enjoyed the reading. "Something most of you don't know," he said, beginning slowly, "is that way back when Marlowe and I first met Chione…." He took his wife's hand, then reached over and squeezed hers, too. "Chione told Marlowe that I shouldn't take my little plane up till I had it checked out." He picked up his fork, took a bite of food and made everyone wait. "She told Marlowe to tell me not to fly—that she feared an explosion."

"Chione said that?" Kenneth asked.

"Yeah, and get this. This seer said that Chione told my wife that something was wrong with the plane. Back then, the plane was just serviced, but Chione insisted. I decided to have the plane checked out again, mostly to be safe. Partly to see what this Chione girl was all about."

"And?" Clifford asked. He had stopped eating.

"The mechanic found an oil-soaked rag left on the engine from the time it was cleaned. Maybe later in flight, the rag would have caught fire. Could've blown us to smithereens!"

No one said a word. Finally, Kenneth said, "The seer down the road knew about this incident that happened, what? Years ago?"

"Yep," Dr. Withers said. "So now I'm beginning to believe." That was not all he was beginning to believe. He and Clifford wore gallibayas and Chione knew with certainty what possessed him to make himself look Egyptian.

447

Chione felt vindicated but hid her smile, not wishing to appear smug. "What else did the seer tell you?" She suspected Marlowe took her husband for a reading to get him acclimated to the changes taking place, a good move on Marlowe's part. It would have prepared Dr. Withers for what was to come.

"This woman... as incredible as it seems—"

"C'mon, man," Clifford said. "I'm afraid to take a drink here because what you're about to say is gonna make me choke. I just know it."

"I was told," he said, raising fingers to show quotes, " 'a woman in our group is going to change history.' "

"We've already heard that," Kenneth said before anyone could react. True, that bit of news was repetitious.

Chione and Aaron were ready to divulge some astonishing new information, and she felt confident. "Maybe it's me," she said. "That is, Aaron and me."

Their colleagues were not blind and had noticed the changes in her before Dr. withers sent them to Cairo. They were still thinking the child was Aaron's, so the truth would hit the team harder than it had them.

When the group settled again, Chione stood and quietly began. "Each of you has accepted that we've been deeply affected by this tomb, it's ancient spells and magic, right?" All heads nodded. Aaron waited patiently. She took a breath. "Do you remember that one morning Kendra and Clifford noticed one of Tut's bowls was missing?" Again, they nodded. "Well... I took the bowl intentionally."

"Wha-at?"

"Wait, not intentionally," Chione said. She was nervous, not telling things quite right. "What I mean is, I grabbed a bowl to use, not knowing it was Tutankhamon's."

"Use for what?"

Bebe's eyes got big and fearful. She wouldn't have told everyone about performing her spell. Chione gave her a reassuring smile to let her know she was not about to divulge Bebe's secret.

"One of the numerous papyri we found," Chione said, "contained one of Tauret's spells to help women become pregnant."

The group leaned over the table toward her.

"Did you do what I think you're about to tell us?" Dr. Withers asked.

"I did the spell." She thought she had not said it loud enough. "I performed Tauret's spell." She lifted her chin proudly. They were already familiar with the ancient practice of writing in lampblack and drinking the fluid.

"And?" Bebe asked pretentiously.

Kenneth stood suddenly and paced. "I don't know if I can accept what you're about to say," He kept taking side-glances at her belly. "Don't scare us, Chione. This is too spooky."

"It gets spookier," Aaron said quietly. He put an assuring hand on the back of her waist as she stood beside him.

"I took a bowl from Inventory to make the spell more real. I didn't know till the next morning that it was Tut's bowl."

"It made the spell authentic, didn't it?" Bebe asked, seeming joyous.

"Yes, it did," Chione said. They were about to find out just how authentic.

Kenneth paced like he could not throw off the nervous energy fast enough.

"Kenneth, you come and sit down here," Bebe said. "What you're about to hear isn't going to kill us."

"Honey," Kenneth said as he stood behind her. He put both hands on her shoulders and leaned around sideways to look at her. "Don't tell me you're buying into this."

Bebe pulled at her husband's hand. "Sit down, Kenneth."

He kept shaking his head. "It's too much. I've already had one magical bomb dropped on me—"

"Was that bomb similar to dropping the curtains to the doors of your cubicle?" Clifford asked with another silly grin.

Kenneth's shoulders drooped. He looked as if he did not know how to save himself. He sat down as if his legs had weakened.

"Back when Aaron and I accompanied Tauret's coffin to Cairo," Chione said. "I performed a pregnancy test."

"No," Kenneth said, shaking his head. "No, I can't believe this."

If anyone had shocked this special group of people, it had been her with her dreams and visions. The information she and Aaron now had to relate would stretch reality beyond the limit. Yet, she could not quit.

"Tell us," Dr. Withers said. "That you and Aaron have been close all along... and that you're having a good laugh at our expense. Tell us that."

"I never touched her," Aaron said respectfully. "Not until we were married, less than two months ago." She wondered when he might speak. He seemed confident in her relating the facts. Still, he was not about to have his integrity attacked.

"Whose baby is this?" Dr. Withers asked.

"Sterling, you're not getting it," Marlowe said. "Remember the spell? 'Beware two who would enter. The spell is cast, till all of time has passed.' "

"Tauret cast a spell," Aaron said, "that her child by Pharaoh would be born, in order to live a life to take into the Afterlife."

"Umi clearly stated that in his scratchings," Bebe said, excited at having remembered. "Remember, Chione? It was Clifford who said we'd find our proof in Umi's scratchings."

"How did you know what was in them before the glyphs were interpreted, Clifford?" Kenneth asked.

Just how did Clifford know what some of Umi's scratchings might tell? Dr. Withers stared wide-eyed as if asking where the hell did this come from? As Chione watched each person's reaction, the point that they had changed since being in Egypt was driven home. The plates in front of them contained only local foods, and they guzzled Karkade and Yansun instead of coffee.

"When did you drink that spell, Chione?" Kenneth asked. He spoke like a person intending to discredit what he could not believe.

"We hadn't been here two weeks," Chione said. "Not quite four months ago." The team seemed confused by Kenneth's disruptions. "On this last trip, we had a prenatal test done."

"Amniocentesis?" Marlowe asked. She shivered erratically. "Isn't that where they stick a needle—?"

"Drinking a spell had nothing to do with it," Kenneth said angrily. He stood, paced again. It was almost hilarious to watch him.

"Right and wrong," Chione said. "I now know that drinking the spell was only ritual acceptance and amniocentesis validated it."

"With the DNA," Aaron said.

With the mention of DNA, everyone came to attention. With what they knew about Randy's involvement with DNA, Chione sensed pieces of the puzzle coming together in each of their minds.

Aaron pulled some papers out of his notebook and spread them on the tabletop. "When Chione and I were in Cairo when we got married, we had Randy do our personal DNA prints." He paused, letting the others absorb slowly. The pages contained columns with small soft rectangular spots clearly but sporadically marked. "Check these out," he said, pointing. "This one is Chione's and this one is mine." Then he laid another two pages just below those. "Randy already had copies of Tutankhamon's and now Tauret's, from her teeth." Everyone looked closely.

"The reason I decided to have an amniocentesis is that the amniotic fluid contains cells sloughed off by the fetus."

"We had our baby's DNA printed as well," Aaron said. Just the word *baby* made some gasp.

Bebe's hands shook. She dropped her fork. She knew! Marlowe gave her husband a sideways glance, anticipating that he was about to be hit with irrefutable proof that she and Aaron were being honest; irrefutable DNA proof in which the good Dr. Withers believed wholeheartedly. Marlowe glowed in the revelation of participating in another paranormal experience.

Kenneth sat, unblinking, in denial. "Tell me again how long ago you did do that spell."

"Just under four months ago."

Aaron separated Tauret and Tut's charts and slid another sheet of prints in between. "This one's from our baby."

Everyone studied the new page. Kenneth saw it first. Then Clifford noticed and elbowed Dr. Withers. "Looks like you got your psychic reading just in time, Sterling," Clifford said. "Hope you understand what's going on here."

"If you'll notice," Chione said as she pointed to the charts, "Our baby's DNA doesn't match Aaron's or mine in the least."

"But look," Aaron said, pointing to the similarities. "It's a perfect match between Tauret and Tutankhamon."

They all pounced upon the prints and sent dishes and other tableware flying. You would think they had just received a list of lotto winners knowing one of them was on it. After taking a good look, the group quieted, took their seats, and stared at her and Aaron.

Dr. Withers stared out through the tent fly with a strange look of knowing glimmering in his eyes. After a while, he sat forward, adjusted his gallibaya and then quietly said, "It took a lot of lifetimes for each of us to come together again." His voice had a strange otherworldly ring to it.

Clifford took a deep breath like he could not get enough air. He seemed exhausted. He rubbed his temples and said, "I was hoping we wouldn't have to die yet again before this kid was born." His voice sounded familiar, but it was not Clifford's voice.

"Are we to believe because of this spell you did just after we arrived here, you're now four months pregnant?" Kenneth asked.

Tauret was pregnant almost through the second trimester. Chione thought of the Cairo doctor's recent shocking diagnosis that confirmed the very first time she felt ill. It was about the time the onslaught of dreams that ultimately brought the team to Egypt began; two months before anyone left for Egypt. Unbeknownst to her, Tauret's spells were already implanted.

"Four months we've been here. You're saying four months?" Kenneth asked again.

"No. It started with the first dream I had, even before I told anyone about my dreams that brought us all here," Chione said. She rubbed her hand lovingly across her belly. "I'm six months."

Dear reader,

We hope you enjoyed reading *The Ka*. Please take a moment to leave a review, even if it's a short one. Your opinion is important to us.

Discover more books by Mary Deal at https://www.nextchapter.pub/authors/mary-deal-romance-mystery-author.

Want to know when one of our books is free or discounted for Kindle? Join the newsletter at http://eepurl.com/bqqB3H.

Best regards,
Mary Deal and the Next Chapter Team

You could also like:
Ascension by Lorelei Bell

To read the first chapter for free, head to:
https://www.nextchapter.pub/books/ascension-urban-fantasy

Glossary

18th Dynasty – During the New Kingdom period, 1570 – 1070 BC.

Akhenaten – Heretic tenth Pharaoh of the 18th Dynasty, 1352-1336 B.C., possibly Tutankhamon's half-brother or his father.

Akhen – Translates to "he who serves the sun."

Akhetaten – Name for the town that Akhenaten built for worshippers of the Aten. Located in Tel el Amarna.

Akhet – Translates to "Horizon of the Aten," based on how the sun rose over the distant hills, as seen from Tel el Amarna, the town Akhenaten built.

Al-Qurn – Pyramid Mountain, *Peak of the West*. Believed to be a natural pyramid placed by Ancient Gods, which led the Ancient Egyptians to choose Valley of the Kings and Valley of the Queens for royal burial sites.

Amarnian figures – Statues and etchings from Akhenaten's era, at Tel el-Amarna and other locations, show both men and women with full rounded stomachs, hips, and thighs.

Amniocentesis – Needle procedure to draw amniotic fluid to test cells sloughed off by the fetus.

Amulet – Carved figurine of various life forms, or other symbolic trinkets.

Ankh – The symbolic representation of both Physical and Eternal life. It is known as the original cross, which is a powerful symbol created by Africans in Ancient Egypt. The Ankh is commonly known to mean life in the language of Ancient Kemet (land of the Blacks) renamed Egypt by the Greeks. A symbol for the power to give and sustain life, the Ankh is typically associated with material things such as water (which was believed by Egyptians to regenerate life), air, sun, as well as with the Gods, who are frequently pictured carrying an Ankh. The Egyptian king is often associated with the Ankh also, either in possession of an Ankh (providing life to his people) or being given an Ankh (or stream of Ankhs) by the Gods. Numerous examples have been found that were made from metal, clay, and wood. It is usually worn as an amulet to extend the life of the living and placed on the mummy to energize the resurrected spirit. The Gods and the Kings are often shown carrying the Ankh to distinguish them from mere mortals. The Ankh symbolized eternal life and bestowed immortality on anyone who possessed it. It is believed that life energy emanating from the Ankh can be absorbed by anyone within a certain proximity. An Ankh serves as an antenna or conduit for the divine power of life that permeates the universe. The amulet is a powerful talisman that provides the wearer with protection from the evil forces of decay and degeneration.

Ankhesenpa – Also, Ankhesenpa-Aten or Ankhesenamun. Tutankhamon's only wife.

Armed Guard – Questionable group of area police who wear gallibayas and look like the laborers.

Aspergillus Niger – A pathogenic fungus or mold with black spores that cause infection in the ears.

Aysh – Arabic or Egyptian pita-type bread made from white flour. An alternative is made from coarse whole-wheat, which is called *aysh baladi*. The most common way to eat the aysh is to stuff it with bean paste and eat it as a sandwich.

Bebaghanoug – Eggplant paste.

Bersim – A grain, grown as fodder for livestock.

Beq – Symbol of a pregnant woman.

Bilharzia – Potentially life-threatening infection caused by drinking water tainted with schistosomes, a by-product of snails.

Giovani Battista Belzoni – Weightlifter-turned-explorer in the early Nineteenth Century, who damaged or destroyed a lot of tombs and valuable history while using strong-arm methods of getting to the artifacts.

Bolis – Common term for the official Egyptian Police Force, who wear white uniform tunics over dark trousers.

Birket Habu – An important archaeological site located at the southern end of the Necropolis of Thebes. This was the town and palace site of Amenhotep III of the Eighteenth Dynasty, along with the Palace of Malkatta with its man-made lake. The complex included a large number of buildings, courts and parade grounds, houses for the inhabitants, and a large temple of Amon as well as the royal palaces.

Cache of royal mummies – See "Victor Loret."

Canopic jars – Central to ancient Egyptian religious beliefs was the need to preserve the body. The ancient Egyptians developed a method of artificial preservation, called mummification. Mummification was a complicated and lengthy process that lasted up to 70 days. It began with the body being delivered to the embalmer. He would then bathe the body and lay it out. In preparation, the priests would shave their entire bodies and the priest in charge would wear the mask of a jackal representing the god Anubis. At this point, the brains were removed through the nostrils and discarded, and then an incision was made in the side of the body. All of the major organs were removed and placed in canopic jars. Four organs to be removed each time, with four canopic jars to guard them. The organs were placed in the following jars: Lungs went into the jar with the head of *Hapi* (baboon); stomach into the jar with the head of *Duamutefla* (dog); liver in the jar with the head of *Imseti* (human); and, intestines into jar with the head of *Qebehsenuef* (falcon).

Capstan – A broad revolving cylinder for winding a heavy rope or cable.

Cartouche – Usually a small rectangular shaped impression with rounded corners; contains symbols translating to the owner's name.

The outer band symbolized continuity, which enclosed a god's or pharaoh's name. Its use was not unlike a modern logo.

Copts – The Copts are the descendants of the Ancient Egyptians who accepted Christianity in the First Century. *Copt* was derived from the word Aigyptos, which meant *Egypt* in Greek. The Arabs who invaded Egypt in 641 AD corrupted the word. The Arabs, then, couldn't pronounce it as such and instead, they pronounced it as *Gypt* or *Kipt.* To them, they called Egypt, the Land of the Kipt, or Copt.

Jean-Francois Champollion – 1790-1832, French Egyptologist, acknowledged as the father of modern Egyptology. Best known for his work interpreting the *Rosetta Stone,* which led to translations of hieroglyphs. It was his deciphering of the hieroglyphics contained on the Stone that laid the foundations for Egyptian archaeology.

Chateau d-Egypte Rose' – A modern-day Egyptian wine.

Cloak – Usually worn by women, similar to a vest. It did not have sleeves but did have armholes. The front was fastened around and under or over the breasts and sometimes attached to the front of the skirt.

Coffinettes – Small hollowed, carved figurines, into which was placed the deceased's internal organs; the figurines then inserted into the canopic jars.

Cowry shells – Represented a desire of the wearer to bear children.

Dado – Chamber lower walls or pedestals covered with gypsum plaster and painted yellow.

Dakarai – Happy.

Dier el-Bahri – Discovered in 1743 on the West Bank of the Nile. The funeral Temple of *Queen Hatshepsut,* (1490 BC-1468BC), was built by the architect *Senenmut.* Located South of Valley of the Kings in the Necropolis of Thebes.

Dier el-Medina – Southwest of Dier el-Bahri. From the New Kingdom. In Arabic meaning *monastery of the city,* was also known by workmen as *Pa demi,* simply, *the town,* though it was also called *Set Maa, the place of truth.* It is one of the most well-preserved ancient settlements in all Egypt. It lies within the Necropolis of Thebes between Dier el-Bahri and Valley of the Queens. It was a highly skilled community of craftsmen who passed their expertise on from father to son, all dedicated to building the great tombs of the Egyptian Kings and Queens. The community included the workmen and their wives, children and other dependents, as well as coppersmiths, carpenters, potters, basket makers, and a part-time physician. The workers belonged to what we today call the middle class, having no royal or noble connections.

Diorite – Hardest stone in nature. Igneous rock similar to granite but with less quartz. Normal rock contains light-colored white and pink feldspar and dark biotite and hornblende minerals, giving it a salt and pepper appearance. The rock crystallized slowly, deep beneath the surface, indicated by the coarse grains.

Djed – A djed-pillar amulet. The *Tet*(Djed)-pillar was one of the most significant symbols of the Egyptian religion. It symbolized the idea of stability and duration. This symbol may well have been an ancient fetish that was adopted by the Osiris cult. It came to be regarded as the backbone of the god, and later as a representation of Osiris himself. Some interpretations claim that it represents columns imitating a bundle of stalks tied together or is derived from sheaves of rushes or similar vegetable growths, lengthened by the expedient of inserting one bundle inside another and firmly tying the neck of each sheaf to prevent the next slipping within it. While some saw in the Tet(Djed) an architectural support without any meaning, others found mystical interpretations for this symbol that have purely theological concepts. It was suggested that it represented the mother goddess Hathor, pregnant with the god or king since she was referred to, in a late text, as the female Tet(Djed)-pillar, who concealed Ra from his enemies. Whereas in the Osirian myth, Osiris was concealed in a pillar.

Douceur – The gentle sweetness of the local people.

Egyptian Zodiac – Egypt was one of the first cultures to devise a zodiac—a series of animals along the sun's path through the sky. Important animals in the zodiac included the hippo and alligator among others. Gods and goddesses were also included.

Faience – Egyptian faience is a glazed, non-clay ceramic material. It is composed mainly of quartz with amounts of lime and natron or plant ash. The body of a faience creation is coated with soda-lime silica glaze. Adding different metals and their oxides cause color changes. The glazed composition can be modeled into the shape of an amulet or bowl or vase. Sometimes the molding is done by hand. Faience was not used as an inexpensive substitute for more costly materials but for its association with light and rebirth.

Falaafil – Deep-fried patties of minced beans, mixed with a variety of spices.

Farseekh – Dried fish.

Fellahin – Farmers along the Nile. DNA tests add evidence that farmers along the Nile are the closest relatives of the laborers and workers who built the Pyramids. When the inundation occurred, farmers could not work the fields and went, instead, to help build the pyramids.

Felucca – Thirty-foot sailing boats on the Nile.

Fenogreek – A wild plant that has a mild bitter chlorophyll taste, refreshing and tasty and very uncommon.

Ful medames – Fava beans.

Fuul – Beans for human consumption.

Gallibaya – Ankle length tunic, common dress of Egyptian men, sometimes worn over regular clothing.

Hamitic – The Egyptians are a fairly homogeneous people of Hamitic origin: Mediterranean and Arab influences appear in the north, and there is some mixing in the south with the Nubians of northern Sudan. Ethnic minorities include a small number of Bedouin Arab nomads in the eastern and western deserts and in the Sinai, as well as some 50,000-100,000 Nubians clustered along the Nile in Upper Egypt.

Hapi's mud – Ancient Egyptians knew the black mud found along the banks of the Nile River to be fertile and made crops grow. They used the mud as a treatment, applied to the faces of women who had difficulty conceiving. Hapi was probably a Predynastic name for the Nile. As a water god, Hapi was a deity of fertility - he provided water, food and the yearly inundation of the Nile. He was also known as *Lord of the Fishes and Birds of the Marshes,* indicating that he provided these creatures to the Egyptians along with the Nile itself. Without Hapi,

Egypt would have died, and so he was sometimes revered even above *Ra*, the sun god. The depiction of Hapi himself, though, was that of a rather well-fed, blue or green man with the false beard of the pharaoh on his chin. Other than showing his status as a god of fertility by his color, the Egyptians showed Hapi as having rather large breasts, like those of a mother with a baby.

Helva – Sweet tahini rich in sesame and walnut or pistachios; when mixed with herbs like fenogreek, used for medicinal purposes.

Horus – The god, Horus, had a body of a man and a head of a hawk. Thus, the markings of a hawk eye for the wadjet amulet.

Ini-Herit – Related to royalty.

Iniuts – Lotus blossom buds.

Jibade – Related to royalty.

Ka – Spirit. Egyptians believed that part of the personality, called the *Ka*, remained in the tomb.

Kamuzu – Medical, as in Kamuzu University. *University for Medicine.*

Karkade – A red hibiscus tea that can be drunk hot or cold.

Karnak – The Temple of Karnak was actually three main temples, smaller enclosed temples, and several outer temples, located in Thebes.

Khamsin wind – Violent sandstorm, also known as the *Wind of 50 Days.* Usually occurs from February to April.

Khepri – Morning sun.

Kheperu-Ra – See *Neb-Kheperu-Ra Tutankh-Amon.*

Khufu – Also known as *Cheops*, second Pharaoh of *The Old Kingdom*, 4th Dynasty, 2613-2494 B.C. The Great Pyramid at Giza was built for this Pharaoh.

King Tut – See *Tutankhamon* or *Neb-Kheperu-Ra Tutankh-Amon.*

Kohl – Thick dark eye paint, which deflected sunlight.

Koushari – A mix of macaroni and rice, chickpeas and lentils in oil.

Kilt – Short pleated skirts worn by men and boys.

Lateen sails – Triangular sails on feluccas.

Lord Carnarvon – Patron of Howard Carter's expedition that discovered Tutankhamon's tomb in 1922.

Luxor – The present-day name for the ancient city of Thebes.

Victor Loret – On March 9, 1898, Victor Loret found the tomb of Amenhotep II - which had provided safety for another cache of royal mummies for around 3000 years. In an antechamber, Loret found an unwrapped mummy laid on a ceremonial boat. In a side-room of the main burial chamber, he found three unwrapped and badly damaged mummies. And in another side room he was stunned to find the bodies of no less than 8 Pharaohs: Tuthmosis IV, Amenhotep III, Seti II, Siptah, Merneptah, and Rameses IV, V and VI. The mummies from tomb #DB320 were moved to Cairo, but it took a modern-day robbery in the tomb of another Pharaoh, Amenhotep II, to encourage the authorities to move the mummies to the relative safety of the Cairo Museum. As the mummies were transported down the Nile, villagers along the Nile banks wailed, shot guns and threw dirt on their heads: all a sign of respect, not only for the dead, but for royalty.

Madu – *Of the people* as in Madu Museum: The *People's Museum.*

Mashrabia – Ornate, turned wood spool-work panels, made of beech and mahogany wood, used to provide privacy, shadow, light, and ventilation.

Mastabas – Low rectangular brick or stone structures. Like the pyramids, they were built on the west side of the Nile (symbol of death, where the sun falls into the Underworld).

Masud – Lucky.

Menat – The menat was a broad collar or necklace that comprised several rows of beads with a counterpoise that hung down the back when worn. The collar symbolized religious significance and was imbued with the power of healing from *Het-Hert* (*Hathor*). It was often used as a percussion instrument like the sistrum.

Mes – Symbol of a woman giving birth.

Mena – Symbol of a woman nursing a child.

Meskhenet – Destiny.

Museum Spirit – An insect that decays mummies.

Naeem – Benevolent one.

Natron – A salt compound of sodium carbonate and sodium chloride used for dehydration in the mummification process.

Neb-Kheperu-Ra-Tutankh-Amon – Neb Kheperu-Ra was Tutankhamon's throne name. It meant, *The Lord of forms is Ra*. This is the name the people of his time would have known him by. The name Tutankhamon is more personal and less important.

Necropolis – Cemetery or entire valley of cemeteries.

Nefertauret – Nefer means *the beautiful divine*. Tauret means *midwife*. Hence, *The beautiful divine midwife*.

Nemes – Royal head cloth with a Wadjet and symbolic cobra heads attached on top. The nemes headdress came in several styles and colors and was worn by Pharaohs.

Nouveau riche – People who have recently become rich and who display their wealth in an obvious or tasteless way.

Oud – Egyptian or Arabic musical instrument. The oud is the most popular instrument in Middle Eastern music. Its name derives from the Arabic for *wood*, and this refers to the strips of wood used to make its rounded body. The neck of the oud, which is short in comparison to the body, has no frets and this contributes to its unique sound. The most common string combination is five pairs of strings tuned in unison and a single bass string, although up to thirteen strings may be found. Strings are generally made of nylon or gut, and are plucked with a plectrum known as a *risha* or *mizrap*. Another distinctive feature of the oud is its head, with the tuning pegs bent back at an angle to the neck.

Palace of Malkatta – See *Birket Habu*.

Paparazzi – Usually refers to photographers and journalists who seek out sensational stories.

Papyrus – A material made in ancient Egypt from the stem of a water plant, used for writing or painting on.

Piasters – The Egyptian Pound (often symbolized by the letters L.E.) is divided into 100 piasters of 10 milliemes each. The rate of exchange in mid-2002 was about LE 3.40 = US $ 1, or LE 1 = around US $.30.

Portcullis – A monolithic stone carved to fit a passageway shaft or opening and which, when dropped into place, sealed a tomb for all eternity.

Praziquantel – A medication to treat Bilharzia.

Predynastic – Time period before the Dynasties were established.

Punt – Modern-day Somalia.

Quaashie – Born on Sunday.

Queen Tyi – Grandmother of Tutankhamon. Some historical interpretations list her as Tutankhamon's mother.

Ramadan – The ninth month of the Muslim calendar. The Month of Ramadan is also when it is believed the *Holy Quran* was sent down from heaven, guidance unto men, a declaration of direction, and a means of Salvation. It is during this month that Muslims fast. It is called the Fast of Ramadan and lasts the entire month. Ramadan is a time when Muslims concentrate on their faith and spend less time on the concerns of their everyday lives. It is a time of worship and contemplation. During the Fast of Ramadan strict restraints are placed on the daily lives of Muslims. They are not allowed to eat or drink during the daylight hours. Smoking and sexual relations are also forbidden during fasting. At the end of the day, the fast is broken with prayer and a meal called the *iftar*. In the evening following the iftar, it is customary for Muslims to go out visiting family and friends. The fast is resumed the next morning.

Renen – Symbol of a woman playing with children.

Sarcophagus – Carved outer stone coffin, to hold inner sarcophagi, coffins and funerary masks.

Schistosomes – Bacteria found in the waste of snails living in and along the Nile River.

Shabti – Carved, stone figures or painted on walls, said to jump to the command of Osiris to work, if the dead preferred not to work in the Afterlife.

Sheesh – Hair covering worn by women.

Sistrum – The sistrum was an ancient musical instrument, like a rattle in shape, combined with the function of a modern tambourine. It had two basic designs, the *naos* and the hoop. Most in the late period were of the hoop design. Most commonly it featured a representation of Het-Hert (Hathor) on the handle. It was used in sacred rituals, most particularly for Het-Hert but later associated with *Imen (Amun)* and *Aset (Isis)*. The women musicians and chantresses who served in the temple used it. The sound was believed to ward off the powers of chaos.

Smenkhkare – Possibly Tutankhamon's half-brother; possibly Queen Nefertiti's assumed identity in a bid for the throne after the death of her husband, Akhenaten.

Sorghum – A grain, millet, grown as fodder for livestock.

Stele – Stone writing tablet of any size.

Sugs – Markets that are set up in the open air, or small shops or vendors along a specific street.

Tahini – A sesame-seed sauce.

Ta'miyya – Deep fried patties of minced beans, mixed with a variety of spices.

Tarik – Name of a warrior.

Tel el-Amarna – Several hundred miles north of Thebes, sixty miles north of *Asyut*, in Middle Egypt. Formally known as Akhetaten. The new name came from a local village called *El Till*. The word Amarna came from the Bedouin tribe that settled in this village. The word Tel, in Arabic, means a mound or a small hill. But interestingly enough, Tel El Amarna is a flat area of land beside the Nile Valley. The ancient name, Akhetaten, means *the horizon of the solar disk*. It is very similar to the meaning of *Amun Dwelt* at Thebes, *Ptah* at Memphis and other gods at their favored places. Pharaoh Akhenaten offered this place to be the home for his god Aten. The area is a plain field, separated from the Nile Valley by a strip of palm trees. It stretches 12 kilometers from north to south. The area is covered mostly with sand and outlined with ruins of temples, palaces and houses uncovered by archeologists.

Ten – Symbol meaning to split or separate, as in giving birth.

Thebes – In the heart of Upper Egypt and within reach of the Eastern Desert. Thebes counter-balanced Memphis, the hub of Lower Egypt. The city proper, now known as Luxor, with its state temples, stood on the east bank; the necropolis, with its funerary temples and rock cut tombs, lay on the west bank. Luxor having been Thebes, the capital of the New Kingdom, held a population as high as 1 million. Center of

Amon worship, the city suffered from Akhenaten's attempts to force a monotheistic religion on the citizens. During that time, Thebes ceased being the capital. But Akhenaten never succeeded, and at his death, power returned to Thebes.

Tutankhamon – Better known as King Tut or the Boy King, once ruled Egypt in the Eighteenth Dynasty, approximately 1333- 1323 BC. He ruled for a short period, assuming the throne at the age of eight or nine, and died at age eighteen or nineteen. Although not very popular during his time, he remains today the most famous pharaoh.

Umi – Life.

Uro – An ancient Egyptian beverage, possibly similar to beer, with flavoring from nettles before hops began to be used.

Usi – Smoke.

Valley of the Kings – Located on the northeast corner of the Necropolis of Thebes. Shortly after 1500 BC, concealed tombs cut into rock replaced pyramid burial chambers. Almost all the New Kingdom Pharaohs, and some queens, were buried in the Valley of the Kings. The site, chosen by the Ancients because of the outcrop, also known as al-Qurn or Peak of the West, resembled a pyramid.

Valley of the Queens – Located in the western portion of Necropolis of Thebes, west of Dier el-Medina. Between 75 and 80 tombs have been found in the Valley of the Queens. These belong to Queens of the 18th, 19th and 20th Dynasties, including Nefertari, the favored wife of Rameses II. When Nefertari's mummy was found and unveiled, it crumpled into dust, presumably from lack of proper mummification.

Victory Day – A national holiday, celebrated on December 23rd, in memory of 1956 when Egypt stopped England, France and Israel from attacking Egypt through Port Said.

Wadjet – The left eye of God Horus, symbolizing the process of making whole and healing. The great Pharaohs were entombed with Wadjet amulets hung around their necks. It symbolized both the vengeful eye of the Sun God and the eye of the God Horus, torn out by *Seth* (a God of evil) in the struggle for the throne of Egypt. Because the eye was magically restored, the wadjet was said to protect everything behind it.

Wimple – Covering not only for the hair but for the neck and sides of the face.

Yafeu: - Bold.

Yansun – A tea made from aniseed.

Yurt – A tent, usually round, from small to house sizes.

Egyptian Conversational Phrases

Ahmar – Red.

An iznukum, esmaHuli – Saying "excuse me" to a group.

Ari – Guardian.

Ay? – What?

Ay el-hekaya? – What is the matter?

Baksheesh – Word cried out by beggars when asking for a handout.

El hahoonay! – Help!

Enta bititkallim Inglizi – Telling a male to "Speak English."

Inglizi – English.

Iwah – Yes.

Min Fadlukum – Saying "please" to a group.

Oba – Tauret's name for Tutankhamon, meaning *King*.

Ohrma alaya – She has fainted.

Umayma – Little mother.

Yahya – Gift of God Aten. Tutankhamon's name for the unborn baby.

Gods and Goddesses

Amon, Amen, Amun – Myth god of united Egypt.

Amon-Ra, Amen-Ra – Myth, personification of the power of the universe.

Amunet – Myth goddess of mystery.

Anubis – Myth god of the dead. Jackal god of Embalming. In primitive times Anubis was merely the jackal god, associated with the dead because the jackal was generally seen prowling about the tombs. His worship is ancient, probably older than that of *Osiris*. Associated with the Eye of Horus, his duty was to guide the dead through the Underworld and on to Osiris.

Aten – Myth sun disk.

Bes – Myth dwarf god, brings joy.

Goddess Isis – Protects the sarcophagus, faces inward on the southwest corner or guards the Canopic jars. Goddess of magic. Isis was a great enchantress. She taught mankind the secrets of medicine. She was the embalmer and guardian of Osiris. She is often rendered on the foot of coffins with long wings spread to protect the deceased.

Goddess Neith – Protects the sarcophagus, faces inward from the southeast corner, or guards the canopic jars. As protector of the dead, she is often seen standing with Nephthys at the head of coffins or assisting Isis, Nephthys, and Selket, to guard the Canopic jars. As *Opener of the Ways*, she was a guide in the Underworld, a female Anubis. In the Eighteenth Dynasty, she took on the attributes of Hathor, as a protector of women. A creative deity, she was said to be the wife of Khnum.

Goddess Nephthys – Protects the sarcophagus; faces inward from the northwest corner. Goddess of silence, solace, warmth, protector; one who guides people through the changes of life and of death. She and her sister, Isis, protect the dead.

Goddess Selket – Protects the sarcophagus; faces inward from the northeast corner. Selket's divine role was not limited to funerary duties. She was chiefly noted for her control of magic and, in particular, for treating scorpion stings by means of magic.

Horus – Myth hawk god of the sky.

Khentimentiu – Predynastic myth god of the dead's destiny, seen as the guardian *dog of the dead.*

Khnum – Myth god of the reborn sun. The ram god thought responsible for the Creation of mankind, which he molded from the mud of the Nile on a potter's wheel.

Osiris – A king who married his sister, Isis, slain by their brother *Set*. Isis put the parts of Osiris back together, performing the first mummification, preparatory for the trip to the heavens.

Ra – Sun god.

Re-Harakhty – Myth, *Horus of the Horizon.*

Tauret - Myth goddess of pregnant women.

Taweret – Goddess of childbirth; the pregnant hippopotamus that appeared ferocious, to ward off evil during childbirth.

About the Author

Mary Deal writes in several genres and receives many of her plots through dreams. She woke one morning with Egyptian scenes parading through her mind. Startled by the foreign spectacle, she lay quietly watching. Only when a bizarre event appeared, which fully woke her, did she realize she had the ending scene of a new story, presented here and titled *The Ka*.

She spent four years researching 3,500 years of Egyptian dynasties to find the proper period in which to weave her threads of fantasy. During the research period, she completed three additional novel manuscripts and published two. Another four years of writing, rewriting, and polishing produced *The Ka*. Then, giving the completed *Ka* manuscript a rest, she completed another thriller.

Mary is an Amazon bestselling, multi-genre author. Among her many awards:

Mary's first feature screenplay, *Sea Storm*, was nominated into the Semi-Finals in a *Moondance International Film Festival* competition.

One of Mary's many short stories, *The Last Thing I Do*, appeared in the anthology, *Freckles to Wrinkles*, by *Silver Boomer Books*, and was nominated for the coveted *Pushcart Prize*.

A native of Walnut Grove, California in the Sacramento River Delta, Mary Deal has lived in England, the Caribbean, the Hawaiian Islands, and presently resides in Scottsdale, Arizona.

Find Her Online

Her Website: http://www.marydeal.com
Amazon Author Page: http://tinyurl.com/y9ca5u8t
Barnes & Noble: http://tinyurl.com/o7keqf7
FaceBook Social: http://www.facebook.com/mdeal
Facebook Author Page: https://www.facebook/MaryDealBooks
Facebook 4 & 5 STAR Book Reviews:
https://www.facebook/com.groups/powerwriters
Twitter: http://twitter.com/Mary_Deal or @Mary_Deal
Linked In: http://www.linkedin.com/in/marydeal
Goodreads: https://www.goodreads.com/MaryDeal
BookTown: http://booktown.ning.com/members/MaryDeal
Instagram: https://www.instagram.com/mary.l.deal

Her Art Galleries

Mary Deal Fine Art
http://www.marydealfineart.com
Island Image Gallery
http://www.islandimagegallery.com
Mary Deal Fine Art and Photography
https://www.facebook.com/MDealArt
Pinterest
https://www.pinterest.com/1deal

Made in the USA
Middletown, DE
23 October 2022

13315073R00286